WITH KITCHENER IN THE SOUDAN

MORE WILDSIDE CLASSICS

WITH KITCHENER IN THE SOUDAN

A Story Of Atbara And Omdurman

G. A. HENTY

WILDSIDE PRESS

WITH KITCHENER IN THE SOUDAN

This edition published in 2006 by Wildside Press, LLC.
www.wildsidepress.com

PREFACE.

The reconquest of the Soudan will ever be mentioned as one of the most difficult, and at the same time the most successful, enterprises ever undertaken. The task of carrying an army hundreds of miles across a waterless desert; conveying it up a great river, bristling with obstacles; defeating an enormously superior force, unsurpassed in the world for courage; and, finally, killing the leader of the enemy and crushing out the last spark of opposition; was a stupendous one.

After the death of Gordon, and the retirement of the British troops, there was no force in existence that could have barred the advance of the fanatical hordes of the Mahdi, had they poured down into Egypt. The native Egyptian army was, as yet, in the earliest stage of organization; and could not be relied upon to stand firm against the wild rush of the Dervishes. Fortunately, time was given for that organization to be completed; and when, at last, the Dervish forces marched north, they were repulsed. Assouan was saved, and Wady Halfa became the Egyptian outpost.

Gradually, preparations were made for taking the offensive. A railway was constructed along the banks of the Nile, and a mixed force of British and Egyptians drove the enemy beyond Dongola; then, by splendidly organized labour, a railroad was made from Wady Halfa, across the desert, towards the elbow of the great bend from Dongola to Abu Hamed. The latter place was captured, by an Egyptian brigade moving up from the former place; and from that moment, the movement was carried on with irresistible energy.

The railway was pushed forward to Abu Hamed; and then southward, past Berber, up to the Atbara river. An army of twenty thousand men, under one of the Khalifa's sons, was attacked in a strong position and defeated with immense loss. Fresh British troops were then brought up; and, escorted by gunboats and steamers carrying provisions, the army marched up the Nile, crushed the Khalifa's great host before Omdurman, and recovered possession of Khartoum.

Then, the moving spirit of this enterprise, the man whose marvellous power of organization had secured its success, was called to other work. Fortunately, he had a worthy successor in Colonel Wingate; who, with a native force, encountered that which the Khalifa had again gathered, near El Obeid, the scene of the total destruction of the army under Hicks Pasha; routed it with ease, killing the Khalifa and all his principal emirs. Thus a land that had been turned into a desert, by the terrible tyranny of the Mahdi and his successor, was wrested from barbarism and restored to civilization; and the stain upon British honour, caused by the desertion of Gordon by the British ministry of the day, was wiped out.

It was a marvellous campaign—marvellous in the perfection of its organization, marvellous in the completeness of its success.

G. A. Henty.

CHAPTER 1:

Disinherited.

"Wanted, an active and intelligent young man, for general work, in a commercial house having a branch at Alexandria. It is desirable that he should be able to write a good hand; and, if necessary, to assist in office work. Wages, 2 pounds per week. Personal application to be made at Messieurs Partridge and Company, 453 Leadenhall Street."

This advertisement was read by a man of five or six and twenty, in a small room in the upper story of a house in Lupus Street, Pimlico. He was not the only inmate of the room, for a young woman, apparently not more than eighteen, was sitting there sewing; her work interrupted, occasionally, by a short, hacking cough. Her husband, for this was the relation in which he stood to her, put down the paper carelessly, and then got up.

"I am going out, dear, on my usual search. You know, we have agreed that it is of no use my trying to live by my pen. I get an article accepted, occasionally, but it's not enough to provide more than bread and cheese. I must look for something else."

"But you must succeed, presently, Gregory."

"Yes, dear; but while the grass grows, the horse starves. At any rate, I will try for something else. If I get anything, it won't prevent my writing; and when my genius is recognized, I can drop the other thing, and take to literature regularly, again."

"Well, I won't be away longer than I can help. Anyhow, I will be back to our midday banquet. I will bring a couple of rashers of bacon in with me. We have potatoes enough, I think."

So saying, he kissed his wife tenderly, and went out.

Gregory Hartley belonged to a good family. He was the second son of the Honorable James Hartley, brother of the Marquis of Langdale. He had been educated at Harrow and Cambridge; and, after leaving the university, had gone out to Egypt with a friend of his father's, who was an enthusiast in the exploration of the antiquities of that country. Gregory had originally intended to stay there a few months, at most, but he was infected by the enthusiasm of his companion, and remained in Egypt for two years; when the professor was taken ill and died, and he returned home.

A year later, he fell in love with the governess in a neighbouring family. His feeling was reciprocated, and they became engaged. His father was furious, when his son told him what had taken place.

"It is monstrous," he said, "after the education that you have had, and the place that I, if I survive him; or, if not, your brother, will take at the death of your uncle; that you should dream of throwing yourself away, in this manner. I have looked to your making a good marriage; for, as you know, I am not what may be called a rich man. Your brother's tastes are expensive; and what with his education, and yours, and the allowances I have made you both, it is as much as I have been able to do to keep up our position. And there are your sisters to be provided for. The idea of your falling in love with this young woman is monstrous."

"Young lady, Father. She is a clergyman's daughter."

"I won't hear of such a thing—I will not hear of it for a moment; and if you persist in this mad folly, I tell you, fairly, that from this moment I shall have nothing more to say to you! You have to choose between me, and this penniless beggar."

"I am sorry you put it in that way, sir. My choice is made. I am engaged to this young lady, and shall certainly marry her. I trust that, when your present anger has subsided, you will recognize that my honour was involved in the matter; and that even if I wished it, I could not, without showing myself to be a downright cad, draw back."

And so, Gregory Hartley married the girl of his choice. She had, for some time, refused to allow him to sacrifice himself; but when she found that he was as determined as his father, and absolutely refused to release her from the engagement, she had given way; and had, after a quiet marriage, accompanied him to London.

There he had endeavoured to get literary work, but had found it much harder than he had expected. The market was overcrowded, and they had moved from comfortable lodgings into small rooms; and so, step by step, had come to the attic in Lupus Street. He was doing a little better now, and had hopes that, ere long, he would begin to make his way steadily up.

But the anxiety had told on his wife. Never very strong, she had developed a short, hard cough; and he had drawn upon his scanty reserves, to consult a specialist.

"There is undoubtedly lung trouble," the latter said. "If you can manage it, I should say that she ought certainly to be taken to a warm climate. The damage is not extensive, as yet; and it is probable that, under favourable circumstances, she might shake it off; but I fear that, if she continues to live in London, her chances are not great."

This, Gregory felt, was almost equivalent to a death sentence; and he had begun to consult the advertisements in the papers, for some post abroad. He had, unknown to her, applied for several situations, but without success.

When he first read the advertisement that morning, he had hardly thought of applying for the situation. His pride revolted at the idea of becoming a mere messenger; but his wife's cough had decided him.

What did it matter, so that he could save her life?

"I may not get it," he said to himself, as he went out; "but my knowledge of Arabic, and the native dialect, is all in my favour. And at least, in a year or two, she may have thoroughly shaken off the cough, and that is everything.

"At any rate, I have a better chance of getting this than I had of the other places that I applied for. There can hardly be a rush of applicants. When I am out there, I may hear of something better.

"However, I will take another name. Fortunately I have a second one, which will do very well. Hilliard will do as well as Hartley; and as I never write it in full as my signature, no one would recognize it as my name. There is nothing to be ashamed of, in accepting such a post.

"As for the marquis, as he has never been friendly with us, it does not matter. He is, I have heard, a very tough sort of man; and my father is not likely to survive him. But I do not think it would be fair to Geoffrey, when he comes into his peerage, that anyone should be able to say that he has a brother who is porter, in a mercantile house at Alexandria. We have never got on very well together. The fact that he was heir to a title spoilt him. I think he would have been a very good fellow, if it hadn't been for that."

On arriving at the office in Leadenhall Street, he was, on saying he wished to speak to Mr. Partridge, at once shown in. A good many of his personal belongings had been long since pledged; but he had retained one or two suits, so that he could make as good an appearance as possible, when he went out. The clerk had merely said, "A gentleman wishes to speak to you, sir," and the merchant looked up enquiringly at him, as he entered.

"I have come to see you, sir, with reference to that advertisement, for a man at your establishment at Alexandria."

A look of surprise came over the merchant's face, and he said:

"Have you called on your own account?"

"Yes; I am anxious to go abroad, for the sake of my wife's health, and I am not particular as to what I do, so that I can take her to a warm climate. I may say that I have been two years in Egypt, and speak Arabic and Koptic fluently. I am strong and active, and am ready to make myself useful, in any way."

Mr. Partridge did not answer, for a minute. Certainly this applicant was not at all the sort of man he had expected to apply for the place, in answer to his advertisement. That he was evidently a gentleman was far from an advantage, but the fact that he could speak the languages would add much to his value.

"Can you give me references?" he said, at last.

"I cannot, sir. I should not like to apply to any of my friends, in such a matter. I must ask you to take me on trust. Frankly, I have quarrelled with my family, and have to strike out for myself. Were it not for my wife's health, I could earn my living; but I am told it is essential that she should go to a warm climate, and as I see no other way of accomplishing this, I have applied for this situation, hoping that my knowledge of the language, and my readiness to perform whatever duties I may be required to do, might induce you to give me a trial."

"And you would, if necessary—say, in the case of illness of one of my clerks—be ready to help in the office?"

"Certainly, sir."

"Will you call again, in half an hour? I will give you an answer, then."

By the time Gregory returned, the merchant's mind was made up. He had come to the conclusion that the story he had heard was a true one. The way it had been told was convincing. The man was undoubtedly a gentleman. There was no mistake in his manner and talk. He had quarrelled with his family, probably over his marriage; and, as so many had done, found it difficult to keep his head above water. His wife had been ordered to a warm climate, and he was ready to do anything that would enable him to keep her there.

It would assuredly be a great advantage to have one who could act, in an emergency, as a clerk; of course, his knowledge of language would greatly add to his utility. It certainly was not business to take a man without a reference, but the advantages more than counterbalanced the disadvantages. It was not likely that he would stay with him long; but at any rate, the fact that he was taking his wife with him would ensure his staying, until he saw something a great deal better elsewhere.

When Gregory returned, therefore, he said:

"I have been thinking this matter over. What is your name?"

"Gregory Hilliard, sir."

"Well, I have been thinking it over, and I have decided to engage you. I quite believe the story that you have told me, and your appearance fully carries it out. You may consider the matter settled. I am willing to pay for a second-class passage for your wife, as well as yourself; and will give such instructions, to my agents there, as will render your position as easy for you as possible. In the natural course of things, your duties would have included the sweeping out of the offices, and work of that description; but I will instruct him to engage a native to do this, under your supervision. You will be in charge of the warehouse, under the chief storekeeper; and, as you say, you will, in case of pressure of work in the office, take a desk there.

"In consideration of your knowledge of the language, which will render you, at once, more useful than a green hand would be, I shall add ten shillings a week to the wages named in the advertisement, which will enable you to obtain comfortable lodgings."

"I am heartily obliged to you, sir," Gregory said, "and will do my best to show that your confidence in me has not been misplaced. When do you wish me to sail? I shall only require a few hours to make my preparations."

"Then in that case I will take a passage, for you and your wife, in the P. and O. that sails, next Thursday, from Southampton. I may say that it is our custom to allow fifteen pounds, for outfit. If you will call again in half an hour, I will hand you the ticket and a cheque for that amount; and you can call, the day before you go, for a letter to our agents there."

Gregory ascended the stairs to his lodging with a far more elastic step than usual. His wife saw at once, as he entered, that he had good news of some sort.

"What is it, Gregory?"

"Thank God, darling, that I have good news to give you, at last! I have obtained a situation, at about a hundred and thirty pounds a year, in Alexandria."

"Alexandria?" she repeated, in surprise.

"Yes. It is the place of all others that I wanted to go to. You see, I understand the language. That is one thing; and what is of infinitely more consequence, it is a place that will suit your health; and you will, I hope, very soon get rid of that nasty cough. I did not tell you at the time, but the doctor I took you to said that this London air did not suit you, but that a warm climate would soon set you up again."

"You are going out there for my sake, Gregory! As if I hadn't brought trouble enough on you, already!"

"I would bear a good deal more trouble for your sake, dear. You need not worry about that."

"And what are you going to do?" she asked.

"I am going to be a sort of useful man—extra clerk, assistant store-keeper, et cetera, et cetera. I like Egypt very much. It will suit me to a T. At any rate, it will be a vast improvement upon this.

"Talking of that, I have forgotten the rashers. I will go and get them, at once. We sha'n't have to depend upon them as our main staple, in future; for fruit is dirt cheap, out there, and one does not want much meat. We shall be able to live like princes, on two pounds ten a week; and besides, this appointment may lead to something better, and we may consider that there is a future before us.

"We are to sail on Thursday. Look! Here are fifteen golden sovereigns. That is for my outfit, and we can begin with luxuries, at once. We shall not want much outfit: half a dozen suits of white drill for myself, and some gowns for you."

"Nonsense, Gregory! I sha'n't want anything. You would not let me sell any of my dresses, and I have half a dozen light ones. I shall not want a penny spent on me."

"Very well; then I will begin to be extravagant, at once. In the first place, I will go down to that confectioner's, round the corner; and we will celebrate my appointment with a cold chicken, and a bottle of port. I shall be back in five minutes."

"Will it be very hot, Gregory?" she asked, as they ate their meal. "Not that I am afraid of heat, you know. I always like summer."

"No. At any rate, not at present. We are going out at the best time of the year, and it will be a comfort, indeed, to change these November fogs for the sunshine of Egypt. You will have four or five months to get strong again, before it begins to be hot. Even in summer, there are cool breezes morning and evening; and of course, no one thinks of going out in the middle of the day. I feel as happy as a schoolboy, at the thought of getting out of this den and this miserable climate, and of basking in the sunshine. We have had a bad beginning, dear, but we have better days before us."

"Thank God, Gregory! I have not cared about myself. But it has been a trial, when your manuscripts have come back, to see you sitting here slaving away; and to know that it is I who have brought you to this."

"I brought myself to it, you obstinate girl! I have pleased myself, haven't I? If a man chooses a path for himself, he must not grumble because he finds it rather rougher than he expected. I have never, for a single moment, regretted what I have done; at any rate, as far as I, myself, am concerned."

"Nor I, for my own sake, dear. The life of a governess is not so cheerful as to cause one regret, at leaving it."

And so, Gregory Hartley and his wife went out to Alexandria, and established themselves in three bright rooms, in the upper part of a house that commanded a view of the port, and the sea beyond it. The outlay required for furniture was small, indeed: some matting for the floors, a few cushions for the divans which ran round the rooms, a bed, a few simple cooking utensils, and a small stock of crockery sufficed.

Mr. Ferguson, the manager of the branch, had at first read the letter that Gregory had brought him with some doubt in his mind, as to the wisdom of his principal, in sending out a man who was evidently a gentleman. This feeling, however, soon wore away; and he found him perfectly ready to undertake any work to which he was set.

There was, indeed, nothing absolutely unpleasant about this. He was at the office early, and saw that the native swept and dusted the offices. The rest of the day he was either in the warehouse, or carried messages, and generally did such odd jobs as were required. A fortnight after his arrival, one of the clerks was kept away by a sharp attack of fever; and as work was pressing, the agent asked Gregory to take his place.

"I will do my best, sir, but I know nothing of mercantile accounts."

"The work will be in no way difficult. Mr. Hardman will take Mr. Parrot's ledgers; and, as you will only have to copy the storekeeper's issues into the books, five minutes will show you the form in which they are entered."

Gregory gave such satisfaction that he was afterwards employed at office work, whenever there was any pressure.

A year and a half passed comfortably. At the end of twelve months, his pay was raised another ten shillings a week.

He had, before leaving England, signed a contract to remain with the firm for two years. He regretted having to do this, as it prevented his accepting any better position, should an opening occur; but he recognized that the condition was a fair one, after the firm paying for his outfit and for two passages. At the end of eighteen months, Gregory began to look about for something better.

"I don't mind my work a bit," he said to his wife, "but, if only for the sake of the boy" (a son had been born, a few months after their arrival), "I must try to raise myself in the scale, a bit. I have nothing to complain about at the office; far from it. From what the manager said to me the other day, if a vacancy occurred in the office, I should have the offer of the berth. Of course, it would be a step; for I know, from the books, that Hardman gets two hundred a year, which is forty more than I do."

"I should like you to get something else, Gregory. It troubles me, to think that half your time is spent packing up goods in the warehouse, and work of that sort; and even if we got less I would much rather, even if we had to stint ourselves, that your work was more suitable to your past; and such that you could associate again with gentlemen, on even terms."

"That does not trouble me, dear, except that I wish you had some society among ladies. However, both for your sake and the boy's, and I own I should like it myself, I will certainly keep on the lookout for some better position. I have often regretted, now, that I did not go in for a commission in the army. I did want to, but my father would not hear of it. By this time, with luck, I might have got my company; and though the pay would not have been more than I get here, it would, with quarters and so on, have been as much, and we should be in a very different social position.

"However, it is of no use talking about that now; and indeed, it is difficult to make plans at all. Things are in such an unsettled condition, here, that there is no saying what will happen.

"You see, Arabi and the military party are practically masters here. Tewfik has been obliged to make concession after concession to them, to dismiss ministers at their orders, and to submit to a series of humiliations. At any moment, Arabi could dethrone him, as he has the whole army at his back, and certainly the larger portion of the population. The revolution could be completed without trouble or bloodshed; but you see, it is complicated by the fact that Tewfik has the support of the English and French governments; and there can be little doubt that the populace regard the movement as a national one, and directed as much against foreign control and interference as against Tewfik, against whom they have no ground of complaint, whatever. On the part of the army and its generals, the trouble has arisen solely on account of the favouritism shown to Circassian officers.

"But once a revolution has commenced, it is certain to widen out. The peasantry are, everywhere, fanatically hostile to foreigners. Attacks have been made upon these in various country districts; and, should Arabi be triumphant, the position of Christians will become very precarious. Matters are evidently seen in that light in England; for I heard today, at the office, that the British and French squadrons are expected here, in a day or two.

"If there should be a row, our position here will be very unpleasant. But I should hardly think that Arabi would venture to try his strength against that of the fleets, and I fancy that trouble will, in the first place, begin in Cairo; both as being the capital of the country, and beyond the reach of armed interference by the Powers. Arabi's natural course would be to consolidate his power throughout the whole of Egypt, leaving Alexandria severely alone, until he had obtained absolute authority elsewhere.

"Anyhow, it will be a satisfaction to have the fleet up; as, at the first rumour of an outbreak, I can get you and baby on board one of the ships lying in harbour. As a simple measure of precaution, I would suggest that you should go out with me, this evening, and buy one of the costumes worn by the native women. It is only a long blue robe, enveloping you from head to foot; and one of those hideous white cotton veils, falling from below the eyes. I will get a bottle of iodine, and you will then only have to darken your forehead and eyelids, and you could pass, unsuspected, through any crowd."

"But what are you going to do, Gregory?"

"I will get a native dress, too; but you must remember that though, if possible, I will come to you, I may not be able to do so; and in case you hear of any tumult going on, you must take Baby, and go down at once to the port. You know enough of the language, now, to be able to tell a boatman to take you off to one of the steamers in the port. As soon as I get away I shall go round the port, and shall find you without difficulty. Still, I do not anticipate any trouble arising without our having sufficient warning to allow me to come and see you settled on board ship;

and I can then keep on in the office until it closes, when I can join you again.

"Of course, all this is very remote, and I trust that the occasion will never arise. Still, there is no doubt that the situation is critical, and there is no harm in making our preparations for the worst.

"At any rate, dear, I beg that you will not go out alone, till matters have settled down. We will do the shopping together, when I come back from the office.

"There is one thing that I have reason to be grateful for. Even if the worst comes to the worst, and all Christians have to leave the country, the object for which I came out here has been attained. I have not heard you cough, for months; we have laid by fifty pounds; and I have written some forty stories, long and short, and if we go back I have a fair hope of making my way, for I am sure that I write better than I used to do; and as a good many of the stories are laid in Egypt, the local colouring will give them a distinctive character, and they are more likely to be accepted than those I wrote before. Editors of magazines like a succession of tales of that kind.

"For the present, there is no doubt that the arrival of the fleet will render our position here more comfortable than it is, at present. The mere mob of the town would hesitate to attack Europeans, when they know that three or four thousand sailors could land in half an hour. But on the other hand, Arabi and his generals might see that Alexandria was, after all, the most important position, and that it was here foreign interference must be arrested.

"I should not be surprised if, on the arrival of the ships, Tewfik, Arabi, and all the leaders of the movement come here at once. Tewfik will come to get the support of the fleet. Arabi will come to oppose a landing of troops. The war in the beginning of the century was decided at Alexandria, and it may be so, again. If I were sure that you would come to no harm, and I think the chances of that are very small, I own that all this would be immensely interesting, and a break to the monotony of one's life here.

"One thing is fairly certain. If there is anything like a regular row, all commercial work will come to an end until matters are settled; in which case, even if the offices are not altogether closed, and the whole staff recalled to England, they would be glad enough to allow me to leave, instead of keeping me to the two years' agreement that I signed, before starting."

"I should hardly think that there would be a tumult here, Gregory. The natives all seem very gentle and peaceable, and the army is composed of the same sort of men."

"They have been kept down for centuries, Annie; but there is a deep, fanatical feeling in every Mussulman's nature; and, at any rate, the great proportion of the officers of the army are Mussulmans. As for the Kopts, there would be no danger of trouble from them; but the cry of 'death to the Christians' would excite every Mahomedan in the land, almost to madness.

"Unfortunately, too, there is a general belief, whether truly founded or not, that although the French representative here is apparently acting in concert with ours, he and all the French officials are secretly encouraging Arabi, and will take no active steps, whatever. In that case, it is doubtful whether England would act alone. The jealousy between the two peoples here is intense. For years, the French have been thwarting us at every turn; and they may very well think that, however matters might finally go, our interference would make us so unpopular, in Egypt, that their influence would become completely paramount.

"Supremacy in Egypt has always been the dream of the French. Had it not been for our command of the sea, they would have obtained possession of the country in Napoleon's time. Their intrigues here have, for years, been incessant. Their newspapers in Egypt have continually maligned us, and they believe that the time has come when they will be the real, if not the nominal, rulers of Egypt. The making of the Suez Canal was quite as much a political as a commercial move, and it has certainly added largely to their influence here; though, in this respect, a check was given to them by the purchase of the Khedive's shares in the canal by Lord Beaconsfield; a stroke which, however, greatly increased the enmity of the French here, and heightened their efforts to excite the animosity of the people against us.

"Well, I hope that whatever comes of all this, the question as to whose influence is to be paramount in Egypt will be finally settled. Even French domination would be better than the constant intrigues and trouble, that keep the land in a state of agitation. However, I fancy that it will be the other way, if an English fleet comes here and there is trouble. I don't think we shall back down; and if we begin in earnest, we are sure to win in the long run. France must see that, and if she refuses to act, at the last moment, it can only be because Arabi has it in his power to produce documents showing that he was, all along, acting in accordance with her secret advice."

A week later, on the 20th of May, the squadrons of England and France anchored off Alexandria. The British fleet consisted of eight ironclads and five gunboats, carrying three thousand five hundred and thirty-nine men and one hundred and two guns, commanded by Sir Frederick Seymour. Two days before the approach of the fleet was known at Cairo, the French and English consuls proposed that the Khedive should issue a decree, declaring a general amnesty, and that the president of the council, the minister of war, and the three military pashas should quit the country for a year. This request was complied with.

The ministry resigned, in a body, on the day the fleet arrived; on the ground that the Khedive acquiesced in foreign interference. A great meeting was held of the chief personages of state, and the officers and the representatives of the army at once told the Khedive that they refused to obey his orders, and only recognized the authority of the Porte.

At Alexandria all trade ceased at once, when it became known that the troops were busy strengthening the forts, mounting cannon, and preparing for a resistance. That this was done by the orders of Arabi, who was now practically dictator, there could be no question. The native population became more and more excited, being firmly of belief that no vessels could resist the fire of the heavy guns; and that any attempt on the part of the men-of-war to reduce the place would end in their being sunk, as soon as fighting began.

The office and stores were still kept open, but Gregory's duties were almost nominal; and he and Mr. Parrot, who was also married, were told by the manager that they could spend the greater portion of their time at their homes. Part of Gregory's duties consisted in going off to vessels that came into the port with goods for the firm, and seeing to their being brought on shore; and he had no difficulty in making arrangements, with the captain of one of these ships, for his wife and child to go on board at once, should there be any trouble in the town.

"If you hear any sounds of tumult, Annie, you must disguise yourself at once, and go down to the wharf. I have arranged with our boatman, Allen, whom you know well, as we have often gone out with him for a sail in the evening, that if he hears of an outbreak, he shall bring the boat to the steps at the end of this street, and take you off to the Simoon. Of course, I shall come if I can, but our house is one of those which have been marked off as being most suitable for defence. The men from half a dozen other establishments are to gather there and, as belonging to the house, I must aid in the defence. Of course, if I get sufficient warning, I shall slip on my disguise, and hurry here, and see you down to the boat; and then make my way back to our place. But do not wait for me. If I come here and find that you have gone, I shall know that you have taken the alarm in time, and shall return at once to the office.

"Of course, if the outbreak commences near here, and you find that your way down to the water is blocked, you will simply put on your disguise, stain your face, and wait till I come to you, or till you see that the way to the water is clear. Do not attempt to go out into a mob. There are not likely to be any women among them. However, I do not anticipate a serious riot. They may attack Europeans in the street, but with some fourteen or fifteen men-of-war in the port, they are not likely to make any organized assault. Arabi's agents will hardly precipitate matters in that way. Hard as they may work, it will take a month to get the defences into proper order, and any rising will be merely a spasmodic outbreak of fanaticism. I don't think the danger is likely to be pressing until, finding that all remonstrances are vain, the admiral begins to bombard the port."

"I will do exactly as you tell me, Gregory. If I were alone, I could not bring myself to leave without you, but I must think of the child."

"Quite so, dear. That is the first consideration. Certainly, if it comes to a fight, I should be much more comfortable with the knowledge that you and Baby were in safety."

The Egyptian soldiers were quartered, for the most part, outside the town; and for some days there was danger that they would enter, and attack the European inhabitants; but Arabi's orders were strict that, until he gave the command, they were to remain quiet.

The British admiral sent messages to Tewfik, insisting that the work upon the fortifications should cease, and the latter again issued orders to that effect, but these were wholly disobeyed. He had, indeed, no shadow of authority remaining; and the work continued, night and day. It was, however, as much as possible concealed from observation; but, search lights being suddenly turned upon the forts, at night, showed them to be swarming with men.

Things went on with comparative quiet till the 10th of June, although the attitude of the natives was so threatening that no Europeans left their houses, except on urgent business. On that day, a sudden uproar was heard. Pistols were fired, and the merchants closed their stores and barricaded their doors.

Gregory was in the harbour at the time and, jumping into his boat, rowed to the stairs and hurried home. He found that his wife had already disguised herself, and was in readiness to leave.

The street was full of excited people. He slipped on his own disguise, darkened his face, and then, seizing a moment when the crowd had rushed up the street at the sound of firearms at the other end, hurried down to the boat, and rowed off to the Simoon.

"I must return now, dear," he said. "I can get in at the back gate—I have the key, as the stores are brought in through that way. I do not think that you need feel any uneasiness. The row is evidently still going on, but only a few guns are being fired now. Certainly the rascals cannot be attacking the stores, or you would hear a steady musketry fire. By the sound, the riot is principally in the foreign quarter, where the Maltese, Greeks, and Italians congregate. No doubt the police will soon put it down."

The police, however, made no attempt to do so, and permitted the work of massacre to take place under their eyes. Nearly two hundred Europeans were killed. The majority of these dwelt in the foreign quarter, but several merchants and others were set upon, while making their way to their offices, and some seamen from the fleet were also among the victims. The British consul was dragged out of his carriage, and severely injured. The consulate was attacked, and several Frenchmen were killed in the streets.

The Khedive hurried from Cairo, on hearing the news. Arabi was now sending some of his best regiments to Alexandria, while pretending to be preparing for a raid upon the Suez Canal. He was receiving the assistance of Dervish Pasha, the Sultan's representative; and had been recognized by the Sultan, who conferred upon him the highest order of Medjidie.

In the meantime a conference had been held by the Powers, and it was decided that the Sultan should be entrusted with the work of putting down the insurrection, he being nominally lord paramount of Egypt. But conditions were laid down, as to his army leaving the country afterwards.

The Sultan sent an evasive reply. The Khedive was too overwhelmed at the situation to take any decisive course. France hesitated, and England determined that, with or without allies, she would take the matter in hand.

CHAPTER 2:

The Rising In Alexandria.

The harbour was full of merchant ships, as there were, at present, no means of getting their cargoes unloaded. The native boatmen had, for the most part, struck work; and had they been willing to man their boats, they must have remained idle as, in view of the situation, the merchants felt that their goods were much safer on board ship than they would be in their magazines. It was settled, therefore that, for the present, Annie and the child should remain on board the Simoon, while Gregory should take up his residence at the office.

The fleet in the harbour was now an imposing one. Not only were the English and French squadrons there, but some Italian ships of war had arrived, and a United States cruiser; and on the 7th of July, Sir Beauchamp Seymour sent in a decisive message, that he should commence a bombardment of the fort unless the strengthening of the fortifications was, at once, abandoned. No heed was taken of the intimation and, three days later, he sent an ultimatum demanding the cessation of work, and the immediate surrender of the forts nearest to the entrance to the harbour; stating that, if these terms were not complied with in twenty-four hours, the bombardment would commence.

Already the greater part of the European inhabitants had left the town, and taken up their quarters in the merchant ships that had been engaged for the purpose. A few, however, of the bankers and merchants determined to remain. These gathered in the bank, and in Mr. Ferguson's house, to which the most valuable goods in other establishments were removed. They had an ample supply of firearms, and believed that they could hold out for a considerable time. They were convinced that the Egyptian troops would not, for an hour, resist the fire that would be opened upon them, but would speedily evacuate the town; and that, therefore, there would only be the mob to be encountered, and this but for a short time, as the sailors would land as soon as the Egyptian troops fled.

The Egyptians, on the other hand, believed absolutely in their ability to destroy the fleet.

Both parties were wrong. The Europeans greatly undervalued the fighting powers of the Egyptians, animated as they were by confidence in the strength of the defences, by their number, and by their fanaticism; while the Egyptians similarly undervalued the tremendous power of our ships.

That evening, and the next morning, the port presented an animated appearance. Boats were putting off with those inhabitants who had waited on, hoping that the Egyptians would at the last moment give in. Many of the merchantmen had already cleared out. Others were getting up sail. Smoke was rising from the funnels of all the men of war.

An express boat had brought, from France, orders that the French fleet were to take no part in the proceedings, but were to proceed at once to Port Said. This order excited the bitterest feeling of anger and humiliation among the French officers and sailors, who had relied confidently in taking their part in the bombardment; and silently their ships, one by one, left the port. The Italian and American vessels remained for a time; and as the British ships followed, in stately order, their crews manned the rigging and vociferously cheered our sailors, who replied as heartily.

All, save the British men of war, took up their stations well out at sea, in a direction where they would be out of the fire of the Egyptian batteries. It was not until nine o'clock in the evening that the two last British ships, the *Invincible* and *Monarch*, steamed out of port. At half-past four in the morning the ships got under weigh again, and moved to the positions marked out for them.

Fort Mex, and the batteries on the sand hills were faced by the *Penelope*, the *Monarch*, and the *Invincible*; the *Alexandra*, the *Superb*, and the *Sultan* faced the harbour forts, Ada, Pharos, and Ras-el-Teen; the *Temeraire* and *Inflexible* prepared to aid the *Invincible* in her attack on Fort Mex, or to support the three battleships engaged off the port, as might be required; and the five gunboats moved away towards Fort Marabout, which lay some distance to the west of the town.

At seven o'clock, the *Alexandra* began the engagement by firing a single gun. Then the whole fleet opened fire, the Egyptian artillerymen replying with great steadiness and resolution. There was scarcely a breath of wind, and the ships were, in a few instants, shrouded in their own smoke; and were frequently obliged to cease firing until this drifted slowly away, to enable them to aim their guns. The rattle of the machine guns added to the din. Midshipmen were sent aloft, and these signalled down to the deck the result of each shot, so that the gunners were enabled to direct their fire, even when they could not see ten yards beyond the muzzle of the guns.

In a short time, the forts and batteries showed how terrible was the effect of the great shells. The embrasures were torn and widened, there were great gaps in the masonry of the buildings, and the hail of missiles from the machine guns swept every spot near the Egyptian guns; and yet, Arabi's soldiers did not flinch but, in spite of the number that fell, worked their guns as fast as ever.

Had they been accustomed to the huge Krupp guns in their batteries, the combat would have been more equal; and although the end would have been the same, the ships must have suffered terribly. Fortunately, the Egyptian artillerymen had little experience in the working of these heavy pieces, and their shot in almost every case flew high—sometimes above the masts, sometimes between them, but in only a few instances striking the hull. With their smaller guns they made good practice, but though the shot from these pieces frequently struck, they dropped harmlessly from the iron sides, and only those that entered through the portholes effected any damage.

The Condor, under Lord Charles Beresford, was the first to engage Fort Marabout; and, for a time, the little gunboat was the mark of all the guns of the fort. But the other four gunboats speedily came to her assistance, and effectually diverted the fire of the fort from the ships that were engaging Fort Mex.

At eight o'clock the *Monarch*, having silenced the fort opposite to her, and dismounted the guns, joined the *Inflexible* and *Penelope* in their duel with Fort Mex; and by nine o'clock all the guns were silenced except four, two of which were heavy rifled guns, well sheltered. In spite of the heavy fire from the three great ships, the Egyptian soldiers maintained their fire, the officers frequently exposing themselves to the bullets of the machine guns by leaping upon the parapet, to ascertain the effect of their own shot.

The harbour forts were, by this time, crumbling under the shot of four warships opposed to them. The Pharos suffered most heavily, and its guns were absolutely silenced; while the fire from the other two forts slackened, considerably. At half-past ten, it was seen that the Ras-el-Teen Palace, which lay behind the fort, was on fire; and, half an hour later, the fire from that fort and Fort Ada almost died out.

The British Admiral now gave the signal to cease firing, and as the smoke cleared away, the effects of the five hours' bombardment were visible. The forts and batteries were mere heaps of ruins. The guns could be made out, lying dismounted, or standing with their muzzles pointing upwards.

The ships had not come out scatheless, but their injuries were, for the most part, immaterial; although rigging had been cut away, bulwarks smashed, and sides dinted. One gun of the *Penelope* had been disabled, and two of the *Alexandra*. Only five men had been killed, altogether, and twenty-seven wounded.

No sign was made of surrender, and an occasional fire was kept up on the forts, to prevent the Egyptians from repairing damages. At one o'clock, twelve volunteers from the *Invincible* started to destroy the guns of Fort Mex. Their fire had ceased, and no men were to be seen in the fort; but they might have been lying in wait to attack any landing party.

On nearing the shore, the surf was found to be too heavy for the boat to pass through it, and Major Tulloch and six men swam ashore and entered the fort. It was found to be deserted, and all the guns but two ten-inch pieces dismounted. The charges of gun cotton, that the swimmers brought ashore with them, were placed in the cannon; and their muzzles blown off. After performing this very gallant service, the little party swam back to their boat.

The British admiral's position was now a difficult one. There were no signs of surrender; for aught he could tell, fifteen thousand Egyptian troops might be lying round the ruined forts, or in the town hard by, in readiness to oppose a landing. That these troops were not to be despised was evident, by the gallantry with which they had fought their guns. This force would be aided by the mass of the population; and it would be hazardous, indeed, to risk the loss of fifteen hundred men, and the reversal of the success already gained.

At the same time, it was painful to think that the Europeans on shore might be massacred, and the whole city destroyed, by the exasperated troops and fanatical population. It was known that the number of Englishmen there was not large, two or three hundred at most; but there was a much larger number of the lower class of Europeans—port labourers, fishermen, petty shopkeepers, and others—who had preferred taking their chance to the certainty of losing all their little possessions, if they left them.

Anxiously the glasses of those on board the ships were directed towards the shore, in hopes of seeing the white flag hoisted, or a boat come out with it flying; but there were no signs of the intentions of the defenders, and the fleet prepared to resume the action in the morning. Fort Marabout, and several of the batteries on the shore, were still unsilenced; and two heavy guns, mounted on the Moncrieff system (by which the gun rose to a level of the parapet, fired, and instantly sank again), had continued to fire all day, in spite of the efforts of the fleet to silence them.

Next morning, however, there was a long heavy swell, and the ironclads were rolling too heavily for anything like accuracy of aim; but as parties of men could be seen, at work in the Moncrieff battery, fire was opened upon them, and they speedily evacuated it.

All night, the Palace of Ras-el-Teen burned fiercely. Another great fire was raging in the heart of the town, and anxiety for those on shore, for the time, overpowered the feeling of exultation at the victory that had been gained.

At half-past ten a white flag was hoisted at the Pharos battery, and all on board watched, with deep anxiety, what was to follow. Lieutenant Lambton at once steamed into the fort, in the Bittern, to enquire if the government were ready to surrender. It was three o'clock before he steamed out again, with the news that his mission was fruitless; and that the white flag had only been hoisted, by the officer in command of the fort, to enable himself and his men to get away unmolested. Lieutenant Lambton had obtained an interview with the military governor, on behalf of the government, and told him that we were not at war with Egypt, and had simply destroyed the forts because they threatened the fleet; that we had no conditions to impose upon the government, but were ready to discuss any proposal; and that the troops would be allowed to evacuate the forts, with the honour of war.

It was most unfortunate that the fleet had not brought with them two or three thousand troops. Had they done so they could have landed at once, and saved a great portion of the town from destruction; but as he had no soldiers, the admiral could not land a portion of the sailors, as the large Egyptian force in the town, which was still protected by a number of land batteries, might fall upon them.

At five o'clock the *Helicon* was sent in to say that white flags would not be noticed, unless hoisted by authority; and if they were again shown, the British admiral would consider them the signs of a general surrender. It was a long time before the *Helicon* returned, with news that no communication had been received from the enemy, that the barracks and arsenals seemed to be deserted and, as far as could be seen, the whole town was evacuated.

As evening wore on, fresh fires broke out in all parts of the town, and a steam pinnace was sent ashore to ascertain, if possible, the state of affairs. Mr. Ross, a contractor for the supply of meat to the fleet, volunteered to accompany it.

The harbour was dark and deserted. Not a light was to be seen in the houses near the water. The crackling of the flames could be heard, with an occasional crash of falling walls and roofs. On nearing the landing place the pinnace paused, for two or three minutes, for those on board to listen; and as all was quiet, steamed alongside. Mr. Ross jumped ashore, and the boat backed off a few yards.

A quarter of an hour later, he returned. That quarter of the town was entirely deserted, and he had pushed on until arrested by a barrier of flames. The great square was on fire, from end to end; the European quarter generally was in flames; and he could see, by the litter that strewed the streets, that the houses had been plundered before being fired.

When daylight broke, a number of Europeans could be seen, at the edge of the water, in the harbour. Boats were at once lowered; and the crews, armed to the teeth, rowed ashore. Here they found about a hundred Europeans, many of them wounded. When rioting had broken out they had, as arranged, assembled at the Anglo-Egyptian Bank. They were taken off to the merchant steamers, lying behind the fleet, and their information confirmed the worst forebodings of the fugitives there.

When the first gun of the bombardment was fired, Gregory had gone up, with the other employees, to the top of the house; where they commanded a view over the whole scene of action. After the first few minutes' firing they could see but little, for batteries and ships were, alike, shrouded in smoke. At first, there had been some feeling of insecurity, and a doubt whether a shot too highly aimed might not come into the town; but the orders to abstain carefully from injuring the city had been well observed, and, except to the Palace and a few houses close to the water's edge, no damage was done.

Towards evening, all those who had resolved to remain behind gathered at the Anglo-Egyptian Bank, or at Mr. Ferguson's. But a consultation was held later, and it was agreed that next morning all should go to the bank, which was a far more massive building, with fewer entrances, and greater facilities for defence. When the town was quiet, therefore, all were employed in transferring valuable goods there, and the house was then locked up and left to its fate. Against a mere rising of the rabble the latter might have been successfully defended; but there was little doubt that, before leaving the town, the troops would join the fanatics; and in that case, a house not built with a special eye for defence could hardly hope to hold out, against persistent attack.

The bank, however, might hope to make a stout defence. It was built of massive stone, the lower windows were barred, and a strong barricade was built against the massive doors. A hundred and twenty resolute men, all well armed, could hold it against even a persistent attack, if unsupported by artillery.

Early in the afternoon, all felt that the critical moment had approached. Throughout the night a fire had raged, from the opposite side of the great square; where several deserted houses had been broken into, and plundered, by the mob; but the soldiers stationed in the square had prevented any further disorder.

Now, however, parties of troops from the forts began to pour in. It was already known that their losses had been very heavy, and that many of the forts had been destroyed. Soon they broke up and, joining the mob, commenced the work of pillage. Doors were blown in, shutters torn off and, with wild yells and shouts, the native population poured in. The work of destruction had begun.

The garrison of the bank saw many Europeans, hurrying, too late, to reach that shelter, murdered before their eyes. In the Levantine quarter, the cracking of pistols and the shouts of men showed that the work of massacre was proceeding there. Soon every door of the houses in the great square was forced in, and ere long great numbers of men, loaded with spoil of all kinds, staggered out.

So far the bank had been left alone; but it was now its turn, and the mob poured down upon it. As they came up, a sharp fire broke out from every window, answered by a discharge of muskets and pistols from the crowd. Here men fell fast, but they had been worked up to such a pitch of excitement, and fanaticism, that the gaps were more than filled by fresh comers.

All the afternoon and evening the fight continued. In vain the mob endeavoured to break down the massive iron bars of the windows, and batter in the doors. Although many of the defenders were wounded, and several killed; by the fire from the windows of the neighbouring houses, and from the road; their steady fire, at the points most hotly attacked, drove their assailants back again and again.

At twelve o'clock the assault slackened. The soldiers had long left and, so far as could be seen from the roof of the house, had entirely evacuated the town; and as this fact became known to the mob, the thought of the consequences of their action cooled their fury; for they knew that, probably, the troops would land from the British ships next day. Each man had his plunder to secure, and gradually the crowd melted away.

By two o'clock all was quiet; and although, occasionally, fresh fires burst out in various quarters of the town, there could be little doubt that the great bulk of the population had followed the example of the army, and had left the city.

Then the besieged gathered in the great office on the ground floor; and, as it was agreed that there would be probably no renewal of the attack, they quietly left the house, locking the doors after them, and made their way down to the shore. They believed that they were the only survivors, but when they reached the end of the town, they found that the building of the Credit Lyonnais had also been successfully defended, though the Ottoman Bank had been overpowered, and all within it, upwards of a hundred in number, killed.

Gregory had done his full share in the defence, and received a musket ball in the shoulder. His wife had passed a terrible time, while the conflagration was raging, and it was evident that the populace had risen, and were undoubtedly murdering as well as burning and plundering; and her delight was indeed great when she saw her husband, with others, approaching in a man-of-war's boat. The fact that one arm was in a sling was scarcely noticed, in her joy at his return, alive.

"Thank God, you are safe!" she said, as he came up the gangway. "It has been an awful time, and I had almost given up hope of ever seeing you alive, again."

"I told you, dear, that I felt confident we could beat off the scum of the town. Of course it was a sharp fight, but there was never any real danger of their breaking in. We only lost about half a dozen, out of nearly a hundred and twenty, and some twenty of us were wounded. My injury is not at all serious, and I shall soon be all right again. It is only a broken collarbone.

"However, it has been a terrible time. The great square, and almost all the European quarter, have been entirely destroyed. The destruction of property is something frightful, and most of the merchants will be absolutely ruined. Fortunately, our firm were insured, pretty well up to the full value."

"But I thought that they could not break in there?"

"We all moved out, the evening before, to the Anglo-Egyptian Bank. The town was full of troops, and we doubted whether we could hold the place. As the bank was much stronger, we agreed that it was better to join the two garrisons and fight it out there; and I am very glad we did so, for I doubt whether we could have defended our place, successfully."

Mr. Ferguson and the clerks had all come off with Gregory to the Simoon, on board which there was plenty of accommodation for them, as it was not one of the ships that had been taken up for the accommodation of the fugitives. Among the party who came on board was a doctor, who had taken part in the defence of the bank, and had attended to the wounded as the fight went on. He did so again that evening, and told Gregory that in a month he would, if he took care of himself, be able to use his arm again.

The next morning there was a consultation in the cabin. Mr. Ferguson had gone on shore, late the previous afternoon; as five hundred sailors had been landed, and had returned in the evening.

"It is certain," he said, "that nothing can be done until the place is rebuilt. The sailors are busy at work, fighting the fire, but there are continued fresh outbreaks. The bulk of the natives have left; but Arabi, before marching out, opened the prisons and released the convicts; and these and the scum of the town are still there, and continue the destruction whenever they get a chance. A score or two have been caught red handed and shot down, and a number of others have been flogged.

"Another batch of sailors will land this morning, and order will soon be restored; unless Arabi, who is encamped, with some ten thousand men, two miles outside the town, makes an effort to recover the place. I don't think he is likely to do so, for now that the European houses have all been destroyed, there would be no longer any reluctance to bombard the town itself; and even if Arabi did recover it, he would very soon be shelled out.

"By the way, a larger number of people have been saved than was imagined. Several of the streets in the poor European quarters have escaped. The people barricaded the ends, and fought so desperately that their assailants drew off, finding it easier to plunder the better quarters. Even if the mob had overcome the resistance of the defenders of the lanes, they would have found little worth taking there; so some five hundred Europeans have escaped, and these will be very useful.

"Charley Beresford has charge of the police arrangements on shore, and he has gangs of them at work fighting the fire, and all the natives are forced to assist. The wires will be restored in a day or two, when I shall, of course, telegraph for instructions; and have no doubt that Mr. Partridge will send out orders to rebuild as soon as order is completely restored.

"I imagine that most of us will be recalled home, until that is done. Even if the place were intact, no business would be done, as our goods would be of little use to the navy or army; for no doubt an army will be sent. Arabi is as powerful as ever, but now that we have taken the matter in hand, it must be carried through.

"At any rate, there will be no clerks' work to be done here. The plans for a new building will naturally be prepared at home, and a foreman of works sent out. It is a bad job for us all, but as it is we must not complain; for we have escaped with our lives, and I hope that, in six months, we may open again. However, we can form no plans, until I receive instructions from home."

Gregory did not go ashore for the next week, by which time order had been completely restored, the fires extinguished, and the streets made, at least, passable. The sailors had been aided by a battalion of marines, which had been telegraphed for from Malta by the admiral, before the bombardment began. The Khedive had returned to Has-el-Teen, which had only been partly destroyed, as soon as the blue-jackets entered. His arrival put an end to all difficulties, as henceforward our operations were carried on, nominally, by his orders.

The American ships entered the harbour the next day and the naval officer in command landed one hundred and twenty-five men, to assist our blue-jackets; and, two days later, the 38th Regiment and a battalion of the 60th Rifles arrived.

The shops in the streets that escaped destruction gradually re-opened, and country people began to bring in supplies. Many of the refugees on board the ships sailed for home, while those who found their houses still standing, although everything in them was smashed and destroyed, set to work to make them habitable. Soon temporary sheds were erected, and such portions of the cargoes on board the merchantmen as would be likely to find a sale, were landed.

Before the end of the week, Mr. Ferguson had received an answer to his telegram. Three days previously he had received a wire: "Have written fully." The letter came via Marseilles. After congratulations at the escape of himself and the staff, Mr. Partridge wrote:

"As you say that the house and warehouse are entirely destroyed, with all contents, there can be nothing for you and the clerks to do; and you had best return, at once, to England. I will make the best arrangements that I can for you all.

"As I have a plan of the ground, I have already instructed an architect to prepare a sketch for rebuilding, on a larger scale than before. The insurance companies are sending out agents to verify claims. Looking at your last report, it seems to me that the loss of goods, as well as that of buildings, will be fully covered. Should any of the staff determine to remain in Alexandria, and to take their chance of finding something to do, you are authorized to pay them three months' salary, and to promise to reinstate them, as soon as we reopen.

"I anticipate no further disturbances, whatever. A strong force is being sent out, and there can be no doubt that Arabi will be crushed, as soon as it is ready to take the field."

Other directions followed, but these were only amplifications of those mentioned.

"What do you think, Annie?" Gregory said, when Ferguson had read to his staff that portion of the letter that concerned them. "Shall we take the three months' pay and remain here, or shall we go back to England?"

"What do you think, yourself?"

"There are two lights in which to look at it, Annie. First, which would be best for us? And secondly, which shall we like best? Of course, the first is the more difficult point to decide. You see, Partridge doesn't say that we shall be kept on; he only says that he will do his best for us. I don't think that there is any chance of his keeping us on at full pay. If he intended to do so, it would have been cheaper for him to give us our pay here, in which case he would save our passages back to England and out again. I think we could not reckon on getting anything like full pay, while we were in England, and you know I have lost faith in my literary powers. I think I have improved, but I certainly should not like, after our last experience, to trust to that for keeping us, in England.

"The question is, what should I do here? There will be plenty of openings, for men who can speak the native language, as labour overseers. The contractors for food for the army will want men of that sort; and as I know several of them, through my work in the port and being in Partridge's house, I have no doubt I could get employment that way, and carry on very well till trade is open again, and obtain then a good deal better berth than they would offer me. No doubt, one could get employment in the transport or commissariat of the army, when it comes out. That will be a thing to think seriously of.

"My objections to that are personal ones. In the first place, it would lead to nothing when the affair is over. In the second place, I should be certain to meet men I knew at Harrow, or at the University, or since then; and I own that I should shrink from that. As Gregory Hilliard, I don't mind carrying a parcel or helping to load a dray; but I should not like, as Gregory Hartley, to be known to be doing that sort of thing. Personally I feel not the smallest humiliation in doing so, but I don't think it would be fair to Geoffrey. I should not like it myself, if I were an earl, for fellows who knew him to be able to say that my brother was knocking about in Egypt as an interpreter, or mule driver, or something of that sort. That certainly has to be taken into consideration.

"It is not likely that I should get any sort of berth that an officer would be appointed to, for every officer in the army, whose regiment is not coming out here, will be rushing to the War Office to apply for any sort of appointment that would enable him to come out to the war.

"Again, it is almost certain that, when this business is over—and I don't suppose it will last long, after we get an army out here—a fresh Egyptian force will be raised. You may be sure that the greater portion of our troops will be hurried back, as soon as it is over; and that, as the present Egyptian army will be altogether smashed up, it will be absolutely necessary that there should be a force, of some kind or other, that can put a stop to this Mahdi fellow's doings. He has overrun half the Soudan, and inflicted serious defeats on the Egyptian troops there. He has captured a considerable portion of Kordofan; and, of course, it is owing to his insurrection that those rows have occurred down at the Red Sea, where our men have been fighting.

"It is likely enough that they may appoint some British officers to the new force, and I might get a fair position on it. They will want interpreters there. Promotion will be sure to be rapid, and I might have opportunities of distinguishing myself, and get an appointment where I could, without discrediting it, take my own name again.

"These are only among the things that might be; but at the worst, I am certain to get some sort of post, at Alexandria, which would enable us to live without trenching upon the three months' pay that is offered me; and then, if I could see nothing better, I could return to Partridge's employment when they reopen here, and I have no doubt that they would improve my position.

"I don't think that Parrott is likely to come back again. The climate did not suit him, and he is always having attacks of fever. Ferguson has, I know, for he told me so, reported very favourably about my work to headquarters; and, as I have been wounded in defence of the house, I have an additional claim. The others will, of course, be moved up, and I should get the junior clerkship—no advance in the way of remuneration, but a great improvement in position.

"So I think we had better accept the three months' pay, and take our chances. At any rate, there will be no fear of another disturbance at Alexandria. The mob have had a lesson here that they are not likely to forget, and I should fancy that, although we may withdraw the army, two or three regiments will be left here, and at Cairo, for a long time to come. We should be fools, indeed, if we threw away the money that this business will cost, before it is over, and let Egypt slip altogether out of our fingers again. France has forfeited her right to have anything to say in the matter. In our hands it will be a very valuable possession, and certainly our stay here would be of inestimable advantage to the natives, as we should govern Egypt as we govern India, and do away with the tyranny, oppression, and extortion of the native officials."

Mrs. Hilliard quite agreed with her husband; and accordingly, the next day, Gregory informed Mr. Ferguson that he would accept the three months' pay, and his discharge; and should, at any rate for a time, remain in Alexandria.

"I think you are right, Hilliard. There will be lots of opportunities here for a man who knows the language as you do. If you like, I will speak to Mr. Ross. I saw him yesterday, in the town, and he said that two of his assistants had been killed. He has already obtained a fresh contract, and a very heavy one, for the supply of meat for the troops as they arrive; and I have no doubt he would be very glad to engage you, on good terms, though the engagement could only be made during the stay of the army here."

"Thank you, sir. I shall be much obliged to you if you will do so; and I would rather that the engagement should be a temporary one, on both sides, so that I should be free to leave, at a few days' notice."

The contractor, after a chat with Gregory Hilliard, was glad to secure his services. He saw the advantage that it would be to have a gentleman to represent him, with the army, instead of an agent of a very different kind. Other men would do to purchase animals from the Arabs, or to receive them at the ports when they were brought over from Spain and Italy; but it required a variety of qualities, difficult to obtain in the same person, to act as agent with the army. Gregory was exactly the man required, and he was soon on excellent terms, both with the officers of the quartermaster's department, and the contractors who brought in the cargoes of cattle.

As soon as the bulk of the army sailed from Alexandria to Ismailia, he made the latter town his headquarters; and by his power of work, his tact and good temper, he smoothed away all the difficulties that so often arise between contractors and army officials, and won the goodwill of all with whom he came in contact. When the army removed to Cairo, after the defeat and dispersal of Arabi's force at Tel-el-Kebir, Gregory established himself there, and was joined by his wife and child.

As soon as matters settled down, and a considerable portion of the troops had left Egypt, Mr. Ross said to him:

"Of course, our operations in the future will be comparatively small, Mr. Hilliard, and I must reduce my staff."

"I quite understand that," Gregory replied, "and I knew that I should have to look out for something else."

"I shall be very sorry to lose your services, which have indeed been invaluable, and I am sure have been appreciated, by the army men as much as by myself. I certainly should not think of your leaving me, until you get another berth; and it is only because I see an opening, if you like to take it, that might lead to something better, in the future, than anything I can offer you.

"You know that Colonel Hicks arrived here, a fortnight since, and is to take command of the Egyptian army, and to have the rank of pasha. Several officers have received appointments on his staff. He will shortly be going up to Khartoum. I was speaking to him yesterday, and as I was doing so, two of the officers of Wolseley's staff came in. A question of supplies came up, and I mentioned your name, and said that I thought that you were the very man for him, that you were master of Arabic, and an excellent organizer; and, a very important matter where there were so few English officers together, a gentleman.

"One of the officers, who knew the work that you had done, at once confirmed what I had said, and declared that Wolseley's quartermaster general would speak as warmly in your favour. Hicks told me that, until he got up to Khartoum, he could not say what arrangements would be made for the supplies; but that he would, at any rate, be very glad to have you with him, in the capacity of a first-class interpreter, and for general service with the staff, with the temporary rank of captain; with the special view of your services in organizing a supply train, when he moved forward. I said that I should speak to you, and ascertain your views."

"I am very much obliged to you, indeed. I must take twenty-four hours to think it over. Of course I shall be guided, to some extent, by the question whether the appointment would be likely to be a permanent one."

"That I have no doubt. Indeed, Hicks said as much. I asked him the question, and he replied, 'I can hardly make a permanent appointment now, as I am not quite in the saddle; but I have no doubt, from what you say, that Mr. Hilliard will make a valuable officer; and after our first campaign I shall, without difficulty, be able to obtain him a permanent appointment in the Egyptian army.'"

"I thank you, most heartily, Mr. Ross. It seems to me a grand opening. There is no doubt that, as our troops leave, the Egyptian army will be thoroughly reorganized; and there will be many openings for a man who knows the language, and is ready to work hard; and, no doubt, the regiments will be largely officered by Englishmen."

That evening, Gregory had a long talk with his wife.

"I don't like the thought of leaving you, even for a time; but no doubt, when the Mahdi is settled with, you will be able to join me at Khartoum; which, I believe, is by no means an unpleasant place to live in. Of course, I shall come down and take you up. It is a splendid chance, and will really be my reinstatement. Once holding a commission in the Egyptian army, I should resume my own name, and have the future to look forward to. Entering the service as the army is being reorganized, I should have a great pull, and should be sure to get on, and be able to write to my father and brother, without its appearing that I wanted help of any kind."

There were tears in Mrs. Hilliard's eyes, but she said bravely:

"I quite agree with you, Gregory. Of course, I shall be sorry that you should leave me, even for a time; but it seems to me, too, that it is a grand opportunity. You know what a pain it was to me, all the time that we were at Alexandria, that you should be working in such a subordinate position. Now there is an opening by which you will be in a position, ere long, more worthy of your birth and education. I have no doubt I shall get on very well, here. I believe that Hicks Pasha has brought his wife out with him here; and some of his officers will, no doubt, be married men also; and as the wife of one of his officers I shall, of course, get to know them. I should be selfish, indeed, to say a word to keep you back, and shall be delighted to think of you associating with other English gentlemen, as one of themselves."

And so it was settled. The next day, Gregory called on Hicks Pasha. The latter had made some more enquiries respecting him, and was well pleased with his appearance.

"I have already a gentleman named as staff interpreter, Mr. Hilliard, but I can appoint you, at once, interpreter to the quartermaster's department, attached to my personal staff for the present. I can tell you that the Egyptian army will be largely increased, and I shall be able, after a time, to procure you a better appointment. When we have once defeated the Mahdi, and restored order, there will be many appointments open for the reorganization of the Soudan. There are a good many preparations to be made, before I leave, which I expect to do in the course of three or four weeks; and I shall be glad of your assistance, as soon as you can join us."

"I shall be glad to do so, at once. Mr. Ross has kindly told me that I am at liberty to resign my post, under him, as soon as I like."

"Very well, then. You may consider yourself appointed, today. My intention is to go first to Suakim, and thence up to Berber, and so by water to Khartoum."

The next three weeks passed rapidly. Gregory was, on the following day, introduced to the various officers of Hicks Pasha's staff; and, on learning that he was married, the general asked him and his wife to dinner, to make the acquaintance of Lady Hicks, and the wives of three of his fellow officers.

At last, the time came for parting. Annie bore up well; and although, when alone, she had many a cry, she was always cheerful, and went with her husband and saw him off, at the station of the railway for Ismailia, without breaking down badly.

CHAPTER 3:

A Terrible Disaster.

It was an anxious time for his wife, after Gregory started. He, and those with him, had left with a feeling of confidence that the insurrection would speedily be put down. The garrison of Khartoum had inflicted several severe defeats upon the Mahdi, but had also suffered some reverses. This, however, was only to be expected, when the troops under him were scarcely more disciplined than those of the Dervishes, who had always been greatly superior in numbers, and inspired with a fanatical belief in their prophet. But with British officers to command, and British officers to drill and discipline the troops, there could be no fear of a recurrence of these disasters.

Before they started, Mrs. Hilliard had become intimate with the wife of Hicks Pasha, and those of the other married officers, and had paid visits with them to the harems of high Turkish officials. Visits were frequently exchanged, and what with these, and the care of the boy, her time was constantly occupied. She received letters from Gregory, as frequently as possible, after his arrival at Omdurman, and until he set out with the main body, under the general, on the way to El Obeid.

Before starting, he said he hoped that, in another two months, the campaign would be over, El Obeid recovered, and the Mahdi smashed up; and that, as soon as they returned to Khartoum, Hicks Pasha would send for his wife and daughters, and the other married officers for their wives; and, of course, she would accompany them.

"I cannot say much for Omdurman," he wrote; "but Khartoum is a nice place. Many of the houses there have shady gardens. Hicks has promised to recommend me for a majority, in one of the Turkish regiments. In the intervals of my own work, I have got up drill. I shall, of course, tell him then what my real name is, so that I can be gazetted in it. It is likely enough that, even after we defeat the Mahdi, this war may go on for some time before it is stamped out; and in another year I may be a full-blown colonel, if only an Egyptian one; and as the pay of the English officers is good, I shall be able to have a very comfortable home for you.

"I need not repeat my instructions, darling, as to what you must do in the event, improbable as it is, of disaster. When absolutely assured of my death, but not until then, you will go back to England with the boy, and see my father. He is not a man to change his mind, unless I were to humble myself before him; but I think he would do the right thing for you. If he will not, there is the letter for Geoffrey. He has no settled income at present, but when he comes into the title he will, I feel quite certain, make you an allowance. I know that you would, for yourself, shrink from doing this; but, for the boy's sake, you will not hesitate to carry out my instructions. I should say you had better write to my father, for the interview might be an unpleasant one; but if you have to appeal to Geoffrey, you had better call upon him and show him this letter. I feel sure that he will do what he can.

"Gregory."

A month later, a messenger came up from Suakim with a despatch, dated October 3rd. The force was then within a few days' march of El Obeid. The news was not altogether cheering. Hordes of the enemy hovered about their rear. Communication was already difficult, and they had to depend upon the stores they carried, and cut themselves off altogether from the base. He brought some private letters from the officers, and among them one for Mrs. Hilliard. It was short, and written in pencil:

"In a few days, Dear, the decisive battle will take place; and although it will be a tough fight, none of us have any fear of the result. In the very improbable event of a defeat, I shall, if I have time, slip on the Arab dress I have with me, and may hope to escape. However, I have little fear that it will come to that. God bless and protect you, and the boy!

"Gregory."

A month passed away. No news came from Hicks Pasha, or any of his officers. Then there were rumours current in the bazaars, of disaster; and one morning, when Annie called upon Lady Hicks, she found several of the ladies there with pale and anxious faces. She paused at the door.

"Do not be alarmed, Mrs. Hilliard," Lady Hicks said. "Nizim Pasha has been here this morning. He thought that I might have heard the rumours that are current in the bazaar, that there has been a disaster, but he says there is no confirmation whatever of these reports. He does not deny, however, that they have caused anxiety among the authorities; for sometimes these rumours, whose origin no one knows, do turn out to be correct. He said that enquiries have been made, but no foundation for the stories can be got at. I questioned him closely, and he says that he can only account for them on the ground that, if a victory had been won, an official account from government should have been here before this; and that it is solely on this account that these rumours have got about. He said there was no reason for supposing that this silence meant disaster. A complete victory might have been won; and yet the messenger with the despatches might have been captured, and killed, by the parties of tribesmen hanging behind the army, or wandering about the country between the army and Khartoum. Still, of course, this is making us all very anxious."

The party soon broke up, none having any reassuring suggestions to offer; and Annie returned to her lodging, to weep over her boy, and pray for the safety of his father. Days and weeks passed, and still no word came to Cairo. At Khartoum there was a ferment among the native population. No secret was made of the fact that the tribesmen who came and went all declared that Hicks Pasha's army was utterly destroyed. At length, the Egyptian government announced to the wives of the officers that pensions would be given to them, according to the rank of their husbands. As captain and interpreter, Gregory's wife had but a small one, but it was sufficient for her to live upon.

One by one, the other ladies gave up hope and returned to England, but Annie stayed on. Misfortune might have befallen the army, but Gregory might have escaped in disguise. She had, like the other ladies, put on mourning for him; for had she declared her belief that he might still be alive, she could not have applied for the pension, and this was necessary for the child's sake. Of one thing she was determined. She would not go with him, as beggars, to the father who had cast Gregory off; until, as he had said, she received absolute news of his death. She was not in want; but as her pension was a small one, and she felt that it would be well for her to be employed, she asked Lady Hicks, before she left, to mention at the houses of the Egyptian ladies to whom she went to say goodbye, that Mrs. Hilliard would be glad to give lessons in English, French, or music.

The idea pleased them, and she obtained several pupils. Some of these were the ladies themselves, and the lessons generally consisted in sitting for an hour with them, two or three times a week, and talking to them; the conversation being in short sentences, of which she gave them the English translation, which they repeated over and over again, until they knew them by heart. This caused great amusement, and was accompanied by much laughter, on the part of the ladies and their attendants.

Several of her pupils, however, were young boys and girls, and the teaching here was of a more serious kind. The lessons to the boys were given the first thing in the morning, and the pupils were brought to her house by attendants. At eleven o'clock she taught the girls, and returned at one, and had two hours more teaching in the afternoon. She could have obtained more pupils, had she wished to; but the pay she received, added to her income, enabled her to live very comfortably, and to save up money. She had a Negro servant, who was very fond of the boy, and she could leave him in her charge with perfect confidence, while she was teaching.

In the latter part of 1884, she ventured to hope that some news might yet come to her, for a British expedition had started for the relief of General Gordon, who had gone up early in the year to Khartoum;

where it was hoped that the influence he had gained among the natives, at the time he was in command of the Egyptian forces in the Soudan, would enable him to make head against the insurrection. His arrival had been hailed by the population, but it was soon evident to him that, unless aided by England with something more than words, Khartoum must finally fall.

But his requests for aid were slighted. He had asked that two regiments should be sent from Suakim, to keep open the route to Berber, but Mr. Gladstone's government refused even this slight assistance to the man they had sent out, and it was not until May that public indignation, at this base desertion of one of the noblest spirits that Britain ever produced, caused preparations for his rescue to be made; and it was December before the leading regiment arrived at Korti, far up the Nile.

After fighting two hard battles, a force that had marched across the loop of the Nile came down upon it above Metemmeh. A party started up the river at once, in two steamers which Gordon had sent down to meet them, but only arrived near the town to hear that they were too late, that Khartoum had fallen, and that Gordon had been murdered. The army was at once hurried back to the coast, leaving it to the Mahdists—more triumphant than ever—to occupy Dongola; and to push down, and possibly, as they were confident they should do, to capture Egypt itself.

The news of the failure was a terrible blow to Mrs. Hilliard. She had hoped that, when Khartoum was relieved, some information at least might be obtained, from prisoners, as to the fate of the British officers at El Obeid. That most of them had been killed was certain, but she still clung to the hope that her husband might have escaped from the general massacre, thanks to his knowledge of the language, and the disguise he had with him; and even that if captured later on he might be a prisoner; or that he might have escaped detection altogether, and be still living among friendly tribesmen. It was a heavy blow to her, therefore, when she heard that the troops were being hurried down to the coast, and that the Mahdi would be uncontested master of Egypt, as far as Assouan.

She did, however, receive news when the force returned to Cairo, which, although depressing, did not extinguish all hope. Lieutenant Colonel Colborne, by good luck, had ascertained that a native boy in the service of General Buller claimed to have been at El Obeid. Upon questioning him closely, he found out that he had unquestionably been there, for he described accurately the position Colonel Colborne—who had started with Hicks Pasha, but had been forced by illness to return—had occupied in one of the engagements. The boy was then the slave of an Egyptian officer of the expedition.

The army had suffered much from want of water, but they had obtained plenty from a lake within three days' march from El Obeid. From this point they were incessantly fired at, by the enemy. On the second day they were attacked, but beat off the enemy, though with heavy loss to themselves. The next day they pressed forward, as it was necessary to get to water; but they were misled by their guide, and at noon the Arabs burst down upon them, the square in which the force was marching was broken, and a terrible slaughter took place. Then Hicks Pasha, with his officers, seeing that all was lost, gathered together and kept the enemy at bay with their revolvers, till their ammunition was exhausted. After that they fought with their swords till all were killed, Hicks Pasha being the last to fall. The lad himself hid among the dead and was not discovered until the next morning, when he was made a slave by the man who found him.

This was terrible! But there was still hope. If this boy had concealed himself among the dead, her husband might have done the same. Not being a combatant officer, he might not have been near the others when the affair took place; and moreover, the lad had said that the black regiment in the rear of the square had kept together and marched away; he believed all had been afterwards killed, but this he did not know. If Gregory had been there when the square was broken, he might well have kept with them, and at nightfall slipped on his disguise and made his escape. It was at least possible—she would not give up all hope.

So years went on. Things were quiet in Egypt. A native army had been raised there, under the command of British officers, and these had checked the northern progress of the Mahdists and restored confidence in Egypt. Gregory—for the boy had been named after his father—grew up strong and hearty. His mother devoted her evenings to his education. From the Negress, who was his nurse and the general servant of the house, he had learnt to talk her native language. She had been carried off, when ten years old, by a slave-raiding party, and sold to an Egyptian trader at Khartoum; been given by him to an Atbara chief, with whom he had dealings; and, five years later, had been captured in a tribal war by the Jaalin. Two or three times she had changed masters, and finally had been purchased by an Egyptian officer, and brought down by him to Cairo. At his death, four years afterwards, she had been given her freedom, being now past fifty, and had taken service with Gregory Hilliard and his wife. Her vocabulary was a large one, and she was acquainted with most of the dialects of the Soudan tribes.

From the time when her husband was first missing, Mrs. Hilliard cherished the idea that, some day, the child might grow up and search for his father; and, perhaps, ascertain his fate beyond all doubt. She was a very conscientious woman, and was resolved that, at whatever pain to herself, she would, when once certain of her husband's death, go to England and obtain recognition of his boy by his family. But it was pleasant to think that the day was far distant when she could give up hope. She saw, too, that if the Soudan was ever reconquered, the knowledge of the tribal languages must be of immense benefit to her son; and she therefore insisted, from the first, that the woman should always talk to him in one or other of the languages that she knew.

Thus Gregory, almost unconsciously, acquired several of the dialects used in the Soudan. Arabic formed the basis of them all, except the Negro tongue. At first he mixed them up, but as he grew, Mrs. Hilliard insisted that his nurse should speak one for a month, and then use another; so that, by the time he was twelve years old, the boy could speak in the Negro tongue, and half a dozen dialects, with equal facility.

His mother had, years before, engaged a teacher of Arabic for him. This he learned readily, as it was the root of the Egyptian and the other languages he had picked up. Of a morning, he sat in the school and learned pure Arabic and Turkish, while the boys learned English; and therefore, without an effort, when he was twelve years old he talked these languages as well as English; and had, moreover, a smattering of Italian and French, picked up from boys of his own age, for his mother had now many acquaintances among the European community.

While she was occupied in the afternoon, with her pupils, the boy had liberty to go about as he pleased; and indeed she encouraged him to take long walks, to swim, and to join in all games and exercises.

"English boys at home," she said, "have many games, and it is owing to these that they grow up so strong and active. They have more opportunities than you, but you must make the most of those that you have. We may go back to England some day, and I should not at all like you to be less strong than others."

As, however, such opportunities were very small, she had an apparatus of poles, horizontal bars, and ropes set up, such as those she had seen, in England, in use by the boys of one of the families where she had taught, before her marriage; and insisted upon Gregory's exercising himself upon it for an hour every morning, soon after sunrise. As she had heard her husband once say that fencing was a splendid exercise, not only for developing the figure, but for giving a good carriage as well as activity and alertness, she arranged with a Frenchman who had served in the army, and had gained a prize as a swordsman in the regiment, to give the boy lessons two mornings in the week.

Thus, at fifteen, Gregory was well grown and athletic, and had much of the bearing and appearance of an English public-school boy. His mother had been very particular in seeing that his manners were those of an Englishman.

"I hope the time will come when you will associate with English gentlemen, and I should wish you, in all respects, to be like them. You belong to a good family; and should you, by any chance, some day go home, you must do credit to your dear father."

The boy had, for some years, been acquainted with the family story, except that he did not know the name he bore was his father's Christian name, and not that of his family.

"My grandfather must have been a very bad man, Mother, to have quarreled with my father for marrying you."

"Well, my boy, you hardly understand the extent of the exclusiveness of some Englishmen. Of course, it is not always so, but to some people, the idea of their sons or daughters marrying into a family of less rank than themselves appears to be an almost terrible thing. As I have told you, although the daughter of a clergyman, I was, when I became an orphan, obliged to go out as a governess."

"But there was no harm in that, Mother?"

"No harm, dear; but a certain loss of position. Had my father been alive, and had I been living with him in a country rectory, your grandfather might not have been pleased at your father's falling in love with me, because he would probably have considered that, being, as you know by his photograph, a fine, tall, handsome man, and having the best education money could give him, he might have married very much better; that is to say, the heiress of a property, or into a family of influence, through which he might have been pushed on; but he would not have thought of opposing the marriage on the ground of my family. But a governess is a different thing. She is, in many cases, a lady in every respect, but her position is a doubtful one.

"In some families she is treated as one of themselves. In others, her position is very little different from that of an upper servant. Your grandfather was a passionate man, and a very proud man. Your father's elder brother was well provided for, but there were two sisters, and these and your father he hoped would make good marriages. He lived in very good style, but your uncle was extravagant, and your grandfather was over indulgent, and crippled himself a good deal in paying the debts that he incurred. It was natural, therefore, that he should have objected to your father's engagement to what he called a penniless governess. It was only what was to be expected. If he had stated his objections to the marriage calmly, there need have been no quarrel. Your father would assuredly have married me, in any case; and your grandfather might have refused to assist him, if he did so, but there need have been no breakup in the family, such as took place.

"However, as it was, your father resented his tone, and what had been merely a difference of opinion became a serious quarrel, and they never saw each other, afterwards. It was a great grief to me, and it was owing to that, and his being unable to earn his living in England, that your father brought me out here. I believe he would have done well at home, though it would have been a hard struggle. At that time I was very delicate, and was ordered by the doctors to go to a warm climate, and therefore your father accepted a position of a kind which, at least, enabled us to live, and obtained for me the benefit of a warm climate.

"Then the chance came of his going up to the Soudan, and there was a certainty that, if the expedition succeeded, as everyone believed it would, he would have obtained permanent rank in the Egyptian army, and so recovered the position in life that he had voluntarily given up, for my sake."

"And what was the illness you had, Mother?"

"It was an affection of the lungs, dear. It was a constant cough, that threatened to turn to consumption, which is one of the most fatal diseases we have in England."

"But it hasn't cured you, Mother, for I often hear you coughing, at night."

"Yes, my cough has been a little troublesome of late, Gregory."

Indeed, from the time of the disaster to the expedition of Hicks Pasha, Annie Hilliard had lost ground. She herself was conscious of it; but, except for the sake of the boy, she had not troubled over it. She had not altogether given up hope, but the hope grew fainter and fainter, as the years went on. Had it not been for the promise to her husband, not to mention his real name or to make any application to his father unless absolutely assured of his death, she would, for Gregory's sake, have written to Mr. Hartley, and asked for help that would have enabled her to take the boy home to England, and have him properly educated there. But she had an implicit faith in the binding of a promise so made, and as long as she was not driven, by absolute want, to apply to Mr. Hartley, was determined to keep to it.

A year after this conversation, Gregory was sixteen. Now tall and strong, he had, for some time past, been anxious to obtain some employment that would enable his mother to give up her teaching. Some of this, indeed, she had been obliged to relinquish. During the past few months her cheeks had become hollow, and her cough was now frequent by day, as well as by night. She had consulted an English doctor, who, she saw by the paper, was staying at Shepherd's Hotel. He had hesitated before giving a direct opinion, but on her imploring him to tell her the exact state of her health, said gently:

"I am afraid, madam, that I can give you no hope of recovery. One lung has already gone, the other is very seriously diseased. Were you living in England, I should say that your life might be prolonged by taking you to a warm climate; but as it is, no change could be made for the better."

"Thank you, Doctor. I wanted to know the exact truth, and be able to make my arrangements accordingly. I was quite convinced that my condition was hopeless, but I thought it right to consult a physician, and to know how much time I could reckon on. Can you tell me that?"

"That is always difficult, Mrs. Hilliard. It may be three months hence. It might be more speedily—a vessel might give way in the lungs, suddenly. On the other hand, you might live six months. Of course, I cannot say how rapid the progress of the disease has been."

"It may not be a week, doctor. I am not at all afraid of hearing your sentence—indeed, I can see it in your eyes."

"It may be within a week"—the doctor bowed his head gravely—"it may be at any time."

"Thank you!" she said, quietly. "I was sure it could not be long. I have been teaching, but three weeks ago I had to give up my last pupil. My breath is so short that the slightest exertion brings on a fit of coughing."

On her return home she said to Gregory:

"My dear boy, you must have seen—you cannot have helped seeing—that my time is not long here. I have seen an English doctor today, and he says the end may come at any moment."

"Oh, Mother, Mother!" the lad cried, throwing himself on his knees, and burying his face in her lap, "don't say so!"

The news, indeed, did not come as a surprise to him. He had, for months, noticed the steady change in her: how her face had fallen away, how her hands seemed nerveless, her flesh transparent, and her eyes grew larger and larger. Many times he had walked far up among the hills and, when beyond the reach of human eye, thrown himself down and cried unrestrainedly, until his strength seemed utterly exhausted, and yet the verdict now given seemed to come as a sudden blow.

"You must not break down, dear," she said quietly. "For months I have felt that it was so; and, but for your sake, I did not care to live. I thank God that I have been spared to see you growing up all that I could wish; and though I should have liked to see you fairly started in life, I feel that you may now make your way, unaided.

"Now I want, before it is too late, to give you instructions. In my desk you will find a sealed envelope. It contains a copy of the registers of my marriage, and of your birth. These will prove that your father married, and had a son. You can get plenty of witnesses who can prove that you were the child mentioned. I promised your father that I would not mention our real name to anyone, until it was necessary for me to write to your grandfather. I have kept that promise. His name was Gregory Hilliard, so we have not taken false names. They were his Christian names. The third name, his family name, you will find when you open that envelope.

"I have been thinking, for months past, what you had best do; and this is my advice, but do not look upon it as an order. You are old enough to think for yourself. You know that Sir Herbert Kitchener, the Sirdar, is pushing his way up the Nile. I have no doubt that, with your knowledge of Arabic, and of the language used by the black race in the Soudan, you will be able to obtain some sort of post in the army, perhaps as an interpreter to one of the officers commanding a brigade—the same position, in fact, as your father had, except that the army is now virtually British, whereas that he went with was Egyptian.

"I have two reasons for desiring this. I do not wish you to go home, until you are in a position to dispense with all aid from your family. I have done without it, and I trust that you will be able to do the same. I should like you to be able to go home at one-and-twenty, and to say to your grandfather, 'I have not come home to ask for money or assistance of any kind. I am earning my living honourably. I only ask recognition, by my family, as my father's son.'

"It is probable that this expedition will last fully two years. It must be a gradual advance, and even then, if the Khalifa is beaten, it must be a considerable time before matters are thoroughly settled. There will be many civil posts open to those who, like yourself, are well acquainted with the language of the country; and if you can obtain one of these, you may well remain there until you come of age. You can then obtain a few months' leave of absence and go to England.

"My second reason is that, although my hope that your father is still alive has almost died out, it is just possible that he is, like Neufeld and some others, a prisoner in the Khalifa's hands; or possibly living as an Arab cultivator near El Obeid. Many prisoners will be taken, and from some of these we may learn such details, of the battle, as may clear us of the darkness that hangs over your father's fate.

"When you do go home, Gregory, you had best go first to your father's brother. His address is on a paper in the envelope. He was heir to a peerage, and has, perhaps, now come into it. I have no reasons for supposing that he sided with his father against yours. The brothers were not bad friends, although they saw little of each other; for your father, after he left Oxford, was for the most part away from England, until a year before his marriage; and at that time your uncle was in America, having gone out with two or three others on a hunting expedition among the Rocky Mountains. There is, therefore, no reason for supposing that he will receive you otherwise than kindly, when once he is sure that you are his nephew. He may, indeed, for aught I know, have made efforts to discover your father, after he returned from abroad."

"I would rather leave them alone altogether, Mother," Gregory said passionately.

"That you cannot do, my boy. Your father was anxious that you should be at least recognized, and afterwards bear your proper name. You will not be going as a beggar, and there will be nothing humiliating. As to your grandfather, he may not even be alive. It is seldom that I see an English newspaper, and even had his death been advertised in one of the papers, I should hardly have noticed it, as I never did more than just glance at the principal items of news.

"In my desk you will also see my bank book. It is in your name. I have thought it better that it should stand so, as it will save a great deal of trouble, should anything happen to me. Happily, I have never had any reasons to draw upon it, and there are now about five hundred and fifty pounds standing to your credit. Of late you have generally paid in the money, and you are personally known to the manager. Should there be any difficulty, I have made a will leaving everything to you. That sum will keep you, if you cannot obtain the employment we speak of, until you come of age; and will, at any rate, facilitate your getting employment with the army, as you will not be obliged to demand much pay, and can take anything that offers.

"Another reason for your going to England is that your grandfather may, if he is dead, have relented at last towards your father, and may have left him some share in his fortune; and although you might well refuse to accept any help from him, if he is alive, you can have no hesitation in taking that which should be yours by right. I think sometimes now, my boy, that I have been wrong in not accepting the fact of your father's death as proved, and taking you home to England; but you will believe that I acted for the best, and I shrank from the thought of going home as a beggar, while I could maintain you and myself comfortably, here."

"You were quite right, Mother dear. We have been very happy, and I have been looking forward to the time when I might work for you, as you have worked for me. It has been a thousand times better, so, than living on the charity of a man who looked down upon you, and who cast off my father."

"Well, you will believe at least that I acted for the best, dear, and I am not sure that it has not been for the best. At any rate I, too, have been far happier than I could have been, if living in England on an allowance begrudged to me."

A week later, Gregory was awakened by the cries of the Negro servant; and, running to Mrs. Hilliard's bedroom, found that his mother had passed away during the night. Burial speedily follows death in Egypt; and on the following day Gregory returned, heartbroken, to his lonely house, after seeing her laid in her grave.

For a week, he did nothing but wander about the house, listlessly. Then, with a great effort, he roused himself. He had his work before him—had his mother's wishes to carry out. His first step was to go to the bank, and ask to see the manager.

"You may have heard of my mother's death, Mr. Murray?" he said.

"Yes, my lad, and sorry, indeed, I was to hear of it. She was greatly liked and respected, by all who knew her."

"She told me," Gregory went on, trying to steady his voice, "a week before her death, that she had money here deposited in my name."

"That is so."

"Is there anything to be done about it, sir?"

"Not unless you wish to draw it out. She told me, some time ago, why she placed it in your name; and I told her that there would be no difficulty."

"I do not want to draw any of it out, sir, as there were fifty pounds in the house. She was aware that she had not long to live, and no doubt kept it by her, on purpose."

"Then all you have to do is to write your signature on this piece of paper. I will hand you a cheque book, and you will only have to fill up a cheque and sign it, and draw out any amount you please."

"I have never seen a cheque book, sir. Will you kindly tell me what I should have to do?"

Mr. Murray took out a cheque book, and explained its use. Then he asked what Gregory thought of doing.

"I wish to go up with the Nile expedition, sir. It was my mother's wish, also, that I should do so. My main object is to endeavour to obtain particulars of my father's death, and to assure myself that he was one of those who fell at El Obeid. I do not care in what capacity I go up; but as I speak Arabic and Soudanese, as well as English, my mother thought that I might get employment as interpreter, either under an officer engaged on making the railway, or in some capacity under an officer in one of the Egyptian regiments."

"I have no doubt that I can help you there, lad. I know the Sirdar, and a good many of the British officers, for whom I act as agent. Of course, I don't know in what capacity they could employ you, but surely some post or other could be found for you, where your knowledge of the language would render you very useful. Naturally, the officers in the Egyptian service all understand enough of the language to get on with, but few of the officers in the British regiments do.

"It is fortunate that you came today. I have an appointment with Lord Cromer tomorrow morning, so I will take the opportunity of speaking to him. As it is an army affair, and as your father was in the Egyptian service, and your mother had a pension from it, I may get him to interest himself in the matter. Kitchener is down here at present, and if Cromer would speak to him, I should think you would certainly be able to get up, though I cannot say in what position. The fact that you are familiar with the Negro language, which differs very widely from that of the Arab Soudan tribes, who all speak Arabic, is strongly in your favour; and may give you an advantage over applicants who can only speak Arabic.

"I shall see Lord Cromer at ten, and shall probably be with him for an hour. You may as well be outside his house, at half-past ten; possibly he may like to see you. At any rate, when I come down, I can tell you what he says."

With grateful thanks, Gregory returned home.

CHAPTER 4:

An Appointment.

Soon after ten, next morning, Gregory took up his place near the entrance to Lord Cromer's house. It was just eleven when Mr. Murray came down.

"Come in with me," he said. "Lord Cromer will see you. He acknowledged at once, when I told him your story, that you had a strong claim for employment. The only point was as to your age. I told him that you were past sixteen, and a strong, active fellow, and that you had had a good physical training."

They had now entered the house.

"Don't be nervous, Hilliard; just talk to him as you would to me. Many a good man has lost an appointment, from being nervous and embarrassed when he applied for it."

"You want to go up to the Soudan?" Lord Cromer said. "Mr. Murray has told me your reasons for wanting to go. Though I fear it is hardly likely that any new light can be thrown upon the fate of Hicks Pasha, and his officers, I feel that it is a natural desire on your part."

"It was my mother's last wish, sir, and she took particular pains in my training, and education, to fit me for the work."

"You speak Arabic, and the tongue of the Negro blacks, almost as well as English?"

"Yes, sir. Arabic quite as well, and the other nearly as well, I think."

"What sort of post did you hope to get, Mr. Hilliard?"

"Any post for which I may be thought fit, sir. I do not care at all about pay. My mother saved sufficient to keep me for two or three years. I would rather enlist than not go up at all, though I fear I am too young to be accepted; but I am quite ready to turn my hand to anything."

"If it concerned the Egyptian government, or a civil appointment, I would certainly exert my influence in your favour; but this expedition is in the hands of the military. However, if you will take a seat in the anteroom, and do not mind waiting there for an hour or two, I will see what can be done."

"Thank you very much indeed, sir."

Mr. Murray, as they went out together, said:

"I think that you have made a good impression. He told me, before, that it was a matter for Sir Herbert Kitchener, and that he was expecting him in a quarter of an hour. Come and tell me the result, when you leave."

Ten minutes later, a tall man, whom Gregory recognized at once as

Sir Herbert Kitchener, whose figure was well known in Cairo, passed through the room; all who were sitting there rising to their feet, as he did so. He acknowledged the salute mechanically, as if scarcely conscious of it. An hour later a bell was rung, and an attendant went into the room. He returned directly.

"Mr. Hilliard," he said.

Gregory rose, and passed through the door held open. Kitchener was sitting at the table with Lord Cromer. His keen glance seemed, to Gregory, to take him in from head to foot, and then to look at something far beyond him.

"This is Mr. Hilliard," Lord Cromer said, "the young gentleman I have spoken of."

"You want to go up?" the general said shortly, in Arabic.

"Yes, sir."

"You do not mind in what capacity you go?"

"No, sir; I am ready to do anything."

"To work on the railway, or in the transport?"

"Yes, sir. Though I would rather not be on the railway, for the railway cannot get on as fast as the troops; but I would enlist in one of the English regiments, if they would take me."

"And you speak the language of the Nubian blacks?"

The question was put in that language.

"Yes; I do not think I speak it quite as well as Arabic, but I speak it fairly."

"Do you think that you could stand the fatigue?—no child's play, you know."

"I can only say that I hope I can, sir. I have been accustomed to take long walks, and spend an hour a day in gymnastic exercises, and I have had lessons in fencing."

"Can you use a pistol?"

"Yes, fairly; I have practised a good deal with it."

"You are most fitted for an interpreter," the general said, speaking this time in English. "Now the North Staffordshire have come down, there are no British regiments up there, and of course the British officers in the Egyptian army all speak Arabic, to some extent. However, I will send you up to Dongola. Either General Hunter, or Colonel Wingate, of the Intelligence Department, may be able to find some use for you; and when the British troops go up, you can be attached to one of their regiments as their interpreter. You will have temporary rank of lieutenant, with, of course, the pay of that rank.

"Captain Ewart came with me, Lord Cromer. I left him in the anteroom. If you will allow me, I will call him in.

"Captain Ewart," he said, as that officer entered, "Mr. Hilliard here has just received the temporary rank of lieutenant, in the Egyptian army, and is going up to join General Hunter, at Dongola. You are starting in three days, are you not?

"I shall be glad if you will take him under your wing, as far as you go. He speaks the languages, Negro as well as Arabic. You can tell him what kit he had better take, and generally mother him.

"That is all, Mr. Hilliard. Call at my quarters, the day after tomorrow, for the letters for General Hunter and Colonel Wingate."

"I thank you most deeply, sir," Gregory began, but the Sirdar gave a little impatient wave with his hand.

"Thank you most deeply also, Lord Cromer!" Gregory said with a bow, and then left the room.

Captain Ewart remained there for another ten minutes. When he came out, he nodded to Gregory.

"Will you come with me?" he said. "I am going to the bank. I shall not be there many minutes, and we can then have a talk together."

"Thank you, sir! I am going to the bank too. It was Mr. Murray who first spoke to Lord Cromer about me."

"You could not have had a better introduction. Well, you won't have very long to get ready for the start—that is, if you have not begun to prepare for it. However, there is no rush at present, therefore I have no doubt you will be able to get your khaki uniforms in time. As for other things, there will be no difficulty about them."

"You have been up at the front before, sir?"

"Yes, my work is on the railway. I had a touch of fever, and got leave to come down and recruit, before the hot weather came in. I dare say you think it hot here, sometimes, but this is an ice house in comparison with the desert."

They talked until they arrived at the bank.

"You may as well go in first, and see Murray. I suppose you won't be above two or three minutes. I shall be longer, perhaps a quarter of an hour; so if you wait for me, we will go to Shepherd's, and talk your business over in some sort of comfort."

"I am pleased, indeed," Mr. Murray said, when Gregory told him of his appointment. "It is better than I even hoped. It is bad enough there, in the position of an officer, but it would be infinitely worse in any other capacity. Do you want to draw any money?"

"No, sir; I have fifty pounds by me, and that will be enough, I should think, for everything."

"More than ample. Of course, you have plenty of light under-clothing of all sorts, and a couple of suits of khaki will not cost you anything like so much as they would, if you got them at a military tailor's in London. However, if you want more, you will be able to draw it."

"Thank you very much, sir! I will not detain you any longer, now; but will, if you will allow me, come in to say goodbye before I start.

Captain Ewart is waiting to speak to you. He came with me from Lord Cromer's."

Captain Ewart then went in, and after settling the business on which he had come, asked Mr. Murray questions about Gregory, and received a sketch of his story.

"He seems to be a fine young fellow," he said, "well grown and active, not at all what one would expect from a product of Cairo."

"No, indeed. Of course, you have not seen him to advantage, in that black suit, but in his ordinary clothes I should certainly take him, if I had not seen him before, to be a young lieutenant freshly come out to join."

"Did you know the father?"

"No, I was not here at that time; but the mother was a lady, every inch. It is strange that neither of them should have friends in England. It may be that she preferred to earn her living here, and be altogether independent."

"She had a pension, hadn't she?"

"A small one, but she really earned her living by teaching. She gave lessons to the ladies in English, French, and music, and had classes for young boys and girls. I once asked her if she did not intend to go back and settle in England, and she said 'Possibly, some day.'

"I fancy that there must have been some mystery about the affair—what, I can't say; but at any rate, we may take it that such a woman would not have married a man who was not a gentleman."

"Certainly the boy looks a well-bred one," Captain Ewart said, "and I am sure that the Sirdar must have been taken with him. You don't know any more about his father than you have told me?"

"Very little. Once, in talking with his wife, she told me that her husband had been in a commercial house, in Alexandria, for a year; but the place was burned down at the time of the bombardment. Being thus out of harness, he became an assistant to one of the army contractors and, when things settled down at Cairo, obtained a berth as interpreter, with the temporary rank of captain, on Hicks Pasha's staff, as he also spoke Arabic fluently. I can tell you no more about him than that, as I never saw him; though no doubt he came here with his wife, when her account was opened.

"I was interested in her. I looked up the old books, and found that two hundred pounds was paid into her account, before he left. I may say that she steadily increased that amount, ever since; but a few years ago she had the sum then standing transferred to the boy's name, telling me frankly, at the time, that she did so to save trouble, in case anything happened to her. I fancy, from what she said, that for the last year or two she had been going downhill. I had a chat with her, the last time she came in. She told me that she had been consumptive, and that it was for the sake of her health they came out here."

"That accounts for it, Murray. By the date, they were probably only married a year or so before they came out; and a man who loved a young wife, and saw no other way of saving her, would throw up any berth at home, in order to give her the benefit of a warm climate. Still, it is a little curious that, if he had only been out here a year or so before Hicks started, he should have learned Arabic sufficiently well to get a post as interpreter. I have been in the country about three years, and can get on fairly well with the natives, in matters concerning my own work; but I certainly could not act as general interpreter.

"Well, I am glad to have heard this, for you know the sort of men interpreters generally are. From the lad's appearance and manner, there is no shadow of doubt that his mother was a lady. I thought it more than probable that she had married beneath her, and that her husband was of the ordinary interpreter class. Now, from what you have said, I see that it is probable he came of a much better family. Well, you may be sure that I shall do what I can for the lad."

Gregory joined him, as he left the bank.

"I think, Hilliard, we had best go to the tailor, first. His shop is not far from here. As you want to get your things in three days, it is as well to have that matter settled, at once."

The two suits, each consisting of khaki tunic, breeches, and putties, were ordered.

"You had better have breeches," he said. "It is likely you will have to ride, and knickerbockers look baggy."

This done, they went to Shepherd's Hotel.

"Sit down in the verandah," Captain Ewart said, "until I get rid of my regimentals. Even a khaki tunic is not an admirable garment, when one wants to be cool and comfortable."

In a few minutes he came down again, in a light tweed suit; and, seating himself in another lounging chair, two cooling drinks were brought in; then he said:

"Now we will talk about your outfit, and what you had best take up. Of course, you have got light underclothing, so you need not bother about that. You want ankle boots—and high ones—to keep out the sand. You had better take a couple of pairs of slippers, they are of immense comfort at the end of the day; also a light cap, to slip on when you are going from one tent to another, after dark. A helmet is a good thing in many ways, but it is cumbrous; and if there are four or five men in a tent, and they all take off their helmets, it is difficult to know where to stow them away.

"Most likely you will get a tent at Dongola, but you can't always reckon upon that, and you may find it very useful to have a light *tente d'abri* made. It should have a fly, which is useful in two ways. In the first place, it adds to the height and so enlarges the space inside; and in the next place, you can tie it up in the daytime, and allow whatever air there is to pass through. Then, with a blanket thrown over the top, you will find it cooler than a regimental tent.

"Of course, you will want a sword and a revolver, with a case and belt. Get the regulation size, and a hundred rounds of cartridges; you are not likely ever to use a quarter of that number, but they will come in for practice.

"Now, as to food. Of course you get beef, biscuit, or bread, and there is a certain amount of tea, but nothing like enough for a thirsty climate, especially when—which is sometimes the case—the water is so bad that it is not safe to drink, unless it has been boiled; so you had better take up four or five pounds of tea."

"I don't take sugar, sir."

"All the better. There is no better drink than tea, poured out and left to cool, and drunk without sugar. You might take a dozen tins of preserved milk, as many of condensed cocoa and milk, and a couple of dozen pots of jam. Of course, you could not take all these things on if you were likely to move, but you may be at Dongola some time, before there is another advance, and you may as well make yourself as comfortable as you can; and if, as is probable, you cannot take the pots up with you, you can hand them over to those who are left behind. You will have no trouble in getting a fair-sized case taken up, as there will be water carriage nearly all the way.

"A good many fellows have aerated waters sent up, but hot soda water is by no means a desirable drink—not to be compared with tea kept in porous jars; so I should not advise you to bother about it. You will want a water bottle. Get the largest you can find. It is astonishing how much water a fellow can get down, in a long day's march.

"Oh! As to your boots, get the uppers as light as you can—the lighter the better; but you must have strong soles—there are rocks in some places, and they cut the soles to pieces, in no time. The sand is bad enough. Your foot sinks in it, and it seems to have a sort of sucking action, and very often takes the sole right off in a very short time.

"I suppose you smoke?"

"Cigarettes, sir."

"I should advise you to get a pipe, in addition, or rather two or three of them. If they get broken, or lost in the sand, there is no replacing them; and if you don't take to them, yourself, you will find them the most welcome present you can give, to a man who has lost his.

"I should advise you to get a lens. You don't want a valuable one, but the larger the better, and the cheapest that you can buy; it will be quite as good as the best, to use as a burning glass. Matches are precious things out there and, with a burning glass, you will only have to draw upon your stock in the evening.

"Now, do you ride? Because all the white officers with the Egyptian troops do so."

"I am sorry to say that I don't, sir. I have ridden donkeys, but anyone can sit upon a donkey."

"Yes; that won't help you much. Then I should advise you to use all the time that you can spare, after ordering your outfit, in riding. No doubt you could hire a horse."

"Yes; there is no difficulty about that."

"Well, if you will hire one, and come round here at six o'clock tomorrow morning, I will ride out for a couple of hours with you, and give you your first lesson. I can borrow a horse from one of the staff. If you once get to sit your horse, in a workman-like fashion, and to carry yourself well, you will soon pick up the rest; and if you go out, morning and evening, for three hours each time, you won't be quite abroad, when you start to keep up with a column of men on foot.

"As to a horse, it would be hardly worth your while to bother about taking one with you. You will be able to pick one up at Dongola. I hear that fugitives are constantly coming in there, and some of them are sure to be mounted. However, you had better take up a saddle and bridle with you. You might as well get an Egyptian one; in the first place because it is a good deal cheaper, and in the second because our English saddles are made for bigger horses. You need not mind much about the appearance of your animal. Anything will do for riding about at Dongola, and learning to keep your seat. In the first fight you have with Dervish horsemen, there are sure to be some riderless horses, and you may then get a good one, for a pound or two, from some Tommy who has captured one."

"I am sure I am immensely obliged to you, Captain Ewart. That will indeed be an advantage to me."

On leaving the hotel Gregory at once made all his purchases, so as to get them off his mind; and then arranged for the horse in the morning. Then he went home, and told the old servant the change that had taken place in his position.

"And now, what about yourself, what would you like to do?"

"I am too old to go up with you, and cook for you."

"Yes, indeed," he laughed; "we shall be doing long marches. But it is not your age, so much. As an officer, it would be impossible for me to have a female servant. Besides, you want quiet and rest. I have been round to the landlord, to tell him that I am going away, and to pay him a month's rent, instead of notice. I should think the best way would be for you to take a large room for yourself, or two rooms not so large—one of them for you to live in, and the other to store everything there is here. I know that you will look after them, and keep them well.

Of course, you will pick out all the things that you can use in your room. It will be very lonely for you, living all by yourself, but you know numbers of people here; and you might engage a girl to stay with you, for some small wages and her food. Now, you must think over what your food and hers will cost, and the rent. Of course, I want you to live comfortably; you have always been a friend rather than a servant, and my mother had the greatest trust in you."

"You are very good, Master Gregory. While you have been away, today, I have been thinking over what I should do, when you went away. I have a friend who comes in, once a week, with fruit and vegetables. Last year, you know, I went out with her and stayed a day. She has two boys who work in the garden, and a girl. She came in today, and I said to her:

"'My young master is going away to the Soudan. What do you say to my coming and living with you, when he has gone? I can cook, and do all about the house, and help a little in the garden; and I have saved enough money to pay for my share of food.'

"She said, 'I should like that, very well. You could help the boys, in the field.'

"So we agreed that, if you were willing, I should go. I thought of the furniture; but if you do not come back here to live, it would be no use to keep the chairs, and tables, and beds, and things. We can put all Missy's things, and everything you like to keep, into a great box, and I could take them with me; or you could have them placed with some honest man, who would only charge very little, for storage."

"Well, I do think that would be a good plan, if you like these people. It would be far better than living by yourself. However, of course I shall pay for your board, and I shall leave money with you; so that, if you are not comfortable there, you can do as I said, take a room here.

"I think you are right about the furniture. How would you sell it?"

"There are plenty of Greek shops. They would buy it all. They would not give as much as you gave for it. Most of them are great rascals."

"We cannot help that," he said. "I should have to sell them when I come back and, at any rate, we save the rent for housing them. They are not worth much. You may take anything you like, a comfortable chair and a bed, some cooking things, and so on, and sell the rest for anything you can get, after I have gone. I will pack my dear mother's things, this evening."

For the next two days, Gregory almost lived on horseback; arranging, with the man from whom he hired the animals, that he should change them three times a day. He laid aside his black clothes, and took to a white flannel suit, with a black ribbon round his straw hat; as deep mourning would be terribly hot, and altogether unsuited for riding.

"You will do, lad," Captain Ewart said to him, after giving him his first lesson. "Your fencing has done much for you, and has given you an easy poise of body and head. Always remember that it is upon balancing the body that you should depend for your seat; although, of course, the grip of the knees does a good deal. Also remember, always, to keep your feet straight; nothing is so awkward as turned-out toes. Besides, in that position, if the horse starts you are very likely to dig your spurs into him.

"Hold the reins firmly, but don't pull at his head. Give him enough scope to toss his head if he wants to, but be in readiness to tighten the reins in an instant, if necessary."

Each day, Gregory returned home so stiff, and tired, that he could scarcely crawl along. Still, he felt that he had made a good deal of progress; and that, when he got up to Dongola, he would be able to mount and ride out without exciting derision. On the morning of the day on which he was to start, he went to say goodbye to Mr. Murray.

"Have you everything ready, Hilliard?" the banker asked.

"Yes, sir. The uniform and the tent are both ready. I have a cork bed, and waterproof sheet to lay under it; and, I think, everything that I can possibly require. I am to meet Captain Ewart at the railway, this afternoon at five o'clock. The train starts at half past.

"I will draw another twenty-five pounds, sir. I have not spent more than half what I had, but I must leave some money with our old servant. I shall have to buy a horse, too, when I get up to Dongola, and I may have other expenses, that I cannot foresee."

"I think that is a wise plan," the banker said. "It is always well to have money with you, for no one can say what may happen. Your horse may get shot or founder, and you may have to buy another. Well, I wish you every luck, lad, and a safe return."

"Thank you very much, Mr. Murray! All this good fortune has come to me, entirely through your kindness. I cannot say how grateful I feel to you."

CHAPTER 5:

Southward.

At the hour named, Gregory met Captain Ewart at the station. He was now dressed in uniform, and carried a revolver in his waist belt, and a sword in its case. His luggage was not extensive. He had one large bundle; it contained a roll-up cork bed, in a waterproof casing. At one end was a loose bag; which contained a spare suit of clothes, three flannel shirts, and his underclothing. This formed the pillow. A blanket and a waterproof sheet were rolled up with it. In a small sack was the *tente d'abri*, made of waterproof sheeting, with its two little poles. It only weighed some fifteen pounds. His only other luggage consisted of a large case, with six bottles of brandy, and the provisions he had been recommended to take.

"Is that all your kit?" Captain Ewart said, as he joined him.

"Yes, sir. I hope you don't think it is too much."

"No; I think it is very moderate, though if you move forward, you will not be able to take the case with you, The others are light enough, and you can always get a native boy to carry them. Of course, you have your pass?"

"Yes, sir. I received it yesterday, when I went to headquarters for the letter to General Hunter."

"Then we may as well take our places, at once. We have nearly an hour before the train starts; but it is worth waiting, in order to get two seats next the window, on the river side. We need not sit there till the train starts, if we put our traps in to keep our places. I know four or five other officers coming up, so we will spread our things about, and keep the whole carriage to ourselves, if we can."

In an hour, the train started. Every place was occupied. Ewart had spoken to his friends, as they arrived, and they had all taken places in the same compartment. The journey lasted forty hours, and Gregory admitted that the description Captain Ewart had given him, of the dust, was by no means exaggerated. He had brought, as had been suggested, a water skin and a porous earthenware bottle; together with a roll of cotton-wool to serve as a stopper to the latter, to keep out the dust. In a tightly fitting handbag he had an ample supply of food for three days. Along the opening of this he had pasted a strip of paper.

"That will do very well for your first meal, Hilliard, but it will be of no good afterwards."

"I have prepared for that," Gregory said. "I have bought a gum bottle, and as I have a newspaper in my pocket, I can seal it up after each meal."

"By Jove, that is a good idea, one I never thought of!"

"The gum will be quite sufficient for us all, up to Assouan. I have two more bottles in my box. That should be sufficient to last me for a long time, when I am in the desert; and as it won't take half a minute to put a fresh paper on, after each meal, I shall have the satisfaction of eating my food without its being mixed with the dust."

There was a general chorus of approval, and all declared that they would search every shop in Assouan, and endeavour to find gum.

"Paste will do as well," Ewart said, "and as we can always get flour, we shall be able to defy the dust fiend as far as our food goes.

"I certainly did not expect that old campaigners would learn a lesson from you, Hilliard, as soon as you started."

"It was just an idea that occurred to me," Gregory said.

The gum bottle was handed round, and although nothing could be done for those who had brought their provisions in hampers, three of them who had, like Gregory, put their food in bags, were able to seal them up tightly.

It was now May, and the heat was becoming intolerable, especially as the windows were closed to keep out the dust. In spite of this, however, it found its way in. It settled everywhere. Clothes and hair became white with it. It worked its way down the neck, where the perspiration changed it into mud. It covered the face, as if with a cake of flour.

At first Gregory attempted to brush it off his clothes, as it settled upon them, but he soon found that there was no advantage in this. So he sat quietly in his corner and, like the rest, looked like a dirty white statue. There were occasional stops, when they all got out, shook themselves, and took a few mouthfuls of fresh air.

Gregory's plan, for keeping out the dust from the food, turned out a great success; and the meals were eaten in the open air, during the stoppages.

On arriving at Assouan, they all went to the transport department, to get their passes for the journey up the Nile, as far as Wady Halfa. The next step was to go down to the river for a swim and, by dint of shaking and beating, to get rid of the accumulated dust.

Assouan was not a pleasant place to linger in and, as soon as they had completed their purchases, Captain Ewart and Gregory climbed on to the loaded railway train, and were carried by the short line to the spot where, above the cataract, the steamer that was to carry them was lying. She was to tow up a large barge, and two native craft. They took their places in the steamer, with a number of other officers—some newcomers from England, others men who had been down to Cairo, to recruit. They belonged to all branches of the service, and included half a dozen of the medical staff, three of the transport corps, gunners, engineers, cavalry, and infantry. The barges were deep in the water, with their cargoes of stores of all kinds, and rails and sleepers for the railway, and the steamer was also deeply loaded.

The passage was a delightful one, to Gregory. Everything was new to him. The cheery talk and jokes of the officers, the graver discussion of the work before them, the calculations as to time and distance, the stories told of what had taken place during the previous campaign, by those who shared in it, were all so different from anything he had ever before experienced, that the hours passed almost unnoticed. It was glorious to think that, in whatever humble capacity, he was yet one of the band who were on their way up to meet the hordes of the Khalifa, to rescue the Soudan from the tyranny under which it had groaned, to avenge Gordon and Hicks and the gallant men who had died with them!

Occasionally, Captain Ewart came up and talked to him, but he was well content to sit on one of the bales, and listen to the conversation without joining in it. In another couple of years he, too, would have had his experiences, and would be able to take his part. At present, he preferred to be a listener.

The distance to Wady Halfa was some three hundred miles; but the current was strong, and the steamer could not tow the boats more than five miles an hour, against it. It was sixty hours, from the start, before they arrived.

Gregory was astonished at the stir and life in the place. Great numbers of native labourers were at work, unloading barges and native craft; and a line of railway ran down to the wharves, where the work of loading the trucks went on briskly. Smoke pouring out from many chimneys, and the clang of hammers, told that the railway engineering work was in full swing. Vast piles of boxes, cases, and bales were accumulated on the wharf, and showed that there would be no loss of time in pushing forward supplies to Abu Hamed, as soon as the railway was completed to that point.

Wady Halfa had been the starting point of a railway, commenced years before. A few miles have been constructed, and several buildings erected for the functionaries, military and civil; but Gordon, when Governor of the Soudan, had refused to allow the province to be saddled with the expenses of the construction, or to undertake the responsibility of carrying it out.

In 1884 there was some renewal of work and, had Gordon been rescued, and Khartoum permanently occupied, the line would no doubt have been carried on; but with the retirement of the British troops, work ceased, and the great stores of material that had been gathered there remained, for years, half covered with the sand. In any other climate this would have been destructive, but in the dry air of Upper Egypt they remained almost uninjured, and proved very useful, when the work was again taken up.

It was a wonderful undertaking, for along the two hundred and thirty-four miles of desert, food, water, and every necessary had to be carried, together with all materials for its construction. Not only had an army of workmen to be fed, but a body of troops to guard them; for Abu Hamed, at the other end of the line, for which they were making, was occupied by a large body of Dervishes; who might, at any moment, swoop down across the plain.

Had the Sirdar had the resources of England at his back, the work would have been easier, for he could have ordered from home new engines, and plant of every description; but it was an Egyptian work, and had to be done in the cheapest possible way. Old engines had to be patched up, and makeshifts of all kinds employed. Fortunately he had, in the chief engineer of the line, a man whose energy, determination, and resource were equal to his own. Major Girouard was a young officer of the Royal Engineers and, like all white officers in the Egyptian service, held the rank of major. He was a Canadian by birth, and proved, in every respect, equal to the onerous and responsible work to which he was appointed.

However, labour was cheap, and railway battalions were raised among the Egyptian peasants, their pay being the same as that of the soldiers. Strong, hearty, and accustomed to labour and a scanty diet, no men could have been more fitted for the work. They preferred it to soldiering; for although, as they had already shown, and were still further to prove, the Egyptian can fight, and fight bravely; he is, by nature, peaceable, and prefers work, however hard. In addition to these battalions, natives of the country and of the Soudan, fugitives from ruined villages and desolated plains, were largely employed.

The line had now been carried three-quarters of the distance to Abu Hamed, which was still in the hands of the Dervishes. It had been constructed with extraordinary rapidity, for the ground was so level that only occasional cuttings were needed. The organization of labour was perfect. The men were divided into gangs, each under a head man, and each having its own special work to do. There were the men who unloaded the trucks, the labourers who did the earth work, and the more skilled hands who levelled it. As fast as the trucks were emptied, gangs of men carried the sleepers forward, and laid them down roughly in position; others followed, and corrected the distance between each. The rails were then brought along and laid down, with the fish plates, in the proper places; men put these on, and boys screwed up the nuts. Then plate layers followed and lined the rails accurately; and, when this was done, sand was thrown in and packed down between the sleepers.

By this division of labour, the line was pushed on from one to two miles a day, the camp moving forward with the line. Six tank trucks brought up the water for the use of the labourers, daily, and everything worked with as much regularity as in a great factory at home. Troops of friendly tribesmen, in our pay, scoured the country and watched the wells along the road, farther to the east, so as to prevent any bands of Dervishes from dashing suddenly down upon the workers.

At Wady Halfa, Captain Ewart and two or three other officers left the steamer, to proceed up the line. Gregory was very sorry to lose him.

"I cannot tell you, Captain Ewart," he said, "how deeply grateful I feel to you, for the immense kindness you have shown me. I don't know what I should have done, had I been left without your advice and assistance in getting my outfit, and making my arrangements to come up here."

"My dear lad," the latter said, "don't say anything more. In any case, I should naturally be glad to do what I could, for the son of a man who died fighting in the same cause as we are now engaged in. But in your case it has been a pleasure, for I am sure you will do credit to yourself, and to the mother who has taken such pains in preparing you for the work you are going to do, and in fitting you for the position that you now occupy."

As the officers who had come up with them in the train from Cairo were all going on, and had been told by Ewart something of Gregory's story, they had aided that officer in making Gregory feel at home in his new circumstances; and in the two days they had been on board the boat, he had made the acquaintance of several others.

The river railway had now been carried from Wady Halfa to Kerma, above the third cataract. The heavy stores were towed up by steamers and native craft. Most of the engines and trucks had been transferred to the desert line; but a few were still retained, to carry up troops if necessary, and aid the craft in accumulating stores.

One of these trains started a few hours after the arrival of the steamer at Wady Halfa. Gregory, with the officers going up, occupied two horse boxes. Several of them had been engaged in the last campaign, and pointed out the places of interest.

At Sarras, some thirty miles up the road, there had been a fight on the 29th of April, 1887; when the Dervish host, advancing strong in the belief that they could carry all before them down to the sea, were defeated by the Egyptian force under the Sirdar and General Chermside.

The next stop of the train was at Akasheh. This had been a very important station, before the last advance, as all the stores had been accumulated here when the army advanced. Here had been a strongly entrenched camp, for the Dervishes were in force, fifteen miles away, at Ferket.

"It was a busy time we had here," said one of the officers, who had taken a part in the expedition. "A fortnight before, we had no idea that an early move was contemplated; and indeed, it was only on the 14th of March that the excitement began. That day, Kitchener received a telegram ordering an immediate advance on Dongola. We had expected it would take place soon; but there is no doubt that the sudden order was the result of an arrangement, on the part of our government with Italy, that we should relieve her from the pressure of the Dervishes round Kassala by effecting a diversion, and obliging the enemy to send a large force down to Dongola to resist our advance.

"It was a busy time. The Sirdar came up to Wady Halfa, and the Egyptian troops were divided between that place, Sarras, and Akasheh. The 9th Soudanese were marched up from Suakim, and they did the distance to the Nile (one hundred and twenty miles) in four days. That was something like marching.

"Well, you saw Wady Halfa. For a month, this place was quite as busy. Now, its glories are gone. Two or three huts for the railway men, and the shelters for a company of Egyptians, represent the whole camp."

As they neared Ferket the officer said:

"There was a sharp fight out there on the desert. A large body of Dervishes advanced, from Ferket. They were seen to leave by a cavalry patrol. As soon as the patrol reached camp, all the available horse, two hundred and forty in number, started under Major Murdoch. Four miles out, they came in sight of three hundred mounted Dervishes, with a thousand spearmen on foot.

"The ground was rough, and unfavourable for a cavalry charge; so the cavalry retired to a valley, between two hills, in order to get better ground. While they were doing so, however, the Dervishes charged down upon them. Murdoch rode at them at once, and there was a hand-to-hand fight that lasted for twenty minutes. Then the enemy turned, and galloped off to the shelter of the spearmen. The troopers dismounted and opened fire; and, on a regiment of Soudanese coming up, the enemy drew off.

"Eighteen of the Dervishes were killed, and eighty wounded. Our loss was very slight; but the fight was a most satisfactory one, for it showed that the Egyptian cavalry had, now, sufficient confidence in themselves to face the Baggara.

"Headquarters came up to Akasheh on the 1st of June. The spies had kept the Intelligence Department well informed as to the state of things at Ferket. It was known that three thousand troops were there, led by fifty-seven Emirs. The ground was carefully reconnoitred, and all preparation made for an attack. It was certain that the Dervishes also had spies, among the camel drivers and camp followers, but the

Sirdar kept his intentions secret, and on the evening of June 5th it was not known to any, save three or four of the principal officers, that he intended to attack on the following morning. It was because he was anxious to effect a complete surprise that he did not even bring up the North Staffordshires.

"There were two roads to Ferket—one by the river, the other through the desert. The river column was the strongest, and consisted of an infantry division, with two field batteries and two Maxims. The total strength of the desert column, consisting of the cavalry brigade, camel corps, a regiment of infantry, a battery of horse artillery, and two Maxims—in all, two thousand one hundred men—were to make a detour, and come down upon the Nile to the south of Ferket, thereby cutting off the retreat of the enemy.

"Carrying two days' rations, the troops started late in the afternoon of the 6th, and halted at nine in the evening, three miles from Ferket. At half-past two they moved forward again, marching quietly and silently; and, at half-past four, deployed into line close to the enemy's position. A few minutes later the alarm was given; and the Dervishes, leaping to arms, discovered this formidable force in front of them; and at the same time found that their retreat was cut off, by another large body of troops in their rear; while, on the opposite bank of the river, was a force of our Arab allies.

"Though they must have seen that their position was hopeless, the Dervishes showed no signs of fear. They fought with the desperation of rats in a trap. The Egyptians advanced with steady volleys. The Baggara horsemen attacked them furiously, but were repulsed with heavy loss. There was hand-to-hand fighting among their huts; and the second brigade carried, with the bayonet, that rough hill that you see over there.

"It was all over, by seven o'clock. Our loss was only twenty killed, and eighty wounded. About one thousand of the Dervishes were killed, including their chief Emir and some forty of the others, while five hundred were taken prisoners. It was a great victory, and a very important one; but it can hardly be said that it was glorious, as we outnumbered them by three to one. Still, it was a heavy blow to the Dervishes, and the fact that the Khalifa was obliged to send troops down to the Nile, to check an advance that had proved so formidable, must have greatly relieved the pressure on the Italians at Kassala.

"There was a pause, here. It was certain that we should have to meet a much stronger force before we got to Dongola. Well as the Egyptian troops had fought, it was thought advisable to give them a stronger backing.

"The heat was now tremendous, and cholera had broken out. We moved to Koshyeh, and there encamped. The only change we had was a terrific storm, which almost washed us away. In the middle of August, we managed to get the gunboats up through the cataract, and were in hopes of advancing, when another storm carried away twenty miles of the railway, which by this time had come up as far as the cataract."

At Ginnis, twenty miles from Ferket, they passed the ground where, on the 31st of December, 1885, on the retirement of General Wolseley's expedition, Generals Grenfel and Stevenson, with a force of Egyptian troops and three British regiments, encountered the Dervish army which the Khalifa had despatched under the Emir Nejumi, and defeated it. It was notable as being the first battle in which the newly raised Egyptian army met the Mahdists, and showed that, trained and disciplined by British officers, the Egyptian fellah was capable of standing against the Dervish of the desert.

From this point the railway left the Nile and, for thirty miles, crossed the desert. Another twenty miles, and they reached Fareeg.

"It was here," the officer said, "that the North Staffordshires came up and joined the Egyptians. The Dervishes had fallen back before we advanced, after a halt at Sadeah, which we sha'n't see, as the railway cuts across, to Abu Fetmeh. We bivouacked five miles from their camp, and turned out at three next morning. The orders were passed by mouth, and we got off as silently as an army of ghosts.

"I shall never forget our disgust when a small cavalry force, sent on ahead to reconnoitre, reported that the Dervishes had abandoned the place during the night, and had crossed the river in native boats. It was a very clever move, at any rate, on the part of fellows who did not want to fight. There were we facing them, with our whole infantry and cavalry useless, and we had nothing available to damage the enemy except our artillery and the gunboats.

"These opened fire, and the Dervishes replied heavily. They had earthworks, but the boats kept on, pluckily, till they got to a narrow point in the stream; when a couple of guns, which had hitherto been hidden, opened upon them at close range; while a strong force of Dervish infantry poured in such a hot fire that the boats had to fall back.

"After our field guns had peppered the enemy for a bit, the gunboats tried again, but the fire was too hot for them, and the leading boat had to retire.

"Things did not look very bright, till nine o'clock; when we found that, at one point, the river was fordable to a small island, opposite the enemy's lines. Four batteries, and the Maxims, at once moved over, with two companies of Soudanese, and opened fire. The distance across was but six hundred yards, and the fire was tremendous—shell, shrapnel, and rockets—while the Soudanese fired volleys, and the Maxims maintained a shower of bullets.

"It seemed that nothing could stand against it, but the Dervishes stuck to their guns with great pluck. However, their fire was so far kept down, that the three gunboats succeeded in forcing their way up; and, passing the Dervish works, sank a steamer and a number of native boats.

"The Dervishes now began to give way, and the gunboats steamed up the river, making for Dongola. The Dervishes, as soon as they had gone, reopened fire, and the duel continued all day; but the great mass of the enemy soon left, and also made their way towards Dongola.

"It was awfully annoying being obliged to remain inactive, on our side, and it was especially hard for the cavalry; who, if they could have got over, would have been able to cut up and disperse the enemy.

"The next morning the Dervishes were all gone, and that was practically the end of the fighting. The gunboats went up and shelled Dongola; and when we got there, two days later, the Dervishes had had enough of it. Of course, there was a little fighting, but it was the effort of a party of fanatics, rather than of an enemy who considered resistance possible.

"We were greeted with enthusiasm by the unfortunate inhabitants, who had been subject to the Dervish tyranny. As a whole, however, they had not been badly treated here, and had been allowed to continue to cultivate their land, subject only to about the same taxation as they had paid to Egypt. Of course, from what they have done elsewhere, the comparative mildness of the conduct of the Dervishes was not due to any feeling of mercy, but to policy. As the most advanced position, with the exception of scattered and temporary posts lower down the river, it was necessary that there should be food for the considerable body of tribesmen encamped at Dongola; especially as an army invading Egypt would provide itself, there, with stores for the journey. It was therefore good policy to encourage the cultivators of land to stay there."

"Thank you very much!" Gregory said, when the officer had concluded his sketch of the previous campaign. "Of course, I heard that we had beaten the Khalifa's men, and had taken Dongola, but the papers at Cairo gave no details. The Staffordshire regiment went down, directly the place was taken, did they not?"

"Yes. They had suffered heavily from cholera; and as there was now no fear that the Egyptians and Soudanese would prove unequal to withstanding a Dervish rush, there was no necessity for keeping them here."

At Abu Fetmeh they left the train, and embarked in a steamer. Of the party that had left Assouan, only four or five remained. The rest had been dropped at other stations on the road.

The boat stopped but a few hours at Dongola, which had for a time been the headquarters of the advanced force. Great changes had been made, since the place was captured from the Dervishes. At that time the population had been reduced to a handful, and the natives who remained tilled but enough ground for their own necessities; for they knew that, at any time, a Dervish force might come along and sweep everything clear. But with the advent of the British, the fugitives who had scattered among the villages along the river soon poured in.

Numbers of Greek traders arrived, with camels and goods, and the town assumed an aspect of life and business. The General established a court of justice, and appointed authorities for the proper regulation of affairs; and by the time Gregory came up, the town was showing signs of renewed prosperity.

But the steamer stopped at Dongola only to land stores needed for the regiment stationed there. The headquarters had, months before, been moved to Merawi, some eighty miles higher up, situated at the foot of the fourth cataract.

Although he had enjoyed the journey, Gregory was glad when the steamer drew up against a newly constructed wharf at Merawi. Now he was to begin his duties, whatever they might be.

At the wharf were a large number of Soudanese soldiers. A telegram, from the last station they touched at, had given notice of the hour at which the boat would arrive; and a battalion of native troops had marched down, to assist in unloading the stores. A white officer had come down with them, to superintend the operation, and the other officers at once went on shore to speak to him.

Gregory had got all his traps together and, as the Soudanese poured on board, he thought it better to remain with them; as, if his belongings once got scattered, there would be little chance of his being able to collect them again. After a short time, he went up to one of the native officers.

"This is my first visit here," he said in Arabic, "and as I have not brought up a servant with me, I do not like to leave my baggage here, while I go and report myself to General Hunter. Will you kindly tell me what I had better do?"

"Certainly. I will place one of my corporals in charge of your things. It would be as well to get them ashore at once, as we shall want the decks clear, in order that the men may work freely in getting the stores up from below. The corporal will see that your baggage is carried to the bank, to a spot where it will be out of the way, and will remain with it until you know where it is to be taken."

Thanking him for his civility, Gregory went on shore. The officer who had told him the story of the campaign was still talking, to the Major who had come down with the blacks. As Gregory came up, he said:

"I wondered what had become of you, Hilliard. I have been telling Major Sidney that a young lieutenant had come up, to report himself to the General for service."

"I am glad to see you, sir," the Major said, holding out his hand. "Every additional white officer is a material gain, and I have no doubt that General Hunter will find plenty for you to do. I hear you can speak the Negro language, as well as Arabic. That will be specially useful here, for the natives are principally Negro, and speak very little Arabic.

"How about your baggage?"

"One of the native officers has undertaken to get it ashore, and to put a corporal in charge of it, until I know where it is to go."

"Well, Fladgate, as you are going to the General's, perhaps you will take Mr. Hilliard with you, and introduce him."

"With pleasure.

"Now, Mr. Hilliard, let us be off, at once. The sun is getting hot, and the sooner we are under shelter, the better."

Ten minutes' walk took them to the house formerly occupied by the Egyptian Governor of the town, where General Hunter now had his headquarters. The General, who was a brevet colonel in the British Army, had joined the Egyptian Army in 1888. He had, as a captain in the Lancashire regiment, taken part in the Nile Expedition, 1884-85; had been severely wounded at the battle of Ginnis; and again at Toski, where he commanded a brigade. He was still a comparatively young man. He had a broad forehead, and an intellectual face, that might have betokened a student rather than a soldier; but he was celebrated, in the army, for his personal courage and disregard of danger, and was adored by his black soldiers.

He rose from the table at which he was sitting, as Captain Fladgate came in.

"I am glad to see you back again," he said. "I hope you have quite shaken off the fever?"

"Quite, General. I feel thoroughly fit for work again. Allow me to present to you Mr. Hilliard, who has just received a commission as lieutenant in the Egyptian Army. He has a letter from the Sirdar, to you."

"Well, I will not detain you now, Captain Fladgate. You will find your former quarters in readiness for you. Dinner at the usual time; then you shall tell me the news of Cairo.

"Now, Mr. Hilliard," and he turned to Gregory, "pray take a seat. This is your first experience in soldiering, I suppose?"

"Yes, sir."

"I think you are the first white officer who has been appointed, who has not had experience in our own army first. You have not been appointed to any particular battalion, have you?"

"No, sir. I think I have come out to make myself generally useful. These are the letters that I was to hand to you—one is from the Sirdar himself, the other is from his chief of the staff, and this letter is from Captain Ewart."

The General read the Sirdar's letter first. He then opened that from the chief of the staff. This was the more bulky of the two, and contained several enclosures.

"Ah! this relates to you," the General said as, after glancing over the two official despatches, he read through the letter of Captain Ewart, who was a personal friend of his.

The latter had given a full account of Gregory's history, and said that the Sirdar had especially asked him to put him in the way of things; that he had seen a great deal of him on the journey up, and was very greatly pleased with him.

"The lad is a perfect gentleman," he said, "which is certainly astonishing, he being a product of Cairo. I consider him in all respects—except, of course, a classical education—fully equal to the average young officer, on first joining. He is very modest and unassuming; and will, I feel sure, perform with credit any work that you may give him to do."

"I see," he said, laying it down, "you have only joined the army temporarily, and with a special purpose, and I am told to utilize your services as I think best. You have a perfect knowledge of Arabic, and of the Negro dialect. That will be very useful, for though we all speak Arabic, few speak the Negro language, which is more commonly used here.

"Your father fell with Hicks Pasha, I am told, and you have joined us with the object of obtaining news as to the manner in which he met his death?"

"That is so, sir. It was always my mother's wish that I should, when I was old enough, come up to the Soudan to make enquiries. As my father was a good Arabic scholar, my mother always entertained a faint hope that he might have escaped; especially as we know that a good many of the Egyptian soldiers were not killed, but were taken prisoners, and made to serve in the Mahdi's army."

"Yes, there are several of them among the Khalifa's artillerymen, but I am very much afraid that none of the officers were spared. You see, they kept together in a body, and died fighting to the last."

"I have hardly any hopes myself, sir. Still, as my father was interpreter, he might not have been with the others, but in some other part of the square that was attacked."

"That is possible; but he was a white man, and in the heat of the battle I don't think that the Dervishes would have made any exception. You see, there were two correspondents with Hicks, and neither of them has ever been heard of; and they must, I should think, have joined in that last desperate charge of his.

"Well, for the present I must make you a sort of extra aide-de-camp, and what with one thing and another, I have no doubt that I shall find plenty for you to do. As such, you will of course be a member of headquarters mess, and therefore escape the trouble of providing for yourself. You have not brought a servant up with you, I suppose?"

"No, sir. Captain Ewart, who most kindly advised me as to my outfit, said that, if I could find an intelligent native here, it would be better than taking a man from Cairo."

"Quite right; and the fellows one picks up at Cairo are generally lazy, and almost always dishonest. The men you get here may not know much, but are ready enough to learn; and, if well treated, will go through fire and water for their master.

"Go down to the stores, and tell the officer in charge there that I shall be glad if he will pick out two or three fellows, from whom you may choose a servant."

When Gregory had given his message, the officer said:

"You had better pick out one for yourself, Mr. Hilliard. Strength and willingness to work are the points I keep my eye upon; and, except for the foremen of the gangs, their intelligence does not interest me. You had better take a turn among the parties at work, and pick out a man for yourself."

Gregory was not long in making his choice. He selected a young fellow who, although evidently exerting himself to the utmost, was clearly incapable of doing his share in carrying the heavy bales and boxes, that were easily handled by older men. He had a pleasant face, and looked more intelligent than most of the others.

"To what tribe do you belong?" Gregory asked him.

"The Jaalin. I come from near Metemmeh."

"I want a servant. You do not seem to be strong enough for this work, but if you will be faithful, and do what I tell you, I will try you."

The young fellow's face lit up.

"I will be faithful, bey. It would be kind of you to take me. I am not at my full strength yet and, although I try my hardest, I cannot do as much as strong men, and then I am abused. I will be very faithful, and if you do not find me willing to do all that you tell you, you can send me back to work here."

"Well, come along with me, then."

He took him to the officer.

"I have chosen this man, sir. Can I take him away at once?"

"Certainly. He has been paid up to last night."

"Thank you very much! I will settle with him for today."

And, followed by the young tribesman, he went to the headquarters camp, near which an empty hut was assigned to him.

CHAPTER 6:

Gregory Volunteers.

The hut of which Gregory took possession was constructed of dry mud. The roof was of poles, on which were thickly laid boughs and palm leaves; and on these a layer of clay, a foot thick. An opening in the wall, eighteen inches square, served as a window. Near the door the floor was littered with rubbish of all kinds.

"What is your name?"

"Zaki."

"Well, Zaki, the first thing is to clear out all this rubbish, and sweep the floor as clean as you can. I am going down to the river to get my baggage up. Can you borrow a shovel, or something of that sort, from one of the natives here? Or, if he will sell it, buy one. I will pay when I return. It will always come in useful. If you cannot get a shovel, a hoe will do. Ah! I had better give you a dollar, the man might not trust you."

He then walked down to the river, and found the black corporal sitting tranquilly by the side of his baggage. The man stood up and saluted, and on Gregory saying that he had now a house, at once told off two soldiers to carry the things.

Arriving at the hut, he found Zaki hard at work, shovelling the rubbish through the doorway. Just as he came up, the boy brought down his tool, with a crash, upon a little brown creature that was scuttling away.

"What is that, Zaki?"

"That is a scorpion, bey; I have killed four of them."

"That is not at all pleasant," Gregory said. "There may be plenty of them, up among the boughs overhead."

Zaki nodded.

"Plenty of creatures," he said, "some snakes."

"Then we will smoke them out, before I go in. When you have got the rubbish out, make a fire in the middle, wet some leaves and things and put them on, and we will hang a blanket over the window and shut the door. I will moisten some powder and scatter it among the leaves, and the sulphur will help the smoke to bring them down."

This was done, the door closed and, as it did not fit at all tightly, the cracks were filled with some damp earth from the watercourse.

"What did you pay for the shovel, Zaki?"

"Half a dollar, bey. Here is the other half."

"Well, you had better go and buy some things for yourself. Tomorrow I will make other arrangements. Get a fire going out here. There is a sauce pan and a kettle, so you can boil some rice or fry some meat."

Gregory then went again to the officer who was acting as quarter-master.

"I have been speaking to the General," the latter said. "You will mess with the staff. The dinner hour is seven o'clock. I am sure you will soon feel at home."

Gregory now strolled through the camp. The troops were in little mud huts, of their own construction; as these, in the heat of the day, were much cooler than tents. The sun was getting low, and the Soudanese troops were all occupied in cooking, mending their clothes, sweeping the streets between the rows of huts, and other light duties. They seemed, to Gregory, as full of fun and life as a party of school-boys—laughing, joking, and playing practical tricks on each other.

The physique of some of the regiments was splendid, the men aver-aging over six feet in height, and being splendidly built. Other regi-ments, recruited among different tribes, were not so tall, but their sturdy figures showed them to be capable of any effort they might be called upon to make.

One of the officers came out of his tent, as he passed.

"You are a new arrival, I think, sir?" he said. "We have so few white officers, here, that one spots a fresh face at once."

"Yes, I only arrived two or three hours ago. My name is Hilliard. I am not attached to any regiment; but, as I speak the languages well, General Hunter is going, so he said, to make me generally useful. I only received my commission a few days before leaving Cairo."

"Well, come in and have a soda and whisky. The heat out here is frightful. You can tell me the last news from Cairo, and when we are going to move."

"I shall be happy to come in and have a chat," Gregory said, "but I do not drink anything. I have been brought up in Cairo, and am accus-tomed to heat, and I find that drinking only makes one more thirsty."

"I believe it does," the other said, "especially when the liquid is almost as hot as one is, one's self. Will you sit down on that box? Chairs are luxuries that we do not indulge in here. Well, have you heard any-thing about a move?"

"Nothing; but the officers I have spoken to all seem to think that it will soon begin. A good many came up with me, to Wady Halfa and the stations on the river; and I heard that all who had sufficiently recov-ered were under orders to rejoin, very shortly."

"Yes, I suppose it won't be long. Of course we know nothing here, and I don't expect we shall, till the order comes for us to start. This is not the time of year when one expects to be on the move; and if we do go, it is pretty certain that it is because Kitchener has made up his mind for a dash forward. You see, if we take Abu Hamed and drive the Dervishes away, we can, at once, push the railway on to that place; and, as soon as it is done, the troops can be brought up and an advance made to Berber, if not farther, during the cool season—if you can ever call it a cool season, here."

"Is there any great force at Abu Hamed?"

"No; nothing that could stand against this for a moment. Their chief force, outside Omdurman, is at Metemmeh under Mahmud, the Khalifa's favourite son. You see, the Jaalin made fools of themselves. Instead of waiting until we could lend them a hand, they revolted as soon as we took Dongola, and the result was that Mahmud came down and pretty well wiped them out. They defended themselves stoutly, at Metemmeh, but had no chance against such a host as he brought with him. The town was taken, and its defenders, between two and three thousand fighting men, were all massacred, together with most of the women and children.

"By the accounts brought down to us, by men who got away, it must have been an even more horrible business than usual; and the Dervishes are past masters in the art of massacre. However, I think that their course is nearly up. Of late, a good many fugitives from Kordofan have arrived here, and they say that there will be a general revolt there, when they hear that we have given the Dervishes a heavy thrashing."

"And where do you think the great fight is likely to take place?" Gregory asked.

"Not this side of Metemmeh. Except at Abu Hamed, we hear of no other strong Dervish force between this and Omdurman. If Mahmud thinks himself strong enough, no doubt he will fight; but if he and the Khalifa know their business, he will fall back and, with the forces at Omdurman, fight one big battle. The two armies together will, from what we hear, amount to sixty or seventy thousand; and there is no doubt whatever that, with all their faults, the beggars can fight. It will be a tough affair, but I believe we shall have some British troops here to help, before the final advance. We can depend now on both the Soudanese and the Egyptians to fight hard, but there are not enough of them. The odds would be too heavy, and the Sirdar is not a man to risk failure. But with a couple of brigades of British infantry, there can be no doubt what the result will be; and I fancy that, if we beat them in one big fight, it will be all up with Mahdism.

"It is only because the poor beggars of tribesmen regard the Dervishes as invincible, that they have put up so long with their tyranny. But the rising of the Jaalin, and the news we get from Kordofan, show that the moment they hear the Dervishes are beaten, and Khartoum is in our hands, there will be a general rising, and the Dervishes will be pretty well exterminated. We all hope that Mahmud won't fight, for if he does, and we beat him, the Khalifa and his lot may lose heart and retire before we get to Omdurman; and, once away, the tremendous business of trying to follow him will confront us. Here we have got the river and the railway, but we have no land carriage for an army, and he might keep on falling back to the great lakes, for anything that we could do to overtake him. So we all hope that Mahmud will retire to Omdurman without fighting, and with such a host as the Khalifa would then have, he would be certain to give battle before abandoning his capital."

"They are fine-looking fellows, these blacks," Gregory said.

"They are splendid fellows—they love fighting for fighting's sake. It is, in their opinion, the only worthy occupation for a man, and they have shown themselves worthy to fight by the side of our men. They have a perfect confidence in us, and would, I believe, go anywhere we led them. They say themselves, 'We are never afraid—just like English.'"

"There seem to be a good many women about the camps."

"Yes, their women follow them wherever they go. They cook for them, and generally look after them. They are as warlike as their husbands, and encourage them, when they go out to battle, with their applause and curious quavering cries. The men get very little pay; but as they are provided with rations, and draw a certain amount for the women, it costs next to nothing, and I fancy that having the wives with them pays well. I believe they would rather be killed than come back and face their reproaches.

"I could not wish to have more cheery or better fellows with me. They never grumble, they are always merry, and really they seem to be tireless. They practically give no trouble whatever, and it is good to see how they brighten up, when there is a chance of a fight."

"I hope I shall see them at it, before long," Gregory said. "Now I must be going, for I have to change, and put on my mess uniform before dinner. I am rather nervous about that, for I am not accustomed to dine with generals."

"You will find it all very pleasant," the other said. "Hunter is a splendid fellow, and is adored by his men. His staff are all comparatively young men, with none of the stiffness of the British staff officer about them. We are all young—there is scarcely a man with the rank of captain in the British Army out here. We are all majors or colonels in the Egyptian Army, but most of us are subalterns in our own regiments. It is good training for us. At home a subaltern is merely a machine to carry out orders; he is told to do this, and he does it; for him to think for himself would be a heinous offence. He is altogether without responsibility, and without initiative and, by the time he becomes a field officer, he is hidebound. He has never thought for himself, and he can't be expected to begin to do so, after working for twenty years like a machine.

"You will see, if we ever have a big war, that will be our weak point. If it wasn't for wars like this, and our little wars in India, where men do learn to think and take responsibility, I don't know where our general officers would get their training.

"Well, you must be going. Goodbye! We shall often meet. There are so few of us here, that we are always running against each other. I won't ask you to dine with us, for a few days. No doubt you would like to get accustomed to headquarters mess first. Of course, Hunter and the brigade staff dine together; while we have little regimental messes among ourselves, which I prefer. When there are only three or four of us, one can sit down in one's shirt sleeves, whereas at the brigade mess one must, of course, turn up in uniform, which in this climate is stifling."

The meal was a more pleasant one than Gregory had anticipated. On board the steamer he had, of course, dined with the other officers; and he found little difference here. Ten sat down, including the principal medical officer and a captain—the head of the station intelligence department, Major Wingate, being at present at Wady Halfa. Except for the roughness of the surroundings, it was like a regimental mess, and the presence of the General commanding in no way acted as a damper to the conversation.

General Hunter had, before sitting down, introduced him to all the members with a few pleasant words, which had put him at his ease. Gregory had, on his way up, learned a good deal as to the officers who were down at Cairo for their health; and he was able to say who were convalescent, and who had sailed, or were on the point of sailing, for England.

The table was formed of two long benches, and had been constructed by the engineers. It was laid under a large tent, of which the walls had been removed to give a free passage of air.

Although scarcely up to the standard of a mess dinner at home, it was by no means a bad one; consisting of soup, fish from the river, a joint of beef at one end and of mutton at the other, curried kidneys, sweet omelettes and cheese, whisky with water or soda to drink at dinner; and, after the meal, four bottles of claret were placed on the table, and cigars or pipes lit. Half an hour later four of the party sat down to whist, and the rest, going outside the tent, sat or threw themselves down on the sand, and smoked or chatted till it was time to turn in.

Gregory's first step, next morning, was to buy a horse. This he purchased from some fugitives, who had come down from Kordofan. It was a good animal, though in poor condition, and would soon pick up flesh, when well attended and fed. To accustom himself to riding, Gregory went out on it for a couple of hours every morning; getting up before daybreak, so as to take exercise before the work of the day began. He also followed the example of the officers of the Egyptian regiments, and purchased a camel for the conveyance of his own baggage.

"You will find it a great advantage," one of them said to him. "Of course, times may arrive when you will have to leave it behind; but, as a rule, there is no trouble about it at all. You hire a native driver, who costs practically nothing, and he keeps with the baggage. No one asks any questions, and when you halt for a day or two, you have comforts. Of course, with a British regiment you are cut down to the last ounce, but with us it is altogether different. There being only three or four white officers to each regiment, the few extra camels in the train make no appreciable difference. Besides, these black fellows consider it quite natural and proper that their white officers should fare in a very different way from themselves; whereas a British Tommy would be inclined to grumble if he saw his officers enjoying luxuries, while he himself had to rough it."

As the horse only cost three pounds, and the camel only five, Gregory's store of money was not seriously affected by the purchases. For both animals, although in poor condition from their journey from Kordofan, a fortnight's rest and good feeding did wonders.

Zaki had not much to do, but Gregory was well satisfied with the selection he had made. He looked after and groomed the horse, saw that the native with the camel took care of it, and went down regularly to the river to water it every evening, while he himself did the same with the horse. He always had a jug of cold tea ready for Gregory, whenever he came in, and the floor of the tent was kept scrupulously clean. Zaki's only regret was that he could not do more for his master, but he was consoled by being told that the time would soon come when he would be more actively engaged.

From the first day of his arrival, Gregory was kept fully employed. Sometimes he assisted the officer of the Intelligence Department, in interviewing fugitives who had arrived from Berber and other points on the river, from Kordofan, or from villages on the White Nile. Sometimes he carried messages from the General to the officers in command of the two Egyptian brigades. He had to listen to disputes between natives returning to their homes, from which they had been driven by the Dervishes, and those they found in possession of their land. He took notes of the arguments on both sides, and submitted them to the General for his decision.

The work would have been trifling in any other climate, but was exhausting in the sweltering heat of the day, and he was not sorry when the sun sank, and he could take off his khaki tunic and go down to the river for a swim.

One evening, as they were sitting after dinner, General Hunter said:

"It is very annoying that, while these natives making their way down the country are able to tell us a good deal of what is taking place on the Nile, from Omdurman down to Metemmeh; and while we also get news of the state of things at Berber and Abu Hamed; we know nothing whatever of Mahmud's intentions, nor indeed anything of what is doing at Metemmeh, itself, since it was captured by the Dervishes and, as we heard, the whole population destroyed.

"Of course, Mahmud has the choice of three courses. He can stay where he is, he can march his whole force to Berber, or he can advance against us here. I don't suppose that he has any idea of the progress the railway is making from Wady Halfa. He may have heard, and no doubt he has heard, that we are making a road of some sort across the desert in the direction of Abu Hamed; but of the capabilities of the railway he can form no idea, and may well believe that the march of an army, across what is practically a waterless desert, is a matter of impossibility.

"On the other hand, he knows that we are gathering a considerable force here; and, with his limited knowledge, doubtless supposes that we are going to cross the Bayuda desert, to Metemmeh, as the Gordon relief column did; or that, if we are not coming that way, we intend to follow the river bank up to Berber. Unquestionably his best course, if he considers, as we may be sure he does, that the force under his command is strong enough to crush us here, would be to push across the desert, and fall upon us before reinforcements arrive. But it is reported, and I believe truly, that the Khalifa, his father, has positively refused to let him do so; still, sons have disobeyed their fathers before now.

"There is, it is true, the difficulty of water; but that is not so serious, in the case of a Dervish force, as it is with us. In the first place, they can march twice as far as we can. In the second place, they are accustomed to go a long time without water, and are but little affected by the heat. Lastly, they have nothing to carry except their weapons, a few handfuls of dates, and their water gourds. Still, we know that the forces that have, one after another, arrived here have been greatly weakened by the journey. However, Mahmud may attempt it, for he must know, from his spies here, that we have at present no such land transport as would be required, were we intending to advance across the desert. He may, therefore, move at least a portion of his force to Berber; trusting to the fact that, even did we make an advance south from here, with the intention of cutting off his retreat to Khartoum, he would be able to reach Metemmeh before we could get there.

"Undoubtedly, a British general, if commanding a force constituted as Mahmud's is, would make a dash across the desert and fall upon us; unless, indeed, he felt certain that, after the difficulties we encountered last time we attempted to take the desert route, we should be certain to advance by the river, step by step, continuing the policy that we have followed since we began to push forward from Assouan.

"Mahmud is in a very difficult position. He is controlled by his father at Khartoum. Among those with him are many important Emirs, men of almost equal rank with himself; and he could hardly hope that whatever decision he might personally arrive at would be generally accepted by all; and those who opposed him would do so with all the more force, as they could declare that, in making any movement, he was acting in opposition to his father's orders.

"However, our total ignorance as to Mahmud's plans and intentions is most unfortunate; but it can hardly be helped, for naturally the natives coming down from Kordofan give Metemmeh a very wide berth. As to sending up any of the natives here, to find out what is going on, it is out of the question, for they would be detected at once, as their language is so different from that of the Baggara."

Later on, the General retired to his quarters. Gregory went there.

"Can I speak to you for a few minutes, sir?" he asked.

"Certainly, Mr. Hilliard. What can I do for you?"

"I have been thinking over what you were saying, regarding information as to Mahmud's intentions. With your permission, I am ready to undertake to go into his camp, and to find out what the general opinion is as to his plans."

"Impossible, Mr. Hilliard! I admire your courage in making the offer, but it would be going to certain death."

"I do not think so, sir. I talk Baggara better than the Negro dialect that passes here. It is among the Baggara that I am likely to learn something of my father's fate; and, as the old nurse from whom I learnt these languages had been for a long time among that tribe, she devoted, at my mother's request, more time to teaching me their Arab dialect than any other, and I am convinced that I could pass unsuspected among them, as far as language is concerned. There is no great difference between Arab features and European, and I think that, when I am stained brown and have my head partly shaved, according to their fashion, there will be little fear of my being detected.

"As to costume, that is easy enough. I have not seen any of the Dervishes yet, but the natives who have come in from El Obeid, or any other neighbourhood where they are masters, could give me an account of their dress, and the way in which they wear the patches on their clothes, which are the distinguishing mark of the Mahdists."

"I could tell you that. So could any of the officers. Their dress differs very little from the ordinary Arab costume. Nearly all wear loose white trousers, coming down to the ankles. In some cases these are the usual baggy Eastern articles, in others the legs are separate. They almost all wear the white garment coming down to the knee, with of course a sash round the waist, and sleeves reaching down to the elbow or an inch or two below it. Some wear turbans, but the majority simply skullcaps. I could get the dress made up in three or four hours. But the risk is altogether too great, and I do not think that I should be justified in allowing you to undertake it."

"I really do not think that there will be any great danger, sir. If there were no great object to be gained, it would be different; but in view of the great importance, as you said this evening, of learning Mahmud's intentions, the risk of one life being lost, even were it great, is nothing. As you say, the Sirdar's plans might be greatly affected by the course Mahmud adopts; and in such a case, the life of a subaltern like myself is a matter scarcely to be considered.

"From childhood I have been preparing to go among the Dervishes, and this is what I propose doing, as soon as Khartoum is recaptured. Therefore sir if, by anticipating my work by a few months, or possibly a year, I can render a service to the army, I would gladly undertake it, if you will give me permission to do so."

The General was, for a minute or two, silent.

"Well, Hilliard," he said at last, "on thinking it over as you put it, I do not know that I should be justified in refusing your offer. It is a very gallant one, and may possibly meet with success."

"Thank you, sir! I shall be really glad to enter upon the work I have looked forward to. Although it may have no direct bearing upon the discovery of my father's fate, it will be a start in that direction. Do you think that I had better go mounted, or on foot?"

"I should say certainly on horseback, but there is no occasion for any hasty determination. Every step should be carefully considered, and we should, as far as possible, foresee and provide for every emergency that may arise. Think it over well, yourself. Some time tomorrow I will discuss it again with you."

Gregory went straight back to his hut.

"Come in, Zaki, I want to speak to you.

"Light the lamp, and shut the door. Now sit down there. Do you know the country between this and Metemmeh?"

"Yes, master; I travelled there with my father, six years ago."

"Is it difficult to find the way?"

"It is not difficult. There are many signs of the passage of caravans. There are skeletons of the camels of the English expedition; there are very many of them. It would not be difficult, even for one who has never passed them, to find the way."

"And there are wells?"

"There are wells at Howeyat and Abu Halfa, at Gakdul and Abu Klea, also at Gubat."

"That is to say, water will be found nearly every day?"

"Quite every day, to one on horseback. The longest distance is from Gakdul to Abu Klea, but that would not be too long for mounted men, and could even be done by a native on foot, in a long day's march."

"Do you know whether Mahmud's army is in Metemmeh, or outside the town?"

"From what I have heard, most of the Dervish force is on the hills behind the town. They say Metemmeh is full of dead, and that even the Dervishes do not care to live there."

"The Baggara are mostly mounted, are they not?"

"Most of them are so, though there are some on foot. The leaders of the tribesmen who fight for the Khalifa are all on horseback, but most of the army are on foot."

"You do not speak the Baggara language, I suppose?"

Zaki shook his head.

"I know a little Arabic, but not much."

"I suppose most of the Arab tribes in the Soudan speak a dialect very much like the Baggara?"

"Yes; it is everywhere Arabic, and there is but little difference. They can all understand each other, and talk together. May your servant ask why you put these questions?"

"Yes, Zaki, but you must not mention what I tell you to a soul."

"Zaki will be as silent as the grave."

"Well, I am going up dressed as a Mahdist. I can speak the Baggara tongue well. I am going to try and find out what they are going to do: whether they will march to Berber, or come here, or remain at Metemmeh."

Zaki stared at his master, in speechless amazement. Gregory could not help smiling at the expression of his face.

"There does not seem much difficulty in it," he said. "I can speak with you in the dialect of Dongola, but the Baggara language is much easier to me, because I have been accustomed to speak Arabic since I was a child. Of course my skin will be dyed, and I shall wear the Dervish dress. There is no difficulty in this matter."

"But they would cut you in pieces, my lord, if they found out that you were a white."

"No doubt they would, but there is no reason why they should find that out. It would be much more dangerous for you to go into their camp than it would be for me. In the first place, you can scarcely speak any Arabic; and in the second, they would see by your features that you are one of the Jaalin. Whereas my features, when stained, would be much more like those of the Arabs than yours would."

"Where should I be most likely to meet the Dervishes first?"

"I do not think any of them are much this side of Metemmeh, at present. Sometimes parties ride down to Gakdul, and they have even passed on till they are within sight of this camp; but when they have found out that the wells are still unoccupied, and the army here quiet, they go back again."

"If I go on horseback, Zaki, I shall want someone with me who will act as a guide; and who will look after his horse and mine at some place near the river, where he can find a hiding place while I am away in the Dervish camp."

"Would you take me, my lord?" Zaki said quickly.

"I would much rather take you than anyone else, if you are willing to go, Zaki."

"Surely I will go with my lord," the native said. "No one has ever been so good to me as he has. If my lord is killed, I am ready to die with him. He may count on me to do anything that he requires, even to go with him into the Dervish camp. I might go as a slave, my lord."

"That would not do, Zaki. I do not wish to travel as a person who could ride attended by a slave. People might say, 'Who is this man? Where does he come from? How is it that no one knows a man who rides with a slave?'

"My great object will be to enter the camp quietly, as one who has but left half an hour before. When I have once entered it, and they ask whence I came, I must tell them some likely story that I have made up: as, for example, that I have come from El Obeid, and that I am an officer of the governor there; that, finding he could not get away himself, he yielded to my request that I might come, and help to drive the infidels into the sea."

Zaki nodded.

"That would be a good tale, my lord, for men who have escaped from El Obeid, and have come here, have said that the Khalifa's troops there have not been called to join him at Omdurman; for it is necessary to keep a strong force there, as many of the tribes of the province would rise in rebellion, if they had the chance. Therefore you would not be likely to meet anyone from El Obeid in Mahmud's camp."

"How is it, Zaki, that when so many in the Soudan have suffered at the hands of the Dervishes, they not only remain quiet, but supply the largest part of the Khalifa's army?"

"Because, my lord, none of them can trust the others. It is madness for one tribe to rise, as the Jaalin did at Metemmeh. The Dervishes wiped them out from the face of the earth. Many follow him because they see that Allah has always given victory to the Mahdists; therefore the Mahdi must be his prophet. Others join his army because their villages have been destroyed, and their fields wasted, and they see no other way of saving themselves from starvation.

"There are many who fight because they are fond of fighting. You see how gladly they take service with you, and fight against their own countrymen, although you are Christians. Suppose you were to conquer the Khalifa tomorrow, half his army would enlist in your service, if you would take them. A man who would be contented to till his fields, if he could do so in peace and quiet, fears that he may see his produce eaten by others and his house set on fire; and would rather leave his home and fight—he cares not against whom.

"The Mahdist army are badly fed and badly paid. They can scarce keep life together. But in the Egyptian Army the men are well taken care of. They have their rations, and their pay. They say that if they are wounded, or lose a limb, and are no more able to fight, they receive a pension. Is it wonderful that they should come to you and be faithful?"

"Well, Zaki, we won't talk any longer, now. It is agreed, then, that if I go on this expedition, you will accompany me?"

"Certainly, master. Wherever you go I am ready to go. Whatever happens to you will, I hope, happen to me."

On the following afternoon, Gregory was sent for.

"I have given the matter a good deal of thought, Mr. Hilliard," the General said, "and have decided to accept your offer. I suppose that you have been thinking the matter over. Do you decide to go on foot, or mounted?"

"On horseback, sir. My boy is perfectly willing to go with me. He knows the way, and the position of the wells on the road. My plan is that, when we get near Metemmeh, he shall remain with the horses somewhere near the river; and I shall enter the camp on foot. I am less likely to be noticed that way. If questioned, my story will be that my father was at El Obeid, and that the Governor there is, by the Khalifa's orders, holding his force in hand to put down any outbreaks there may be in the province; and that, wishing to fight against the infidel, I have come on my own account. If I am asked why I had not come on horseback, I shall say that I had ridden to within the last two or three miles, and that the horse had then died.

"But I do not expect to be questioned at all, as one man on foot is as nothing, in an army of twenty or thirty thousand, gathered from all over the Soudan."

"You quite understand, Mr. Hilliard, that you are taking your life in your hands? And that there is no possibility, whatever, of our doing anything for you, if you get into trouble?"

"Quite, sir. If I am detected, I shall probably be killed at once. I do not think that there is more risk in it than in going into battle. As I have told you, I have, so far as I know, no relatives in the world; and there will be no one to grieve, if I never come back again.

"As to the clothes, I can easily buy them from one of the natives here. Many of them are dressed in the garments of the Dervishes who were killed when we came up here; except, of course, that the patches were taken off. I will get my man to buy a suit for himself, and one for me. It would be better than having new clothes made; for, even if these were dirtied, they would not look old. When he has bought the clothes, he can give them a good washing, and then get a piece of stuff to sew on as patches.

"I am afraid, sir, that there will be little chance of my being able to obtain any absolute news of Mahmud's intentions; but only to glean general opinion, in the camp. It is not likely that the news of any intended departure would be kept a secret up till the last moment, among the Dervishes, as it would be here."

"Quite so," the General agreed. "We may take it as certain that the matter would be one of common talk. Of course, Mahmud and his principal advisers might change their minds, at any moment. Still I think that, were it intended to make a move against us, or to Berber, it would be generally known.

"I may tell you that we do not intend to cross the Bayuda desert. We shall go up the river, but this is a secret that will be kept till the last moment. And before we start, we shall do all in our power to spread a belief that we are going to advance to Metemmeh. We know that they are well informed, by their spies here, of our movements. We shall send a strong force to make a reconnaissance, as far as Gakdul. This will appear to be a preliminary step to our advance, and should keep Mahmud inactive, till too late. He will not dare advance to Berber, because he will be afraid of our cutting him off from Omdurman.

"You are satisfied with your horse? It is advisable that you should have a good one, and yet not so good as to attract attention."

"Yes; I could not want a better horse, General. He is not handsome, but I have ridden him a great deal, and he is certainly fast; and, being desert bred, I have no doubt has plenty of endurance. I shall, of course, get one for my boy."

"There are plenty in the transport yard. They have been bought up from fugitives who have come in here. I will write you an order to select any one you choose; and if you see one you think better than your own, you can take it also; and hand yours over to the transport, to keep until you return.

"You should take a Martini-Henri with you. I will give you an order for one, on one of the native regiments. They are, as you know, armed with them; and have, of course, a few cases of spare rifles. A good many have fallen into the hands of the Dervishes, at one time or another, so that your carrying such a weapon will not excite any remark. It would not do to take a revolver, but no doubt you will be able to buy pistols that have been brought down by the fugitives. You will certainly be able to get them at some of those Greek shops. They buy up all that kind of thing. Of course, you will carry one of the Dervish long knives.

"Is there anything else that you can think of?"

"Nothing, sir."

"When will you be ready, do you suppose?"

"By the day after tomorrow, sir. I shall start after dark, so that no one will notice my going. With your permission, I will come round before I set off, so that you can see whether the disguise is good enough to pass."

CHAPTER 7:

To Metemmeh.

Zaki at once set to work to collect the articles needed for the journey; and Gregory obtained, from the transport, another horse and two native saddles. He was well satisfied with his own animal; and, even had he found in the transport yard a better horse, he would still have preferred his own, as they were accustomed to each other. He bought pistols for himself and Zaki, and a matchlock for the latter.

Everything was ready by the time Gregory went to the mess to lunch, on the day fixed for his departure. Nothing whatever had been said as to his leaving, as it was possible that some of the native servants, who waited upon them, might have picked up sufficient English to gather that something important was about to take place. When, however, the meal was over and he said carelessly, "I shall not be at mess this evening;" he saw, by the expression of the officers' faces, that they all were aware of the reason for his absence. One after another they either shook hands with him, or gave him a quiet pat on the shoulder, with the words "Take care of yourself, lad," or "A safe journey and a speedy return," or some other kind wish.

Going to his hut, he was shaved by Zaki at the back of the neck, up to his ears; so that the white, closely-fitting cap would completely cover the hair. Outside the tent a sauce pan was boiling with herbs and berries, which the lad had procured from an old woman who was considered to have a great knowledge of simples. At four in the afternoon, Gregory was stained from head to foot, two coats of the dye being applied. This used but a small quantity of the liquor, and the rest was poured into a gourd, for future use. The dresses were ready, with the exception of the Mahdi patches, which were to be sewn on at their first halting place.

Before it was dark, Gregory went across to the General's quarters. The black sentry stopped him.

"The General wants to speak to me," Gregory said, in Arabic.

The man called up the native sergeant from the guard tent, who asked what he wanted.

"I am here by the orders of the General."

The sergeant looked doubtful, but went in. He returned in a minute, and motioned to Gregory to follow him in. The General looked at him, from head to foot.

"I suppose it is you, Hilliard," he said, "but I certainly should not have recognized you. With that yellowish-brown skin, you could pass anywhere as a Soudan Arab. Will the colour last?"

"I am assured that it will last for some days, but I am taking enough with me to renew it, four or five times."

"Well, unless some unexpected obstacle occurs, I think you are safe from detection. Mind you avoid men from El Obeid; if you do not fall in with them, you should be safe. Of course, when you have sewn on those patches, your disguise will be complete.

"I suppose you have no idea how long you will be away?"

"It will take me five days to go there, and five days to come back. I should think that if I am three days in the camp, I ought to get all the information required. In a fortnight I should be here; though, of course, I may be longer. If I am not back within a few days of that time, you will know that it is because I have stayed there, in the hopes of getting more certain news. If I don't return in three weeks, it will be because something has gone wrong."

"I hope it will not be so, lad. As regards appearance and language, I have no fear of your being detected; but you must always bear in mind that there are other points. You have had the advantage of seeing the camps of the native regiments, when the men are out of uniform—how they walk, laugh uproariously, play tricks with each other, and generally behave. These are all natives of the Soudan, and no small proportion of them have been followers of the Mahdi, and have fought against us, so they may be taken as typical of the men you are going among. It is in all these little matters that you will have to be careful.

"Now, I will not detain you longer. I suppose your horses are on board?"

It had been arranged that Gregory should be taken down to Korti, in a native craft that was carrying some stores required at that camp.

"Yes, sir. My boy put them on board, two hours ago."

"Here is the pass by which you can enter or leave the British lines, at any time. The boat will be there before daylight, but the landing of the stores will not, of course, take place until later. Show this pass to the first officer who comes down. It contains an order for you to be allowed to start on your journey, at once.

"This other pass is for your return. You had better, at your first halt, sew it under one of your patches. It is, as you see, written on a piece of linen, so that however closely you may be examined, there will be no stiffness or crackling, as would be the case with paper.

"Now goodbye, Hilliard! It is a satisfaction to me that you have undertaken this journey on your own initiative, and on your own request. I believe that you have a fair chance of carrying it through—more so than men with wider shoulders and bigger limbs would have. If you come to grief, I shall blame myself for having accepted your offer; but I shall at least know that I thought it over seriously, and that, seeing the importance of the object in view, I did not feel myself justified in refusing."

With a cordial shake of the hand, he said goodbye to Gregory. The latter went off to his hut. He did not leave it until dusk, and then went down to the boat, where Zaki had remained with the horses.

As soon as it started they lay down alongside some bales, on the deck of the native craft, and were soon asleep. They did not wake until a slight bump told them they were alongside the wharf, at Korti.

Day was just breaking, so no move was made until an hour later. An officer came down, with the fatigue party, to unload the stores that she had brought down. When the horses were ashore, Gregory handed the pass to the officer, who was standing on the bank. He looked at it, with some surprise.

"Going to do some scouting," he muttered, and then called to a native officer, "Pass these two men beyond the outposts. They have an order from General Hunter."

"Will you be away long?" he asked Gregory, in Arabic.

"A week or more, my lord," the latter replied.

"Ah! I suppose you are going to Gakdul. As far as we have heard, there are no Dervishes there. Well, you must keep a sharp lookout. They may be in hiding anywhere about there, and your heads won't be worth much, if they lay hands on you."

"We intend to do so, sir;" and then, mounting, they rode on, the native officer walking beside them.

"You know the country, I suppose?" he said. "The Dervishes are bad, but I would rather fall into their hands than lose my way in the desert. The one is a musket ball or a quick chop with a knife, the other an agony for two or three days."

"I have been along the road before," Zaki said. "There is no fear of my losing my way; and, even if I did so, I could travel by the stars."

"I wish we were all moving," the native said. "It is dull work staying here, month after month."

As soon as they were beyond the lines, they thanked the officer and went off, at a pace native horses are capable of keeping up for hours.

"Korti is a much pleasanter camp to stay in than Merawi," Gregory said. "It really looks a delightful place. It is quite evident that the Mahdists have never made a raid here."

The camp stood on a high bank above the river. There were spreading groves of trees, and the broad avenues, that had been constructed when the Gordon relief expedition was encamped there, could still be seen. Beyond it was a stretch of land which had been partly cultivated. Sevas grass grew plentifully, and acacia and mimosa shrubs in patches.

They rode to the wells of Hambok, a distance of some five-and-thirty miles, which they covered in five hours. There they halted, watered their horses and, after giving them a good feed, turned them out to munch the shrubs or graze on the grass, as they chose. They then had a meal from the food they had brought with them, made a shelter of bushes, for the heat was intense, and afterwards sewed the Mahdi patches upon their clothes.

When the sun went down they fetched the horses in, gave them a small feed, and then fastened them to some bushes near. As there was plenty of water in the wells, they took an empty gourd down and, stripping, poured water over their heads and bodies; then, feeling greatly refreshed, dressed and lay down to sleep.

The moon rose between twelve and one; and, after giving the horses a drink, they mounted and rode to Gakdul, which they reached soon after daybreak. They had stopped a mile away, and Zaki went forward on foot, hiding himself as much as possible from observation. On his return he reported that no one was at the wells, and they therefore rode on, taking every precaution against surprise.

The character of the scenery had completely changed; and they had, for some miles, been winding along at the foot of the Jebel-el-Jilif hills. These were steep and precipitous, with spurs and intermediate valleys. The wells differed entirely from those at Hambok, which were merely holes dug in the sand, the water being brought up in one of the skin bags they had brought with them, and poured into shallow cisterns made in the surface. At Gakdul the wells were large pools in the rock, at the foot of one of the spurs of the hill, two miles from the line of the caravan route. Here the water was beautifully clear, and abundant enough for the wants of a large force.

"It is lucky I had you with me, Zaki, for I should certainly have gone straight on past the wells, without knowing where they were; and as there are no others this side of Abu Klea, I should have had rather a bad day."

The three forts which the Guards had built, when they came on in advance of General Stewart's column, were still standing; as well as a number of smaller ones, which had been afterwards added.

"It is rather a bad place for being caught, Zaki, for the ground is so broken, and rocky, that the Dervishes might creep up without being seen."

"Yes, sir, it is a bad place," Zaki agreed. "I am glad that none of the Dervishes were here, for we should not have seen them, until we were quite close."

Zaki had, on the road, cut a large faggot of dried sticks, and a fire was soon lighted.

"You must give the horses a good allowance of grain," Gregory said, "for they will be able to pick up nothing here, and it is a long ride to Abu Klea."

"We shall have to be very careful there, my lord. It is not so very far from Metemmeh, and we are very likely to find Baggaras at the wells. It was there they met the English force that went through to Metemmeh.

"I think it would be better for us to halt early, this evening, and camp at the foot of Jebel Sergain. The English halted there, before advancing to Abu Klea. We can take plenty of water in the two skins, to give the horses a drink and leave enough for tomorrow. There is grass in abundance there.

"When the moon rises, we can make our way round to avoid Abu Klea, and halt in the middle of the day for some hours. We could then ride on as soon as the sun is low, halt when it becomes too dark to ride, and then start again when the moon rises. In that way we shall reach the river, before it is light."

"I think that would be a very good plan, Zaki. We should find it very difficult to explain who we were, if we met any Dervishes at Abu Klea. I will have a look at my sketch map; we have found it very good and accurate, so far; and with that, and the compass the General gave me before starting, we ought to have no difficulty in striking the river, as the direction is only a little to the east of south."

He opened a tin of preserved meat, of which he had four with him, and placed it to warm near the fire.

"We should have had to throw the other tins away, if we had gone on to Abu Klea," he said. "It would never have done for them to be found upon us, if we were searched."

When the meat was hot they ate it, using some biscuits as plates. Afterwards they feasted on a melon they had brought with them, and were glad to hear their horses munching the leaves of some shrubs near.

When the moon rose, they started. It was slow work at first, as they had some difficulty in passing the rough country lying behind the hill. Once past it, they came upon a level plain, and rode fast for some hours. At ten o'clock they halted, and lay down under the shelter of the shrubs; mounting again at four, and riding for another three hours.

"How far do you think we are from the river now? By the map, I should think we cannot be much more than twenty miles from it."

"I don't know, my lord. I have never been along here before; but it certainly ought not to be farther than that."

"We have ridden nine hours. We travelled slowly for the first four or five, but we have come fast, since then. We must give the horses a good rest, so we will not move on till the moon rises, which will be about a quarter to two. It does not give a great deal of light, now, and we shall have to make our way through the scrub; but, at any rate, we ought to be close to the river, before morning."

When the sun was low they again lit a fire, and had another good meal, giving the greater portion of their stock of biscuits to the horses, and a good drink of water.

"We must use up all we can eat before tomorrow, Zaki, and betake ourselves to a diet of dried dates. There is enough water left to give the horses a drink before we start, then we shall start as genuine Dervishes."

They found that the calculation they had made as to distance was correct and, before daybreak, arrived on the bank of the Nile, and at once encamped in a grove. In the morning they could see the houses of Metemmeh, rising from the line of sandy soil, some five miles away.

"There seems to be plenty of bush and cover, all along the bank, Zaki. We will stay here till the evening, and then move three miles farther down; so that you may be handy, if I have to leave the Dervishes in a hurry."

"Could we not go into the camp, my lord?"

"It would be much better, in some respects, if we could; but, you see, you do not speak Arabic."

"No, master; but you could say I was carried off as a slave, when I was a boy. You see, I do speak a little Arabic, and could understand simple orders; just as any slave boy would, if he had been eight or ten years among the Arabs."

"It would certainly be a great advantage to have you and the horses handy. However, at first I will go in and join the Dervishes, and see how they encamp. They are, no doubt, a good deal scattered; and if we could find a quiet spot, where a few mounted men have taken up their station, we would join them. But before we did that, it would be necessary to find out whether they came from Kordofan, or from some of the villages on the White Nile. It would never do to stumble into a party from El Obeid."

They remained quiet all day. The wood extended a hundred and fifty yards back from the river, and there was little fear that anyone coming down from Omdurman would enter it, when within sight of Metemmeh. At dusk they rode on again, until they judged that they were within two miles of the town; and then, entering a clump of high bushes by the river, halted for the night.

CHAPTER 8:

Among The Dervishes.

In the morning Gregory started alone, as soon as it was light. As he neared the town, he saw that there were several native craft on the river; and that boats were passing to and fro between the town and Shendy, on the opposite bank. From the water side a number of men were carrying what appeared to be bags of grain towards the hills behind the town, while others were straggling down towards the river.

Without being questioned, Gregory entered Metemmeh, but stopped there for a very few minutes. Everywhere were the bodies of men, women, and children, of donkeys and other animals. All were now shrivelled and dried by the sun, but the stench was almost unbearable, and he was glad to hurry away.

Once beyond the walls he made for the hill. Many tents could be seen there, and great numbers of men moving about. He felt sure that, among so many, no one would notice that he was a newcomer; and after moving among the throng, he soon sat down among a number of Dervishes who were eating their morning meal. Taking some dates out of his bag, he munched them quietly.

From the talk going on, he soon perceived that there was a considerable amount of discontent at the long delay. Some of the men were in favour of moving to Berber, on the ground that they would at least fare better there; but the majority were eager to march north, to drive the infidels from Merawi and Dongola.

"Mahmud would do that, I am sure," one of them said, "if he had but his will; but how could we march without provisions? It is said that Mahmud has asked for a sufficient supply to cross the Bayuda, and has promised to drive the infidels before him to Assouan; but the Khalifa says no, it would be better to wait till they come in a strong body, and then to exterminate them. If we are not to fight, why were we sent here? It would have been better to stay at Omdurman, because there we had plenty of food; or, if it ran short, could march to the villages and take what we wanted. Of course the Khalifa knows best, but to us it seems strange, indeed."

There was a general chorus of assent. After listening for some time Gregory rose and, passing over the ridge, came upon the main camp. Here were a number of emirs and sheiks, with their banners flying before the entrance of their tents. The whole ground was thickly dotted with little shelters, formed of bushes, over which dark blankets were thrown to keep out the rays of the sun. Everywhere women were seated or standing—some talking to each other, others engaged in cooking.

Children played about; boys came in loaded with faggots, which they had gone long distances to cut. In some places numbers of horses were picketed, showing where the Baggara cavalry were stationed.

In the neighbourhood of the emirs' tents there was some sort of attempt at order, in the arrangement of the little shelters, showing where the men of their tribes were encamped. Beyond, straggling out for some distance, were small encampments, in some of which the men were still erecting shelters, with the bushes the women and boys brought in. Most of these were evidently fresh arrivals, who had squatted down as soon as they came up; either from ignorance as to where their friends had encamped, or from a preference for a quiet situation. This fringe of new arrivals extended along the whole semicircle of the camp; and as several small parties came up while Gregory wandered about, and he saw that no notice was taken of them by those already established, he thought that he could bring Zaki, and the horses up without any fear of close questioning. He therefore walked down again to the spot where he had left them; and, mounting, they rode to the camp, making a wide sweep so as to avoid the front facing Metemmeh.

"We could camp equally well, anywhere here, Zaki, but we may as well go round to the extreme left; as, if we have to ride off suddenly, we shall at least start from the nearest point to the line by which we came."

There was a small clump of bushes, a hundred yards or so from the nearest of the little shelters. Here they dismounted, and at once began, with their knives, to cut down some of the bushes to form a screen from the sun. They had watered the horses before they left the river, and had also filled their water skins.

"I don't think we could find a better place, Zaki," Gregory said, when, having completed their shelter and thrown their blankets over it, they lay down in the shade. "No doubt we shall soon be joined by others; but as we are the first comers on this spot, it will be for us to ask questions of them, and, after, for them to make enquiries of us.

"I shall go into the camp as soon as the heat abates, and people begin to move about again. Remember our story—You were carried off from a Jaalin village, in a raid. Your master was a small sheik, and is now with the force at El Obeid. You had been the companion of his son, and when the latter made up his mind to come and fight here your master gave you your freedom, so that you might fight by his son's side. You might say that I have not yet settled under whose banner I shall fight. All I wish is to be in the front of the battle, when we meet the infidels. That will be quite sufficient. There are men here from almost every village in the Soudan, and no one will care much where his neighbours come from.

"Mention that we intend to fight as matchlock men, not on horseback, as the animals are greatly fatigued from their long journey, and will require rest for some time; and, being so far from home, I fear that we might lose them if we went into the fight with them; and in that case might have to journey on foot, for a long time, before we could get others.

"I don't at all suppose that it will be necessary for you to say all this. People will be too much occupied with their own affairs to care much about others; still, it is well not to hesitate, if questioned."

Talk and laughter in the great camp ceased now, and it was not until the sun lost its power that it again began. Gregory did not move, till it began to get dusk.

"I shall be away some time," he said, "so don't be at all uneasy about me. I shall take my black blanket, so that I can cover myself with it and lie down, as if asleep, close to any of the emirs' tents where I hear talk going on; and so may be able to gather some idea as to their views. I have already learned that the tribesmen have not heard of any immediate move, and are discontented at being kept inactive so long. The leaders, however, may have their plans, but will not make them known to the men, until it is time for action."

The camp was thoroughly alive when he entered it. Men were sitting about in groups; the women, as before, keeping near their little shelters, laughing and chatting together, and sometimes quarrelling. From the manner of the men, who either sat or walked about, it was not difficult for Gregory to distinguish between the villagers, who had been dragged away from their homes and forced to enter the service of the Khalifa, and the Baggara and kindred tribes, who had so long held the Soudan in subjection. The former were quiet in their demeanour, and sometimes sullen in their looks. He had no doubt that, when the fighting came, these would face death at the hands of the infidels as bravely as their oppressors, for the belief in Mahdism was now universal. His followers had proved themselves invincible; they had no doubt that they would destroy the armies of Egypt, but they resented being dragged away from their quiet homes, their families, and their fields.

Among these the Baggara strode haughtily. Splendid men, for the most part, tall, lithe, and muscular; men with the supreme belief in themselves, and in their cause, carrying themselves as the Norman barons might have done among a crowd of Saxons; the conquerors of the land, the most trusted followers of the successor of the Mahdi, men who felt themselves invincible. It was true that they had, so far, failed to overrun Egypt, and had even suffered reverses, but these the Khalifa had taught them to consider were due to disobedience of his orders, or the result of their fighting upon unlucky days. All this was soon to be reversed. The prophecies had told that the infidels were about to be annihilated, and that then they would sweep down without opposition, and possess themselves of the plunder of Egypt.

Gregory passed wholly unnoticed among the crowd. There was nothing to distinguish him from others, and the thought that an Egyptian spy, still less one of the infidels, should venture into their camp had never occurred to one of that multitude. Occasionally, he sat down near a group of the Baggara, listening to their talk. They were impatient, too, but they were convinced that all was for the best; and that, when it was the will of Allah, they would destroy their enemy. Still, there were expressions of impatience that Mahmud was not allowed to advance.

"We know," one said, "that it is at Kirkeban that the last great destruction of the infidel is to take place, and that these madmen are coming to their fate; still, we might move down and destroy those at Dongola and along the river, and possess ourselves of their arms and stores. Why should we come thus far from Omdurman, if we are to go no farther?"

"Why ask questions?" another said contemptuously. "Enough that it is the command of the Khalifa, to whom power and knowledge has been given by the Mahdi, until he himself returns to earth. To the Khalifa will be revealed the day and the hour on which we are to smite the infidel. If Mahmud and the great emirs are all content to wait, why should we be impatient?"

Everywhere Gregory went, he heard the same feelings expressed. The men were impatient to be up and doing, but they must wait the appointed hour.

It was late before he ventured to approach the tents of the leaders. He knew that it was impossible to get near Mahmud himself, for he had his own bodyguard of picked men. The night, however, was dark and, enveloping himself from head to foot in his black blanket, he crawled out until well beyond the line of tents, and then very cautiously made his way towards them again. He knew that he should see the white figures of the Dervishes before they could make him out; and he managed, unnoticed, to crawl up to one of the largest tents, and lie down against it. He heard the chatter of the women in an adjoining tent, but there was no sound in that against which he lay.

For an hour all was quiet. Then he saw two white figures coming from Mahmud's camp, which lay some fifty yards away. To his delight, they stopped at the entrance of the tent by which he was concealed, and one said:

"I can well understand, Ibrahim Khalim, that your brother Mahmud is sorely vexed that your father will not let him advance against the Egyptians, at Merawi. I fully share his feelings; for could I not, with my cavalry, sweep them before me into the river, even though no footmen came with me? According to accounts they are but two or three thousand strong, and I have as many horsemen under my command."

"That is so, Osman Azrakyet. But methinks my father is right. If we were to march across the desert, we would lose very many men and great numbers of animals, and we should arrive weakened and dispirited. If we remain here, it is the Egyptians who will have to bear the hardships of the march across the desert. Great numbers of the animals that carry the baggage and food, without which the poor infidels are unable to march, would die, and the weakened force would be an easy prey for us."

"That is true," the other said, "but they may come now, as they came to Dongola, in their boats."

"They have the cataracts to ascend, and the rapid currents of the Nile at its full to struggle against. There is a strong force at Abu Hamed, and our Governor at Berber will move down there, with all his force, when he hears that the Egyptians are coming up the cataracts. Should it be the will of Allah that they should pass them, and reach Berber, we shall know how to meet them. Mahmud has settled this evening that many strong forts are to be built on the river bank here, and if the infidels try to advance farther by water, they will be all sunk.

"I agree with you and Mahmud, and wish that it had been otherwise, and that we could hurl ourselves at once upon the Egyptians and prevent their coming farther—but that would be but a partial success. If we wait, they will gather all their forces before they come, and we shall destroy them at one blow. Then we shall seize all their stores and animals, cross the desert to Dongola, march forward to Assouan, and there wait till the Khalifa brings his own army; and then who is to oppose us? We will conquer the land of the infidel. I am as eager for the day of battle as you are, but it seems to me that it is best to wait here, until the infidels come; and I feel that it is wise of the Khalifa thus to order. Now I will to my tent."

As soon as Ibrahim Khalim had entered his tent, Gregory crawled away, well satisfied that he had gained exactly the information he had come to gather. He had gone but a few paces when he saw a white figure striding along, in front of the tents. He stopped, and threw himself down.

Unfortunately, the path taken by the sheik was directly towards him. He heard the footsteps advancing, in hopes that the man would pass either in front or behind him. Then he felt a sudden kick, an exclamation, and a heavy fall. He leapt to his feet, but the Arab sheik was as quick and, springing up, also seized him, at the same time drawing his knife and uttering a loud shout.

Gregory grasped the Arab's wrist, and without hesitation snatched his own knife from the sash, and drove it deep into his assailant's body. The latter uttered another loud cry for help, and a score of men rushed from behind the tents.

Gregory set off at the top of his speed, dashed over the brow of the bridge, and then, without entering the camp there, he kept along close to the crest, running at the top of his speed and wrapping his blanket as much as possible round him. He heard an outburst of yells behind, and felt sure that the sheik he had wounded had told those who had rushed up which way he had fled. With loud shouts they poured over the crest, and there were joined by others running up from the camp.

When Gregory paused for a moment, after running for three or four hundred yards, he could hear no sound of footsteps behind him. Glancing round, he could not see white dresses in the darkness. Turning sharply off, he recrossed the crest of the hill and, keeping close to it, continued his flight until well past the end of the camp.

The alarm had by this time spread everywhere, and a wild medley of shouts rose throughout the whole area of the encampment. He turned now, and made for the spot where he had left Zaki and the horses. In five minutes he reached it.

"Is that you, my lord?" Zaki asked, as he came up.

"Yes, we must fly at once! I was discovered, and had to kill—or at least badly wound—a sheik, and they are searching for me every-where."

"I have saddled the horses, and put the water skins on them."

"That is well done, Zaki. Let us mount and be off, at once. We will lead the horses. It is too dark to gallop among these bushes, and the sound of the hoofs might be heard. We will go quietly, till we are well away."

Not another word was spoken, till they had gone half a mile.

"We will mount now, Zaki. The horses can see better than we. We will go at a walk. I dare not strike a light to look at the compass, but there are the stars. I do not see the north star, it must be hidden by the mist, lower down; but the others give us the direction, quite near enough to go by.

"It is most unfortunate that the fellow who rushed against me was a sheik. I could see that, by the outline of his robe. If it had been a common man, there would not have been any fuss over it. As it is, they will search for us high and low. I know he wasn't killed on the spot, for he shouted after I had left him; and they are likely to guess, from his account, that I had been down at one of the emirs' tents, and was prob-ably a spy.

"I know that I ought to have paused a moment, and given him another stab, but I could not bring myself to do it. It is one thing to stab a man who is trying to take one's life, but it is quite another when he has fallen, and is helpless."

Zaki had made no reply. He could scarcely understand his master's repugnance to making matters safe, when another blow would have done so, but it was not for him to blame.

They travelled all night and, when the moon rose, were able to get along somewhat faster; but its light was now feeble and uncertain. As soon as day broke, they rode fast, and at ten o'clock had left behind the range of hills, stretching between the wells of Abu Klea and Jebel Sergain.

"We ought to be safe now," Gregory said, as they dismounted. "At any rate, the horses must have a rest. We have done over forty miles."

"We are safe for the present, my lord. It all depends whether or not they think you are a spy. If they come to that conclusion, they will send at once to Abu Klea; and if a strong body is stationed there, they may have sent a party on to Gakdul, or even to El Howeyat, for they will feel sure that we shall make for one of the wells."

"How much water have you got in the bags?"

Zaki examined them.

"Enough for ourselves for five or six days; but only enough for two drinks each, for the horses and for ourselves, for a couple of days."

"That is bad. If we had had any idea of coming away so soon, we would have filled the large bags yesterday. I had intended to send down the horses in the morning, therefore left them only half full, and they must have leaked a good deal to get so low. See if one leaks more than the other."

It was found that one held the water well, but from the other there was a steady drip. They transferred the water from this to the sound bag.

"We must drink as little as we can, Zaki, and give the horses only a mouthful, now and then, and let them munch the shrubs and get a little moisture from them. Do you think there is any fear of the Dervishes following our tracks?"

"No, my lord. In the first place, they do not know that there are two of us, or that we are mounted. When those who camped near us notice, when they get up this morning, that we have moved; they will only think that we have shifted our camp, as there was no talk of horsemen being concerned in this affair. No, I do not think they will attempt to follow us, except along the caravan road, but I feel sure they will pursue us on that line."

They rested for some hours, in the shade of a high rock, leaving the horses to pick what herbage they could find. At four o'clock they started again. They had ridden two hours, when Zaki said:

"See, my lord, there are two men on the top of Jebel Sergain!"

Gregory gazed in that direction.

"Yes, I can notice them now, but I should not have done so, if you had not seen them."

"They are on watch, my lord."

"Well, they can hardly see us, at this distance."

"You may be sure that they see us," Zaki said; "the eyes of an Arab are very keen, and could not fail to catch two moving objects—especially horsemen."

"If they are looking for us, and have seen us, Zaki, they would not be standing stationary there."

"Not if they were alone. But others may have been with them. When they first caught sight of us, which may have been half an hour ago, the others may have gone down to Abu Klea, while those two remained to watch which course we took. The Arabs can signal with their lances, or with their horses, and from there they would be able to direct any party in pursuit of us."

"Well, we must keep on as hard as we can, till dark; after that, we can take it quietly. You see, the difficulty with us will be water. Now that they have once made out two horsemen riding north, they must know that we have some special object in avoiding them; and will, no doubt, send a party to Gakdul, if not farther."

They crossed the rough country as quickly as they could, and then again broke into a canter. An hour later, as they crossed a slight rise, Zaki looked back.

"There are some horsemen in pursuit, my lord. They have evidently come from Abu Klea."

Gregory looked round.

"There are about fifteen of them," he said. "However, they are a good three miles behind, and it will be dark in another half hour. As soon as it is so, we will turn off to the right or left, and so throw them off our track. Don't hurry your horse. The animals have made a very long journey, since we started, and we shall want them badly tomorrow."

In another half hour the sun went down. Darkness comes on quickly in the Soudan, and in another quarter of an hour they had lost sight of their pursuers, who had gained about a mile upon them.

"Another five minutes, Zaki, to allow for their eyes being better than ours. Which way do you think we had better turn?"

"I should say to the left, my lord. There is another caravan route from Metemmeh to Ambukol. It cannot be more than fifteen miles to the west."

"Do you know anything about it?"

"I have never been along there. It is a shorter route than the one to Korti, but not so much used, I believe, because the wells cannot be relied upon."

"Well, I feel sure we shall not be able to get at the wells on the other line, so we had better take that. As we shall be fairly safe from pursuit, we may as well bear towards the northwest. By doing so we shall be longer in striking the track, but the journey will be a good bit shorter than if we were to ride due west.

"Now we can safely dismount. It is getting pitch dark, and we will lead our horses. I can feel that mine is nearly dead beat. In a few minutes we will halt, and give them half a gourd full of water, each. After that, we had better go on for another six or seven miles, so as to be well out of sight of anyone on the hills."

Ten minutes later they heard the dull sound of horses' hoofs on the sand. They waited five minutes, until it died away in the distance, and then continued their course. It was slow work, as they had to avoid every bush carefully; lest, if their pursuers halted, they should hear the crackling of a dry stick in the still air. Zaki, who could see much better in the dark than his master, went on ahead; while Gregory led the two horses.

A good hour passed before they stopped. They gave the horses a scanty drink, and took a mouthful or two each; and then, throwing themselves down, allowed the horses to crop the scanty herbage.

After four hours' halt they pursued their way on foot for three hours, laying their course by the stars. They calculated that they must have gone a good fifteen miles from the point where they turned off, and feared that they might miss the caravan track, if they went on before daybreak.

CHAPTER 9:

Safely Back.

As soon as the sun was up they pursued their journey, Gregory's compass being now available.

In half an hour, Zaki said, "There is a sign of the track, my lord," and he pointed to the skeleton of a camel.

"How many more miles do you think we have to go, Zaki?"

"We must be a good half way, my lord."

"Yes, quite that, I should think. Looking at the map, I should say that we must be about abreast of the line of Gakdul. This route is only just indicated, and there are no halting places marked upon it. Still, there must be water, otherwise caravans could not use it. We have about sixty miles farther to go, so that if the horses were fresh we might be there this evening; but as it is, we have still two, if not three days' journey before us.

"Well, we must hope that we shall find some water. Just let the horses wet their mouths; we can keep on for a bit, before we have a drink.

"How much more is there left?" he asked, after the lad had given a little water to each horse.

"Not above two gourdfuls."

"Well, we must ride as far as we can and, at any rate, must keep one gourdful for tomorrow. If we cover twenty-five miles today—and I don't think the horses can do more—we can manage, if they are entirely done up, to walk the other thirty-five miles. However, as I said, there must be wells, and even if they are dry, we may be able to scratch the sand out and find a little water. What food have we got?"

"Only about two pounds of dates."

"That is a poor supply for two days, Zaki, but we must make the best of them. We will only eat a few today, so as to have a fair meal in the morning. We shall want it, if we have to walk thirty-five miles over the sand."

"It will not be all sand," Zaki said; "there is grass for the last fifteen miles, near the river; and there were cultivated fields about ten miles out, before the Dervishes came."

"That is better. Now we will be moving."

The herbage the horses had cropped during the halt had served, to a certain degree, to supply the place of water; and they proceeded at a brisker pace than Gregory had expected.

"Keep a sharp lookout for water. Even if the wells are dry, you will see a difference in the growth of the bushes round them; and as it is certain that this route has not been used for some time, there may even be grass."

They rode on at an easy canter, and avoided pressing the horses in the slightest degree, allowing them to walk whenever they chose. The heat was very great, and after four hours' riding Gregory called a halt.

"We must have done twenty miles," he said. "The bushes look green about here, and the horses have got something of a feed."

"I think this must be one of the old halting places," Zaki said, looking round as they dismounted. "See, my lord, there are some broken gourds, and some rags scattered about."

"So there are," Gregory said. "We will take the bridles out of the horses' mouths, so that they can chew the leaves up better; and then we will see if we can find where the wells were."

Twenty yards farther away they found a deep hole.

"This was one of them," the lad said, "but it is quite dry. See, there is an old bucket lying at the bottom. I will look about; there may be some more of them."

Two others were discovered, and the sand at the bottom of one of them looked a somewhat darker colour than the others.

"Well, we will dig here," Gregory said. "Bring down those two half gourds; they will help us to shovel the sand aside."

The bottom of the hole was some six feet across, and they set to work in the middle of it. By the time they had got down two feet, the sand was soft and clammy.

"We will get to water, Zaki, if we have to stay here all day!" said Gregory.

It was hard work, and it was not until after four hours' toil that, to their delight, they found the sand wet under their feet. They had taken it by turns to use the scoop, for the labour of making the hole large enough for them both to work at once would have been excessive.

In another hour there was half an inch of water in the hole. Gregory took a gourd, and buried it in the soft soil until the water flowed in over the brim.

"Give me the other one down, Zaki. I will fill that, too, and then we will both start drinking together."

Five minutes later, the two took a long draught. The scoops were then refilled and carried to the horses, who drank with an eagerness that showed how great was their thirst. Three times the gourds were filled, and emptied.

"Now hand me down that water bag."

This was half filled, and then, exhausted with their work, they threw themselves down and slept for some hours. When they awoke, the sun was setting.

"Bring up the horses, Zaki. Let them drink as much as they like."

The gourds had each to be filled six times, before the animals were satisfied. The riders then took another deep drink, ate a handful of dates, and mounted.

"We are safe now, and only have to fear a band of marauding Arabs; and it would be hard luck, were we to fall in with them. We had better ride slowly for the first hour or so. We must not press the horses, after they have had such a drink."

"Very well, master."

"There is no particular reason for hurry, and even if we miss the trail we know that, by keeping straight on, we shall strike the river somewhere near Korti or Ambukol."

For an hour they went at a walk, and then the horses broke into their usual pace, of their own accord. It was getting dark, now, and soon even Zaki could not make out the track.

"The horses will keep to it, my lord," he said; "their sight is a great deal better than ours, and I dare say their smell may have something to do with it. Besides, the track is clear of bushes, so we should know at once, if they strayed from it."

They rode for five hours, and then felt that the horses were beginning to fag.

"We will halt here," Gregory said. "We certainly cannot be more than five-and-twenty miles from the river; and, if we start at dawn, shall be there before the heat of the day begins. We can have another handful of dates, and give the horses a handful each, and that will leave us a few for the morning."

The horses, after being given the dates, were again turned loose; and it was not long before they were heard pulling the leaves off bushes.

"Our case is a good deal better this evening than it was yesterday," Gregory said. "Then it looked as if it would be rather a close thing, for I am sure the horses could not have gone much farther, if we had not found the water. I wish we had a good feed to give them."

"They will do very well on the bushes, my lord. They get little else, when they are with the Arabs; a handful of durra, occasionally, when they are at work; but at other times they only get what they can pick up. If their master is a good one, they may get a few dates. They will carry us briskly enough to the river, tomorrow."

They did not talk long, and were soon sound asleep. Zaki was the first to wake.

"Day is just breaking, master."

"You don't say so!" Gregory grumbled, sleepily. "It seems to me that we have only just lain down."

They ate the remainder of their dates, took a drink of water, and gave two gourdfuls to the horses; and, in a quarter of an hour, were on their way again. They had ridden but two or three miles, when Zaki exclaimed:

"There are some horsemen!"

"Eight of them, Zaki, and they are evidently riding to cut us off! As far as I can see, only four of them have guns; the others have spears.

"I think we can manage them. With my breech-loader I can fire two shots to their one, and we have pistols, as well."

The Arabs drew up ahead of them, and remained quiet there until the others came to within fifty yards, and checked their horses. A man who appeared to be the leader of the party shouted the usual salutation, to which Gregory replied.

The leader said, "Where are my friends going and why do they halt?"

"We are on a mission. We wish to see if the infidels are still at Ambukol."

"For that you will not want guns," the man said, "and we need them badly. I beg of you to give them to us."

"They may be of use to us. We may come upon infidel scouts."

"Nevertheless, my friends, you must hand them over to us. We are, as you see, eight, and you are only two. The law of the desert is that the stronger take, and the weaker lose."

"It may be so, sometimes," Gregory said quietly, "but not in this case. I advise you to ride your way, and we will ride ours."

Then he said to Zaki, "Dismount and stand behind your horse, and fire over the saddle; but don't fire the first shot now."

He threw himself from his saddle. Scarcely had he done so when four shots were fired, and Gregory took a steady aim at the chief. The latter threw up his arms, and fell. With a yell of fury, the others dashed forward. Zaki did not fire until they were within twenty yards, and directly afterwards Gregory fired again. There were now but five assailants.

"Now for your pistols, Zaki!" he cried, glancing round for the first time.

He then saw why Zaki had not fired when he first did so—his horse was lying dead in front of him, shot through the head.

"Stand by me! Don't throw away a shot! You take the man on the other side of the horse. I will take the others."

Steadily the four pistols were fired. As the Arabs rode up, two of them fell, and another was wounded. Dismayed at the loss of so many of their number, the three survivors rode off at full speed.

"Are you hurt, Zaki?"

"A spear grazed my cheek, my lord; that is all. It was my own fault. I kept my last barrel too long. However, it tumbled him over.

"Are you hurt, master?"

"I have got a ball in the shoulder. That fellow without a spear has got pistols, and fired just as I did; or rather, an instant before. That shook my aim, but he has a ball in him, somewhere.

"Just see if they have got some dates on their saddles," for the horses of the fallen men had remained by the side of their masters' bodies.

"Yes, my lord," Zaki said, examining them. "Two bags, nearly full."

"That is satisfactory. Pick out the best horse for yourself, and then we will ride on. But before we go, we will break the stocks of these four guns, and carry the barrels off, and throw them into the bushes, a mile or two away."

As soon as this was done, they mounted and rode on. They halted in a quarter of an hour and, after Gregory's arm had been bound tightly to his side with his sash, both they and their horses had a good meal of dates. Then they rode on again, and in three hours saw some white tents ahead.

There was a slight stir as they were seen coming, and a dozen black soldiers sprang up and ran forward, fixing bayonets as they did so.

"We are friends!" Gregory shouted, in Arabic; and Zaki repeated the shout in his own language.

The soldiers looked doubtful, and stood together in a group. They knew that the Dervishes were sometimes ready to throw away their own lives, if they could but kill some of their enemy.

One of them shouted back, "Stay where you are until I call an officer!"

He went back to the tents, and returned with a white officer, whom Gregory at once recognized as one of those who had come up with him from Wady Halfa.

"Leslie," he shouted in English, "will you kindly call off your soldiers? One of their muskets might go off, accidentally. I suppose you don't remember me. I am Hilliard, who came up with you in the steamer."

The officer had stopped in astonishment, at hearing this seeming Dervish address him, by name, in English. He then advanced, giving an order to his men to fall back.

"Is it really you, Hilliard?" he said, as he approached the horsemen, who were coming forward at a walk. "Which of you is it? For I don't see any resemblance, in either of you."

"It is I, Leslie. I am not surprised that you don't know me."

"But what are you masquerading for, in this dress; and where have you come from?"

"Perhaps I had better not say, Leslie. I have been doing some scouting across the desert, with my boy here. We have had a long ride. In the first place, my arm wants attending to. I have a bullet in the shoulder. The next thing we need is something to eat; for the last three days we have had nothing but dates, and not too many of them.

"Is there any chance of getting taken up to Merawi? We came down from there to Korti, in a native vessel."

"Yes; a gunboat with some native craft will be going up this afternoon. I will give orders, at once, that your horses shall be put on board."

When the ball had been extracted from his shoulder, and the wound dressed and bandaged by the surgeon in charge, Gregory went up to the tents again, where he was warmly received by the three white officers of the Negro regiment. Breakfast already had been prepared, Zaki being handed over to the native officers. After having made a hearty meal, Gregory related the adventure with the Arabs in the desert, merely saying that they had found there were no Dervishes at Gakdul.

"But why didn't you go straight back, instead of coming down here?"

"I wanted to see whether this line was open, and whether there were any wells on it. We only found one, and it took us four or five hours' hard work to get at the water. It is lucky, indeed, that we did so; for our horses were getting very done up, and I had begun to think that they would not reach our destination alive."

In the afternoon, the adventurers started with the boats going up to Merawi and, the next morning, arrived at the camp. The Dervish patches had been removed from their clothes, as soon as they arrived at Ambukol. Gregory could have borrowed a white suit there; but as the stain on his skin, although somewhat lighter than when first put on, was too dark, he declined the offer.

"No one may notice me as I land, now," he said, "but everyone would stare at a man with a brown face and white uniform."

Leaving Zaki to get the horses on shore, Gregory went straight to the General's quarters. He told the sentry that he wished to see the General, on business.

"You cannot go in," the man said. "The General is engaged."

"If you send in word to him that his messenger has returned, I am sure he will see me."

"You can sit down here, then," the sentry said. "When the officer with him comes out, I will give your message to his orderly."

Gregory, however, was in no humour to be stopped; and in an authoritative voice called, "Orderly!"

A soldier came down directly from the guard room.

"Tell the General, at once, that Mr. Hilliard has returned."

With a look of wonder, the orderly went into the tent. Half a minute later, he returned.

"You are to come in," he said.

As the General had seen Gregory in his disguise, before starting, he of course recognized him.

"My dear Hilliard," he said, getting up and shaking him cordially by the hand, "I am heartily glad to see you back. You have been frequently in my thoughts; and though I had every confidence in your sharpness, I have regretted, more than once, that I allowed you to go.

"I suppose you failed to get there. It is hardly possible that you should have done so, in the time. I suppose, when you got to Gakdul, you learned that the Dervishes were at Abu Klea."

"They were at Abu Klea, General; but I made a detour, and got into their camp at Metemmeh."

"You did, and have returned safely! I congratulate you, most warmly.

"I told you, Macdonald," he said, turning to the officer with whom he had been engaged, "that I had the greatest hope that Mr. Hilliard would get through. He felt so confident in himself that I could scarce help feeling confidence in him, too."

"He has done well, indeed!" Colonel Macdonald said. "I should not have liked to send any of my officers on such an adventure, though they have been here for years."

"Well, will you sit down, Mr. Hilliard," the General said, "and give us a full account? In the first place, what you have learned? And in the second, how you have learned it?"

Gregory related the conversations he had heard among the soldiers; and then that of Mahmud's brother and the commander of the Dervish cavalry. Then he described the events of his journey there, his narrow escape from capture, and the pursuit by the Dervishes at Abu Klea; how he gave them the slip, struck the Ambukol caravan road, had a fight with a band of robber Arabs, and finally reached the Egyptian camp.

"An excellently managed business!" the General said, warmly. "You have certainly had some narrow escapes, and seem to have adopted the only course by which you could have got off safely. The information you have brought is of the highest importance. I shall telegraph, at once, to the Sirdar that there will assuredly be no advance on the part of Mahmud from Metemmeh; which will leave him free to carry out the plans he has formed. I shall of course, in my written despatch, give him full particulars of the manner in which I have obtained that information."

"It was a very fine action," Macdonald agreed. "The lad has shown that he has a good head, as well as great courage.

"You will make your way, Mr. Hilliard—that is, if you don't try this sort of thing again. A man may get through it once, but it would be just tempting providence to try it a second time."

"Now, Mr. Hilliard," the General said, "you had best go to your quarters. I will ask the surgeon to attend to you, at once. You must keep quiet, and do no more duty until you are discharged from the sick list."

Ten days later, orders were issued that the brigade under Macdonald; consisting of the 3rd Egyptians, and the 9th, 10th, and 11th Soudanese, together with a mule battery; were to move forward the next day to Kassinger, the advanced post some ten miles higher up the river. This seemed only a preliminary step, and the general opinion was that another fortnight would elapse before there would be a general movement.

A reconnaissance with friendly Arabs had, however, been made ahead towards Abu Hamed, and had obtained certain information that the garrison at that place was by no means a strong one. The information Gregory had gathered had shown that Mahmud had no intention of advancing against Merawi; and that no reinforcements had, as yet, started to join the force at Abu Hamed; the Dervish leader being convinced that the Nile was not yet high enough to admit of boats going up the cataract.

Thus, everything favoured the Sirdar's plan to capture Abu Hamed, and enable the railway to be constructed to that place before Mahmud could receive the news that the troops were in motion. He therefore directed General Hunter to push forward, with only one brigade, leaving the rest to hold Merawi; and ordered the camel corps, and the friendly Arabs, to advance across the desert as far as the Gakdul wells, where their appearance would lead Mahmud to believe that they were the advance guard of the coming army.

Two days later Gregory, on going to the headquarters tent, was told that General Hunter and his staff would start, in an hour's time, to inspect the camp at Kassinger.

"Do you think you are fit to ride?" the chief of the staff asked him.

"Perfectly, sir. The doctor discharged me yesterday as fit for duty, but advised me to keep my arm in a sling, for a time."

"In that case, you may accompany us.

"It is a little uncertain when we shall return," the officer said, with a smile; "therefore I advise you to take all your belongings with you. Have them packed up quietly. We do not wish any suspicions to arise that we are not returning this evening."

"Thank you, sir!" Gregory said, gratefully. "I shall be ready to start in an hour."

He returned in high glee to his hut, for he felt certain that an immediate advance was about to take place.

"Zaki," he said, "I am going to ride with the General; and, as it is possible I may be stationed at Kassinger for a short time, you had better get the camel brought up, and start as soon as you have packed the things on it. I am going to ride over with the staff, in an hour, and shall overtake you by the way. How long will you be?"

"Half an hour, bey."

"I will be there by that time, and will take my horse; then you can go on with the camel."

Behind the headquarter camp the work of packing up was also going on; the camels being sent off in threes and fours, as they were laden, so as to attract no attention. Half an hour later the General came out, and without delay started with the staff, Captain Fitton remaining behind to see that the rest of the stores were sent off, and a small tent for the use of the General. All heavy packages were to be taken up by water.

The arrival of the General at Kassinger excited no surprise, as he had ridden over the day before; but when, in the afternoon, orders were issued that the camels should all be laden, in preparation for a march that evening; the Soudanese could with difficulty be restrained from giving vent to their exuberant joy that, at length, their long halt was at an end, and they were to have another chance of getting at the enemy.

A large train of camels had been quietly collected at Kassinger, sufficient to carry the necessary supplies for the use of the column, for some three weeks' time; and it was hoped that, before long, the gunboats and many of the native craft, with stores, would join them at Abu Hamed.

The force started at sunset. The distance to be travelled was a hundred and eighteen miles, and the road was a very difficult one. The ground rose steeply, almost from the edge of the river; and at times had to be traversed in single file.

As night came on, the scene was a weird one. On one side the rocky ascent rose, black and threatening. On the other, the river rushed foaming, only broken by the rocks and little islands of the cataract.

Gregory had been ordered to remain with the camel train; to keep them, as much as possible, together, and prevent wide gaps from occurring in the ranks. It was tedious work; and the end of the train did not arrive, until broad daylight, at the spot where the infantry halted. He at once told Zaki to pitch his little tent, which he had already shown him how to do, while he went to see if there were any orders at headquarters.

He found the staff were just sitting down to a rough breakfast. Being told, after the meal, that he would not be wanted during the day; but that at night he was to continue his work with the camels; he went back to his tent, and threw himself on his bed. But, in spite of the fly being fastened up, and a blanket thrown over the tent, the heat was so great that he was only able to doze off occasionally.

He observed that even the black troops suffered from the heat. They had erected screens, with their blankets placed end to end, supported by their guns; and lay there, getting what air there was, and sheltered from the direct rays of the sun. Few slept. Most of them talked, or smoked.

There was some argument, among the officers, as to the relative advantages of night and day marches. All agreed that, if only one march had to be done, it was better to do it at night; but when, as in the present case, it would last for seven or eight days, many thought that, terrible as would be the heat, it would be better to march in the day, and permit the troops to sleep at night. This opinion certainly seemed to be justified; for, at the end of the third day, the men were so completely worn out from want of sleep that they stumbled as they marched; and were with difficulty restrained from throwing themselves down, to get the much-needed rest.

Gregory always went down, as soon as the column arrived at its halting place, as he did before starting in the evening, to bathe in some quiet pool or backwater; and, much as he had set himself against taking spirits, he found that he was unable to eat his meals, unless he took a spoonful or two with his water, or cold tea.

On the evening of the third day, they passed the battlefield of Kirkeban, where General Earle fell when the River Expedition was attacked by the Dervishes. Next day they halted at Hebbeh, where Colonel Stewart, on his way down with a number of refugees from Khartoum, was treacherously murdered. A portion of the steamer was still visible in the river.

Day after day the column plodded on, for the most part strung out in single file, the line extending over many miles; and, late on the evening of the 6th of August, they reached a spot within a mile and a half of Abu Hamed, the hundred and eighteen miles having been accomplished in seven days and a half.

So far as they knew, the enemy had, as yet, received no news of their approach. Three hours' rest was given the troops, and then they marched out, in order of battle.

A fair idea of the position had been obtained from the friendly natives. Abu Hamed lay on the river. The desert sloped gradually down to it, on all sides; with a sharp, deep descent within two hundred yards of the town. The houses were all loopholed, for defence.

When within a mile of the town, they must have been sighted by the Dervish sentries on a lofty watchtower. No movement, however, was visible, and there was a general feeling of disappointment, as the impression gained ground that the enemy had retreated. The 9th and 10th Soudanese made a sweep round, to attack from the desert side. The 11th, and half of the Egyptian battalion—the other half having been left to guard the baggage—followed the course of the river.

Major Kincaid rode forward, to the edge of the steep slope that looked down to the town. He could see no one moving about. The Dervish trenches, about eighty yards away, appeared empty; and he was about to write a message to the General, saying that the place was deserted, when a sharp fire suddenly opened upon him. He turned to ride back to warn the General, but he was too late; for, at the same moment, Hunter with his staff galloped up to the edge of the slope, and was immediately saluted by a heavy volley; which, however, was fired so wildly that none of the party was hit.

The artillery were now ordered to bombard the place. At first, they could only fire at the tops of the houses; but, changing their position, they found a spot where they could command the town. For half an hour this continued. The infantry were drawn up just beyond the brow, where they could not be seen by the defenders. The Dervishes gave no signs of life, and as the artillery could not depress their guns sufficiently to enable them to rake the trenches, the infantry were ordered to charge.

As soon as they reached the edge of the dip, a storm of musketry broke out from the Dervish trenches, but, fortunately, the greater portion of the bullets flew overhead. Macdonald had intended to carry the place at the point of the bayonet, without firing; but the troops, suddenly exposed to such a storm of musketry, halted and opened fire without orders; the result being that they suffered a great deal more than they would have done, had they crossed the eighty yards, which divided them from the trench, by a rush. Standing, as they did, against the skyline, the Dervishes were able to pick them off; they themselves showing only their heads above the trenches. Two of the mounted officers of the 10th were killed, and two had their horses shot under them.

Macdonald and his officers rushed along in front of the line, knocking up the men's muskets; and abusing them, in the strongest terms, for their disobedience to orders. The moment the fire ceased, the troops rushed forward; and the Dervishes at once abandoned their trenches, and ran back to the line of houses. These were crowded together, divided by narrow winding lanes, and here a desperate struggle took place.

The Dervishes defended themselves with the greatest tenacity, sometimes rushing out and hurling themselves upon their assailants, and defending the houses to the last, making a stand when the doors were burst open, until the last of the inmates were either shot or bayoneted. So determined was the defense of some of the larger houses, that it was necessary to bring up the guns and batter an entrance. Many of the houses were found, when the troops burst in, to be tenanted only by dead; for the Soudanese always heralded their attack by firing several volleys, and the bullets made their way through and through the mud walls, as if they had been paper.

About seventy or eighty horsemen and a hundred Dervish infantry escaped, but the rest were either killed or made prisoners, together with Mahomed Zein, the governor. A quantity of arms, camels, and horses were also captured. The loss on our side was two British officers killed, and twenty-one of the black troops; and three Egyptian officers, and sixty-one men wounded.

When the convoy halted, previous to the troops marching to the attack, Gregory, whose duties with the baggage had now ended, joined the General's staff and rode forward with them. Hunter had glanced round, as he rode up, and answered with a nod when he saluted, and asked if he could come.

He felt rather scared on the Dervishes opening fire so suddenly, when the General's impatience had led him to ride forward, without waiting for Major Kincaid's report. After the troops rushed into the town, the General maintained his position at the edge of the dip, for the narrow streets were so crowded with men that a group of horsemen could hardly have forced their way in, and it would be impossible to see what was going on, and to issue orders.

Mahomed Zein had not followed the example of some of his followers, and died fighting to the last. He was found hiding under a bed, and was brought before General Hunter; who asked him why he fought, when he must have known that it was useless; to which he replied:

"I knew that you had only three times as many as I had, and every one of my men is worth four of yours. You could not fire till you were quite close up, and at that range our rifles are as good as yours."

The General asked what he thought Mahmud would do, to which he replied:

"He will be down here in five days, and wipe you out!"

It was necessary to halt at Abu Hamed, until stores came up. Captain Keppel, Royal Navy, and the officers commanding the gunboats were toiling at the cataracts to bring them up. Nevertheless one of these was capsized, and only three got through safely. Major Pink, with a large number of troops from Merawi, succeeded in hauling the sailing boats through.

A large column of laden camels was, at the same time, being pushed forward by the caravan route from Korosko. It was a time of much anxiety, till stores began to arrive; for, had Mahmud advanced at once, the passage up the river would have been arrested, and the land column cut off; in which case the little force would have been reduced to sore straits, as they must have stood on the defensive until reinforcements reached them.

There was, too, some anxiety as to the safety of the forces at Ambukol and Korti; for Mahmud, on learning that the garrisons had been weakened by the despatch of troops to Abu Hamed, might have crossed the desert with all his force and fallen upon them. Mahmud had indeed, as it turned out, believed that the expedition to Abu Hamed was only undertaken to cover the flank of the Egyptian army from attack, from that quarter; and still believed that it was from Merawi that the main British force would advance against him.

Before the supplies had all arrived, the position changed; as news came that Berber was being evacuated by the Dervishes. The information was telegraphed to the Sirdar, who at once ordered that a force of the friendly Arabs, escorted by a gunboat, should go up to Berber to find if the news was true. One gunboat had already arrived, and General Hunter decided on going up in her himself. Two hundred of the Arabs, under Ahmed Bey, were to ride along the bank. They were to be mounted on the fastest camels that could be picked out; so that, if they encountered the Dervishes, they would have a fair chance of escaping, and getting under cover of the gunboat's fire.

"Mr. Hilliard," the General said, "I shall be obliged if you will accompany Ahmed Bey. The Arabs are always more steady, if they have an English officer with them. They will be ready to start in an hour. A signaller from the 11th Soudanese shall go with you; and you can notify, to us, the approach of any strong party of the enemy, and their direction; so that the gunboat can send a shell or two among them, as a hint that they had better keep out of range."

As his baggage camel was by no means a fast one, Gregory at first decided to leave it behind in charge of Zaki; but on going across to the Arab camp, Ahmed Bey at once offered to place a fast one at his disposal. He accordingly sent his own animal into the transport yard, committed the heavy wooden case, with the greater portion of his remaining stores, to the charge of the sergeant of the mess, retaining only three or four tins of preserved milk, some tea, four or five tins of meat, a bottle of brandy, and a few other necessaries. To these were added half a sheep and a few pounds of rice. These, with his tent and other belongings, were packed on the Arab camel; and Zaki rode beside it with great satisfaction, for he had been greatly cast down when his master first told him that he would have to remain behind. All the preparations were made in great haste, but they were completed just as Ahmed Bey moved out of his camp, with his two hundred picked men and camels.

Five minutes later, a whistle from the steamer told them that General Hunter, and the party with him, were also on the point of starting. The distance to be traversed to Berber was a hundred and thirty miles, and the expedition was undoubtedly a hazardous one. Even if the news was true, that the five thousand Dervishes who had been holding Berber had evacuated the town, it was quite possible that a part of the force had been sent down the river, to oppose any advance that might be made; or, if unable to do this, to carry the news of the advance to Mahmud. The Arabs were to keep abreast of the gunboat; and would, where the shores were flat, be covered by its guns. But at spots where the ground was high and precipitous, this assistance could scarcely avail them in case of an attack, unless the hundred soldiers on board the steamer could be landed.

As they rode along, Ahmed Bey explained to Gregory the plan that he should adopt, if they were attacked in such a position, and found their retreat cut off.

"The camels will all be made to lie down, and we shall fight behind them, as in an entrenchment. My men are all armed with rifles the government has given them, and we could beat off an attack by a great number; while, if we were on our camels and pursued, we should soon lose all order, and our shooting would be bad."

"I think that would be by far the best plan, sheik. Your two hundred men, and the hundred the gunboat could land, ought to be able to make a tough fight of it, against any number of the enemy.

"How long do you think we shall be, on the way?"

"About four days. The camels can easily travel thirty-five miles a day. We have six days' provisions with us, in case the gunboat cannot make its way up. Fortunately we have not to carry water, so that each camel only takes twenty pounds of food, for its rider; and forty pounds of grain, for itself. If we were pursued, we could throw that away, as we should only have to ride to some point where the gunboat could protect us. We could not hope to escape by speed, for the Dervishes could ride and run quite as fast as the camels could go."

CHAPTER 10:

Afloat.

The first three days' journey passed without any adventure. From the natives who still remained in the little villages they passed, they learned that the report that the Dervishes had left Berber was generally believed; but whether they had marched for Metemmeh, or for some other point, was unknown. The people were delighted to see the gunboat; as, until its arrival, they had been in hourly fear of raiding parties. They had heard of the capture of Abu Hamed, by the British, from horsemen who had escaped; but all these had said, confidently, that Mahmud would speedily drive them out again; and they had been in hourly fear that the Dervishes would swoop down upon them, and carry off the few possessions still remaining to them.

When within thirty miles of Berber the Arabs had halted on the bank, watching the gunboat as, with great difficulty, it made its way up a cataract. Suddenly it was seen to stop, and a great bustle was observed on board. An exclamation of grief burst from the Arabs.

"She has struck on a rock!" Ahmed Bey exclaimed.

"I am afraid she has," said Gregory; who had, all along, ridden by his side at the head of the party. "I am afraid so. I hope she is not injured."

Unfortunately, the damage was serious. A hole had been knocked through her side, under water, and the water poured in, in volumes. A rush was made by those on board; and beds, pillows, and blankets were stuffed into the hole. This succeeded, to some extent, and she was brought alongside the bank.

The sheik and Gregory went down to meet her. General Hunter came to the side.

"A large hole has been knocked in her," he said, to the sheik. "We shall have to get the guns and stores on shore, to lighten her; and then heel her over, to get at the hole. It will certainly take two or three days; by that time, I hope, the other gunboat will be up.

"In the meantime, you must go on to Berber. I think there can be no doubt that the Dervishes have all left, but it is most important that we should know it, for certain. You must push straight on, and as soon as you arrive there, send word on to me by the fastest camel you have. If you are attacked, you will, of course, defend yourselves. Take up a position close to the river, and hold it until you are relieved. If you can send off news to me by a camel, do so; if not, seize a boat—there are some at every village—and send the news down by water. I will come on at once, with everyone here, to assist you."

"I will do as you order," the sheik said; "and if you see us no more, you will know that we died as brave men."

"I hope there is no fear of that," the General said, cheerfully. "You will defend yourselves as brave men if you are attacked, I am sure; but as I am convinced that the Dervishes have left Berber, I think there is little fear of your falling in with them."

Then he went on, in English, to Gregory.

"Keep them moving, Mr. Hilliard. Let them go as fast as they can. They are less likely to get nervous, if they are riding hard, than they would be if they dawdled along. If they press their camels, they will be in Berber this afternoon. See that a man starts at once, to bring me the news."

"Very well, sir. I will keep them at it, if I can."

The sheik rejoined his band, which gathered round to hear the result of his interview with the white general.

"The steamer is injured," he said, "but she will soon be made right, and will follow us. We are to have the honour of going on and occupying Berber, and will show ourselves worthy of it. There is little chance of our meeting the Dervishes. Had they been in Berber, we should have heard of them before this. If we meet them we will fight; and you, Abu, who have the fastest camel among us, will ride back here at all speed, and the General and his soldiers will come up to help us.

"Now, let us not waste a moment, but push forward. In five hours we shall be at Berber; and throughout your lives, you will be proud to say that you were the first to enter the town that the Dervishes have so long held."

A few of the men waved their guns, and shouted. The rest looked grave. However, they obeyed their chief's orders, and the cavalcade at once started. As they did so, Gregory drew his horse up alongside Zaki.

"Look here," he said, "if we see the Dervishes coming in force, I shall come to you, at once. You shall take my horse, it is faster than yours. I shall give you a note for the General, and you will ride back at full gallop, and give it to him. The horse is fast, and there will be no fear of their catching you, even if they chase; which they will not be likely to do, as they will be thinking of attacking us."

"Very well, master. I will do as you order me, but I would rather stop and fight, by your side."

"That you may be able to do some other time, Zaki. This time, you have got to fetch aid."

Then he rode on to join the chief. There was no talking along the line, every man had his rifle unslung and in his hand, every eye scanned the country. Hitherto, they had had unlimited faith in the power of the gunboat to protect them; now that they might have to face the Dervishes unaided, they felt the danger a serious one. They had come to fight the Dervishes, and were ready to do so, in anything like equal numbers; but the force they might meet would possibly be greatly stronger than their own—so strong that, although they might sell their lives dearly; they would, in the end, be overpowered.

For the first three hours, the camels were kept going at the top of their speed; but as they neared Berber, there was a perceptible slackness. Ahmed Bey and Gregory rode backwards and forwards along the line, keeping them together, and encouraging them.

"We shall get in without fighting," the Bey said. "We should have heard before this, had they been there. Do you think that they would have remained so long in the town, if they had learned that there are but two hundred of us, and one steamer? Mahmud would never have forgiven them, had they not fallen upon us and annihilated us. I only hope that two hundred will have been left there. It will add to our glory, to have won a battle, as well as taken the town. Your children will talk of it in their tents. Your women will be proud of you, and the men of the black regiments will say that we have shown ourselves to be as brave as they are.

"We will halt for half an hour, rest the camels, and then push on at full speed again; but mind, you have my orders: if you should see the enemy coming in force, you are to ride at once to the river bank, dismount, and make the camels lie down in a semicircle; then we have but to keep calm, and shoot straight, and we need not fear the Dervishes, however many of them there may be."

After the halt they again pushed forward. Gregory saw, with pleasure, that the Arabs were now thoroughly wound up to fighting point. The same vigilant watch was kept up as before; but the air of gloom that had hung over them, when they first started, had now disappeared; each man was ready to fight to the last. As the town was seen, the tension was at its highest; but the pace quickened, rather than relaxed.

"Now is the moment!" the Bey shouted. "If they are there, they will come out to fight us. If, in five minutes, they do not appear; it will be because they have all gone."

But there were no signs of the enemy, no clouds of dust rising in the town, that would tell of a hasty gathering. At last, they entered a straggling street. The women looked timidly from the windows; and then, on seeing that their robes did not bear the black patches worn by the Dervishes, they broke into loud cries of welcome.

"Are the Dervishes all gone?" Ahmed Bey asked, reining in his camel.

"They are all gone. The last left four days ago."

The sheik waved his rifle over his head; and his followers burst into loud shouts of triumph, and pressed on, firing their muskets in the air. As they proceeded, the natives poured out from their houses in wild delight. The Arabs kept on, till they reached the house formerly occupied by the Egyptian governor.

"I should say that you had better take possession of this, Bey. There seems to be a large courtyard, where you can put your camels. It is not likely that the Dervishes will return, but it is as well to be prepared. The house is strong, and we could hold out here against a host, unless they were provided with cannon.

"I have money, and you had better buy up as much food as possible, so that we could stand a siege for some time. I shall give my horse a good feed and an hour's rest, and then send my man down to the General, telling him that the Dervishes have deserted the town, and that we have taken possession of the place, and can defend it for a long time should they return."

An hour later, Zaki started with Gregory's report. The inhabitants, finding that they would be paid, brought out their hidden stores; and by evening, enough was collected to last the garrison ten days.

Zaki returned at noon next day, with a letter from General Hunter to the sheik, praising him highly for the energy and courage of his men and himself. He also brought a note for Gregory, saying that he hoped to get the repairs finished the next day; and that he expected, by that time, the other two steamers would be up, when he should at once advance to Berber.

On the third day the smoke of the steamers was seen in the distance; and an hour later the gunboats arrived, and were greeted with cries of welcome by the natives, who thronged the bank. The three boats carried between three and four hundred men. These were disembarked on an island, opposite the town, and the gunboats moored alongside.

General Hunter at once landed, with those of his staff who had accompanied him. He shook hands, very cordially, with the sheik.

"You have done well, indeed!" he said. "It was a dangerous enterprise and, had I not known your courage, and that of your men, I should not have ventured to send you forward. You have fully justified my confidence in you.

"In the first place, I will go and see the house you have occupied. I shall leave you still in possession of it, but I do not intend that you should hold it. In case Mahmud comes down upon you, at once embark in boats, and cross to the islands. It will be some time before I can gather, here, a force strong enough to hold the town against attack. Indeed, it will probably be some weeks; for, until the railway is finished to Abu Hamed, I can only get up stores sufficient for the men here; certainly we have no transport that could keep up the supply for the whole force. However, all this will be settled by the Sirdar, who will very shortly be with us."

It was now the 6th of September and, the same afternoon, two gun-boats were sent up to Ed Damer, an important position lying a mile or two beyond the junction of Atbara river with the Nile. On the opposite bank of the Nile, they found encamped the Dervishes who had retired from Berber. The guns opened fire upon them, and they retired inland; leaving behind them fourteen large boats, laden with grain. These were at once sent down to Berber, where they were most welcome; and a portion of the grain was distributed among the almost starving population, nearly five thousand in number, principally women and children.

Supplies soon began to arrive from below, being brought up in native craft, from Abu Hamed, as far as the cataract; then unloaded and carried up past the rapids on camels; then again placed in boats, and so brought to Berber. Macdonald's brigade started a fortnight after the occupation, their place at Abu Hamed having been taken by a brigade from Kassinger, each battalion having towed up boats carrying two months' supply of provisions.

A fort was now erected at the junction of the two rivers, and occupied by a small force, under an English officer. Two small steamers were employed in towing the native craft from Abu Hamed to Berber. Still, it was evident that it would be impossible to accumulate the necessary stores for the whole force that would take the field; accordingly, as soon as the railway reached Abu Hamed, the Sirdar ordered it to be carried on as far as Berber. He himself came up with Colonel Wingate, the head of the Intelligence Department; and, diligently as all had worked before, their exertions were now redoubled.

On the morning after the Sirdar's arrival, an orderly came across to General Hunter's quarters, with a request that Mr. Hilliard should at once be sent to headquarters. Gregory had to wait nearly half an hour, until the officers who had been there before him had had their audience, and received their orders. He was then shown in.

"You have done very valuable service, Mr. Hilliard," the Sirdar said. "Exceptionally valuable, and obtained at extraordinary risk. I certainly did not expect, when I saw you a few months ago in Cairo, that you would so speedily distinguish yourself. I was then struck with your manner, and thought that you would do well, and you have much more than fulfilled my expectations. I shall keep my eye upon you, and shall see that you have every opportunity of continuing as you have begun."

That evening, General Hunter suggested to Colonel Wingate that Gregory should be handed over to him.

"There will be nothing for him to do with me, at present," he said; "and I am sure that you will find him very useful. Putting aside the expedition he undertook to Metemmeh, he is a most zealous young officer. Although his wound was scarcely healed, he took charge of the baggage animals on the way up from Merawi to Abu Hamed, and came forward here with Ahmed Bey and his followers, and in both cases he was most useful. But at the present, I cannot find any employment for him."

"I will have a talk with him," Colonel Wingate said. "I think I can make good use of him. Captain Keppel asked me, this morning, if I could furnish him with a good interpreter. He is going up the river in a day or two, and as neither he nor the other naval officers know much Arabic, Mr. Hilliard would be of considerable service to them, in questioning any prisoners who may be captured as to hidden guns, or other matters. I should think, from what you tell me, Mr. Hilliard will be very suitable for the post."

"The very man for it. He is a very pleasant lad—for he is not more than that—quiet and gentlemanly, and yet full of life and go, and will be certain to get on well with a naval man."

On returning to his quarters, General Hunter sent for Gregory.

"You will please go to Colonel Wingate, Mr. Hilliard. I have been speaking to him about you; and, as it may be months before things are ready for the final advance, and I am sure you would prefer to be actively employed, I proposed to him that he should utilize your services; and it happens, fortunately, that he is able to do so. The gunboats will be running up and down the river, stirring up the Dervishes at Metemmeh and other places; and as neither Keppel, nor the commanders of the other two boats can speak Arabic with anything like fluency, it is important that he should have an interpreter.

"I think you will find the berth a pleasant one. Of course, I don't know what arrangements will be made, or whether you would permanently live on board one of the boats. If so, I think you would be envied by all of us, as you would get away from the dust, and all the discomforts of the encampment."

"Thank you very much, sir! It would indeed be pleasant, and I was beginning to feel that I was very useless here."

"You have not been useless at all, Mr. Hilliard. The Sirdar asked me about you, and I was able to give him a very favourable report of your readiness to be of service, for whatever work I have found for you to do. I have told him that I had great doubts whether Ahmed Bey would have pushed forward to this place, after he had lost the protection of the gunboats, if you had not been with him."

Gregory at once went to the quarters of Colonel Wingate, and sent in his name. In two or three minutes he was shown in. A naval officer was in the room with the colonel.

"You have come at the right time, Mr. Hilliard. I was just speaking of you to Captain Keppel. I suppose General Hunter has told you how I proposed utilizing your services?"

"Yes, sir, he was good enough to tell me."

"You speak both Arabic and the Negro dialect perfectly, I am told?"

"I speak them very fluently, almost as well as English."

"Just at present, you could not be of much use to me, Mr. Hilliard. Of course, I get all my intelligence from natives, and have no occasion to send white officers out as scouts. Otherwise, from the very favourable report that I have received from General Hunter, I should have been glad to have you with me; but I have no doubt that you would prefer to be in one of the gunboats. They are certain to have a more stirring time of it, for the next few weeks, than we shall have here."

"I should like it greatly, sir, if Captain Keppel thinks I shall do."

"I have no doubt about that," the officer said, with a smile. "I shall rate you as a first lieutenant and midshipman, all in one; and I may say that I shall be very glad to have a white officer with me. There are one or two spare cabins, aft, and you had better have your traps moved in, at once. I may be starting tomorrow."

"Shall I take my servant with me, sir?"

"Yes, you may take him if you like. I suppose you have a horse?"

"Yes, sir, a horse and a camel; but I shall have no difficulty in managing about them. Excuse my asking, sir, but I have a few stores. Shall I bring them on board?"

"No, there is no occasion for that. You will mess with me. Thank goodness, we left naval etiquette behind us when we came up the Nile, and it is not imperative that I should dine in solitary state. Besides, you have been on Hunter's staff, have you not?"

"Yes."

"I know his staff all mess together. I shall be very glad to have you with me. It is lonely work, always messing alone.

"My boat is the Zafir, you know. You had better come on board before eight o'clock, tomorrow morning. That is my breakfast hour."

Gregory needed but little time to make his arrangements. The transport department took over Zaki's horse and camel, and gave him a receipt for them; so that, when he returned, those or others could be handed over to him. One of the staff, who wanted a second horse, was glad to take charge of his mount. The tent, and the big case, and his other belongings were handed over to the stores.

Zaki was delighted, when he heard that he was going up in a gunboat that would probably shell Metemmeh, and knock some of the Dervish fortifications to pieces.

"What shall I have to do, master?" he asked.

"Not much, Zaki. You will brush my clothes, and make my bed, and do anything that I want done; but beyond that I cannot tell you. I am really taking you, not because I think you will be of much use, but because I like to have you with me. Besides, I sha'n't have much to do, and the English officer who commands will have plenty to look after, so that I shall be glad to talk, occasionally, with you.

"However, as I know the gunboats carry Maxim guns, and each have two sergeants of the marine artillery, I will hand you over to them, and ask them to put you in the Maxim crew. Then you will have the satisfaction of helping to fire at your old enemies."

Zaki's eyes glistened at the prospect.

"They killed my mother," he said, "and carried off my sisters, and burned our house. It will be good to fire at them. Much better this, bey, than to load stores at Merawi."

Gregory was much gratified, that evening after mess, at the kindly manner in which the members of the staff all shook hands with him, and said that they were sorry that he was going to leave them. General Hunter was dining with the Sirdar. The next morning, when Gregory went to say "Goodbye" to him, he said:

"I was telling Sir Herbert Kitchener, yesterday evening, that you were transferred to the naval branch. He said:

"'The gunboats will all take up troops, and there will be native officers on board. It is a rule in our army, you know, that all white officers have the honorary rank of major, so as to make them senior to all Egyptian officers. Will you tell Mr. Hilliard that I authorize him to call himself Bimbashi? There is no occasion to put it in orders. My authorization is sufficient. As long as he was on your staff it did not matter; but as, presently, he may be attached to an Egyptian regiment, it is as well that he should bear the usual rank, and it may save misunderstanding in communicating with the natives. He will be much more respected, as Bimbashi, than he would be as lieutenant, a title that they would not understand.'

"A good many lieutenants in the British Army are Bimbashis, here, so that there is nothing unusual in your holding that honorary rank."

"I would just as soon be lieutenant, sir, so far as I am concerned myself; but of course, I feel honoured at receiving the title. No doubt it would be much more pleasant, if I were attached to an Egyptian regiment. I do not know whether it is the proper thing to thank the Sirdar. If it is, I shall be greatly obliged if you will convey my thanks to him."

"I will tell him that you are greatly gratified, Hilliard. I have no doubt you owe it, not only to your ride to Metemmeh, but to my report that I did not think Ahmed Bey would have ventured to ride on into Berber, had you not been with him; and that you advised him as to the defensive position he took up here, and prepared for a stout defence, until the boats could come up to his assistance. He said as much to me."

At the hour named, Gregory went on board the Zafir; Zaki accompanying him, with his small portmanteau and blanket.

"I see you are punctual, Mr. Hilliard," the commander said, cheerily; "a great virtue everywhere, but especially on board ship, where everything goes by clockwork. Eight bells will sound in two minutes, and as they do so, my black fellow will come up and announce the meal. It is your breakfast, as much as mine; for I have shipped you on the books this morning, and of course you will be rationed. Happily, we are not confined to that fare. I knew what it was going to be, and laid in a good stock of stores. Fortunately, we have the advantage over the military, that we are not limited as to baggage."

The breakfast was an excellent one. After it was over, Commander Keppel asked Gregory how it was that he had—while still so young—obtained a commission, and expressed much interest when he had heard his story.

"Then you do not intend to remain in the Egyptian Army?" he said. "If you have not any fixed career before you, I should have thought that you could not do better. The Sirdar and General Hunter have both taken a great interest in you. It might be necessary, perhaps, for you to enter the British Army and serve for two or three years, so as to get a knowledge of drill and discipline; then, from your acquaintance with the languages here you could, of course, get transferred to the Egyptian Army, where you would rank as a major, at once."

"I have hardly thought of the future yet, sir; but of course, I shall have to do so, as soon as I am absolutely convinced of my father's death. Really, I have no hope now; but I promised my mother to do everything in my power to ascertain it, for a certainty. She placed a packet in my hands, which was not to be opened until I had so satisfied myself. I do not know what it contains, but I believe it relates to my father's family.

"I do not see that that can make any difference to me, for I certainly should not care to go home to see relations to whom my coming might be unwelcome. I should greatly prefer to stay out here, for a few years, until I had obtained such a position as would make me absolutely independent of them."

"I can quite understand that," Captain Keppel said. "Poor relations seldom get a warm welcome, and as you were born in Alexandria, they may be altogether unaware of your existence. You have certainly been extremely fortunate, so far; and if you preferred a civil appointment, you would be pretty certain of getting one when the war is over.

"There will be a big job in organizing this country, after the Dervishes are smashed up; and a biggish staff of officials will be wanted. No doubt most of these will be Egyptians, but Egyptian officials want looking after, so that a good many berths must be filled by Englishmen; and Englishmen with a knowledge of Arabic and the Negro dialect are not very easily found. I should say that there will be excellent openings, for young men of capacity."

"I have no doubt there will," Gregory said. "I have really never thought much about the future. My attention, from childhood, has been fixed upon this journey to the Soudan; and I never looked beyond it, nor did my mother discuss the future with me. Doubtless she would have done so, had she lived; and these papers I have may give me her advice and opinion about it."

"Well, I must be going on deck," Captain Keppel said. "We shall start in half an hour."

The three gunboats were all of the same design. They were flat bottomed, so as to draw as little water as possible; and had been built and sent out, in sections, from England. They were constructed entirely of steel, and had three decks, the lower one having loophole shutters for infantry fire. On the upper deck, which was extended over the whole length of the boat, was a conning tower. In the after portion of the boat, and beneath the upper deck, were cabins for officers. Each boat carried a twelve-pounder quick-firing gun forward, a howitzer, and four Maxims. The craft were a hundred and thirty-five feet long, with a beam of twenty-four feet, and drew only three feet and a half of water. They were propelled by a stern wheel.

At half-past nine the Zafir's whistle gave the signal, and she and her consorts—the Nazie and Fatteh—cast off their warps, and steamed out into the river. Each boat had on board two European engineers, fifty men of the 9th Soudanese, two sergeants of royal marine artillery, and a small native crew.

"I expect that we shall not make many more trips down to Berber," the Commander said, when they were once fairly off. "The camp at Atbara will be our headquarters, unless indeed Mahmud advances; in which case, of course, we shall be recalled. Until then we shall be patrolling the river up to Metemmeh; and making, I hope, an occasional rush as far as the next cataract."

When evening came on, the steamer tied up to an island, a few miles north of Shendy. So far they had seen no hostile parties—indeed, the country was wholly deserted.

Next morning they started before daybreak. Shendy seemed to be in ruins. Two Arabs, only, were seen on the bank. A few shots were fired into the town, but there was no reply.

Half an hour later, Metemmeh was seen. It stood half a mile from the river. Along the bank were seven mud forts, with extremely thick and solid walls. Keeping near the opposite bank, the gunboats, led by the Zafir, made their way up the river. Dervish horsemen could be seen, riding from fort to fort, doubtless carrying orders.

The river was some four thousand yards wide and, at this distance, the gunboats opened fire at the two nearest forts. The range was soon obtained to a nicety, and the white sergeants and native gunners made splendid practice, every shell bursting upon the forts, while the

Maxims speedily sent the Dervish horsemen galloping off to the distant hills, on which could be made out a large camp.

The Dervish gunners replied promptly, but the range was too great for their old brass guns. Most of the shot fell short, though a few, fired at a great elevation, fell beyond the boats. One shell, however, struck the Zafir, passing through the deck and killing a Soudanese; and a shrapnel shell burst over the Fatteh.

After an hour's fire, at this range, the gunboats moved up opposite the position; and again opened fire with shell and shrapnel, committing terrible havoc on the forts, whose fire presently slackened suddenly. This was explained by the fact that, as the gunboats passed up, they saw that the embrasures of the forts only commanded the approach from the north; and that, once past them, the enemy were unable to bring a gun to bear upon the boats. Doubtless the Dervishes had considered it was impossible for any steamer to pass up, under their fire; and that it was therefore unnecessary to widen the embrasures, so that the guns could fire upon them when facing the forts, or going beyond them.

Suddenly, as all on board were watching the effect of their fire, an outburst of musketry broke out from the bushes that lined the eastern bank, a hundred yards away. Fortunately, the greater part of the bullets flew overhead, but many rattled against the side. The Maxims were instantly turned upon the unseen enemy, the Soudanese fired volleys, and their rash assailants went at once into the thicker bush, many dropping before they gained it.

The gunboats now steamed slowly up the river; and then, turning, retired downstream again, shelling the enemy's position as they passed. As they were going down they came upon a number of Dervishes, who were busy unloading half a dozen native craft. The Maxim soon sent them flying; and the boats, which contained horses, donkeys, grain, and other goods, were taken in tow by the gunboats, which anchored at the same island as on the previous night.

"Well, Bimbashi," Captain Keppel said, when the work for the day was over, "so you have had your first brush with the enemy. What do you think of it?"

"I would rather that you did not call me Bimbashi, Captain Keppel. The title is ridiculous for me, and it was only given me that it might be useful when with Egyptian or Soudanese soldiers. I should feel really obliged, if you would simply call me Hilliard.

"I felt all right, sir, during the fight; except that I envied the gunners, who were doing something, while I had nothing to do but look on. It certainly made me jump, when that shell struck the boat, because I had quite made up my mind that their guns would not carry so far, and so it was a complete surprise to me."

"Yes, it was a very harmless affair. Still, it was good as a preparation for something more severe. You have got accustomed to the noise, now, and that is always as great a trial to the nerves as actual danger."

"I wish I could be doing something, sir. Everyone else had some duty, from yourself down to the black firemen—even my servant made himself useful, in carrying up shot."

"I tell you what I will do, Mr. Hilliard. I will get those marine sergeants to instruct you in the working of the Maxim, and in the duties of the men attending on it. Then next time we come up, I will put you in command of one of them. Your duties will not be severe, as you would simply direct the men as to the object at which they are to aim, watch the effect and direction of the bullets, and see that they change their aim, as circumstances may direct. The black gunners are well trained, and know their work; still, if by any chance the gun jams, it will be useful for you to be able to show them what to do; even though they know it as well as, or better than, you do yourself. The blacks like being commanded by a white officer, and will feel pleased, rather than otherwise, at your being appointed to command their gun. Your lessons cannot begin for a day or two, for I have not done with Metemmeh, yet."

"I am very much obliged to you, indeed," Gregory said warmly. "I will take care not to interfere with the men's working of the gun."

"No, you will not have to do that; but a word or two of commendation, when they make good practice, pleases them immensely; and they will work all the better, and faster, for your standing by them."

At daybreak next morning the gunboats went up again, and engaged the forts, as before. The Dervishes had placed more guns in position, but again the shells fell short, while those of the boats played havoc with the enemy's defences. Some ten thousand of the Dervish horse and foot came down near the town, in readiness to repel any attempt at a landing.

After some hours' bombardment, the gunboats retired. As they steamed away, the Dervish host were shouting and waving their banners, evidently considering that they had won a great victory.

Having fulfilled their object, which was to retain Mahmud at Metemmeh by showing him that, if he advanced against Merawi and Dongola, we had it in our power to occupy the town; and so cut off his retreat, and prevent reinforcements or stores from reaching him from Omdurman, the gunboats returned to Berber.

So far, Gregory had had no duties to perform in his capacity of interpreter, for no prisoners had been taken. On the way down the river, one of the artillery sergeants explained the working of the Maxim to him, taking the weapon to pieces, and explaining to him how each part acted, and then showing him how to put it together again. The sergeant having done this several times, Gregory was then told to perform the operation himself, and the lessons continued after their arrival at Berber.

In the course of a week he was able to do this smartly; and had learned, in case of a breakdown, which parts of the mechanism would most probably have given way, and how to replace broken parts by spare ones, carried up for the purpose.

There was no long rest at Berber, and on the 1st of November the gunboats again went up the river, reinforced by the Metemmeh, which had now arrived. Each boat, as before, carried fifty soldiers; and Major Stuart-Wortley went up, as staff officer. The evening before starting, they received the welcome news that the railway line had, that day, reached Abu Hamed.

This time there was but a short pause made opposite Metemmeh, and after shelling the forts, which had been added to since the last visit, they proceeded up the river. Shortly after passing the town, a large Dervish camp was seen in a valley, and this, they afterwards found, was occupied by the force that had returned from Berber. A heavy fire of shell and shrapnel was opened upon it, and it was speedily destroyed.

The gunboats then went up as high as the sixth cataract. The country was found to be absolutely deserted, neither a peasant nor a Dervish being visible. Having thus accomplished the object of their reconnaissance, the flotilla returned, exchanged fire with the Metemmeh batteries, and then kept on their way down to Berber.

CHAPTER 11:

A Prisoner.

Rather than remain unoccupied on board the gunboat, Gregory went to Colonel Wingate's headquarters and said that he should be very glad if he would allow him, while the flotilla remained at Berber, to assist in interrogating the fugitives who arrived from the south, and the spies employed to gain early information of the intentions and movements of the enemy. The position of the Dervishes at Metemmeh was becoming critical. The Khalifa was desirous that Mahmud should return with his force to Omdurman, there to take part in the battle in which, as he was convinced, the invaders would be annihilated. Mahmud, who was of an eager and impetuous disposition, was anxious to take the offensive at once, and either to march upon Merawi and Dongola, or to drive the British out of Berber.

There could be no doubt that his view was a more sagacious one than that of his father; and that the best tactics to be adopted were to harass the British advance, fall upon their convoys, cut their communications, and so oblige them to fall back for want of supplies. The Khalifa's mistake was similar to that made by Theodore in Abyssinia, and Koffee Kalkalli in Ashanti. Had either of these leaders adopted the system of harassing the invaders, from the moment they left the coast, it would have been next to impossible for the latter to arrive at their destination. But each allowed them to march on, unmolested, until within striking distance; then hazarded everything on the fortune of a single battle, and lost.

Mahmud made no movement in obedience to the Khalifa's orders to retire to Omdurman, and the latter thereupon refused to send any further supplies to him, and Mahmud's army was therefore obliged to rely upon raids and plunder for subsistence. These raids were carried out with great boldness, and villages situated within a few miles of Berber were attacked. The Dervishes, however, met with a much warmer reception than they had expected, for rifles and ammunition had been served out freely to the villagers; and these, knowing the fate that awaited them were the Dervishes victorious, offered so obstinate a resistance that the latter fell back, discomfited.

Early in January, the Sirdar learned that the Khalifa had changed his mind, and had sent peremptory orders to Mahmud to advance and drive the British out of Berber, and destroy the railway. Mahmud had now been joined by Osman Digna, with five thousand men; and as the Egyptian troops, well as they had fought, had never yet been opposed to so formidable a force as that which Mahmud commanded, the

Sirdar telegraphed to England for white troops.

His request was at once complied with. The Warwickshires, Lincolnshires, and Cameron Highlanders were ordered to proceed from Cairo and Alexandria to the front; and the Seaforth Highlanders at Malta, and the Northumberland Fusiliers at Gibraltar were also despatched, without delay. Major General Gatacre was appointed to the command of the brigade.

At the end of the third week in January, the three regiments from Lower Egypt had arrived at Wady Halfa, and the Seaforths at Assouan. At the beginning of February the British brigade was carried, by railway, to Abu Dis. Here they remained until the 26th, when they marched to Berber, and then to a camp ten miles north of the Atbara, where they arrived on the 4th of March, having covered a hundred and forty-four miles in six days and a half, a great feat in such a climate.

Mahmud had made no movement until the 10th of February, when he began to cross the Nile to Shendy. This movement had not been expected by the Sirdar, and was hailed by him with satisfaction. Had Mahmud remained at Metemmeh he could, aided by the forts, his artillery, and the walled town, have offered a very formidable resistance. Had he marched along the banks of the Nile, he would have been exposed to the fire of the gunboats, but these could not have arrested his course. The country round Berber was favourable to the action of his cavalry, and if defeated he could have fallen back, unmolested, through Metemmeh on Omdurman; but by crossing the river he practically cut himself off from the Dervish base, and now had only a desert behind him; for we had taken over Kassala from the Italians, and the Egyptian battalion there, and a large force of friendly Arabs, would prevent him from retiring up the banks of the Atbara.

Mahmud's plan was to march along the Nile to Ahab, then to cross the desert to Hudi, at an angle of the river; whence a direct march, of twenty-five miles, would take him to Berber, and in this way he would avoid our strong position at the junction of the Atbara and the Nile. It would have been easy for the gunboats to prevent Mahmud from crossing the Nile, but the Sirdar was glad to allow him to do so. The movement afforded him time to concentrate his force, and to get up large supplies. For, each day, the distance that these could be transported by the railway had increased; and he saw that, when the time for fighting came, the victory would be a decisive one; and that few, indeed, of Mahmud's men would ever be able to make their way to Omdurman, and swell the Khalifa's force there.

On one occasion, however, the gunboats went up to watch what was going on, and take advantage of any opportunity that might offer to destroy some of Mahmud's boats, and thus render the work of his getting his force over slower and more difficult. An entrenchment had been thrown up at the point where the Dervishes crossed, and this had been manned by two hundred and fifty riflemen. The Zafir steamed up close to the bank and opened fire with her Maxims. Another gunboat sank one large craft and captured two others, and the troops landed and, covered by the fire of the guns, captured a fourth which had grounded in shallow water.

A smaller boat was halfway across the river when the gunboats arrived. It was seen that there were several women on board, and as the capture would have been of no value, no regard was paid to it. As it would have been as dangerous to return as to keep on, the boatmen plied their hardest to get across, but the stream carried them down near the Zafir. The boat was quite unnoticed, all eyes being intent upon the shore. She was passing about thirty yards astern of the gunboat, when a badly aimed shell from a Dervish battery struck her, and she sank almost instantly.

Gregory, who was superintending the working of the Maxim nearest the stern, looked round at the sound of the explosion. Several of the occupants had evidently been killed, but two or three of the boatmen started to swim to shore. Only two of the women came to the surface, struggling wildly and screaming for help. With scarcely a thought of what he was doing, Gregory unclasped his sword belt, dropped his pistol, and sprang overboard.

One of the women had sunk before he reached them, the other was on the point of doing so, when he caught her by the arm. She at once clung to him, and he had hard work to disengage her arm from his neck; then, after turning her so that her face was above water, he looked round. The gunboat was already a hundred yards away. Her wheel was revolving, so as to keep her in her place facing the redoubt, and the stream was driving him fast away from her.

Within ten yards of him was a black head, and a moment later Zaki was beside him. He had been working at Gregory's Maxim, and had suddenly missed his master. Looking round, he had seen him struggling with the woman in the stream, and without hesitation had leapt overboard.

"I am sorry you came," Gregory said, "for it is only throwing away your life. It is of no use shouting, for they could not hear us in that din; and if they happened to catch sight of us, would take us for two of the black boatmen. I see the stream is taking us nearer to the bank."

Zaki had taken hold of the woman while he was speaking.

"We might swim a long way down, master, if we let go of her."

"I won't do that, Zaki. I know now that I was a fool to jump overboard; but now that I have done so, I will save her life. Besides, I could not swim very far even without her. I am feeling the weight of my boots and clothes.

"Will you swim with us till I can touch the ground, and then leave us? Strike right into the river again—I know that you are a good swimmer—and drop down the stream until you reach one of the islands, and then you can land and hail the gunboats as they come down. Tell Captain Keppel why I jumped over."

"I am not going to leave you, master. No doubt the Dervishes will shoot me, but my life is of no consequence, and I shall be glad to die by the side of so good a master."

The woman, who had ceased to struggle when Gregory shook off her grasp, was now conscious; as, with one of them supporting her on each side, her head was above water.

"They will not kill you," she said. "You have saved me, and they will be grateful."

Gregory had no faith whatever in Dervish gratitude.

"Well, Zaki," he said, "if you will not leave us, we will strike at once for the shore. The gunboats are nearly half a mile away now. There is just a chance that we may not have been noticed by the Dervishes, and may be able to hide in the bushes till the gunboats return. When they see me, they will at once send a boat ashore, under cover of their fire, and take us off."

"There is a good chance of that, master," Zaki said cheerfully, "and the Dervishes are busy up there fighting, and will not think much of a little boat."

Three or four minutes later they were in shallow water. As soon as they landed, Gregory threw himself down, utterly exhausted; and the woman sank down beside him, but not before hastily rearranging her veil. In a couple of minutes, Gregory roused himself.

"I can climb the bank, now," he said, "and the sooner we are hidden among the bushes, the better."

But as he spoke he heard the sound of galloping horsemen, and almost immediately an Emir, on a magnificent animal, followed by a dozen Dervishes, dashed up.

"Mahmud!" the woman cried, as she rose to her feet; "it is I, Fatma!"

Mahmud gave a cry of joy, and waved his hand to his followers, who had already pointed their rifles at Gregory.

"These have saved me, my lord," the woman went on. "They jumped from their boat, and reached me just as I was sinking, and have borne me up. For my sake you must spare their lives."

Mahmud frowned. He dismounted and went up to his wife.

"Have I not sworn, Fatma," he said, "that I would slay every unbeliever who falls into my hands? How, then, can I spare even one who has saved your life?"

"Others have been spared who have been of service, my lord," she said. "There are Greeks and Egyptians who work your guns, and they were spared because they were useful. There is Neufeld, who lives under the protection of the Khalifa. Surely these men have done far more to deserve, not only life, but honour at your hands. They risked their lives to save mine. What follower of the Prophet could do more? They could not have known who I was, a woman they saw drowning. Are there any among the bravest of the tribes who would have done the same?"

"I have sworn an oath," Mahmud said, gloomily.

"But you have not sworn to slay instantly. You can keep them, at least, until you can take them before the Khalifa, and say to him:

"'Father, I have sworn to kill unbelievers, but these men have saved Fatma's life; and I pray you to absolve me from the oath, or order them to be taken from me, and then do you yourself pardon them and set them free for the service that they have rendered me.'

"If he refuses, if these men are killed, I also swear that, as my life is due to them, I myself will perish by my own hands, if they die for saving it!"

"It needs not that, Fatma. You think that I am ungrateful, that I do not feel that these men have acted nobly, thus to risk their lives to save a strange woman whose face they have never seen. It is my oath that lies heavily upon me. I have never been false to an oath."

"Nor need you be now," Fatma said earnestly. "You swore to slay any unbeliever that fell into your hands. This man has not fallen into your hands. I have a previous claim to him. He is under my protection. I cover him with my robe"—and she swept a portion of her garment round Gregory—"and as long as he is under it he is, according to tribal laws, safe even from the vengeance of my husband!

"As to the other, he is not an unbeliever. Your oath concerns him not. Him you can honour and reward, according to the value you place upon my life."

The Arab's face cleared.

"Truly you have discovered a way out of it, Fatma, at any rate for the present."

He turned to Gregory for the first time.

"Do you speak our tongue?" he asked.

"Yes, Emir, as well as my own."

"Then you understand what we have said. Had I not been bound by my oath, I would have embraced you as a brother. We Arabs can appreciate a brave deed, even when it is done by an enemy. When one of the boatmen ran into the battery where I was directing the guns against your boat, and said that the boat in which my wife, with other women, were crossing had been sunk, by a shell from our batteries on the other side, I felt that my blood was turned to water. He said he believed that all had been killed or drowned, but that he looked back as he swam, and saw a white man jump overboard, and a short time after another followed him; and that, when he reached the shore, they were supporting a woman in the water.

"I rode hither, having but small hope indeed that it was my wife, but marvelling much that a white officer should thus risk his life to save a drowning woman. My oath pressed heavily upon me, as I rode. Even had it been but a slave girl whom you rescued, I should no less have admired your courage. I myself am said to be brave, but it would never have entered my mind thus to risk my life for a stranger. When I found that it was my wife who was saved, I still more bitterly regretted the oath that stood between me and her preserver, and truly glad am I that she has herself shown me how I can escape from its consequences.

"Now I see you, I wonder even more than before at what you have done; for indeed, in years, you are little more than a boy."

"What I did, Emir, I believe any white officer who was a good swimmer would have done. No Englishman would see a woman drowning without making an effort to save her, if he had it in his power. As to the fact that she was not of the same race or religion, he would never give it a thought. It would be quite enough for him that she was a woman."

"And you," Mahmud said, turning to Zaki, "you are a Jaalin, are you not?"

"I am."

"Jaalin or Baggara, you are my friend," Mahmud said, placing his hand on Zaki's shoulders. "And so you, too, leapt overboard to save a woman?"

"No, Emir," he replied, "I jumped over because my master jumped over. I had not thought about the woman. I jumped over to aid him, and it was to give him my help that I took my share in supporting the woman. The Bimbashi is a good master, and I would die for him."

Mahmud smiled at this frank answer.

"Nevertheless, whatever may have been your motive, you were enabled to save the life of my wife, and henceforth you are my friend."

Then he turned to the horsemen, who were still grouped on the bank above.

"You have heard what has been said? The white man is under the protection of my harem; the Jaalin is henceforth my friend."

Mahmud was a fine specimen of the tribesmen of the Soudan—tall, well built, and with pure Arab features. He was the Khalifa's favourite son; and was generous, with kindly impulses, but impatient of control. Of late, he had given way to outbursts of passion, feeling acutely the position in which he was placed. He had advanced from Omdurman confident that he should be able to drive the infidels before him, and carry his arms far into Egypt. His aspirations had been thwarted by the Khalifa. His requests for stores and camels that would have enabled him to advance had been refused, and he had been ordered to fall back. His troops had been rendered almost mutinous, from the want of supplies.

He had seen the invaders growing stronger and stronger, and accomplishing what had seemed an impossibility—the bringing up of stores sufficient for their sustenance—by pushing the railroad forward towards Berber. Now that their forces had been very greatly increased, and the issue of the struggle had become doubtful, he had received the order for which he had been craving for months; and had been directed to march down and attack the Egyptian army, drive them across the Nile, and destroy the railway.

By means of spies he had heard that, ere long, a large force of British soldiers would come up to reinforce the Egyptians; so that what might have been easy work, two months before, had now become a difficult and dangerous enterprise. The manner in which the Dervishes had been defeated in their attacks upon Wolseley's desert column, and in the engagements that had since taken place, showed how formidable was the fighting power, not only of the British troops, but of the native army they had organized; and his confidence in the power of the tribesmen to sweep all before them had been shaken.

The Dervishes scowled, when they heard that they were not to have the satisfaction of massacring this Englishman, whose countrymen were still keeping up a terrible fire on their redoubt. It was not one of their wives who had been rescued, and Gregory's act of jumping overboard seemed to them to savour of madness; and if that plea had been advanced, they would have recognized it as rendering the person of the man who had performed it inviolable. However, as he was under the protection of their leader's harem, there was nothing more to be said; and at an order from Mahmud all but four of them rode off, while the others fell in behind him.

Mahmud did not mount again, but walked with his wife to a deserted mud hut, two hundred yards away. There he left her, telling Gregory and Zaki to sit down outside, and placing the four men on guard.

"I must rejoin my men," he said, as he mounted. "When your vessels have gone, I will return."

Half an hour later, the fire ceased. Soon afterwards Mahmud rode up with a score of men, followed by some dozen women, and a slave leading a donkey. On this Fatma took her seat, and the women surrounded her. Gregory and Zaki walked close behind them. Mahmud, with his horsemen, rode in front.

After proceeding for a mile, they came upon a group of tents.

Mahmud's banner was flying on a pole in front of the largest of these. Behind, and touching it, was another almost as large. This was the abode of the ladies of Mahmud's harem. The other tents were occupied by his principal Emirs. A hundred yards away was the encampment of the army, which was sheltered in hastily constructed huts, or arbours, made of bushes.

By Mahmud's order, a small tent was erected, with blankets, close to the after entrance into the harem tent, for Gregory's use; so that, should he be attacked by fanatics, he could at once take refuge in the harem, whose sanctity not even the most daring would dare to violate.

A handsome robe was brought for Zaki; and as Mahmud presented it to him, he said:

"You are my friend, but you must now go back to your vessels, or to Berber. My orders were to kill all the Jaalin, and we have spared none who fell into our hands, at Metemmeh or since. I cannot keep you here. As long as you stay by my side, you will be safe; but you could not leave me for a moment. It is as much as I can do to save the life of this infidel officer, and it is to him that I owe most, for it was he who first leapt into the river.

"The white men's boats have already fastened up, behind the island where they before stationed themselves. Make your way down there, at daybreak, and wave a white cloth. Doubtless they will send a boat ashore, thinking that you bear a message from me; or if you see they do not do this, you can swim out to them."

"I would rather stay with my master. Cannot you let him go, too?"

"That is impossible," Mahmud said shortly. "It is known throughout the camp that I have a white man here. The news will travel fast to the Khalifa. My actions have already been misrepresented to him, and were I to let this officer go, my father might recall me to Omdurman and send another to command here.

"He must stay, but you may go without harm. You can scarcely have been noticed yet, and I can well declare, should the Khalifa hear of you, that you have escaped."

"May I speak with my master?" Zaki said. "If he says stay, I shall stay, though it might cost me my life. If he says go, I must go."

"You may speak to him," Mahmud said.

Zaki went round to Gregory's tent, and told him what Mahmud had said.

"Go, certainly, Zaki. You can do me no good by remaining here, and might even do me harm; for if you were killed I also might be murdered. Moreover, I wish to send the news of my capture, and how it occurred. I do not think any, save yourself, noticed that I was missing; and when the fight was over, and they found that I was absent, they might suppose that I had been shot and had fallen overboard.

"I will write a note for you to carry. It is, in all respects, better that you should go. Were we to be seen talking together, it might be supposed that we were planning some way of escape, and I should be more closely watched. As it is, I see that Mahmud will have difficulty in protecting me. Were you to ride about with him, as he says, your presence would remind his followers that he has a white man a captive here; whereas, if I remain almost in concealment near the harem, the fact that there is a white man here will pass out of the minds of those who know it, and will not become the common talk of the camp.

"Mahmud is running some risk in having spared my life, and I do not wish to make it harder for him. Go, therefore, and tell him that you will leave tonight. I cannot write now; my pocketbook is soaked through. But I will tear out some leaves and dry them in the sun; and write what I have to say, before you start. I shall speak highly of you in my letter, and recommend you to Colonel Wingate; who will, I have no doubt, give you employment.

"I hope I shall see you again, before long. I am very sorry that we must part, but it is best for us both."

Very reluctantly, Zaki returned to Mahmud.

"My master says I must go, Emir; and I must obey his orders, though I would rather stay with him. Tonight, I will leave."

"It is well. I would that I could let him go, also, but my oath prevents me from giving him his freedom. I trust, however, that when the Khalifa hears of his noble action, and how he has made me his debtor, he will say that Allah himself would not blame me for that. Gratitude is even more binding than an oath.

"Still, until I hear from him, I can do nothing. We have not seen matters in the same light, for some time. When I wanted to strike, he was unwilling that I should do so. Now, when it seems to me that the time for that has passed, and that I had best retire on Omdurman, he says go forward and fight. It is not for me to question his commands, or his wisdom. But I may not give him cause for anger.

"My advice to you is, when you get to Berber, do not stay there. We shall assuredly be there before long, and as none would know that you were under my protection, you would be slain. Go straight to Abu Hamed; and when you hear that we have defeated the infidels, and have entered Berber, leave by this road they have made, upon which, as they tell me, carriages run without horses, and stay not until you reach Cairo.

"There you can live quietly, until you hear that the Khalifa's army is approaching. After that, fly. I cannot say whither, but seek a shelter until the black flag waves over the whole of the land. When there is no more fighting, then come to me and I will give you a post of honour."

"I will do so, Emir. When the time comes, I will remind you of your promise."

"I have neither silver nor gold with which I can reward you, now; but we shall gather these things in Egypt, and I will make you wealthy."

Zaki thought that it would be unwise to wander from Mahmud's encampment, and he accordingly sat down by his tent. Presently, one of the slaves came out, with a large dish of food that Mahmud had sent him. As evening approached, he went round to Gregory's little tent, with the intention of trying to persuade him to attempt to escape with him; but two of the tribesmen, with rifles in their hands, were stationed there. They offered no opposition to his entry, but their presence showed that Mahmud was determined that his master should appear to be a close prisoner; as, indeed, his escape might well jeopardize the Emir's position, even among his followers.

Gregory had a letter ready for him to carry to Captain Keppel. It ran as follows:

"Dear Captain Keppel,

"I am a prisoner in Mahmud's hands. This is the result of my own impetuosity—I will not say folly, for I cannot regret that I yielded to the sudden impulse that seized me. A boat containing some women was sunk by a shell, when but a few yards astern of the gunboat. Most of its occupants were killed, but I saw a woman struggling in the water and, without thinking of the consequences, jumped overboard to save her, my servant following me. When we reached her, we found that the current was too strong to regain the gunboat, and so landed about half a mile down, hoping to find shelter in the bushes until the boat came down the stream. What I did, however, had been observed by the Dervishes; and as soon as I landed a party rode up, headed by Mahmud himself, who was aware that his favourite wife was in the boat that had sunk.

"Most fortunately, it turned out that she was the woman I had saved. Upon her appeal Mahmud spared our lives. He has released my man, who will carry this to you; but, having sworn that he would spare no white man, he retains me in his hands as a prisoner, until he can lay the facts before the Khalifa and obtain his permission to let me go. I trust that all will be well, and that some day I may rejoin the army. However, there is no saying how matters may turn out.

"I am happy in knowing that there is no one who, if the worst comes to the worst, will grieve over my loss. I recommend my faithful servant to you. I should wish the balance of pay coming to me to be handed to him, as well as my camel and horse, and all other belongings. By the sale of these he would be able, at the end of the war, to buy a piece of land and settle down among his own people.

"Will you kindly report my capture to Colonel Wingate or General Hunter? Thanking you for your kindness to me, I remain,

"Yours faithfully,

"Gregory Hilliard.

"P. S. In my cabin is a tin box containing documents of importance to me. I shall be greatly obliged if you will take charge of these, until—as I hope will be the case—I rejoin you."

He handed the paper to Zaki, who took his hand and raised it to his forehead, with tears in his eyes.

"I go because you order me, master," he said, in a broken voice; "but I would a thousand times rather remain, and share your fate, whatever it might be."

Then he turned, and abruptly left the tent.

Twice that day, Gregory had received food from a female slave of the harem. Although he knew that he should miss Zaki greatly, he was very glad that he had been sent away; for he felt that, although for the time he had been reprieved, his position was very precarious, and that his servant's would have been still more so. A white prisoner was a personage of some consequence, but the death of a Jaalin was a matter that would disturb no one. Thousands of them had been massacred; and one, more or less, could not matter at all. But, however much the Dervishes might hate a white infidel, it would be a serious matter for even the most powerful Emir to harm a prisoner under the protection of the harem of the Khalifa's son.

Mahmud had been very popular among them, but his position had been gravely shaken by the events of the last six months. Having unlimited confidence in themselves; the Baggara had seen, with increasing fury, the unopposed advance of the Egyptians. They could not understand why they should not have been allowed, after the capture of Metemmeh, to march across the desert to Merawi, and annihilate the infidels assembled there. It was true that these had repulsed the force defending Dongola, but this was a comparatively small body; and it was the gunboats, and not the Egyptian troops, who had forced them to evacuate the town.

The fall of Abu Hamed had added to their discontent, and they were eager to march with all speed to Berber, to join the five thousand men comprising its garrison, and to drive the invaders back across the Nile.

But they had been kept inactive, by the orders of the Khalifa and by the want of stores. They had, for months, been suffering great privations; and while remaining in enforced inactivity, they had known that their enemy's strength was daily increasing; and that what could have been accomplished with the greatest of ease, in August, had now become a very serious business.

Mahmud had chafed at the situation in which he found himself placed, by his father's refusal to support him or to allow him to take any action. This had soured his temper, and he had taken to drinking heavily. He had become more harsh with his men, more severe in the punishment inflicted for any trifling disobedience of orders. Although no thought that the rule of the Khalifa could be seriously threatened entered their minds, fanatical as they were, they could not but feel some uneasiness at the prospect.

A great army was gathering at Berber. Kassala was in the hands of the British, and the forces that had been beleaguering it had been defeated, with heavy loss. Abyssinia had leagued itself against them. The insurrection of the Jaalin had been crushed, but there were signs of unrest in Kordofan, and other parts.

Of course, all this would be put right. An army of sixty thousand men was at Omdurman; and this, with Mahmud's command, would suffice to sweep away all their enemies. Their enthusiasm would never have wavered, had they been called upon for action; but these months of weary waiting, and of semi-starvation, without the acquisition of any booty or plunder—for little, indeed, had been obtained at the capture of Metemmeh—sapped their energy; and the force that crossed the Nile for an advance upon Berber was far less formidable than it would have been, had it been led forward against Merawi and Dongola directly after the capture of Metemmeh. Still, it needed only the prospect of a battle to restore its spirits.

A fortnight after Gregory's capture, the Dervish army was set in motion. A few thousand men had already been sent forward, along the banks of the river, to check any advance that might be made from Fort Atbara. Had it not been for this, Gregory might have attempted to escape. It would not have been very difficult for him to creep out at the back of his little tent, unperceived by his guards; but the dangers to be encountered in making his way to the British fort would have been immense.

It would have been necessary for him to keep by the river, for from this source alone could water be obtained. The country had been stripped of its crops, of all kinds, by the Dervishes; the villages had been razed to the ground; and the last head of maize, and other grain, gleaned by the starving people who had taken refuge in the bush and jungle.

Therefore, although by keeping near the river he could quench his thirst at will, he would assuredly have to face starvation. Moreover, he would have no chance of searching for any ears of corn which might have escaped the eyes of the searchers, for he must travel only by night and lie up by day, to avoid capture by one or other of the bands that had gone on; in which case he would at once be killed, being beyond the influence of Mahmud, and the protection of the harem.

On the other hand, he had nothing to complain of, except the monotony and uncertainty of his position. Fatma kept him well supplied with food; and, from the gossip of the slaves who brought this to him, he learnt how matters were progressing. He was longing for the Dervish army to make a move, for he felt that when they neared the British position, the greater would be the chance of escape; and none among the followers of Mahmud rejoiced more than he did, when he knew that the long-expected advance was about to take place.

Once in motion, the spirits of the Dervishes revived. At last they were going to meet these insolent invaders, and none doubted that they would easily defeat them. The greater portion of the harem and attendants were left behind, at Shendy, for but few camels were available. Fatma and another of Mahmud's wives rode on one. A tent was carried by another. Half a dozen slaves followed, and Gregory walked with these.

He could not help admiring the attitude of the tribesmen—tall, powerful men, inured to hardship, and walking or riding with an air of fierce independence, which showed their pride in themselves, and their confidence in their prowess.

The party always started early in the morning, so as to get the tents erected at the halting place before the main body of the Dervishes came up. On the march, they kept some distance from the river and, being but a small group, the gunboats did not waste their shot upon them; but each day there was a sharp exchange of fire between them and Mahmud's force.

Gregory supposed that Mahmud's plan was to cross the Atbara, which was fordable at several points, and to attack the fort there; in which case, he had no doubt the Arabs would be driven off, with much loss. The Sirdar was of the same opinion, and in order to tempt them to do so, he maintained only one Egyptian brigade in the fort, the remainder of the force being concentrated at Kennur, four miles away. From this point they would be able to advance and take the Dervishes in flank, while they were engaged in the attack of the fort.

Mahmud, however, was kept well informed of the movements of the troops, and instead of continuing his course down the river bank when he reached Gabati, he struck across the desert; and, after two days' march, crossed the Atbara at Nakheila. From this point, owing to the bend in the river, he would be able to march direct to Berber, avoiding the Atbara fort and the force gathered round it.

Altogether the desert march, although only lasting two days, was a trying one. The heat was overpowering, and even the ladies of the harem had the scantiest supply of water. They had, at starting, given Gregory a gourd of water for his own use. This he had taken sparingly, and it lasted him until they reached the Atbara.

It was now dead low water, and the river offered no obstacle to crossing, as the bed was for the most part dry, with pools here and there. The Arab encampment was formed in a thick grove of trees, which afforded some shelter from the sun.

Day after day passed. Mahmud was now informed as to the strength of the force he should have to encounter, and for the first time felt some doubt as to the issue of the fight. He determined, therefore, to stand on the defensive. This decision, however, he kept to himself. The Dervishes were burning to be led to the assault, and became almost mutinous, on account of the delay. Mahmud was obliged to take the strongest measures, and several of those who were loudest in their dis-satisfaction were summarily executed. The rest were pacified with the assurance that he was only waiting for a fortunate day.

In the meantime, the men were employed in fortifying the posi-tion. Deep holes were dug along the edge of the wood, and behind these were trenches and pitfalls. Mahmud's own temper grew daily more sullen and fierce. His own fighting instinct was in favour of the attack his followers longed to deliver, but in his heart he was afraid that the result might be fatal. It was not the rifles of the infantry that he feared—of these he had no experience—but the artillery, which he had learned, already, could be used with terrible effect.

As Mahmud was drinking heavily, and as the fact that the white soldiers were near at hand added to the fanatical hatred of the emirs and tribesmen, Fatma sent a message by a slave to Gregory, warning him not to show himself outside the little shelter tent, composed of a single blanket, in which he now lived.

At length it became known that the English host was approaching. As soon as the gunboats brought down news that the Dervishes were no longer following the river bank, but were disappearing into the desert, the Sirdar guessed their intentions. Nothing could have suited him better. A battle now must be a decisive one. There was no way of retreat open to the Dervishes, except to cross the waterless desert; or to fly south, keeping to the course of the Atbara, which would take them farther and farther from the Nile with every mile they marched.

Bringing up all his force, therefore, from Kennur and the Atbara fort, which one battalion was left to guard, the Sirdar took up his post at Hudi. The position was well chosen. It lay halfway between Mahmud's camp at Nakheila and the Atbara fort, and left Mahmud only the option of attacking him; or of making a long detour, through the desert to the east, in order to reach Berber. The British, on the other hand, could receive their supplies by camels from the Atbara fort.

The cavalry went out to reconnoitre, and had constant skirmishes with the enemy's horse; but when day after day passed, and Mahmud did not come, as the Sirdar had expected, to attack him, it was deter-mined to take the offensive. General Hunter was ordered to move forward, with the whole of the cavalry and a Maxim-gun battery, to discover the exact position of the enemy.

The camp had been well chosen; for, like Abu Hamed, it lay in a depression, and could not be seen until an enemy came within six hundred yards of it. Thus the superiority of range of the British rifles was neutralized, and their guns could not be brought into play until within reach of the Dervish muskets. The wood was surrounded by a high zareba, behind which a crowd of Dervishes were assembled. They had anticipated an attack, and held their fire until the cavalry should come nearer. This, however, General Hunter had no intention of doing, and he retired with the information he had gained. His account of the strength of the position showed the difficulty of taking it by assault.

Next day he again went out with the same force, but this time the Dervishes were prepared. Their mounted men dashed out from the wood, and galloped round to cut off the cavalry; while the footmen crowded out to attack them in front. The cavalry fell back in perfect order, and one squadron charged forty of the Dervish cavalry, who barred the line of retreat. These they drove off, but the main body still pressed forward, and the Maxims opened upon them. The hail of bullets was too much for the horsemen, and they drew off. Several times they gathered again for a charge, but on each occasion the Maxims dispersed them. The unmounted Dervishes were soon left behind, but the horsemen, in spite of the lesson they had received, followed almost to the camp.

On the afternoon of the 7th of April, the Anglo-Egyptian force marched out. They started at five in the afternoon, and halted at seven. The horses were first taken down to water, the infantry by half battalions; all then lay down to sleep. At one o'clock the word to advance was passed round quietly. The moon was full and high overhead, so there was no difficulty in avoiding obstacles. Each brigade marched in square, accompanied by the guns and the Maxims, and the camels with provisions and spare ammunition.

At four o'clock they halted again. They had been well guided, and were now but a short distance from the enemy's position. At sunrise the men were again on their feet, and advanced to within two hundred yards of the position from which they were to deliver their attack. The British brigade—the Camerons, Warwicks, Seaforths, and Lincolns—were on the left. Next to them came Macdonald's brigade—the three Soudanese regiments in front, the 2nd Egyptian in support. Farther still to the right, and touching the river, was Maxwell's brigade, comprising also three Soudanese regiments and an Egyptian one. Two of the three Egyptian battalions of Lewis's brigade were placed on the left rear of the British brigade, the third battalion was in square round the camels. Two field batteries were in front of the infantry, and two to the right of Maxwell's brigade.

Half a mile from the zareba the infantry halted, and the artillery and Maxims opened fire. For an hour a tremendous fire was poured into the enemy's position, but not a shot was fired in reply, although the Dervishes could be seen moving among the trees, apparently unconcerned at the storm of shell and bullets.

Gregory's position had been growing more critical every day. Food was extremely short; the scanty supplies that the force had brought with them had been long since exhausted, and they were now subsisting upon palm nuts. Of these, two were served out daily to each man, a quantity barely sufficient to keep life together. In spite of the vigilant watch kept by the more fanatical of Mahmud's followers, desertions had become frequent, notwithstanding the certain death that awaited those who were overtaken.

The evening after the cavalry made their first reconnaissance, the slave who brought Gregory's food told him that Fatma wished to speak to him. It was but three paces to the entrance of the tent, and his guards made no objection. The entrance was closed as the slave entered, but half a minute later it was opened an inch or two, and, without showing herself, Fatma said:

"Listen to me."

"I am listening," Gregory replied.

"I am in great fear for you. You are in much danger. The Emirs say to Mahmud that you ought to be killed; their followers are well-nigh starving—why should an infidel prisoner be eating? His friends are now close to us, and there will be a battle. None will be spared on either side—why should this man be spared?

"Mahmud has many cares. The men are furious because he will not lead them out to fight. Even the emirs are sullen; and Osman Digna, who was on bad terms with him a short time ago, and who, Mahmud suspects, is intriguing with them against him, is foremost in urging that an attack should take place; though everyone knows he is a coward, and never shows himself in battle, always running away directly he sees that things are going against him. Still, he has five thousand followers of his own.

"Mahmud told me today that he had done all in his power but, placed as he was, he could not withstand the words of the emirs, and the complaints of the tribesmen. When the battle comes—as it must come in a day or two—it will need all his influence and the faith of the men with him to win; and with so much at stake, how can he risk everything for the sake of a single life, and that the life of an infidel? If you would agree to aid in working his guns, as the Greeks and Egyptians do, it would content the emirs."

"That I cannot do," Gregory said. "If I am to be killed, it is the will of God; but better that, a thousand times, than turn traitor!"

"I knew that it would be so," Fatma said sorrowfully. "What can we do? At other times, the protection of the harem would cover even one who had slain a chief; but now that the Baggara are half starving, and mad with anger and disappointment, even that no longer avails. If they would brave the anger of the son of the Khalifa, they would not regard the sanctity of the harem. I wish now that I had advised you to try and escape when we left Shendy, or even when we first came here. It would have been difficult, but not impossible; but now I can see no chance. There is the thorn hedge round the wood, with few openings, and with men on watch all round to prevent desertion. Several tried to escape last night—all were caught and killed this morning. Even if it were possible to pass through, there are bands of horsemen everywhere out on the plain, keeping watch alike against the approach of the enemy and the desertion of cowards.

"I have been in despair, all day, that I cannot save the life of one who saved mine. I have told Mahmud that my honour is concerned, and that I would give my life for yours. Months ago, he would have braved the anger of all his army for me, but he has changed much of late. It is not that he loves me less, but that he has been worried beyond bearing, and in his troubles he drinks until he forgets them.

"My only hope is that your people will attack tomorrow. Mahmud says that they will assuredly be beaten; they will be shot down as they approach, and none will ever be able to get through the hedge. Then, when they fall back, the Baggara will pour out, horse and foot, and destroy them. They will then see how right he has been in not letting them go out into the plain to fight. His influence will be restored, and your life will be safe.

"We are to be removed to the farther side of the wood, when the fighting begins; and there all the women are to be gathered, and wait, till the infidels are utterly destroyed.

"If your people come tomorrow morning, you may be saved. Otherwise I fear the worst."

"I thank you for what you have done for me," replied Gregory, "and whatever comes of it, be sure that I shall feel grateful to you, and shall not blame you for not having been able to do what was impossible. I hope my friends may come tomorrow, for, whatever my fate may be, anything is better than uncertainty."

"May Allah protect you!" the woman said, with a sob; "and go now. I hear Mahmud calling me."

CHAPTER 12:

The Battle of Atbara.

Gregory had little sleep that night. It was clear to him that there was absolutely no chance of making his escape. Even were his two guards withdrawn, it would not improve his position. He had no means of disguise, and even if he had an Arab dress and could stain his face, he could not hope to make his way through the crowds of sleeping men, the pitfalls and trenches, and pass out through the jealously guarded zareba. There was nothing, for him, but to wait till the end.

He could not blame Mahmud. A leader on the eve of a great battle could not, for the sake of a single captive, risk his influence and oppose the wishes of his followers. It was much that he had, for his wife's sake, postponed the fulfilment of his oath; and had so long withstood the wishes of his most influential emirs. More could not be expected. At any rate, he was better off than others who had been in the same position. He had not, so far as he knew, a relation in the world—no one who would be anywise affected by his death; and at least he would have the satisfaction of knowing that it was a kind action which had brought him to his end. He prayed earnestly, not that his life might be spared, but that his death might be a painless one; and that he might meet it as an English officer should, without showing signs of fear.

The next day he heard orders given, and a great stir in camp; and he gathered, from those who passed near the tent, that the enemy's cavalry were again approaching; and that the mounted men were to ride out and cut them off from retreating, while the dismounted men were to pour out and annihilate them. Then, for a time, all was silence in the camp.

Suddenly an outburst of shouts and cries broke out and, almost simultaneously, he heard the rattle of Maxim guns—the fight had begun. Would the Egyptian horsemen stand firm, or would they give way to panic? If they broke and fled, none whatever would return to their camp through the host of Baggara horsemen.

For a time, the roll of the fire from the machine guns was incessant. Then there was a pause. Two or three minutes later it broke out again, but it was evidently somewhat farther off; and so it went on, with intervals of silence, but ever getting farther away. It was clear that the horsemen had not been able to bring the cavalry to a standstill, and that these were steadily falling back, covered by the fire of the Maxims. At last the sound grew faint in the distance and, soon afterwards, the noise in the camp showed that the infantry were returning.

It was not till two hours later that he heard the mounted men ride in; and gathered, from the talk outside, that they had lost nearly two hundred men, and had been unable to prevent the Egyptian cavalry from returning to camp. Towards evening he heard angry talking, and could distinguish Mahmud's voice. Then the blanket was pulled off its supports, and two men ordered him to follow them.

This was doubtless the end, and he nerved himself for what was to come; and, with head erect and a steady face, he accompanied the men to the front of Mahmud's tent. The chief was standing, with frowning face; and several Emirs were gathered in front of him, while a number of tribesmen stood a short distance away.

"Now," Mahmud said, "let one of you speak."

One of the Emirs stepped forward.

"I, Osman Digna, demand that this infidel be put to death. His countrymen have slain many of my men, and yours."

Feeling now that Mahmud, after doing his best, had ceased to struggle for him, and that his death was certain, Gregory took a step forward towards the speaker, and said scornfully:

"So you are Osman Digna! I am one of the first of my countrymen to see your face, though many have seen your back, at a distance."

Instead of provoking a pistol shot, as he had intended, his remark was followed by a roar of laughter from the emirs; for Osman's cowardice was a byword among them, and his nickname was "One who always runs."

Osman, indeed, had put his hand on the stock of one of the pistols in his belt, but Mahmud said imperiously:

"The man's life is mine, not yours, Osman Digna. If you shoot him, I shoot you!"

The fearlessness of the lad had pleased the other emirs; for, recklessly brave themselves, the Baggara appreciated and esteemed courage and honour. One of the others said:

"This is a brave young fellow and, infidels as his people are, we admit that they are brave. Were it for ourselves only, we would say let him live, until we see what comes of it. But our people complain. They say his folk, with whom we had no quarrel, come here and aid the Egyptians against us. They slew many yesterday. It is not right that this man should be living among us, when his countrymen are fighting against us."

There was a murmur of assent among the others, then Mahmud spoke.

"I have promised that he should not be killed, unless by order of the Khalifa. But this I will do: he shall be placed in the front rank. If Allah wills it, he will be killed by the bullets of his countrymen. If, when the fight is over, he is unharmed, you shall all agree that the matter be left for the Khalifa to decide. But, mind, I wash my hands of his death.

On the eve of a battle, it is not for me to set my wishes above those of my emirs and my tribesmen; and I yield to your demands, because it is necessary that all be of one mind. If he is killed, which surely he will be, unless Allah protects him, his blood be upon your heads!"

He waved his hand, and the men came forward and again took Gregory to his tent.

The latter was well contented with the decision that he should be killed. He had no doubt that, at least, his death would be swift and sudden; he would not be speared, or cut to pieces with knives. He would see his countrymen advancing. He would know that he would be speedily avenged.

Two days passed, when the news came that the Egyptians had advanced to Umdabieh, seven miles nearer; and, on the following morning, the Dervish camp was disturbed early. There was joy in every face, and renewed vigour in the bearing of the men. Scouting Dervishes had brought in word that the infidels had marched, during the night, and were now halting but a mile and a half away.

The hour had come, at last. They were confident in themselves, and their trust in their leader was renewed. The fight, two days before, had shown them that the guns of the white men were terrible on the plain; and that it was, after all, wise to await them in the position which had been made impregnable, and against which the foe would hurl themselves in vain; then they were to pour out, and annihilate them.

The slave came to Gregory's tent, at daybreak.

"Fatma is praying to Allah for your safety," he said.

There was no time for more, for already the tents were being pulled down, and soon the women were hurried away to the rear. Four men surrounded Gregory, and led him to the edge of the camp, and there fastened him to the stump of a tree that had been cut off six feet from the ground, the upper portion being used in the construction of the zareba. Ten or twelve men were similarly fastened, in a line with him. These had been detected in trying to sneak away.

Gregory had not seen anything of the camp before and, as he was taken along, he was astounded at the amount of work that had been done. Everywhere the ground was pitted with deep holes, capable of sheltering from fifteen to twenty men. The hedge was a high one, and was formed for the most part of prickly bushes. The position was, indeed, a formidable one; manned, as it was, by nearly twenty thousand desperate fighters.

At six o'clock the first gun was fired; and, for an hour and a half, the camp was swept with shell, shrapnel, and Maxim bullets. Most of the Baggara were lying in the pits. Many, however, walked about calmly, as if in contempt of the fire. More than half of the wretched men bound to the trees were killed.

At last the fire of the guns slackened and, on the crest of the position, in a semicircle round the wood, a long line of steadily marching men appeared. The assault was about to begin.

The Dervishes sprang from their hiding places, and lined the trenches behind the zareba. The troops halted, and waited. The Maxims moved in front of the British brigade, and then opened fire. A bugle sounded, and the whole line, black and white, advanced like a wall. When within three hundred yards, the men knelt down and opened fire, in volleys of sections. At the same instant the Dervishes, with difficulty restrained until now, opened fire in return.

The Maxims, and the storm of British bullets swept the wood, filling the air with a shower of falling leaves. Gregory murmured a prayer, shut his eyes, and awaited death.

Suddenly he felt his ropes slacken and fall from him, and a voice said, "Drop on your face, master!"

Almost mechanically he obeyed, too astonished even to think what was happening; then a body fell across him.

"Lie still and don't move, master. They must think you are dead."

"Is it you, Zaki?" Gregory said, scarcely able, even now, to believe that it was his faithful follower.

"It is I, master. I have been in the camp three days, and have never had a chance of getting near you, before."

"Brave fellow! good friend!" Gregory said, and then was silent.

Speech was almost inaudible, amid the roar of battle. The pipes of the Camerons could, however, be heard above the din. The men advanced steadily, in line, maintaining their excellent volley firing. The three other regiments, in close order, followed; bearing away farther to the right, so as to be able to open fire and advance. On that side the black regiments were advancing no less steadily, and the half brigade of Egyptians were as eager as any. Steadily and well under control, all pushed forward at a run; firing occasionally, but thirsting to get hand to hand with those who had desolated their land, destroyed their villages, and slain their friends.

The British were suffering, but the blacks suffered more; for the volleys of the Camerons kept down the fire of those opposed to them, better than the irregular fire of the Soudanese. The latter, however, first reached the zareba; and, regardless of thorns or of fire, dashed through it with triumphant shouts, and fell upon the defenders.

It was but a minute or two later that the Camerons reached the hedge. Formidable as it looked, it took them but a short time to tear down gaps, through which they rushed; while close behind them the Seaforths, the Lincolns, and the Warwicks were all in, bursting through the low stockade and trenches behind it, and cheering madly.

Now, from their holes and shelters, the Dervishes started up. Brave though they were, the storm that had burst upon them with such suddenness scared them, and none attempted to arrest the course of the Highlanders and red coats. Firing as they ran, the Dervishes made for the river. Many remained in their pits till the last, firing at the soldiers as they rushed past, and meeting their death at the point of the bayonet.

Hotly the troops pursued, often falling into the pits, which were half hidden by thorns and long grass. There was no attempt at regularity in these holes—nothing to show where they were. It was a wild and confused combat. The officers kept their men as well together as it was possible, on such ground; but it was sharp work, for from flank and rear, as well as in front, the shots rang out from their hidden foes, and these had to be despatched as they pushed forward.

As the troops burst through, Gregory sprang to his feet, seized a rifle that had dropped from the hands of a Dervish who had fallen close by and—shouting to Zaki "Lie still as if dead!"—joined the first line of troops. No questions were asked. Every man's attention was fixed on the work before him, and no thought was given to this white officer, who sprang from they knew not where. He had no cartridges, and the Dervishes did not carry bayonets; but, holding the rifle club-wise, he kept in the front line, falling into pits and climbing out again, engaged more than once with desperate foemen.

Striking and shouting, he fought on until the troops reached the river bank; and, having cleared all before them, poured volleys into the mass of fugitives crossing its dry bed. Other hordes were seen away to the left, similarly driven out by Lewis's Egyptians, by whom a terrible fire was kept up until the last of the fugitives disappeared in the scrub on the opposite bank, leaving the river bed thickly dotted with dead bodies; while, on the right, Macdonald's and Maxwell's blacks similarly cleared the wood.

Then the Soudanese and whites alike burst into cheers. Men shook each other by the hand, while they waved their helmets over their heads. The Soudanese leapt and danced like delighted children. Presently an officer left a group of others, who had been congratulating each other on their glorious victory, and came up to Gregory.

"May I ask who you are, sir?" he said, courteously but coldly.

"Certainly, sir. My name is Hilliard. I have been a captive in the hands of the Dervishes; who, when you attacked, tied me to the stump of a tree as a target for your bullets; and I should certainly have been killed, had not a faithful servant of mine, a black, taken the opportunity, when the Dervishes rushed into the trenches and opened fire upon you, to cut my ropes.

"I have no doubt, sir," he went on, as he saw the officer look somewhat doubtful, "that General Hunter is here. I am known personally to him, and served for a time on his staff."

"That is quite sufficient," the officer said, more cordially. "I congratulate you on your escape. I confess it astonished us all, when a strange white officer, whom none of us knew, suddenly joined us. You will find General Hunter somewhere over on the left. He is certain to have led the charge of the Soudanese."

"Thank you! I will go and find him; but first, I must return to where I left my man. He had, of course, the Mahdist's patch on his clothes; and I told him to lie still, as if dead, till I came for him; as, in the melee, it would have been impossible for me to have protected him."

Gregory found Zaki still lying where he left him, head downward and arms thrown forward; in so good an imitation of death that he feared, for a moment, the lad had been shot after he left him. At the sound of his master's voice, however, the native sprang to his feet.

"You have saved my life, Zaki," Gregory said, taking his hand. "I must have fallen—every man tied to a tree is, as you see, dead; but before we say anything else, cut that patch off your clothes, or you might be shot as a Dervish by the first man you come across.

"Keep close to me. I am going to General Hunter. At present, I know none of the officers of the white regiments. When I get among the Soudanese, I shall be more at home."

In ten minutes, he came to where General Hunter was speaking to the Sirdar. Gregory stopped at a short distance, before the general's eyes fell upon him, and he gave an exclamation of pleasure.

"That is Hilliard, General; the young fellow who jumped from one of the gunboats, off Metemmeh, to rescue the woman. The act was unnoticed at the time, but a black he had with him was released, and brought word that his master was a prisoner in their camp."

"I heard of it, at the time," the Sirdar said, and motioned to Gregory to come up. "I am glad to find that you have escaped the fate we feared had befallen you, but your action was altogether wrong. An officer's life is no longer his own, but belongs to the country he serves; and you had no right whatever to risk it when on duty, even in an action which, at any other time, would do you great credit."

He spoke sharply and sternly. Gregory again saluted.

"I knew afterwards that I had done wrong, sir; but I did not stop to think, and acted on the impulse of the moment."

"That may be," the Sirdar said; "but officers should think, and not act on the impulse of the moment."

Gregory again saluted, and fell back. Three or four minutes later, the two generals separated. General Hunter came up to him, and shook him warmly by the hand.

"You must not mind what the Sirdar said, Hilliard. It was a very noble action, and did you credit, and I can assure you that that was the opinion of all who knew you; but to the Sirdar, you know, duty is everything, and I think you are lucky in not being sent down, at once, to the base. However, he said to me, after you had left him:

"'I shall be too busy this evening, but bring the young fellow with you, tomorrow evening. I must hear how it was that Mahmud spared him.'

"I told him that I understood, from your black, that the woman was Mahmud's favourite wife, and that she took you under her care.

"By the way, have you heard that Mahmud is captured? Yes, he is caught, which is a great satisfaction to us; for his being sent down, a prisoner, will convince the tribesmen that we have gained a victory, as to which they would otherwise be incredulous. I hear that the Egyptian brigade, which was to the extreme left, has captured Mahmud's wife, and a great number of women."

"With your permission, sir, I will go over there at once, and ask Colonel Lewis that she may receive specially good treatment. She has been extremely kind to me, and it is to her influence over Mahmud that I owe my life. Up to this morning Mahmud would have spared me, but Osman Digna insisted that I should be killed, and he was obliged to give way. They fastened me to a tree behind the trench, just inside the zareba, and I should certainly have been killed by our own musketry fire, had not my boy, who had come into the camp in disguise, cut my cords. I fell as if shot, and he threw himself down on me; until the Camerons burst in, when I at once joined them, and did what little I could in the fight."

"I will give you a line to Colonel Lewis, to tell him that Mahmud's wife, whom you will point out, is to be treated with respect; and that her people may be allowed to make her an arbour of some sort, until the Sirdar decides what is to be done with her. Probably she will be sent down to Berber. No doubt we shall all fall back."

"Then you will not pursue, sir?"

"No. The cavalry have already gone off in pursuit of their horsemen, but they are not likely to catch them; for we hear that Osman Digna is with them, and he seems to enjoy a special immunity from capture. As for the other poor beggars, we could not do it if we wanted to. I expect the campaign is over, for the present. Certainly, nothing can be done till the railway is completed; then the gunboats can tow the native craft, abreast of us, as we march along the river bank.

"Shendy has been captured, and we found twelve thousand Jaalin prisoners there, women and children, and a large quantity of stores. That is what makes the position of the Dervish fugitives so hopeless. There is nothing before them but to find their way across the desert to Omdurman, and I fancy that few of them will get there alive.

"No doubt some will keep along by the Atbara, and others by the

Nile. The latter will have the best chance, for the friendlies at Kassala will be on the lookout for fugitives. I am sorry for the poor wretches, though they richly deserve the worst that can befall them. They have never shown mercy. For twenty years they have murdered, plundered, and desolated the whole land, and have shown themselves more ferocious and merciless than wild beasts."

He took out his pocketbook, wrote the order to Colonel Lewis; and then, tearing the leaf out, handed it to Gregory, who at once made his way, followed closely by Zaki, to the spot where two Egyptian battalions had halted. They had no difficulty in finding Colonel Lewis, who was receiving a report, from the officers of the two battalions, of the casualties they had sustained. Gregory had met the Colonel several times, at Berber, and the latter recognized him at once.

"Ah! Major Hilliard," that officer said, as he came up; "I am glad to see you. I heard that you had been captured by the Dervishes, and killed; but I suppose, as I see you here, that it was only the usual canard."

"No, sir. I was captured; but, as you see, not killed, though it has been a pretty close thing. This is a note, sir, that General Hunter requested me to give you."

Colonel Lewis read the order.

"The women are down over there, a couple of hundred yards away," he said. "I will send a sergeant and four men with you. If you will point out Mahmud's wife, I will see that she is made as comfortable as possible."

"Thank you, sir! It is to her I owe my life, and I am most anxious to do all I can to repay the debt."

"You came along through the other brigades. Do you know what their losses have been?"

"The British losses are not heavy, sir, considering the fire they have been exposed to. Macdonald's brigade suffered most, I believe."

"Yes; I saw one of the officers just now. It seems they came down upon Mahmud's picked bodyguard, and these fought desperately. They found Mahmud in the usual attitude in which the Dervish emirs await death, when they are conquered. He was sitting quietly on his mat, with his arms laid down beside him; and was, I should imagine, somewhat surprised at finding that he was not cut to pieces, at once."

"I am glad he was not, sir, for he certainly behaved well to me. It was through the influence of his wife, I admit; but in sparing me he really risked serious disaffection among his followers, and at last gave way only to coercion."

The sergeant and men had now come up, and Gregory went off with them. Three or four hundred women were seated on the ground together, with half a dozen Egyptian soldiers standing as sentry over them. More or less closely veiled as they were, Gregory could not distinguish Fatma among them; and indeed, except when he first reached her in the water, he had not got a glimpse of her features. The question, however, was speedily settled when a woman rose, in the middle of the group, with a cry of gladness.

"So you are saved!" she exclaimed, "I have feared so that you were killed. Have you news of Mahmud?"

"Yes, lady. He is a prisoner, but well and unharmed. I have obtained an order, from the General, that you are to be treated with honours, as his wife. We cannot do much for you, at present, but all that is possible will be done. I have represented your kindness to me, and these soldiers will at once erect an arbour for you, and food will be brought for you all, as soon as matters have settled down a little."

The Egyptian soldiers had already begun to cut down saplings. Accustomed as they were to the work, in half an hour they had erected an arbour. Fatma was then assisted into it, with the other women of the harem. The sergeant gave orders, to the sentries, that no one was to be allowed to interfere in any way with them; and then Gregory took his leave, saying that he would return, later on.

He again joined General Hunter, who seemed to be his natural chief, now that his service in the gunboat was over.

The list of casualties was now being brought in. The Camerons, who had led the attack in line, had lost most heavily. They had fifteen killed and forty-six wounded, among them being two officers killed, and one mortally wounded. The Seaforths had one officer killed and one mortally wounded, and four others less severely; in all, six killed and twenty-seven wounded. The Lincolns had one killed and eighteen wounded; the Warwicks two killed and eighteen wounded. Many of the wounded afterwards died.

The Egyptians had lost more heavily. The casualties among them were fifty-seven killed; and four British and sixteen native officers, and three hundred and sixty-seven non-commissioned officers and men, wounded.

The Dervish loss was terrible. Three thousand men were killed, among whom were nearly all the emirs; and two thousand were taken prisoners. The rest were hopeless fugitives, and a vast number of these must have been wounded.

There was but a short rest for the troops. When the wounded had been collected, and carried to a neighbouring palm grove, where the surgeons did all that could then be done for them; and the trophies of the fight—banners and spears, guns of all sorts, swords and knives—had been gathered, principally by the exultant Soudanese and Egyptians, the force prepared for a start.

"May I ask, General, what is to be done with the women?" Gregory said.

"I have been speaking to the Sirdar about them, and I was just going to ask you to go with me to them. They are, of course, not to be considered as prisoners. They cannot stay here, for they would die of hunger. Therefore they had best follow the troops, at any rate as far as the Atbara camp. They will have food given them, and must then decide for themselves what they are to do. It is a difficult question, altogether. The only thing that can, at present, be settled is that they mustn't be allowed to die of hunger, and they must be protected against molestation.

"The troops will march at four o'clock. The Egyptian brigade have volunteered to carry the wounded. They will start later. The women had better follow them. No doubt, some of them will find their husbands among the prisoners, so that there will be no trouble about them."

"What will be done with the men, sir?"

The General smiled.

"Tomorrow they will probably enlist in our service, to a man, and will fight just as sturdily as the other Soudanese battalions, against their brethren in Khartoum. All the prisoners we have hitherto taken who are fit for the work have done so; and, as has been shown today, are just as ready to fight on our side as they were against us. They are a fighting people, and it is curious how they become attached to their white officers, whom formerly they hated as infidels."

When the matter was explained to them, the women accepted the situation with the resignation that is natural to the Mahometan woman. Gregory was able to assure Fatma that, in a short time, she would undoubtedly be allowed to join Mahmud, and accompany him wherever he was sent.

"But will they not kill him?" she said.

"We never kill prisoners. Even the bitterest enemy that may fall into our hands is well treated. Mahmud will doubtless be sent down to Cairo, and it will then be settled where he is to be taken to; but you may be sure that, wherever it may be, he will be well treated and cared for."

"In that case, I shall be happy," she said. "When you saved me, I saw that the ways of you Christians were better than our ways. Now I see it still more. To be always raiding, and plundering, and killing cannot be good. It used to seem to me natural and right, but I have come to think differently."

At four o'clock the troops marched. At Gregory's request, he was allowed to remain behind and accompany the Egyptians. He had bought for a few shillings, from the soldiers, a dozen donkeys that had been found alive in some of the pits. These he handed over to Fatma, for her conveyance and that of the wives of some of the emirs, who were of the party.

The Egyptians started at half-past eight, carrying their own wounded and those of the British. By the route by which the army had marched, the night before, the distance was but nine miles; but there had been some rough places to pass, and to avoid these, where the wounded might have suffered from jolting, they made a circuit, thereby adding three miles to the length of the march; and did not reach Umdabieh camp until two o'clock in the morning. General Hunter, who never spared himself, rode with them and acted as guide.

During the fight he, Colonel Macdonald, and Colonel Maxwell had ridden at the head of their brigades, the white regimental officers being on foot with the men, as was their custom; and it was surprising that the three conspicuous figures had all come through the storm of fire unscathed.

The next morning was a quiet one, and in the afternoon all marched off to the old camp, at Abadar. On Sunday they rested, and on Monday the British brigade marched to Hudi, and then across the desert to Hermali, where they were to spend the summer. The Sirdar rode, with the Egyptian brigades, to Fort Atbara. Macdonald's brigade was to go on to garrison Berber, Maxwell's to Assillem, and that of Lewis to remain at Atbara.

The question of the prisoners was already half solved. Almost all of them willingly embraced the offer to enlist in the Egyptian army. Many of the women found their husbands among the prisoners. Others agreed, at once, to marry men of the Soudanese battalion. The rest, pending such offers as they might receive in the future, decided to remain at Atbara. At Berber their lot would have been a hard one, for they would have been exposed to the hatred and spite of the Jaalin women there, whose husbands had been massacred at Metemmeh.

Fatma, with two attendants only, accompanied Macdonald's brigade to Berber. On arriving outside the town, the force encamped. Next day the Sirdar, with his staff and General Hunter, came up; and, on the following morning, made a triumphant entry into the town, followed by the Soudanese brigade.

Berber was prepared to do honour to the occasion. Flags waved, coloured cloths and women's garments hung from the windows, and the whole population lined the streets, and received the conquerors with cries of welcome and triumph. They had anticipated a very different result, and had fully expected that the army would have been well-nigh annihilated; and that, again, the triumphant Dervishes would become their masters. But the sight of Mahmud walking, a prisoner, with two guards on each side of him, convinced them that the reports that had reached them were true, that the Dervishes had been signally defeated, and that there was no fear of their ever again becoming lords of Berber.

The Sirdar, by whose side General Hunter rode, headed the procession, followed by his staff. Then, leading his brigade, came Macdonald—stern and hard of face, burnt almost black with years of campaigning in the desert—and his staff, followed by the black battalions, erect and proud, maintaining their soldierly bearing amid the loud quavering cries of welcome from the women.

Gregory had, on his arrival with the brigade the day before, gone into the town; and engaged a small house, in its outskirts, as the abode of Fatma and her two attendants, purchased suitable provisions, and made what arrangements he could for her comfort. Late in the evening he had escorted her there, and left Zaki to sleep in an outhouse attached to it, to secure them from all intrusion.

Then he went down to the river and, finding the Zafir lying there, went on board. He was received as one returned from the dead by Captain Keppel, Lieutenant Beatty, and Lieutenant Hood—the commanders of the other gunboats—who had been dining on board. He had become a general favourite, during the time he had spent with them, and their congratulations on his safe return were warm and hearty.

"You may imagine our surprise when, after the fight was over," said Captain Keppel, "it was discovered that you were missing. No one could imagine what had become of you. One of the blacks who had been working your Maxim said they had not noticed your leaving them; and that, when they found you were not there, they supposed you had come to confer with me. Then I sent for your man; but he, too, was missing. We searched everywhere, but no signs of you, dead or alive, and no marks of blood were to be found. So it seemed that the matter must remain a mystery. Early the next morning, however, we saw a white rag waving on the bank, and then a black entered the water and swam out towards us. I sent the boat to meet him, and when he came on board I found that he was your man, and the mystery was explained. I fancy I used some strong language; for I never before heard of a man being so hare-brained as to spring overboard, in the middle of a battle, and pick up a woman, without saying a word to anyone of what he was doing, and that with the boat still steaming ahead. Of course, your man told us that it was Mahmud's wife you had saved, and that she had taken you under her protection; but I did not expect that, among those fanatics, your life would be spared.

"Now, tell us all about your adventures, and how you got down here just in time to see our fellows enter, in triumph. I suppose you managed to give them the slip, somehow?"

Gregory then told his story. When he had concluded, Captain Keppel said:

"Well, you have the luck of the old one! First, you have got hold of as faithful a fellow as is to be found in all Egypt, or anywhere else; and, in the second place, you have been in the battle of Atbara, while we have been kicking our heels here, and fuming at being out of it altogether, except for our bloodless capture of Shendy.

"So you say the Sirdar blew you up? I am not surprised at that. You know the story of the man who fell overboard, in the old flogging days, and the captain sentenced him to two dozen lashes, for leaving the ship without orders."

"I don't think he was really angry; for when I went to him, the next evening, he was a good deal milder. Of course, he did say again that I had done wrong, but not in the same tone as before; and he seemed a good deal interested in what I told him about Mahmud, and how my boy had risked his life to rescue me, and had succeeded almost by a miracle. He said there is a lot of good in these black fellows, if one could but get at it. They have never had a chance yet; but, given good administration, and the suppression of all tribal feuds with a stern hand, they might be moulded into anything."

"And are you coming back to us now, Mr. Hilliard?"

"I have no idea. I don't suppose anything will be settled, for a time. There is not likely to be much doing, anyway, except on the railway; and even your gunboats will have an easy time of it, as there is not an enemy left on this side of the sixth cataract.

"The Dervishes who escaped are pretty sure to cross the Atbara. There are enough of them still, when they rally, to beat off any attacks that might be made by our tribesmen from Kassala."

CHAPTER 13:

The Final Advance.

A few days after the return of headquarters to Berber, Mahmud was sent down country, and Fatma was permitted to accompany him. She expressed to Gregory, in touching terms, her gratitude for what he had done for her.

"We have been of mutual assistance," said Gregory. "I have the same reason to be grateful to you, as you have to thank me. I saved your life, and you saved mine. You were very kind to me, when I was a captive—I have done as much as I could for you, since you have been with us. So we are quits. I hope you will be happy with Mahmud. We do not treat our prisoners badly, and except that he will be away from the Soudan, he will probably be more comfortable than he has ever been in his life."

Gregory was now employed in the transport department, and journeyed backwards and forwards, with large convoys of camels, to the head of the railway. The line was completed to Berber, but the officers charged with its construction were indefatigable; and, as fast as the materials came up, it was pushed on towards the Atbara. Complete as had been the victory on that river, the Sirdar saw that the force which had been sufficient to defeat the twenty thousand men, under Mahmud, was not sufficiently strong for the more onerous task of coping with three times that number, fighting under the eye of the Khalifa, and certain to consist of his best and bravest troops. He therefore telegraphed home for another British brigade, and additional artillery, with at least one regiment of cavalry—an arm in which the Egyptian Army was weak.

Preparations were at once made for complying with the request. The 21st Lancers, 1st battalion of Grenadier Guards, 2nd battalion of the Rifle Brigade, 2nd battalion of the 5th Lancashire Fusiliers, a field battery, a howitzer battery, and two forty-pounders, to batter the defences of Omdurman, should the Khalifa take his stand, were sent. A strong detachment of the Army Service Corps and the Royal Army Medical Corps was to accompany them, but they had yet some months to wait, for the advance would not be made until the Nile was full, and the gunboats could ascend the cataract.

However, there was much to be done, and the troops did not pass the time in idleness. Atbara Fort was to be the base, and here the Egyptian battalions built huts and storehouses. The Soudanese brigades returned to Berber, and the transport of provisions and stores for them was thus saved. The British at Darmali were made as comfortable as possible, and no effort was spared to keep them in good health, during the ensuing hot weather. A small theatre was constructed, and here smoking concerts were held. There was also a race meeting, and one of the steamers took parties, of the men who were most affected by the heat, for a trip down the Nile. They were practised in long marches early in the morning, and although, of course, there was some illness, the troops on the whole bore the heat well.

Had there been a prospect of an indefinitely long stay, the result might have been otherwise; but they knew that, in a few months, they would be engaged in even sterner work than the last battle, that Khartoum was their goal, and with its capture the power of the Khalifa would be broken for ever, and Gordon avenged.

Early in April the railway reached Abadia, a few miles from Berber, and in a short time a wonderful transformation took place here. From a sandy desert, with scarce a human being in sight, it became the scene of a busy industry. Stores were sorted and piled as they came up by rail.

Three gunboats arrived in sections, and these were put together. They were stronger, and much better defended by steel plates than the first gunboats; and each of them carried two six-pounder quick-firing guns, a small howitzer, four Maxims, and a searchlight. They were, however, much slower than the old boats, and could do very little in the way of towing.

Besides these, eight steel double-deck troop barges were brought up, in sections, and put together. Three Egyptian battalions came up from Merawi to aid in the work, which not only included building the gunboats and barges, but executing the repairs to all the native craft, and putting them in a thoroughly serviceable state.

In June the railway reached the Atbara, and for the first time for two years and a half, the officers who had superintended its construction had a temporary rest. The stores were now transferred from Abadia to the Atbara, and two trains ran every day, each bringing up something like two hundred tons of stores.

In the middle of July two Egyptian battalions left Atbara and proceeded up the Nile, one on each bank, cutting down trees and piling them for fuel for the steamers. As the river rose, four steamers came up from Dongola, together with a number of sailing boats; and in the beginning of August the whole flotilla, consisting of ten gunboats, five unarmed steamers, eight troop barges, and three or four hundred sailing boats, were all assembled.

By this time the reinforcements from home were all at Cairo, and their stores had already been sent up. It was arranged that they were to come by half battalions, by squadrons, and by batteries, each one day behind the other. To make room for them, two Egyptian battalions were sent up to the foot of the Shabluka cataract.

The six black battalions left Berber on July 30th, and arrived at Atbara the next day. There were now four brigades in the infantry divisions instead of three, two battalions having been raised from the Dervishes taken at the battle of Atbara. These were as eager as any to join in the fight against their late comrades.

This was scarcely surprising. The Baggara, the tyrants of the desert, are horsemen. The infantry were, for the most part, drawn from the conquered tribes. They had enlisted in the Khalifa's force partly because they had no other means of subsistence, partly from their innate love of fighting. They had, in fact, been little better than slaves; and their condition, as soldiers in the Egyptian Army, was immeasurably superior to that which they had before occupied.

Broadwood, with nine squadrons of Egyptian cavalry, was already on the western bank of the river opposite Atbara; and was to be joined at Metemmeh by the camel corps, and another squadron of horse from Merawi.

On the 3rd of August the six Soudanese battalions left Fort Atbara for the point of concentration, a few miles below the cataract. To the sides of each gunboat were attached two of the steel barges; behind each were two native craft. All were filled as tightly as they could be crammed with troops. They were packed as in slavers, squatting by the side of each other as closely as sardines in a box. The seven steamers and the craft they took with them contained six thousand men, so crowded that a spectator remarked that planks might have been laid on their heads, and that you could have walked about on them; while another testified that he could not have shoved a walking stick between them anywhere. White men could not have supported it for an hour, but these blacks and Egyptians had a hundred miles to go, and the steamers could not make more than a knot an hour against the rapid stream, now swollen to its fullest.

While they were leaving, the first four companies of the Rifle Brigade arrived. Every day boats laden with stores went forward, every day white troops came up. Vast as was the quantity of stores sent off, the piles at Atbara did not seem to diminish. Ninety days' provisions, forage, and necessaries for the whole force had been accumulated there, and as fast as these were taken away they were replaced by others from Berber.

Like everyone connected with the transport or store department, Gregory had to work from daybreak till dark. Accustomed to a warm climate, light in figure, without an ounce of spare flesh, he was able to support the heat, dust, and fatigue better than most; and, as he himself said, it was less trying to be at work, even in the blazing sun, than to lie listless and sweating under the shade of a blanket. There was no necessity, now, to go down the line to make enquiries as to the progress of the stores, or of the laden craft on their way up. the telegraph was established, and the Sirdar, at Atbara, knew the exact position of every one of the units between Cairo and himself; and from every station he received messages constantly, and despatched his orders as frequently.

There was no hitch, whatever. The arrangements were all so perfect that the vast machine, with its numerous parts, moved with the precision of clockwork. Everything was up to time. For a train or steamer, or even a native boat, to arrive half an hour after the time calculated for it, was almost unheard of.

The Sirdar's force of will seemed to communicate itself to every officer under him, and it is safe to say that never before was an expedition so perfectly organized, and so marvellously carried out. At Atbara the Sirdar saw to everything himself. A brief word of commendation, to those working under him, cheered them through long days of toil—an equally curt reproof depressed them to the depths.

Twice, when Gregory was directing some of the blacks piling large cases, as they were emptied from the train; anathematizing the stupid, urging on the willing, and himself occasionally lending a hand in order to show how it should be done; the Sirdar, who, unknown to him, had been looking on, rode up and said shortly, "You are doing well, Mr. Hilliard!"—and he felt that his offence of jumping overboard had been condoned.

General Hunter, himself indefatigable, had more occasion to notice Gregory's work; and his commendations were frequent, and warm.

The lad had not forgotten the object with which he had come to the front. After Atbara, he had questioned many of the prisoners who, from their age, might have fought at El Obeid; but none of these had done so. The forces of the Khalifa came and went, as there was occasion for them. The Baggara were always under arms, but only when danger threatened were the great levies of foot assembled; for it would have been impossible, in the now desolate state of the Soudan, to find food for an army of a hundred thousand men.

All agreed, however, that, with the exception of the Egyptian artillerymen, they heard that no single white man had escaped. Numbers of the black soldiers had been made slaves. The whites had perished—all save one had fallen on the field. That one had accompanied a black battalion, who had held together and, repulsing all attacks, had marched away. They had been followed, however, and after repeated attacks had dwindled away, until they had finally been broken and massacred.

With the Khalifa's army were several emirs who had fought at El Obeid; and these would, no doubt, be able to tell him more; but none of those who were taken prisoners, at the Atbara, had heard of any white man having escaped the slaughter of Hicks's army.

Just as the general movement began, the force was joined by three companies of Soudanese. These had marched from Suakim to Berber, two hundred and eighty-eight miles, in fifteen days, an average of nineteen miles a day—a record for such a march, and one that no European force could have performed. One day, after marching thirty miles, they came to a well and found it dry, and had to march thirty miles farther to another water hole, a feat probably altogether without precedent.

"You had better fall back upon your old work, Hilliard," the General said, the day before they started. "As my aide I shall find plenty for you to do, now that I command the whole division."

"Thank you very much, sir! I don't think that I shall find any work hard, after what I have been doing for the past four months."

"You have got your horse?"

"Yes; he is in good condition, for I have had no riding to do, for some time."

"Well, you had better get him on board one of the gyasses we shall tow up, tomorrow. All our horses will embark this evening. We shall be on board at daybreak. Our private camels are going with the marching column; you had better put yours with them. No doubt they will join us somewhere. Of course, your kit will be carried with us."

It was a delight to Gregory to be on the water again. There was generally a cool breeze on the river, and always an absence of dust. He was now halfway between seventeen and eighteen, but the sun had tanned him to a deep brown, and had parched his face; thus adding some years to his appearance, so that the subalterns of the newly-arrived regiments looked boyish beside him. The responsibilities of his work had steadied him, and though he retained his good spirits, his laugh had lost the old boyish ring. The title of Bimbashi, which had seemed absurd to him seven months before, was now nothing out of the way, for he looked as old as many of the British subalterns serving with that rank in the Egyptian army.

Returning to the little hut that Zaki, with the aid of some of the blacks, had built for him; he gave his orders, and in a short time the camel—a very good one, which he had obtained in exchange for that which he had handed over to the transport—started, with its driver, to join those that were to carry up the baggage and stores of General Hunter, and his staff. These were in charge of a sergeant and three privates, of one of the Soudanese battalions. Gregory had got up a case of whisky, one of bottled fruit, and a stock of tea and sugar from Berber. No tents could be carried, and he left his *tente d'abri* at the stores with his canteen; taking on board, in his own luggage, a plate, knife, fork, and spoon, and a couple of tumblers. When the camels had started, he saw his horse put on board, and then took a final stroll round the encampment.

The change that had occurred there, during the past fortnight, was striking. Then none but black faces could be seen. Now it was the encampment of a British force, with its white tents and all their belongings.

The contrast between the newly-arrived brigade, and the hardy veterans who had fought at the Atbara, was striking. Bronzed and hearty, inured to heat and fatigue, the latter looked fit to go anywhere and do anything, and there was hardly a sick man in the four regiments. On the other hand, the newcomers looked white and exhausted with the heat. Numbers had already broken down, and the doctors at the hospital had their hands full of fever patients. They had scarcely marched a mile since they landed in Egypt, and were so palpably unfit for hard work that they were, if possible, to proceed the whole way in boats, in order to be in fighting condition when the hour of battle arrived.

The voyage up the river was an uneventful one. It seemed all too short to Gregory, who enjoyed immensely the rest, quiet, and comparative coolness. The Sirdar had gone up a week before they landed at Wady Hamed. Here the whole Egyptian portion of the army, with the exception of the brigade that was to arrive the next day, was assembled. The blacks had constructed straw huts; the Egyptians erected shelters, extemporized from their blankets; while the British were to be installed in tents, which had been brought up in sailing boats. The camp was two miles in length and half a mile wide, surrounded by a strong zareba.

The Egyptian cavalry and the camel corps had arrived. On the opposite side of the river was a strong body of friendly Arabs, nominally under the Abadar sheik, but in reality commanded by Major Montague Stuart-Wortley. By the 23rd of August the whole force had arrived; and the Sirdar reviewed them, drawn up in battle array, and put them through a few manoeuvres, as if in action. General Gatacre commanded the British division—Colonel Wauchope the first brigade, and Lyttleton the second. As before, Macdonald, Maxwell, and Lewis commanded the first three Egyptian brigades, and Collinson that newly raised, General Hunter being in command of the division.

The force numbered, in all, about twenty thousand; and although destitute of the glitter and colour of a British army, under ordinary circumstances, were as fine a body of men as a British general could wish to command; and all, alike, eager to meet the foe. The British division had with them two batteries and ten Maxims, and the Egyptian division five batteries and ten Maxims.

As Gregory was strolling through the camp, he passed where the officers of one of the British regiments were seated on boxes, round a rough table, over which a sort of awning had been erected.

"Come and join us, Hilliard. We are having our last feast on our last stores, which we got smuggled up in one of the gunboats," the Major called out.

"With pleasure, sir."

The officer who was sitting at the head of the table made room beside him.

"You men of the Egyptian Army fare a good deal better than we do, I think," the Major went on. "That institution of private camels is an excellent one. We did not know that they would be allowed. But, after all, it is not a bad thing that we did not have them, for there is no doubt it is as well that the soldiers should not see us faring better than they. There is bother enough with the baggage, as it is. Of course, it is different in your case. There are only two or three white officers with each battalion, and it would not strike your black troops as a hardship that you should have different food from themselves. They are living as well as, or better than, they ever did in their lives. Three camels make no material addition to your baggage train, while, as there are thirty or forty of us, it would make a serious item in ours, and the General's keen eyes would spot them at once."

"Our camels are no burden to the army," Gregory said. "They only have a few pounds of grain a day, and get their living principally on what they can pick up. When they go on now, they will each carry fifty pounds of private grain. They get five pounds when there are no bushes or grass, so that the grain will last them for a fortnight."

"I suppose you think that the Dervishes mean fighting?"

"I think there is no doubt about it. All the fugitives that come in say that the Khalifa will fight, but whether it will be in the defence of Omdurman, or whether he will come out and attack us at Kerreri, none can say. The Khalifa keeps his intentions to himself."

"By the bye, Hilliard, I don't think you know my right-hand neighbour; he only joined us an hour before we started, having been left behind at Cairo, sick.

"Mr. Hartley, let me introduce you to Mr. Hilliard—I should say Bimbashi Hilliard. He is on General Hunter's staff."

The young lieutenant placed an eyeglass in his eye, and bowed to Gregory.

"Have you been in this beastly country long?" he asked.

"If you include Lower Egypt, I have been here eighteen years."

"Dear me!" the other drawled; "the climate seems to have agreed with you."

"Fairly well," Gregory replied. "I don't mind the heat much, and one doesn't feel it, while one is at work."

"Hartley has not tried that, yet," one of the others laughed. "Work is not in his line. This most unfortunate illness of his kept him back at

Cairo, and he brought such a supply of ice with him, when he came up, that he was able to hand over a hundredweight of it to us when he arrived. I don't think, Major, that in introducing him you should have omitted to mention that, but for a temporary misfortune, he would be the Marquis of Langdale; but in another two years he will blossom out into his full title, and then I suppose we shall lose him."

Gregory, whose knowledge of the English peerage was extremely limited, looked puzzled.

"May I ask how that is?" he said. "I always thought that the next heir to a title succeeded to it, as soon as his father died."

"As a rule that is the case," the Major said, "but the present is an exceptional one. At the death of the late marquis, the heir to the title was missing. I may say that the late marquis only enjoyed the title for two years. The next of kin, a brother of his, had disappeared, and up to the present no news has been obtained of him. Of course he has been advertised for, and so on, but without success. It is known that he married, but as he did so against the wish of his father, he broke off all communication with his family; and it is generally supposed that he emigrated. Pending any news of him, the title is held in abeyance.

"He may have died. It is probable that he has done so, for he could hardly have escaped seeing the advertisements that were inserted in every paper. Of course, if he has left children, they inherit the title.

"After a lapse of five years Mr. Hartley's father, who was the next heir, and who died five years ago, applied to be declared the inheritor of the title; but the peers, or judges, or someone decided that twenty-one years must elapse before such an application could be even considered. The income has been accumulating ever since, so that at the end of that time, it is probable that Mr. Hartley will be allowed to assume the title.

"Will the estates go with the title, Hartley?"

"Oh, I should say so, of course!" the other drawled. "The title would not be of much use, without them."

"Nonsense, my dear fellow!" another said. "Why, a fellow with your personal advantage, and a title, would be able to command the American market, and to pick up an heiress with millions."

The general laugh that followed showed that Hartley was, by no means, a popular character in the regiment.

"The fellow is a consummate ass," the man on Gregory's left whispered. "He only got into the service as a Queen's cadet. He could no more have got in, by marks, than he could have flown. No one believes that he had anything the matter with him, at Cairo; but he preferred stopping behind and coming up by himself, without any duties, to taking any share in the work. He is always talking about his earldom—that is why the Major mentioned it, so as to draw him out."

"But I suppose he is really heir to it?"

"Yes, if no one else claims it. For aught that is known, there may be half a dozen children of the man that is missing, knocking about somewhere in Canada or Australia. If so, they are safe to turn up, sooner or later. You see, as the man had an elder brother, he would not have counted at all upon coming to the title. He may be in some out-of-the-way place, where even a colonial newspaper would never reach him; but, sooner or later, he or some of his sons will be coming home, and will hear of the last earl's death, and then this fellow's nose will be put out of joint.

"I am sure everyone in the regiment would be glad, for he is an insufferable ass. I suppose, when he comes into the title, he will either cut the army altogether, or exchange into the Guards."

The party presently broke up, having finished the last bottle of wine they had brought up. Gregory remained seated by the Major, discussing the chances of the campaign, and the points where resistance might be expected. The other officers stood talking, a short distance off. Presently Gregory caught the words:

"How is it that this young fellow calls himself Bimbashi, which, I believe, means major?"

"He does not call himself that, although that is his rank. All the white officers in the Egyptian Army have that rank, though they may only be lieutenants, in ours."

"I call it a monstrous thing," the drawling voice then said, "that a young fellow like this, who seems to be an Egyptian by birth, should have a higher rank than men here, who have served fifteen or twenty years."

The Major got up, and walked across to the group.

"I will tell you why, Mr. Hartley," he said, in a loud voice. "It is because, for the purpose of the war in this country, they know infinitely more than the officers of our army. They talk the languages, they know the men. These blacks will follow them anywhere, to the death. As for Mr. Hilliard, he has performed feats that any officer in the army, whatever his rank, would be proud to have done. He went in disguise into the Dervish camp at Metemmeh, before Hunter's advance began, and obtained invaluable information. He jumped overboard from a gunboat to save a drowning Dervish woman, although to do so involved almost certain capture and death at the hands of the Dervishes. In point of fact, his escape was a remarkable one, for he was tied to a tree in the first line of the Dervish defences at Atbara, and was only saved by what was almost a miracle. He may not be heir to an earldom, Mr. Hartley, but he would do more credit to the title than many I could name. I hear him well spoken of, by everyone, as an indefatigable worker, and as having performed the most valuable services. Captain

Keppel, on whose gunboat he served for two or three months, spoke to me of him in the highest terms; and General Hunter has done the same.

"I fancy, sir, that it will be some years before you are likely to distinguish yourself so highly. His father was an officer, who fell in battle; and if he happened to be born in Egypt, as you sneeringly said just now, all I can say is that, in my opinion, had you been born in Egypt, you would not occupy the position which he now does."

Gregory had walked away when the Major rose, and he did not return to the party. It was the first time that he had run across a bad specimen of the British officer, and his words had stung him. But, as he said to himself, he need not mind them, as the fellow's own comrades regarded him, as one of them said, as "an insufferable ass." Still, he could not help wishing, to himself, that the missing heir might turn up in time to disappoint him.

General Hunter started next day, at noon, with two of his brigades and the mounted troops; the other two brigades following, at nightfall. The previous night had been one of the most unpleasant Gregory had ever spent. The long-expected rain had come at last. It began suddenly; there was a flash of lightning, and then came a violent burst of wind, which tore down the tents and the flimsy shelters of the Egyptians and Soudanese. Before this had ceased, the rain poured down in a torrent; lightning, wind, and rain kept on till morning, and when the start was made, everyone was soaked to the skin. The Egyptian baggage left at the same time, in native craft.

That evening they arrived at the mouth of the Shabluka Cataract. Here it had been expected that the advance would be opposed, as strong forts had been erected by the enemy, the river narrowed greatly, and precipitous rocks rose on either side. Through these the course was winding, and the current ran with great strength, the eddies and sharp bends making it extremely difficult for the gunboats to keep their course. Indeed, it would have been impossible for them to get up, had the forts been manned; as they would have had to pass within two hundred yards of the guns. But although the forts could hardly have been attacked by the gunboats, they were commanded by a lofty hill behind them; and the scouts had discovered, some weeks before, that the Dervishes had retired from the position, and that the passage would be unopposed.

Maxwell's and Colville's brigades started at four that afternoon, and the next day the whole division was established at El Hejir, above the cataracts.

Lyttleton's brigade started, at five o'clock A.M. on the 25th, the gunboats and other steamers moving parallel with them along the river. At five in the afternoon the first brigade followed and, two days afterwards, the camp was entirely evacuated, and the whole of the stores well on their way towards El Hejir. On the previous day, two regiments of Wortley's column of friendly natives also marched south. The Sirdar and headquarters, after having seen everything off, went up in a gunboat, starting at nine in the morning.

As usual, the Soudanese troops had been accompanied by a considerable number of their wives, who were heavily laden with their little household goods, and in many cases babies. They trudged patiently along in the rear of the columns, and formed an encampment of their own, half a mile away from the men's, generally selecting a piece of ground surrounded by thick bush, into which they could escape, should Dervish raiders come down upon them.

The stores arrived in due course. One of the gunboats, however, was missing—the Zafir, with three gyasses in tow, having suddenly sunk, ten miles north of Shendy, owing to being so deeply loaded that the water got into the hold. Those on board had just time to scramble into the boats, or swim to shore. No lives were lost, though there were many narrow escapes. Among these were Commander Keppel and Prince Christian Victor, who were on board. Fortunately, another steamer soon came along and took the gyasses, with the ship-wrecked officers and crew on board, and towed them up to El Hejir.

It had been intended to stay here some little time, but the Nile continued to rise to an altogether exceptional height, and part of the camp was flooded. At five o'clock, therefore, the Egyptian brigades started, with the guns on their right and the steamers covering their left, while the cavalry and camel corps were spread widely out, in advance to give notice of any approaching Dervish force. As usual the soldiers' wives turned out, and as the battalions marched past, shouted encouragement to their husbands; calling upon them to behave like men, and not to turn back in battle. The presence of the women had an excellent effect on the soldiers, and in addition to their assistance in carrying their effects, they cooked their rations, and looked after them generally. The Sirdar, therefore, did not discourage their presence in the field, and even supplied them with rations, when it was impossible for them to obtain them elsewhere.

In the afternoon the two white brigades also moved forward. At nine o'clock they arrived at their camping ground, and the whole army was again collected together. Next morning the four squadrons of Egyptian horse, with a portion of the cavalry, went forward to reconnoitre, and one of the gunboats proceeded a few miles up the river. Neither saw anything of the enemy.

There had been heavy rain during the night. This had ceased at daybreak, and a strong wind speedily dried the sands, raising such clouds of dust that it was difficult to see above a few yards. The storm had also the effect of hindering the flotilla.

On the other side of the river, Stuart-Wortley's friendlies had a sharp brush with some Dervishes, whom they had come upon raiding a village, whose inhabitants had not obeyed the Khalifa's orders to move into Omdurman.

As the rainstorms continued, it was decided, by a council of war, that the health of the troops would suffer by a longer stay. On the 29th, therefore, the army set out in order of battle, ready to encounter the Khalifa's attack, but arrived without molestation at Um Teref, a short distance from Kerreri, where it was expected the enemy would give battle.

The camp was smaller than those hitherto made, and was protected by a strong zareba. The sentries were doubled, and patrols thrown out. Heavy rain set in after sunset, and almost a deluge poured down. The tents had been left behind, and as the little blanket shelters were soon soaked through, their occupants were speedily wet to the skin.

It was still raining when, at half-past five, the force again started. As before, the army was marching in fighting order. The day was cool and cloudy, and at one o'clock they halted at a village called Merreh, or Seg. The cavalry had come into touch with the Dervish patrols, but the latter, although numerous, avoided combat.

In one of the deserted villages was found one of Wingate's spies, in Dervish attire. He had left Omdurman thirty hours before, and brought the news that the Khalifa intended to attack at Kerreri. This place had been chosen because there was current an old prophecy, by a Persian sheik, to the effect that English soldiers would one day fight at Kerreri, and be destroyed there. It had, therefore, become an almost holy place to the Mahdists, and was called the death place of all the infidels; and, once a year, the Khalifa and his followers made a pilgrimage to it.

A few shots were fired during the night, and fires blazed on the hills to notify, to Omdurman, our precise position. The troops started again soon after daylight, facing now to the right and marching westward, to leave the bush and broken ground, and get out in the open desert, stretching away to Omdurman. The cavalry were widely spread out, and the Lancers ascended to the top of the hill of El Teb, from which a view of the Dervish camp was obtained.

It lay some ten miles due south. The Dervishes were disposed in three long lines, stretching from within two thousand yards of the Nile out into the desert, being careful to get, as they believed, beyond the range of the four gunboats that steamed quietly up.

After a short march the force halted near the river, two miles north of Kerreri. The place was convenient for camping, but the banks of the river were steep, and there was much difficulty in watering the horses and transport animals.

"We are in for another bad night," one of the General's staff said to Gregory, as the evening approached.

"It looks like it. Clouds are banking up fast. If the rain would but come in the daytime, instead of at night, one would not object to it much. It would lay the dust and cool the air. Besides, on the march we have other things to think of; and though, of course, we should be drenched to the skin, we should not mind it. But it is very unpleasant lying in a pool of water, with streams running in at one's neck."

"As to one's blanket, it is like a sponge, five minutes after the rain begins," the officer said.

"I am better off in that respect," Gregory remarked; "for, when I left my little tent behind, I kept a waterproof sheet instead of my second blanket. I had intended to use it tent fashion, but it was blown down in a minute, after the first storm burst. Now I stand up, wrap my blanket tightly round me, while my boy does the same with the waterproof sheet; and I keep moderately dry, except that the water will trickle in at the end, near my neck. But, on the other hand, the wrapping keeps me so hot that I might almost as well lie uncovered in the rain."

The staff had intended taking a few tents with them, but these were practically of no use at all, as all canvas had to be lowered by the time that "lights out" sounded, and after that hour no loud talking was permitted in the camp. This might have been a privation, had the weather been fine, but even the most joyous spirit had little desire for conversation, when the rain was falling in bucketfuls over him.

The officers of the white division lay down by their men, in the position they would occupy if an attack by the enemy took place. The officers of the Egyptian regiments lay together, just in rear of their men. As soon as the "last post" sounded, absolute silence reigned. The sentries, placed a very short distance out, kept their senses of sight and hearing on the alert; and with eye and ear strove to detect the approach of a lurking foe. Jaalin scouts were stationed outside the zareba, so as to give an early warning of the approach of the enemy; but no reliance could be placed upon them; for, altogether without discipline, they would probably creep under bushes, and endeavour to find some shelter from the pitiless downpour.

Had the Khalifa known his business, he would have taken advantage of the tempestuous night, and launched his warriors at the camp. Confident as the officers of the expedition were, in the ability of their men to repulse any assault that might be made in the daylight, it was felt that such an attack would cause terrible loss, and possibly grave disaster, if delivered at night. The enemy might not be discovered until within a few yards of the camp. The swish of the rain, and the almost incessant crash of thunder, would deaden the sound of their approach;

and, long before the troops could leap to their feet and prepare to receive them calmly, the Dervishes would be upon them. As the latter were enormously stronger in numbers, the advantage of superior weapons would be lost in a hand-to-hand fight, and in the inevitable confusion, as the troops in reserve would be unable to open fire, while ignorant of the precise position of friends and foes.

The Khalifa, however, was relying upon prophecy. It was at Kerreri that the infidel army was to be utterly destroyed, and he may have thought that it would be tempting fate, were he to precipitate an action before the invaders reached the spot where their doom had been pronounced.

Even more miserable than night was the hour before dawn. Lying still, drenched to the skin as they were, Nature prevailed, and the men obtained some sleep; but when they rose to their feet, and threw off the sodden blankets, they felt the full misery of eight hours' drenching. They were cold now, as well as wet, and as they endeavoured to squeeze the water from their clothes, and to restore circulation by swinging their arms, but few words were spoken; and the rising of the sun, which was regarded as a terrible infliction during the day, was eagerly looked for. No sooner did it appear above the horizon than the spirits of the men rose rapidly, and they laughed, joked, and made light of the inconveniences of the situation.

An hour later, their clothes were nearly dry. By that time they were all well on their way, the brigades, as before, marching in echelon—Wauchope's brigade on the left, Lyttleton's farther to the right but more to the rear, the three Egyptian brigades farther out on the plain, the 21st Lancers scouting the ground in front of the British division, and the native cavalry and camel corps out beyond the right of the Egyptians.

All expected that, at least, they should have a skirmish before they reached Kerreri, where they were to encamp; but, as they advanced, it was found that the Dervishes had fallen back from that line, and had joined the Khalifa's main force near Omdurman.

By ten in the morning the army had arrived at its camping place, which was in the southern part of the ground occupied by the straggling village. As usual, both extremities of the line rested on the Nile, forming a semicircle, in which the baggage animals and stores were placed, in charge of Collinson's brigade. The gunboats took up their position, to cover the ground over which an enemy must approach to the attack.

While the infantry were settling down, the cavalry and camel corps went out scouting. Signallers soon mounted a rugged hill, named Surgham, and from here a fine view was obtained of Omdurman, and the Khalifa's army. Omdurman was six miles away, covering a wide tract of ground, with but few buildings rising above the general level, the one conspicuous object being the great tomb of the Mahdi, with its white dome.

In the outskirts of the town were the white tents of the Dervish army. For the present these were unoccupied, the whole force being drawn up, in regular line, out on the plain; about halfway between the town and Surgham Hill. It was formed in five divisions, each of which was bright with banners of all colours, sizes, and shapes. The Khalifa's own division was in the centre, where his great black banner, waving from a lofty flagstaff, could be plainly made out.

The Lancers, Egyptian cavalry, and camel corps continued to advance, capturing several parties of footmen, principally Jaalins, who probably lagged purposely behind the retiring Dervishes, in order to be taken. At times the cavalry attempted to charge the Dervish horsemen, when these approached, but in no case did the latter await the attack.

Presently, above the occasional musketry fire, came the boom of a heavy gun. There was a thrill of excitement in the camp. The gunboats had arrived opposite Omdurman, and had opened fire upon the Dervish riverside forts. These were strongly constructed; but, as in the forts at Metemmeh and Shabluka, the embrasures were so faultily constructed that the guns could only be brought to bear upon the portion of the river directly facing them, and the four gunboats passed them without receiving any material damage, and were so able to maintain the bombardment without receiving any fire in return. At the same time, they landed the forty-pounder guns on an island but a short distance from the town, and thence opened fire with lyddite shells upon it. The howitzers were trained upon the Mahdi's tomb, and soon great holes were knocked in the dome.

It could be seen, from the top of the hill, that this caused great excitement in the Dervish lines, and a number of their horsemen rode out against the Lancers, and drove in their advance scouts; but, on the main body of the regiment moving forward, they fell back to their line; and almost immediately a heavy body of infantry moved out, their intention evidently being to surround and cut off the regiment, while at the same time a general advance took place. The Colonel of the Lancers dismounted a portion of his men, and these checked the advance of the enemy, until the rest fell back.

The news of the advance was signalled to General Kitchener, and the whole force at once took their position, in fighting order. Believing that a general attack on the camp would now be made, the cavalry fell back on either flank, so as to clear the way for the fire of the artillery and infantry.

The Dervishes had a good view of our camp from the top of Surgham, but the Khalifa apparently considered that it was too late in the day for a general attack, and drew off his men to their former position, and the rest of the afternoon and evening passed quietly. As the men ate their meal, of tinned meat and biscuit, they were in higher spirits than they had been since the advance began. Hitherto, they had been in constant apprehension lest the Dervishes should shun a battle, and would retire across the desert to El Obeid, or elsewhere; and that they would have to perform interminable desert marches, only to find, on arriving at the goal, that the enemy had again moved off. The events of the day, however, seemed to show that this fear was groundless, and that the Khalifa had determined to fight a decisive battle for the defence of his capital.

The British soldier is ready to support any fatigue, and any hardship, with a prospect of a fight at the end; and, during the advance, he is always haunted by the fear that the enemy will retire, or give in on his approach. This fear was stronger than usual on this expedition, for there was no question as to the greatly superior mobility of the Dervishes; and it was evident that, if they chose to avoid fighting, they had it in their power to do so.

CHAPTER 14:

Omdurman.

The night passed quietly, except that shots were occasionally fired by Dervishes who crept up within range; and that, once, a mounted man, who had apparently lost his way, rode fearlessly into camp; and then, finding himself close to the troops, turned his horse and galloped off again. No shot followed him, as the orders were strict that the camp was not to be alarmed, unless in the case of a serious attack.

At half past three the bugle sounded, and the troops were soon astir. The animals were watered and fed, and the men had a breakfast of cocoa or tea, with biscuits and tinned meat. At half past four Colonel Broadwood, commanding the Egyptian cavalry, sent out a squadron to the hills on the west, and another to Surgham Hill.

The latter arrived at their destination at two minutes past five, when daylight had just broken. The officer in command saw at once that the Dervish army had been reinforced in the night, and were marching to attack us. News was at once sent back to the camp, where all was in readiness for an advance.

No news could have been more welcome. It was one thing to attack the Dervishes in their chosen position, and to carry the narrow streets of Omdurman at the point of the bayonet—the Dervishes had shown, at Abu Hamed, how desperately they could fight under such circumstances—and another to meet them while attacking our position, in the open. This was protected, along the line occupied by the white troops, by a hedge; while the three Egyptian brigades had constructed shelter trenches. These afforded a vastly better defence against a foe advancing by daylight, although they would not be so effective in checking a sudden and determined rush, in the darkness.

Preparations were at once made to oppose the enemy. The Sirdar and his staff were already mounting, when the news arrived. The horses were now taken to the rear, the reserve ammunition boxes lifted from the mules' backs, and the animals led to a sheltered position, behind some huts.

The guns were wheeled up into positions between the infantry brigades. The troops were disposed in line, two deep; two companies of each battalion, with the stretchers and bearers, taking post at a short distance farther back, to reinforce the front line if hardly pressed, and to supply it from the reserve store of ammunition.

Already the gunboats had recommenced the bombardment of Omdurman, and the mosque of the Mahdi, but as soon as news came that the Dervishes were advancing to the attack, they were signalled to return to cover the flank of the zareba. On their arrival, they took up a position whence they could shell the line by which the Dervishes were advancing, and which would bring them apparently five or six hundred yards west of Surgham Hill.

The Lancers at once started forward to cover the left flank of the position. In a few minutes they reached Surgham Hill, and joined the Egyptian squadron there.

The sight from the crest of Surgham Hill was grand. The enemy's front extended over three miles. The lines were deep and compact, and the banners floated above them. They were advancing steadily and in good order, and their battle cries rose and fell in measured cadence. Their numbers were variously estimated at from fifty to seventy thousand—a superb force, consisting of men as brave as any in the world, and animated by religious fanaticism, and an intense hatred of those they were marching to assail.

In the centre were the Khalifa's own corps, twenty thousand strong. On their right was the banner of Yacoub, his brother, and beyond, two divisions led by well-known emirs; while on his left was the division led by his son, Osman, known as Sheik Ed Din, the nominal commander-in-chief of the whole force.

The 21st Lancers, out in skirmishing order, were speedily driven back by the Dervishes, and retired into the zareba. When the latter came near enough to see the small British force, a shout of exultation rose from their ranks, for they felt certain now of surrounding and annihilating the infidels, according to the prophecy.

On our side the satisfaction was no less marked. The front line moved forward to the thorny hedge, and prepared to open fire above it. The black troops uttered a joyful shout of defiance, as they took their places in their trenches.

When the enemy were two thousand eight hundred yards away, the three batteries on the left of the zareba opened fire; and two batteries on the right, and a number of Maxims, joined in pouring shell and bullets into the thickest of the Dervish mass round the Khalifa's banner. The effect was terrible. For a moment the Dervish lines halted, astonished at the storm to which they were exposed. But it was only for a moment. The wide gaps were filled up, and at a quicker pace than before, the great line swept on; the banner bearers and Baggara horsemen pushing forward to the front, to encourage the infantry.

Seeing how persistently they were coming on, the Sirdar ordered the men of Lyttleton's brigade to open fire at long range. The Grenadiers were the first to begin, firing volleys in sections. The other regiments of the brigade were soon hard at it, but neither they nor the Maxims appeared to be doing serious execution, while the terrible effect of the shell fire could really be seen. But, although great numbers of the enemy were killed or wounded by the bursting shells, there was no halt in the forward movement.

Suddenly, over the crest and sides of the Surgham Hill, the division of the Dervish right, reinforced by a portion of Yacoub's division, appeared; and over fifteen thousand men came streaming down the hill, waving banners and shouting their war cries. They were led by their emirs, on horseback; but the infantry kept pace with these, occasionally discharging their rifles at random.

The guns of the three batteries, and one of the Maxims, were swung round and opened upon them. They were less than a mile away, and the whole of Gatacre's division opened a terrific fire. Still the Dervishes held on, leaving the ground they passed over white with fallen men. From seventeen hundred yards the sights had to be lowered rapidly, but at a thousand yards they held their foe. No man could cross the ground swept by the hail of balls. So rapid and sustained was the fire, that men had to retire to refill their pouches from the reserve ammunition, and the rifles were so heated that they could no longer be held. In some cases the men changed their weapons for those of the companies in reserve, in others these companies closed up and took the places of the front line. Not for a moment was there any cessation in the fire.

Unable to do more, Yacoub's men moved towards the front and joined the main body, whose advance had been checked by the fire of Maxwell's Egyptian brigade. A few rounds had been fired by the three cannon that the Khalifa had brought out with him, but they all fell short.

On our side the casualties had been few. In their desperate attempt to get at close quarters, the Dervish riflemen had not stopped to reload the weapons they had discharged, and there was practically no return to the awful fire to which they had been exposed.

But while Yacoub's force had been terribly punished, and the main body, brought to a standstill at a distance of fourteen hundred yards, had suffered almost as heavily, the battle had not gone so well to the right of our position, towards which the Khalifa was now moving. Broadwood's horse, and the camel corps, had been driven off the hill they occupied; and so fierce was the attack that three of the guns of the horse battery had to be left behind. The camel corps were ordered to retire rapidly, and make for shelter to the right rear of the camp. The force made two or three stands, and the Egyptian cavalry more than once charged the pursuing horsemen. The gunboats opened fire, and covered the final retirement of the camel corps, which had lost eighty men.

The cavalry did not retire to the zareba, but continued to fall back, occasionally turning and facing the enemy, until they were five miles away; when the Dervishes gave up the pursuit, and sat down to rest after their tremendous exertions. Although forced to retire, the cavalry had done good service, for they had drawn off a great body of the enemy at a critical moment, and these were unable to return and take part in the battle still raging.

At length, the Khalifa moved off with all his force behind the western hills, and for a short time there was a lull in the battle. Many of the wounded tribesmen crawled up to within seven or eight hundred yards of the zareba, and there opened fire. Their aim was good, and men began to drop fast, in spite of the volleys fired to clear off the troublesome foe. But their fire was soon disregarded for, from the ravines in the range of low hills, behind which the Khalifa's force had disappeared, a mass of men burst out at a hard run. From their shelter behind Surgham Hill, a portion of the force who were there also swept down to join the Khalifa, while Yacoub advanced from the southwest, and another body from the west.

Instantly the infantry and artillery fire broke out again. On the previous day, the distance had been measured and marked on several conspicuous objects; and the storm of shells tore the ranks of the enemy, and the rifles swept them with a rain of bullets. But, in face of all this, the Dervishes continued to advance at a run, their numbers thinning every minute.

Two or three hundred horsemen, with their emirs, dashed at the zareba at full gallop. Shrapnel, Maxim and rifle bullets swept their ranks, but nearer and nearer they came, with lessening numbers every yard, until the last of them fell within about two hundred yards of Maxwell's line. Animated by the example, the infantry rushed forward. The black flag was planted within nine hundred yards of Maxwell's left; but, in addition to the Egyptian fire, the crossfire of the British divisions poured upon those around it.

The main body began to waver, but the Khalifa and his emirs did their best to encourage and rally them. The flag was riddled with balls, and the men who held it were shot down; but others seized the post of honour, until a pile of bodies accumulated round it.

At last, but one man remained standing there. For a minute he stood quietly immovable, then fell forward dead. Then the Dervishes lost heart, and began to fall back in ones and twos, then in dozens, until the last had disappeared behind the hills.

The troops then turned their attention to the men who, lying in shelter, were still maintaining their fire. There were fully a thousand of these, and the greater portion of our casualties took place from their fire, while the troops were occupied in repelling the main attack. It was not long, however, before bullets and shell proved too much for them; and those who survived crawled away, to join their kinsmen behind the hills.

It was eight o'clock now, and the victory had apparently been won. Some ten thousand of the Khalifa's best troops had been killed or wounded. In the British division, one officer and one man had been killed, and three officers and sixty-five men wounded. The latter were at once placed on board the hospital barges. Fresh ammunition was served out and, half an hour after the last shot was fired, the army prepared to march on Omdurman.

It was most important that they should arrive at the town before Ed Din's Dervishes should reach it; for unless they could do so, the loss that would be incurred in capturing it would be vastly greater than that which had been suffered in the battle. At nine o'clock the start was made. The troops advanced in brigades. Lyttleton led on the left, Wauchope was on his right, Maxwell somewhat in the rear, while still more to the right came Lewis, and farther out on the plain Macdonald. They formed roughly half a semicircle. Lyttleton, followed by Wauchope, was to march between the river and Surgham Hill. Maxwell was to cross over the hill, while Lewis and Macdonald were to keep farther out to the right. Collinson's Egyptian brigade was to guard the stores and materials left behind.

The 21st Lancers scouted ahead of the British brigades, to discover if any foe were lurking behind Surgham Hill. When about half a mile south of the hill, they saw a small party of Dervish cavalry and some infantry, who were hiding in what looked like a shallow water course. The four squadrons rode forward at a gallop. A sharp musketry fire opened upon them, but without hesitation they dashed headlong at the Dervishes, when they found that, instead of a hundred and fifty foemen as they had supposed, some fifteen hundred Dervishes were lying concealed in the water course.

It was too late to draw rein, and with a cheer the cavalry rode down into the midst of the foe. There was a wild, fierce fight, lance against spear, sabre against sword, the butt-end of a rifle or the deadly knife. Some cut their way through unscathed. Others were surrounded and cut off. Splendid feats of heroism were performed. Many of those who got over returned to rescue officers or comrades, until at last all the survivors climbed the bank.

The brunt of the fighting fell upon the two central squadrons. Not only were the enemy thickest where they charged, but the opposite bank of the deep nullah was composed of rough boulders, almost impassable by horses. These squadrons lost sixteen killed and nineteen wounded. Altogether, twenty-two officers and men were killed, and fifty wounded; and there were one hundred and nineteen casualties among the horses.

Once across, the survivors gathered at a point where their fire commanded the water course; and, dismounting, speedily drove the

Dervishes from it. On examining it afterwards, it was found that sixty dead Dervishes lay where the central squadrons had cut their way through.

The charge, in its daring and heroism, resembled that of the 23rd Light Dragoons at Talavera. The fall into the ravine, on that occasion, was much deeper than that into which the Lancers dashed; but it was not occupied by a desperate force, and although many were injured by the fall, it was in their subsequent charge, against a whole French division, that they were almost annihilated.

Both incidents were, like the Balaclava charge, magnificent; but they were not war. A desperate charge, to cover the retreat of a defeated army, is legitimate and worthy of all praise, even if the gallant men who make it are annihilated; but this was not the case at Talavera, nor at Omdurman. It was a brilliant but a costly mistake. The bravery shown was superb, and the manner in which officers and men rode back into the struggling mass, to rescue comrades, beyond all praise; but the charge should never have been made, and the lives were uselessly sacrificed.

As yet, all was quiet at other points. Bodies of the enemy could be seen, making their way towards Omdurman. The battery opposite the town had, from early morning, been keeping up a fire from its heavy guns upon it; but, save for the occasional shot of a lurking Dervish, all was quiet elsewhere.

While the cavalry charge was in progress, Gregory had moved along the line of the Egyptian brigades with General Hunter. Suddenly, from behind the hills where the Khalifa had fallen back with his defeated army, a column of fully twelve thousand men, led by the banner bearers and emirs, poured out again. A strong body sprang forward from another valley, and made for the southeastern corner of Macdonald's brigade, which had moved almost due west from the position it had occupied in the zareba; while the large force that had chased away the Egyptian cavalry were seen, returning to attack him in the rear.

General Hunter, who was riding between Macdonald's and Lewis's brigades, which were now a good mile apart, exclaimed to Gregory, who happened to be the nearest officer to him:

"Ride to Macdonald, and tell him to fall back, if possible!"

Then he turned, and galloped off to fetch up reinforcements. But the need was already seen. The sudden uproar had attracted the attention of the whole army, and the Sirdar instantly grasped the situation. The moment was indeed critical. If Macdonald's brigade were overwhelmed, it might have meant a general disaster; and the Sirdar at once sent orders to Wauchope's brigade, to go, at the double, to Macdonald's aid.

Fortunately Colonel Long, who commanded the artillery, had sent three batteries with Macdonald's brigade. Collinson's brigade were far away near the river, Lewis's were themselves threatened. It was evident, at once, that no assistance could reach Macdonald in time. When Gregory reached him, the Dervishes were already approaching.

"It cannot be done," Macdonald said sternly, when Gregory delivered the message. "We must fight!"

Indeed, to retreat would have meant destruction. The fire would have been ineffective, and the thirty thousand fierce foes would have been among them. There was nothing to do but to fight.

Macdonald had marched out with the 11th Soudanese on his left, the 2nd Egyptians in the centre, and the 10th Soudanese on the right—all in line. Behind, in column, were the 9th Soudanese. The last were at once brought up into line, to face the advancing enemy.

Fortunately, the Sheik Ed Din's force was still some little distance away. The batteries took their place in the openings between the battalions, and the Maxim-Nordenfeldts were soon carrying death into the advancing foe; while the Martini-Henry, with which the black and Egyptian troops were armed, mowed them down as by a scythe. The Soudanese battalions fired, as was their custom, individually, as fast as they could load; the Egyptian battalion by steady volleys.

Still the enemy pressed on, until they were within two hundred yards of the line. The emirs and other leaders, Baggara horse and many spearmen, still held on; until they fell, a few feet only from the steady infantry. The rear ranks of the Dervishes now began to fall back, and the desperate charges of their leaders grew feebler; but Ed Din's division was now within a thousand yards. Macdonald, confident that the main attack was broken, threw back the 9th Soudanese to face it, and wheeled a couple of his batteries to support them.

The already retreating Dervishes, encouraged by the arrival of Ed Din's division, returned to the attack. The 11th Soudanese swung round, to aid the 9th in their struggle with Ed Din's troops. The charges of the Dervishes were impetuous in the extreme. Regardless of the storm of shell and bullets they rushed on, and would have thrust themselves between the 9th and 11th, had not the 2nd Egyptians, wheeling at the double, thrown themselves into the gap.

The Dervishes pressed right up to them, and bayonet and spear frequently crossed; but in a fight of this kind, discipline tells its tale. The blacks and Egyptians maintained their lines, steadily and firmly; and against these, individual effort and courage, even of the highest quality, were in vain.

The ground being now cleared, the gunboats opened with Maxim and cannon upon the rear of the Dervishes. The camel corps coming up, each man dismounted and added his fire to the turmoil; and, finally, three of Wauchope's battalions arrived, and the Lincolns, doubling to the right, opened a terrible flank fire. The Dervishes broke and fled; not, as usual, sullenly and reluctantly, but at full speed, stooping low to escape the storm of bullets that pursued them.

Zaki had, throughout the day, kept close to Gregory, ready to hold his horse when he dismounted; but, quick-footed as he was, he was left behind when his master galloped across to Macdonald. He was up, however, in the course of a minute or two, and Gregory was glad to see him, for the horse was kicking and plunging at the roar of the approaching enemy; and was almost maddened when to this was added the crash of the batteries and musketry.

"Put my blanket round his head, Zaki," Gregory said, when the black ran up. "Wrap it round so that he cannot see. Hold the bridle with one hand, and stroke him with the other, and keep on talking to him; he knows your voice. I don't want to dismount if I can help it, for with my field glasses I see everything that is taking place, and I will tell you how matters are going."

For the moment, it seemed as if the surging crowd streaming down must carry all before it; but the steadiness with which the 9th Soudanese moved into their place on the flank of the line, and the other regiments remained, as if on parade, soon reassured him. The terrible slaughter that was taking place in the ranks of the Dervishes soon showed that, in that quarter at least, there was no fear of things going wrong; but he could not but look anxiously towards the great mass of men approaching from the north.

It was a matter of minutes. Would the present attack be repulsed in time for the position to be changed, to meet the coming storm? Occasionally, Gregory looked back to see if reinforcements were coming. Wauchope's brigade was visible over the tops of the scattered bushes. The movements of the line showed that they were coming on at the double, but they were farther away than Ed Din's host, and the latter were running like deer.

He felt a deep sense of relief when the 9th Soudanese were thrown back, performing the movement as quietly and steadily as if on a drill ground; and two batteries of artillery galloped across to their support. He had hardly expected such calm courage from the black battalion. As to the bravery of the Soudanese troops, there was no question. They were of the same blood and race as their foes, and had shown how bravely they could fight in many a previous battle; but he was not prepared for the steady way in which they worked, under such novel circumstances; and although they, too, must have known that every moment was of consequence, they moved without haste or hurry into the new position, scarcely glancing at the torrent which was rushing on towards them.

Not less steadily and quietly did the 11th, considered to be the crack regiment of the brigade, swing round; and as calmly and firmly did the Egyptian battalion—composed of the peasants who, but twenty years before, had been considered among the most cowardly of people, a host of whom would have fled before a dozen of the dreaded Dervishes—march into the gap between the two black regiments, and manfully hold their own.

And yet, he could not but feel sorry for the valiant savages who, under so awful a fire, still pressed forward to certain death; their numbers withering away at every step, until they dwindled to nothing, only to be replaced by a fresh band, which darted forward to meet a similar fate; and yet, when he remembered the wholesale slaughter at Metemmeh, the annihilation of countless villages and of their inhabitants, and, above all, the absolute destruction of the army of Hicks Pasha, the capture of Khartoum, the murder of Gordon, and the reduction to a state of slavery of all the peaceful tribes of the Soudan, he could not but feel that the annihilation of these human tigers, and the wiping out of their false creed, was a necessity.

When the last shot was fired, he dismounted and leant against his horse, completely unnerved by the tremendous excitement that had been compressed into the space of half an hour. Zaki was in ecstasy at the victory. The ruthless massacre of so many of his tribesmen, the ruin of his native village, and the murder of his relations was avenged, at last. The reign of the Dervishes was over. Henceforth men could till their fields in peace. It was possible that, even yet, he might find his mother and sisters still alive, in the city but a few miles away, living in wretched existence as slaves of their captors.

Tears of joy streamed down his cheeks. He would have liked to help to revenge the wrongs of his tribe, but his master needed him; and moreover, there was no place for an untrained man in the ranks of the Soudanese regiments. They were doing their work better than he could. Still, it was the one bitter drop in his intense joy, that he had not been able to aid in the conflict.

He expressed this to Gregory.

"You have had your share in the fight, Zaki, just as I have had. I have not fired a shot, but I have been in the battle, and run its risks, and so have you. Each of us has done his duty, and we can say, for the rest of our lives, that we have borne our share in the great battle that has smashed up the power of the Khalifa, and the rule of the Dervishes."

CHAPTER 15:

Khartoum.

There was no pause or rest for the troops who had been fighting, for so many hours, in the heat of the African sun. It was all important to occupy Omdurman before the remnants of the Khalifa's army reached it; and as it was known that the Khalifa himself had returned there, it was hoped that he might be captured.

It was ten o'clock when Macdonald's brigade fired their last shot. In half an hour, the troops went forward again. The field presented a terrible appearance, being thickly dotted with dead, from the Surgham Hill across the plain; and round, by the Kerreri Hills, to the spot where Macdonald's brigade had made their stand. There were comparatively few wounded; for, wiry and hardy as they were, the wounded Dervishes, unless mortally hit, were for the most part able to crawl or walk away; which they had done unmolested, for on each occasion after the bugle sounded cease firing, not a shot was fired at them. But of dead there were fully ten thousand, scattered more or less thickly over the plain.

From the position in which they were placed, the Egyptian troops, as they marched south, passed the spot where the Khalifa's flag was still flying, as it had been left after its last defenders had fallen. Slatin, who was with the army, rode over the plain at the Sirdar's request, to ascertain if any of the Dervish leaders were among the fallen. He recognized many, but the Khalifa, his son Ed Din, and Osman Digna were not among them. The last-named had ever been chary of exposing himself, and had probably, as was his custom, viewed the battle from a safe distance. But round the flag were the Khalifa's brother, Yacoub, and ten or twelve of the leading emirs.

On our side, the loss had been comparatively light. Our total number of casualties, including the wounded, was five hundred and twenty-four; towards which Macdonald's brigade contributed one hundred and twenty-eight. Marching steadily on, the force halted in the outlying suburb of Omdurman, at midday, to obtain much needed food and water. As soon as the cavalry had watered their horses, they were sent round to the south of the town to cut off fugitives, and some of the gunboats moved up to their support.

Deputations of the townsfolk, Greeks and natives, came out and offered to surrender. They said that the Khalifa was in his house, and that he had about a thousand of his bodyguard with him, but that they could not offer any successful resistance. The town was full of fugitive Dervishes; many thousands of them were there—among them a great number of wounded.

At half past four the Sirdar, with his staff, entered the town; accompanied by Maxwell's Egyptian brigade. Only a few shots were fired. The Dervish courage was broken. It was to the followers of the Prophet, and not to the infidels, that the plains of Kerreri had proved fatal. It was their bodies, and not those of the white soldiers, that were strewn there so thickly. The promise of the Khalifa had been falsified, the tomb of the Mahdi was crumbling into ruins, the bravest of their troops had fallen—what more was there to be done?

As Slatin Pasha rode in at the head of the troops, he was instantly recognized by the people, among whom, for years, he had been a prisoner; and on his assurances that mercy would be shown to all, if there was no resistance, numbers of the Dervishes came out from their houses and huts, and laid down their arms.

The women flocked out into the streets, uttering their long and quavering cries of welcome. To them the entry of the British was a relief from a living death, as almost all were captives taken in war, or in the Dervish raids upon quiet villages. They could scarce even yet believe that they were free—that their tyrants were slain or fugitives.

Intense was the surprise and relief of the population, when they were told that there would be no looting—no harm done to any by the conquerors; that all would be free, if they chose, to depart to their homes, and to take their few belongings with them.

The scene in the town was awful—the stench overpowering! The Dervishes were absolutely ignorant of all sanitary methods—pools of the foulest slush abounded, and thousands of dead animals, in all stages of decomposition, lay about the streets. Among them were numerous dead bodies, principally of girls and women, who had been killed by their brutal husbands or masters, to prevent them from falling into the hands of the British. There were also many dead Dervishes, and others desperately wounded.

Strangely enough, the latter did not seem to regard their victorious enemy with the hate that had been exhibited by many of the wounded in the field; and some of them half raised themselves, and saluted the Sirdar and his staff as they passed along.

Presently, there was a commotion in the crowd. The wall of the great granary had been breached, by some of the lyddite shells, and the grain had poured out into the street. The natives near ran up to gather it; and, finding that they were not molested by the British, the news spread rapidly. The crowds in the streets melted away; and the inhabitants, for the most part half starved, made a mad rush to the spot, where in a short time many thousands of men, women, and children were hard at work, gathering and carrying off the grain.

In the meantime the Sirdar, with a party of Maxwell's brigade, passed along by the side of the great wall enclosing the buildings, and square mile of ground, in which were the Khalifa's house, the tomb of the Mahdi, the arsenal, storehouses, and the homes of the principal emirs.

As soon as they had turned the corner of the wall, in view of the tomb and the Khalifa's house, a brisk fire was opened by the garrison. Fortunately, the wall was not loopholed, and they had to get on the top of it, or on to the flat roofs of the houses, to fire. Maxwell's men soon silenced them, and on the troops passing in through the breaches, and along the wall, most of the Dervishes at once surrendered.

For a time, further advance was barred by an inner wall, that still intervened between them and the Khalifa's house. After the gunboats' fire had cleared away a number of the Dervishes clustered outside the south wall, the Sirdar and his staff entered by a gateway, and moved towards the Khalifa's house. This was searched by Slatin Pasha, and several officers and soldiers; but, to the general disappointment, it was found that the Khalifa had escaped but a short time before, carrying with him his treasure; his wives having been sent off, as soon as he returned from the field of battle.

The Mahdi's tomb was a ruin. A large portion of the dome had been knocked away, and the falling fragments had smashed the iron railings that surrounded the tomb, itself.

There was nothing more to be done. The pursuit of the Khalifa, mounted, as he would be, on fresh horses, was out of the question. It was already almost dark, and men and horses had been at work since before daybreak. The town was in a very disturbed state—large numbers of the Dervishes were still possessed of their arms, and the greater portion of the troops were withdrawn from the pestilential town. Next morning a larger force was marched in, and the work of disarmament completed.

The cavalry went out and scouted the country, and brought in large numbers of prisoners. The men belonging to the tribes that had renounced Mahdism—Jaalin and others—were at once allowed to leave for their homes; and numbers of others, whose appearance was peaceful, and who had at once given up their arms, were also released; but there were still no fewer than eleven thousand prisoners, among them some of the Khalifa's emirs.

Many of the townspeople had started, the previous evening, for the field of battle; to bury the bodies of their friends who had fallen, and to bring in the wounded. Of the latter, after our own men had been attended to, fully nine thousand received aid and attention from the British doctors.

On the morning after the occupation, the work of purification began. Great numbers of the unwounded prisoners, and of the townspeople, were set to work to clean the streets; and, in a couple of days, the wider thoroughfares and avenues had been thoroughly cleansed.

Having but little to do, Gregory went into the Khalifa's arsenal. This building was full of war material of all kinds; including a perfectly appointed battery of Krupp guns, numbers of old cannon, modern machine-guns, rifles and pistols; mixed up with musical instruments, suits of chain armour, steel helmets, hundreds of battle flags, and thousands of native spears, swords, and shields. Besides these the collection comprised ivory, percussion caps, lead, copper, and bronze, looms, pianos, sewing machines, boilers, steam engines, agricultural implements, ostrich feathers, wooden and iron bedsteads, paints, India rubber, leather water bottles, clothes, three state coaches, and an American buggy. There were also a modern smithy, where gunpowder, shell, bullets, and cartridge cases were made and stored; and a well-appointed engineers' shop and foundry, with several steam engines, turning lathes, and other tools. The machinery had been brought from Gordon's arsenal at Khartoum, where the foreman had been employed; and the workmen were, for the most part, Greeks.

The battle was fought on Friday, the 2nd of September. On Sunday a flotilla of boats, containing detachments from all the British and Egyptian regiments, and every officer who could be spared from duty, proceeded up the river to Khartoum. The ruined and deserted city looked delightful, after the sand, dirt, and wretchedness of Omdurman. The gardens of the governor's house, and other principal buildings, had run wild; and the green foliage was restful indeed, to the eye, after the waste of sand, rock, and scrub that had been traversed by the army on its way from Wady Halfa.

The vessels drew up opposite a grove of tall palms. Beyond them appeared what had been the government house. The upper story was gone, the windows were filled up with bricks, and a large acacia stood in front of the building.

The troops formed up before the palace, in three sides of a square—the Egyptians were to the left, looking from the river, and the British to the right—the Sirdar, and the generals of the divisions and brigades, facing the centre. Two flagstaffs had been raised on the upper story. The Sirdar gave the signal, and the British and Egyptian flags were run up. As they flew out, one of the gunboats fired a salute, the Guards' band struck up "God Save the Queen!" and the band of the 11th Soudanese then played the Khedive's hymn, while the Generals and all present stood in salute, with their hands to the peak of their helmets. The Sirdar's call for three cheers for the Queen was enthusiastically responded to, every helmet being raised. Similar cheers were then given for the Khedive, the bands again struck up, and twenty-one guns were fired.

As the last gun echoed out, the Guards played the Dead March, in Saul; and the black band the march called Toll for the Brave, the latter in memory of the Khedive's subjects, who had died with Gordon. Then minute guns were fired, and four chaplains—Anglican, Presbyterian, Methodist, and Catholic—by turns read a psalm or a prayer. The pipers then wailed a dirge, and finally the Soudanese bands played Gordon's favourite hymn, Abide with Me.

At the conclusion, General Hunter and the other officers shook hands with the Sirdar, one by one. Kitchener himself was deeply moved, and well he might be! Fourteen years of his life had been spent in preparing for, and carrying out, this campaign; and now the great task was done. Gordon was avenged. Of the Dervish host, the remnant were scattered fugitives. The Mahdi's cause, the foulest and most bloodstained tyranny that had ever existed, transforming as it did a flourishing province into an almost uninhabited desert, was crushed forever; and it was his patient and unsparing labour, his wonderful organization, that had been the main factor in the work. No wonder that even the Iron Sirdar almost broke down, at such a moment.

The bugles sounded, and the troops broke up their formation; and, for half an hour, wandered through the empty chambers of the palace, and the wild and beautiful garden. Another bugle call, and they streamed down to the water's edge, took to the boats, and returned to Omdurman.

The long-delayed duty, which England owed to one of her noblest sons, had been done. Gordon had had his burial. None knew where his bones reposed, but that mattered little. In the place where he was slain, all honour had been done to him; and the British flag waved over the spot where he disappeared, forever, from the sight of his countrymen.

On Gregory's return, he found Zaki in a state of the highest excitement.

"Why, what is the matter with you, Zaki?"

"Oh, master, I have found my two sisters!"

"That is good news, indeed. I am very glad to hear it, Zaki. How did you find them?"

"While you were away, Master, I had been walking through the town; and when I was passing near the outskirts, a woman came to a door, and looked very hard at me. Then she suddenly drew aside the cloth from her face and cried, 'Surely it is Zaki!'

"Then I knew her—she was my elder sister. Then another woman came to the door—it was my younger sister, and you can imagine my joy. Both had been married to Baggaras, who had carried them off. Their husbands had gone to the battle, and had not returned; and some neighbours who had gone to the battlefield, next day, brought back news that they had found both bodies; so one sister came to stay with the other. People had told them that it was safe to go out, and that no one was injured who did so; but they had a store of grain in the house, and they decided to wait and see what happened.

"One of them, seeing me come along, and observing that I belonged to the Jaalin, came out to ask me the news; and they were as delighted as I was, at our meeting."

"And your mother, do they know anything of her?"

"She was killed, Master," Zaki said sorrowfully. "I thought possibly it would be so. The Dervishes did not carry off old women. They killed them, and the little children. I had never hoped to see her again; but I did think, when we entered Omdurman, that my sisters might be here."

"What are they going to do?"

"They will go down to Berber. I have told them that many of the people here are going down, and that they will find no difficulty in joining a party. They are sure to find people they know, at Berber, for most of the Jaalin who have escaped have gone there, since we occupied the place. I told them that I would give them what money I had; for, since I have been in my lord's service, I have had no occasion to spend aught that he has paid me."

"I have no doubt, Zaki, that I can arrange for them to go down in one of the empty store boats. I believe that many of the captives who have been released will be sent down that way; and, of course, I shall be glad to give your sisters enough to keep them, for some time, at Berber."

"My lord is too good," Zaki said gratefully.

"Nonsense, Zaki! You saved my life, and I owe you a great deal. I will go down, at once, to the river—that is, if your sisters are ready to start tomorrow—and I have no doubt the transport officer will give me an order, for them, to go in one of the boats."

As he had expected, he had no difficulty in making arrangements. Several of the native boats, that had already landed their stores, would leave on the following day; and Gregory obtained an order for the passage of the two women. He then drew some money from the paymaster and, on his return to headquarters, gave Zaki a hundred dollars for his sisters.

The black was overpowered with joy and, going off, returned with the two girls—for they were little more. Each took one of Gregory's hands, and pressed it to her forehead and heart, and murmured her thanks.

"Do not thank me," he said. "It is but a small part of the debt that I owe your brother. I do not know whether he has told you that he saved my life, at the risk of his own."

"I have been thinking, my lord," Zaki said, "that it would be well for them to go down in the boat as far as Dongola. Our village is not many miles from that place, and many of our people fled there; and doubtless they will return to their villages, and plant their fields, now that they have no longer any fear of the Dervishes. At any rate, they are certain to meet friends, at Dongola."

"Very well, I will get the order altered. There will be no difficulty about that. I shall be very glad to know that you will have a home to go to, when this war is quite over."

"I shall never go, as long as my lord will keep me," Zaki said, fervently.

"I certainly shall not part with you, Zaki, as long as I remain in this country, which will probably be for a long time."

The next day, Zaki aided in carrying his sisters' goods down to the river bank, and saw them on board one of the native craft, which carried also fifteen or twenty other fugitives.

"Now, Mr. Hilliard," General Hunter said, that morning, "you can devote yourself to the object for which you came here. Unquestionably, there must be many among the prisoners who fought at El Obeid. You may gather all particulars of the battle, from their lips.

"The greater portion of the white troops will march down the country, at once. Of course, I don't know what your plans may be; but unless you have a very good reason to the contrary, I should certainly advise you to retain your position in the Egyptian army. A great deal of work will have to be done, before matters are quite settled down; and then civil administration of some sort will, of course, be formed, under which you would certainly obtain a far better post than you could hope to get, at home."

"I have quite made up my mind to do so, sir. Certainly, when I left Cairo, I had no idea of remaining permanently in the service; but I have been so exceptionally fortunate, owing largely to your kindness, that I have been seriously thinking the matter over; and am quite determined that, if I can obtain an appointment, I will remain here. I have no ties, whatever, either in Lower Egypt or in England; no way of earning my living there; and possibly, as I have begun so early, I may rest, in time, in what will no doubt become an important branch of the Egyptian administration."

"I am glad to hear that you take that view. We all grumble at the Soudan, and yet there are few of us but would be sorry to leave it; and there can be no doubt whatever that, under our administration, it will, in time, become a magnificently rich and fertile province."

Being relieved from other duty, at present, Gregory went to the great yard near the mosque, called the Praying Square, where the majority of the Dervish prisoners were confined. Addressing a man of some five-and-forty years, he asked him, in Arabic, whether many among the prisoners had fought against Hicks, at El Obeid.

The man hesitated.

"I am not asking on the part of the Sirdar," Gregory said; "and you may be sure that, if no punishment is inflicted against those who have fought against us now, there can be no thought of punishment, for a thing that happened so many years ago. My father was, I believe, one of the English officers killed there; but as he spoke Arabic well, it is just possible he was not killed; but, like Slatin and Neufeld, was kept as a slave, in case he might be useful."

"There are many here who fought against Hicks," the native said. "I myself fought there, and nearly all the Baggara who are as old as I am were there, also. I have never heard of a white man who escaped death. When we broke into the square, the English General and his officers charged into the middle of us, and all fell. I was not close at the time, but I saw their bodies, an hour afterwards."

"My father was not a fighting officer. He was the interpreter, and may not have been near the others. When the attack by your people was made, I have heard that one of the Soudanese regiments held together, and marched away, and that there was a white officer with them."

"That was so. Two days afterwards, we surrounded them. They fought hard; and at last, when we had lost many men, we offered that, if they would surrender and become the Mahdi's men, they would be spared. Most of them did so, just as some of our tribesmen, taken by you at Atbara, have now taken service with you."

"But the white officer—what became of him?"

"I cannot say," the native said. "I have no memory of him. He may have fallen before they surrendered—who can say? Certainly, I do not remember a white man being killed, after they did so. I will ask others who were there, and tomorrow will tell you what they say."

It was a busy day, in Omdurman. The army that had made such efforts, and achieved so great a triumph, marched in military order, with bands playing, through the town. The Sirdar had a double motive, in ordering them to do so. In the first place, it was a legitimate triumph of the troops, thus to march as conquerors through the town. In the second place the sight would impress, not only the inhabitants, but the Dervish prisoners, with a sense of the power of those who, henceforth, would be their masters; and, undoubtedly, the show had the desired effect. The orderly ranks, as they swept along, the proud demeanour of the men, their physique and equipment, created a profound impression among the natives. Half of them were their own kinsmen, many of whom had fought for the Khalifa, and had now aided in defeating him. This was what had been accomplished by drill and discipline, and the influence of white officers. The Soudanese were evidently well fed and cared for; not even the haughty Baggara held their heads so high.

Especially admired were the artillery, battery following battery, in perfect order. These were the guns that had carried death into the ranks of the Dervishes, against whose fire even the fanatical bravery of the followers of the Khalifa was unable to stand. When the march past was concluded, there was scarce one of the prisoners who would not gladly have enlisted.

On the following day, Gregory again went to the Praying Square. The man he had the morning before seen, at once came up to him.

"I have enquired of many who were at El Obeid, my lord," he said. "All say that there was no white man in the camp, when the black battalion surrendered, though one had been seen while the fighting was going on. Nor was the body of one found, where the fight had taken place on the previous day. It was a matter of talk among the Dervishes, at the time; for they had lain in a circle round the enemy, and were convinced that no one passed through their lines. Those who surrendered said that he had taken the command, and had exposed himself to the hottest fire, and encouraged them; telling them that the more bravely they defended themselves, the more likely they were to obtain favourable terms. The night before, he had advised them to accept any offer the Dervishes might make, but on the following morning he was missing, and none could give any account of what had become of him. The same tale is told by all to whom I have spoken."

The story made a profound impression upon Gregory. It seemed possible that the father, of whom he had no remembrance, might have been the sole white survivor of Hicks's army. True, there was nothing to prove that he was the white man who had joined the black battalion that escaped the first day's massacre. There were other non-combatants: Vizitelly, the artist of the Illustrated London News, and O'Donovan, the correspondent of the Daily News. Either of these might also have been at any other portion of the square, when the attack commenced, and unable to join Hicks and his officers, in their final charge into the midst of the enemy.

Still, it was at least possible that his father was the man who had retired from the field, with the black battalion; and who had, afterwards, so strangely disappeared. If so, what had become of him, all these years? Had he made off in disguise, only to be murdered by wandering bands? Had he been concealed, for months, in the hut of a friendly tribesman? What had he been doing, since? Had he been killed, in trying to make his way down? Had he been enslaved, and was he still lingering on, in a wretched existence?

He could hardly hope that he had fallen into friendly hands; for, had he been alive, he would surely have managed, with his knowledge of the country, to make his way down; or to reach Khartoum, when it was still held by the Egyptians.

At any rate, Gregory concluded that he might find out whether any European had arrived there, during the siege. He went down to the river, and took a native boat across to Khartoum. At the ceremony, on Sunday, many natives watched the arrival of the flotilla; and some of these might have been there, in Gordon's time. He had no great hopes of it, but there was just a chance.

The flags were still flying over the governor's house, when he landed, and a detachment of Egyptian troops was stationed there. A native officer came down, when he landed.

"I have come across to question some of the natives," he said. "I believe some are still living here."

"Oh, yes, Bimbashi! there are a good many, scattered about among the ruins. They come in, bringing fruit and fish for sale. I think they mostly live down by the riverside."

Gregory kept on, till he came to the huts occupied by the fishermen, and men who cultivated small plots of ground. He found several who had lived at Khartoum, when it was captured; and who had escaped the general massacre, by hiding till nightfall, and then making their way up the river, in boats. None of them could give him the information he sought, but one suggested that he was more likely to hear from the Greeks and Turks, who worked in the Khalifa's arsenal and foundries; as they had been spared, for the services they would be able to render to the Mahdi.

Returning to Omdurman, he went to the machine shop. Here work had already been resumed, as repairs were needed by several of the gunboats. He went up to the foreman, a man of some sixty years of age.

"You were engaged in the city during the siege, were you not?" he said, in Arabic, with which he knew the foreman must be thoroughly acquainted.

"Yes, sir, I had been here ten years before that."

"I am very anxious to learn whether any white man, who had survived the battle of El Obeid, ever reached this town before its capture."

The man thought for some time.

"Yes," he said, "a white man certainly came here, towards the end of the siege. I know, because I happened to meet him, when I was going home from work; and he asked me the way to the governor's. I should not have known him to be a white man, for he had a native attire; and was as black, from exposure to the sun, as any of the Arabs. I gave him directions, and did not ask him any questions; but it was said, afterwards, that he was one of Hicks's officers. Later, I heard that he went down in the steamer with Colonel Stewart."

"You did not hear his name?" Gregory asked, anxiously.

"No, sir."

"Did he talk Arabic well?"

"Extremely well. Much better than I did, at the time."

"Do you remember how long he arrived before the steamer

started?"

"Not very long, sir, though I really cannot tell you how long it was."

"After you were cut off, I suppose?"

"Certainly it was, but I cannot say how long."

"No one else, here, would know more about it than you do?"

"No, sir; I should think not. But you can ask them."

He called up some of the other workmen. All knew that a white officer, of Hicks Pasha's army, was said to have returned. One of them remembered that he had come down once, with Gordon, to see about some repairs required to the engines of a steamer; but he had never heard his name, nor could he recall his personal appearance, except that he seemed to be a man about thirty. But he remembered once seeing him, again, on board Stewart's steamer; as they had been working at her engines, just before she started.

After thanking the foreman, Gregory returned to the hut, where he and two other officers of Hunter's staff had taken up their quarters. He was profoundly depressed. This white man might well have been his father; but if so, it was even more certain than before that he had fallen. He knew what had been the fate of Stewart's steamer, the remains of which he had seen at Hebbeh. The Colonel, and all with him, had accepted the invitation of the treacherous sheik of that village, and had been massacred. He would at least go there, and endeavour to learn, from some of the natives, the particulars of the fate of those on board; and whether it was possible that any of the whites could have escaped.

After sitting for some time, in thought, he went to General Hunter's quarters, and asked to see him. The General listened, sympathetically, to his story.

"I never, for a moment, thought that your father could have escaped," he said; "but from what you tell me, it is possible that he did so, only to perish afterwards. But I can well understand how, having learnt so much, you should be anxious to hear more. Certainly, I will grant your request for leave to go down to Hebbeh. As you know, that place was taken and destroyed, by the river column under Earle; or rather under Brackenbury, for Earle had been killed in the fight at Kirkeban. Numerous relics were found of the massacre, but the journal Stewart was known to have kept was not among them. Had it been there it would, no doubt, have mentioned the survivor of Hicks's army, who was coming down the river with him.

"The place was deserted when Brackenbury arrived. It certainly was so, when we came up. Since then, some of the inhabitants have probably returned; and may know of places where plunder was hidden away, on the approach of Brackenbury's column. No doubt the offer of a reward would lead to their production.

"You may not have to be absent long. The British regiments are to go down at once, and several steamers will start tomorrow. I will give you an order to go with them. You will have no difficulty in getting back, for the Sirdar has already decided that the railway is to be carried on, at once, from Atbara to Khartoum; and has, I believe, telegraphed this morning that material and stores are to be sent up, at once. Most of these will, no doubt, be brought on by rail; but grain, of which large quantities will be required, for the use of our troops and of the population of the town, will come on by water.

"But, no doubt, your quickest way back will be to ride to Abu Hamed, and take the train up to Atbara."

"I will be back as soon as I can, General. I am much obliged to you, for letting me go."

"I will tell the Sirdar that I have given you leave, and why. It is not absolutely necessary, but it is always well that one's name should be kept to the front."

The next day, Gregory saw the General again.

"I mentioned, to the Sirdar, that you wanted a fortnight's leave, and told him why. He simply nodded, and said, 'Let him have a month, if he wants it.'

"He had other things to think of; for, this morning, a small Dervish steamer came down the White Nile. They had the Khalifa's flag flying, and had not heard of what had taken place, till one of the gunboats ran alongside her. Of course she surrendered, at once.

"It is a curious story they told. They left Omdurman a month ago with the Sapphire, which carried five hundred men. The object of the voyage was to collect grain. When they reached the old station of Fashoda, they had been fired upon by black troops, with some white men among them, who had a strange flag flying. The firing was pretty accurate, for they had forty men killed and wounded; and the emir in command had disembarked, and encamped his troops from the Sapphire on the opposite bank, and had sent the small steamer back, to ask the Khalifa for orders.

"The story seemed so strange, and improbable, that I went down with the Sirdar to the boat, which had been brought alongside. There was no doubt that it had been peppered with balls. Some of the General's staff cut one of the bullets out of the woodwork, and these fully confirmed the story. They were not leaden balls, or bits of old iron, but conical nickel bullets. They could only have been fired from small-bore rifles, so there were certainly white men at Fashoda. Of course, no one can form any opinion as to who they are, or where they come from. They may be Belgians from the Congo. They may—but that is most improbable—be an expeditionary party of Italians. But Italy is withdrawing, and not pushing forward, so I think it is out of the question that they are concerned in the matter.

"The question seems to lie between Belgians and French, unless an expedition has been sent up from our possessions on the great lakes. The Dervishes in the steamer can only say that the flag is not at all like ours; but as their ignorance of colour is profound, they give all sorts of contradictory statements. Anyhow, it is a serious matter. Certainly, no foreign power has any right to send an expedition to the Nile; and as certainly, if one of them did so, our government would not allow them to remain there; for, beyond all question, Fashoda is an Egyptian station, and within Egyptian territory; which is, at present, as much as to say that a foreign power, established there, would be occupying our country."

"It seems an extraordinary proceeding, sir."

"Very extraordinary. If it were not that it seems the thing has absolutely been done, it would seem improbable that any foreign power could take such an extraordinary, and unjustifiable, course. It is lucky for them, whoever they are, that we have smashed up the Dervishes; for they would have made very short work of them, and the nation that sent them would probably never have known their fate."

Chapter 16:

A Voice From The Dead.

That afternoon, Gregory heard that orders had been issued for five of the gunboats to start up the river, the first thing in the morning; that the Sirdar himself was going, and was to take up five hundred men of the 11th Soudanese. An order was also issued that all correspondents were to leave, the next day, for Cairo. Gregory had met one of them, that evening.

"So you are all off, I hear, Mr. Pearson?"

"Yes; we did have a sort of option given us, but it was really no choice at all. We might go down instantly, or we must stay till the last of the white troops had gone down. That may be a very long time, as there is no saying what may come of this Fashoda business. Besides, the Khalifa has fairly escaped; and if, out of the sixty thousand men with him, some thirty thousand got off, they may yet rally round him: and, in another two or three months, he may be at the head of as large a force as ever. I don't think, after the way the Egyptians fought the other day, there will be any need for white troops to back them. Still, it is likely that a battalion or two may be left. However, we had practically to choose between going at once, or waiting at least a month; and you may be sure that the censorship would be put on, with a round turn, and that we should not be allowed to say a word of the Fashoda business, which would be the only thing worth telegraphing about. So we have all voted for going.

"Of course, we understand that this pressure has been put upon us, on account of this curious affair at Fashoda. Fortunately, none of us are sorry to be off. There is certain to be a pause, now, for some time; and one does not want to be kicking one's heels about, in this ghastly town; and though it is rather sharp and peremptory work, I cannot say that I think the Sirdar is wrong. Whoever these men may be, they must go, that is certain; but of course it will be a somewhat delicate business, and France—that is, if they are Frenchmen who are there—is sure to be immensely sore over the business; and it is certainly very desirable that nothing should be written, from here, that could increase that feeling. I have no doubt the Sirdar telegraphed home, for instructions, as soon as he got the news of the affair; and I imagine that his going up in the morning, with five gunboats, is proof that he has already received instructions of some sort.

"I hope this force is not French. The feeling against us is tremendously strong, in France, and they certainly will not like backing down; but they will have to do that or fight and, with all their big talk, I don't think they are ready to risk a war with us; especially as, though their occupation of Fashoda would be an immense annoyance to us, it would be of no possible utility to them.

"By the way, we have all got to sell our horses. There is no possibility of taking them down, and it is a question of giving them away, rather than of selling; for, of course, the officers of the British regiments do not want to buy. I have a horse for which I gave twenty-five pounds, at Cairo. You are welcome to him. You can give me a couple of pounds, for the saddle and things."

"I am very much obliged to you, but it would be robbery."

"Not at all. If you won't take him, I shall have him shot, tonight. A horse could not possibly pick up food here, and would die of starvation without a master; and it would be still more cruel to give him to a native, for they are brutal horse masters."

"Well, in that case I shall be glad, indeed, to have him; and I am extremely obliged to you."

"That is right. If you will send your man round, I will hand it over to him."

"As you are going tomorrow, it is likely that I shall go with you; for I am going down, also, as far as Abu Hamed, for ten days."

"That will be pleasant, though I do not know that it will be so for you; for I own the majority of us are rather sour-tempered, at present. Though we may be glad enough to go, one does not care to be sent off at a moment's notice, just as fractious children are turned out of a room, when their elders want a private chat. However, for myself, I am not inclined to grumble. I want to go, and therefore I do not stand on the order of going."

Later, General Hunter gave Gregory an order, for a passage in a steamer on which the correspondents of the various newspapers were going down.

"What shall we take, master?" Zaki asked.

"Just the clothes we stand in, Zaki. I have got a couple of the Dervish Remingtons, and several packets of ammunition. I will take them, and I can get four more. We will take them all down, as we know the people about Hebbeh are not disposed to be friendly. I don't suppose, for a minute, that they are likely to show any hostile feeling; for you may be sure that the fall of Omdurman has spread, by this time, over the whole land, and they will be on their best behaviour. Still, it is just as well to be able to defend ourselves, and I shall engage four men at Abu Hamed to go with us. I shall leave all my kit here."

It was a pleasant run down the river, to Atbara. The correspondents were all heartily glad to be on their way home; and the irritation they had at first felt, at being so suddenly ordered away, at the moment when so unexpected and interesting a development occurred, had subsided. They had witnessed one of the most interesting battles ever fought, had seen the overthrow of the Mahdi, and were looking forward to European comforts and luxuries again.

At Atbara all left the steamer, which was to take in stores, and go up again at once; and proceeded, by a military train, with the first of the returned European regiments.

At Abu Hamed, Gregory left them. His first enquiry was whether any boats were going down the river. He learned that several native craft were leaving, and at once engaged a passage in one of them to Hebbeh. He had no difficulty, whatever, in engaging four sturdy Arabs from among those who were listlessly hanging round the little station. While he was doing this, Zaki bought food for six men, for a week; and in less than two hours from his arrival at Abu Hamed, Gregory was on board.

The boat at once dropped down the river and, as the current was running strongly, they were off Hebbeh next morning, at eight o'clock. A boat put off, and took Gregory and his party ashore. As they were seen to land, the village sheik at once came down to them.

"Is there anything I can do for my lord?" he asked.

"Yes; I have come here to ascertain whether any of those, who were present at the attack upon the party who landed from the steamer over there, are still living here. There is no question of punishment. On the contrary, I have come here to obtain information as to some private matters, and anyone who can give me that information will be well rewarded."

"There are but three men alive who were here at the time, my lord. There were more, but they fled when the boats with the white troops came up, from Merawi. I believe they went to the Dervish camp at Metemmeh.

"The three here are quiet and respectable men. They were asked many questions, and guided the white officers to the place where Wad Etman stood—it was there that those who landed from the steamer first rested—and to the place where the great house of Suleiman Wad Gamr, Emir of Salamat, stood.

"It was there that the much to be regretted attack on the white men was made. When the white army came up, six months afterwards, they blew up the house, and cut down all the palm trees in the village."

"I was with the force that came up from Merawi, last year. Will you bring me the three men you speak of? I would question them, one by one. Assure them that they need not be afraid of answering truthfully, even if they themselves were concerned in the attack upon the white officers, and the crew of the steamer, for no steps will be taken against them. It is eighteen years since then; and, no doubt, their houses were destroyed and their groves cut down, when the British column came here and found the place deserted. I am ready to reward them, if I obtain the information I require from them."

The three men were presently brought to the spot where Gregory had seated himself, in the shade of one of the huts. Zaki stood beside him, and the four armed men took post, a short distance away.

The first called up was a very old man. In reply to Gregory's questions, he said:

"I was already old when the steamboat ran ashore. I took no hand in the business; the white men had done me no harm, while the followers of the Mahdi had killed many of my family and friends. I heard what was going to be done, and I stayed in my house. I call upon Allah to witness that what I say is true!"

"Do you know if any remains of that expedition are still in existence?"

"No, my lord. When the white troops came here, some months afterwards, I fled, as all here did; but I know that, before they destroyed Wad Gamr's house, they took away some boxes of papers that had been brought ashore from the ship, and were still in the house. I know of nothing else. The clothes of the men on board the steamboat were divided among those who took part in the attack, but there was little booty."

Gregory knew that, at Wad Gamr's house, but few signs of the tragedy had been found when General Brackenbury's troops entered. Bloodstained visiting cards of Stewart's, a few scraps of paper, and a field glass had, alone, been discovered, besides the boxes of papers.

The next man who came up said that he had been with the party who fell upon the engineers and crew of the boat, by the riverside.

"I was ordered to kill them," he said. "Had I not done so, I should have been killed, myself."

"Do you know whether any booty was hidden away, before the English came?"

"No, my lord, there was no booty taken. No money was found on board the steamer. We stripped her of the brass work, and took the wood ashore, to burn. The sheik gave us a dollar and a half a man, for what we had done. There may have been some money found on the ship, but as his own men were on board first, and took all that they thought of value, I have naught to say about it."

"And you never heard of anything being hidden, before the British troops arrived?"

The Arab shook his head.

"No, my lord, but there may have been, though I never heard of it. I went and fought at Kirkeban; and when we were beaten, I fled at once to Berber, and remained there until the white troops had all gone down the country."

"I may want to question you again tomorrow," Gregory said. "Here are two dollars. I shall give you as much more, if I want you again."

The third man was then called up. He was evidently in fear.

"Do not be afraid to answer me truly," Gregory said. "If you do so, no harm will come to you, whatever share you may have had in the affair. But if you answer falsely, and the truth is afterwards discovered, you will be punished. Now, where were you when this business took place?"

"We were all ordered, by Wad Gamr, to gather near his house; and, when the signal was given, we were to run in and kill the white men. We saw them go up to the house. They had been told to leave their arms behind them. One of the sheik's servants came out and waved his arms, and we ran in and killed them."

"What happened then?"

"We carried the bodies outside the house. Then we took what money was found in their pockets, with watches and other things, in to the sheik; and he paid us a dollar and a half a head, and said that we could have their clothes. For my share, I had a jacket belonging to one of them. When I got it home, I found that there was a pocket inside, and in it was a book partly written on, and many other bits of paper."

"And what became of that?" Gregory asked, eagerly.

"I threw it into a corner. It was of no use to me. But when the white troops came up in the boats, and beat us at Kirkeban, I came straight home and, seeing the pocketbook, took it and hid it under a rock; for I thought that when the white troops got here, they would find it, and that they might then destroy the house, and cut down my trees. Then I went away, and did not come back until they had all gone."

"And where is the pocketbook, now?"

"It may be under the rock where I hid it, my lord. I have never thought of it, since. It was rubbish."

"Can you take me to the place?"

"I think so. It was not far from my house. I pushed it under the first great rock I came to, for I was in haste; and wanted to be away before the white soldiers, on camels, could get here."

"Did you hear of any other things being hidden?"

"No. I think everything was given up. If this thing had been of value I should, perhaps, have told the sheik; but as it was only written papers, and of no use to anyone, I did not trouble to do so."

"Well, let us go at once," Gregory said, rising to his feet. "Although of no use to you, these papers may be of importance."

Followed by Zaki and the four men, Gregory went to the peasant's house, which stood a quarter of a mile away.

"This is not the house I lived in, then," the man said. "The white troops destroyed every house in the village; but, when they had gone, I built another on the same spot."

The hill rose steeply, behind it. The peasant went on, till he stopped at a large boulder.

"This was the rock," he said, "where I thrust it under, as far as my arm would reach. I pushed it in on the upper side."

The man lay down.

"It was just about here," he said.

"It is here, my lord. I can just feel it, but I cannot get it out. I pushed it in as far as the tips of my fingers could reach it."

"Well, go down and cut a couple of sticks, three or four feet long."

In ten minutes, the man returned with them.

"Now take one of them and, when you feel the book, push the stick along its side, until it is well beyond it. Then you ought to be able to scrape it out. If you cannot do so, we shall have to roll the stone over. It is a big rock, but with two or three poles, one ought to be able to turn it over."

After several attempts, however, the man produced the packet. Gregory opened it, with trembling hands. It contained, as the man had said, a large number of loose sheets, evidently torn from a pocketbook, and all covered with close writing.

He opened the book that accompanied them. It was written in ink, and the first few words sufficed to tell him that his search was over. It began:

"Khartoum. Thank God, after two years of suffering and misery, since the fatal day at El Obeid, I am once again amongst friends. It is true that I am still in peril, for the position here is desperate. Still, the army that is coming up to our help may be here in time; and even if they should not do so, this may be found when they come, and will be given to my dear wife at Cairo, if she is still there. Her name is Mrs. Hilliard, and her address will surely be known, at the Bank."

"These are the papers I was looking for," he said to Zaki. "I will tell you about them, afterwards."

He handed ten dollars to the native, thrust the packet into his breast pocket, and walked slowly down to the river. He had never entertained any hope of finding his father, but this evidence of his death gave him a shock.

His mother was right, then. She had always insisted there was a possibility that he might have escaped the massacre at El Obeid. He had done so. He had reached Khartoum. He had started, full of hope of seeing his wife and child, but had been treacherously massacred, here.

He would not, now, read this message from the grave. That must be reserved for some time when he was alone. He knew enough to be able to guess the details—they could not be otherwise than painful. He felt almost glad that his mother was not alive. To him, the loss was scarcely a real one. His father had left him, when an infant. Although his mother had so often spoken of him, he had scarcely been a reality to Gregory; for when he became old enough to comprehend the matter, it seemed to him certain that his father must have been killed. He could, then, hardly understand how his mother could cling to hope.

His father had been more a real character to him, since he started from Cairo, than ever before. He knew the desert, now, and its fierce inhabitants. He could picture the battle and since the fight at Omdurman he had been able to see, before him, the wild rush on the Egyptian square, the mad confusion, the charge of a handful of white officers, and the one white man going off, with the black battalion that held together.

If, then, it was a shock to him to know how his father had died, how vastly greater would it have been, to his mother! She had pictured him as dying suddenly, fighting to the last, and scarce conscious of pain till he received a fatal wound. She had said, to Gregory, that it was better to think of his father as having died thus, than lingering in hopeless slavery, like Neufeld; but it would have been agony to her to know that he did suffer for two years, that he had then struggled on through all dangers to Khartoum, and was on his way back, full of hope and love for her, when he was treacherously murdered.

The village sheik met him, as he went down.

"You have found nothing, my lord?"

"Nothing but a few old papers," he said.

"You will report well of us, I hope, to the great English commander?"

"I shall certainly tell him that you did all in your power to aid me."

He walked down towards the river. One of the men, who had gone on while he had been speaking to the sheik, ran back to meet him.

"There is a steamer coming up the river, my lord."

"That is fortunate, indeed," Gregory exclaimed. "I had intended to sleep here, tonight, and to bargain with the sheik for donkeys or camels to take us back. This will save two days."

Two or three native craft were fastened up to the shore, waiting for a breeze to set in, strong enough to take them up. Gregory at once arranged, with one of them, to put his party on board the steamer, in their boat. In a quarter of an hour the gunboat approached, and they rowed out to meet her.

As she came up, Gregory stood up, and shouted to them to throw him a rope. This was done, and an officer came to the side.

"I want a passage for myself and five men, to Abu Hamed. I am an officer on General Hunter's staff."

"With pleasure.

"Have you come down from the front?" he asked, as Gregory stepped on board, with the five blacks.

"Yes."

"Then you can tell me about the great fight. We heard of it, at Dongola, but beyond the fact that we had thrashed the Khalifa, and taken Omdurman, we received no particulars.

"But before you begin, have a drink.

"It is horribly annoying to me," he went on, as they sat down under the awning, and the steward brought tumblers, soda water, some whisky, and two lemons.

Gregory refused the whisky, but took a lemon with his cold water.

"A horrible nuisance," the officer went on. "This is one of Gordon's old steamers; she has broken down twice. Still, I console myself by thinking that, even if I had been in time, very likely she would not have been taken up.

"I hope, however, there will be work to do, yet. As you see, I have got three of these native craft in tow, and it is as much as I can do to get them up this cataract.

"Now, please tell me about the battle."

Gregory gave him an outline of the struggle, of the occupation of Omdurman, and of what might be called the funeral service of Gordon, at Khartoum. It was dark before the story was finished.

"By the way," the officer said, as they were about to sit down to dinner, "while we were on deck, I did not ask about your men. I must order food to be given them."

"They have plenty," Gregory said. "I brought enough for a week with me. I thought that I might be detained two or three days, here, and be obliged to make the journey by land to Abu Hamed."

"I have not asked you what you were doing at this out of the way place, and how long you have been here."

"I only landed this morning. I came down to search for some relics. My father was on board Stewart's steamer, and as there would be nothing doing at Omdurman, for a few days, I got leave to run down. I was fortunate in securing a boat at Abu Hamed, on my arrival there; and I have been equally so, now, in having been picked up by you; so that I shall not be away from Omdurman more than seven days, if I have equal luck in getting a steamer at Atbara. I do not think I shall be disappointed, for the white troops are coming down, and stores are going up for the Egyptian brigade, so that I am certain not to be kept there many hours. The Sirdar has gone up to Fashoda, or I don't suppose I should have got leave."

"Yes. I heard at Merawi, from the officer in command, that some foreign troops had arrived there. I suppose nothing more is known about it?"

"No; no news will probably come down for another fortnight, perhaps longer than that."

"Who can they be?"

"The general idea is that they are French. They can only be French, or a party from the Congo States."

"They had tremendous cheek, whoever they are," the officer said. "It is precious lucky, for them, that we have given the Khalifa something else to think about, or you may be sure he would have wiped them out pretty quickly; unless they are a very strong force, which doesn't seem probable. I hear the Sirdar has taken a regiment up with him."

"Yes, but I don't suppose any actual move will be made, at present."

"No, I suppose it will be a diplomatic business. Still, I should think they would have to go."

"No one has any doubt about that, at Omdurman," Gregory said. "After all the expense and trouble we have had to retake the Soudan, it is not likely that we should let anyone else plant themselves on the road to the great lakes.

"When will you be at Abu Hamed, sir?"

"We shall be there about five o'clock—at any rate, I think you may safely reckon on catching the morning train. It goes, I think, at eight."

"I am sure to catch a train, soon, for orders have been sent down that railway materials shall be sent up, as quickly as possible; as it has been decided that the railway shall be carried on, at once, to Khartoum. I expect that, as soon as the Nile falls, they will make a temporary bridge across the Atbara."

It was six in the morning, when the steamer arrived at Abu Hamed.

Gregory at once landed, paid his four men, went up to the little station; and, an hour later, was on his way to Atbara Fort. He had but two hours to wait there, and reached Omdurman at three o'clock, on the following afternoon. As he landed, he met an officer he knew.

"Is there any news?" he asked.

"Nothing but Fashoda is talked about. It has been ascertained that the force there is undoubtedly French. The betting is about even as to whether France will back down, or not. They have made it difficult for themselves, by an outburst of enthusiasm at what they considered the defeat of England. Well, of course, that does not go for much, except that it makes it harder for their government to give in."

"And has any news been received of the whereabouts of the Khalifa?"

"No. Broadwood, with two regiments of Egyptian cavalry and the camel corps, started in pursuit of the Khalifa and Osman, an hour after it was found that they had got away. Slatin Pasha went with them. But as the horses had been at work all day, they had to stop at half past eight. They could not then get down to the water, and bivouacked where they had halted. At four in the morning they started again, and at half past eight found a spot where they could get down to the river; then they rode fifteen miles farther.

"They were now thirty-five miles from Omdurman. One of the gunboats had gone up with supplies, but owing to the Nile having overflowed, could not get near enough to land them. Next morning they got news that the Khalifa was twenty-five miles ahead, and had just obtained fresh camels, so they were ordered to return to the town. They had picked up a good many of the fugitives, among them the Khalifa's favourite wife; who, doubtless with other women, had slipped away at one of his halting places, feeling unable to bear the constant fatigues and hardships of the flight in the desert.

"The cavalry have since been out again, but beyond the fact that the Khalifa had been joined by many of the fugitives from the battle, and was making for Kordofan, no certain news has been obtained. At present, nothing can be done in that direction.

"That horse you bought is all right."

"I really did not like taking him, for I already had one; and it looked almost like robbery, giving him two pounds for it, and the saddle."

"Others have done as well," the officer laughed. "One of the brigade staff bought a horse for a pound from Burleigh, who had given forty for it at Cairo. There was no help for it. They could not take horses down. Besides, it is not their loss, after all. The newspapers can afford to pay for them. They must have been coining money, of late."

"That reconciles me," Gregory laughed. "I did not think of the correspondents' expenses being paid by the papers."

"I don't know anything about their arrangements, but it stands to reason that it must be so, in a campaign like this. In an ordinary war, a man can calculate what his outlay might be; but on an expedition of this kind, no one could foretell what expenses he might have to incur.

"Besides, the Sirdar has saved the newspapers an enormous expenditure. The correspondents have been rigidly kept down to messages of a few hundred words; whereas, if they had had their own way, they would have sent down columns. Of course, the correspondents grumbled, but I have no doubt their employers were very well pleased, and the newspapers must have saved thousands of pounds, by this restriction."

"You are back sooner than I expected," General Hunter said, when Gregory went in and reported his arrival. "It is scarce a week since you left."

"Just a week, sir. Everything went smoothly, and I was but three or four hours at Hebbeh."

"And did you succeed in your search?"

"Yes, sir. I most fortunately found a man who had hidden a pocketbook he had taken from the body of one of the white men who were murdered there. There was nothing in it but old papers and, when Brackenbury's expedition approached, he had hidden it away; and did not give it a thought, until I enquired if he knew of any papers, and other things, connected with those on board the steamer. He at once took me to the place where he had hidden it, under a great stone, and it turned out to be the notebook and journals of my father; who was, as I thought possible, the white man who had arrived at Khartoum, a short time before the place was captured by the Dervishes, and who had gone down in the steamer that carried Colonel Stewart."

"Well, Hilliard," the General said, kindly, "even the certain knowledge of his death is better than the fear that he might be in slavery. You told me you had no remembrance of him?"

"None, sir; but of course, my mother had talked of him so often, and had several photographs of him—the last taken at Cairo, before he left—so that I almost seem to have known him. However, I do feel it as a relief to know that he is not, as I feared was remotely possible, a slave among the Baggara. But I think it is hard that, after having gone through two years of trials and sufferings, he should have been murdered on his way home."

"No doubt that is so. Have you read your father's diary, yet?"

"No, sir; I have not had the heart to do so, and shall put it off, until the shock that this has given me has passed away. I feel that a little hard work will be the best thing for me. Is there any chance of it?"

"You have just returned in time. I am going up the Blue Nile, tomorrow morning, to clear out the villages; which, no doubt, are all full of fugitives. I am glad that you have come back. I was speaking of you today to General Rundle, who is in command.

"One of the objects of the expedition is to prevent Fadil from crossing the river. He was advancing from Gedareh, at the head of ten thousand troops, to join the Khalifa; and was but forty miles away, on the day after we took this place; but when he received the news of our victory, he fell back. If he can cross, he will bring a very formidable reinforcement to the Khalifa.

"We know that Colonel Parsons started from Kassala, on the 7th, his object being to capture Gedareh, during the absence of Fadil. He is to cross the Atbara at El Fasher, and will then march up this bank of the river, till he is at the nearest point to Gedareh. It is probable that he will not strike across before the 18th, or the 20th. His force is comparatively small, and we do not know how large a garrison Fadil will have left there.

"Altogether, we are uneasy about the expedition. It is very desirable that Parsons should know that Fadil is retiring, and that, so far as we can learn from the natives, he has not yet crossed the Blue Nile. Gedareh is said to be a strong place, and once there, Parsons might hold it against Fadil until we can send him reinforcements.

"In order to convey this information to him, we require someone on whom we can absolutely rely. I said that, if you were here, I felt sure that you would volunteer for the service. Of course it is, to a certain extent, a dangerous one; but I think that, speaking the language as you do, and as you have already been among the Dervishes, you might, even if taken prisoner, make out a good story for yourself."

"I would undertake the commission, with pleasure," Gregory said. "I shall, of course, go in native dress."

"I propose that we carry you a hundred miles up the river, with us, and there land you. From that point, it would not be more than sixty or seventy miles across the desert to the Atbara, which you would strike forty or fifty miles above El Fasher. Of course you would be able to learn, there, whether Parsons had crossed. If he had, you would ride up the bank till you overtake him. If he had not, you would probably meet him at Mugatta. He must cross below that, as it is there he leaves the river."

"That seems simple enough, sir. My story would be that I was one of the Dervishes, who had escaped from the battle here; and had stopped at a village, thinking that I was safe from pursuit, until your boats came along; and that I then crossed the desert to go to Gedareh, where I thought I should be safe. That would surely carry me through. I shall want two fast camels—one for myself, and one for my boy."

"These we can get for you, from Abdul Azil, the Abadah sheik. Of course, you will put on Dervish robes and badges?"

"Yes, sir."

"I will go across and tell General Rundle, and obtain written instructions for you to carry despatches to Parsons. I will give them to you when you go up on the boat, in the morning. I will see at once about the camels, and ask the Intelligence people to get you two of the Dervish suits. You will also want rifles."

"Thank you, sir! I have a couple of Remingtons, and plenty of ammunition for them. I have two spears, also, which I picked up when we came in here."

"We are off again, Zaki," he said, when he returned to his hut; where the black was engaged in sweeping up the dust, and arranging everything as usual.

"Yes, master." Zaki suspended his work. "When do we go?"

"Tomorrow morning."

"Do we take everything with us?"

"No. I start in uniform. We shall both want Dervish dresses, but you need not trouble about them—they will be got for us."

"Then we are going among the Dervishes, again?"

"Well, I hope we are not; but we may meet some of them. We are going with the expedition up the Blue Nile, and will then land and strike across the desert, to the Atbara. That is enough for you to know, at present. We shall take our guns and spears with us."

Zaki had no curiosity. If his master was going, it was of course all right—his confidence in him was absolute.

In about an hour, a native from the Intelligence Department brought down two Dervish dresses, complete. They had still three hours before mess, and Gregory sat down on his bed, and opened his father's pocketbook, which he had had no opportunity to do, since it came into his possession.

Chapter 17:

A Fugitive.

"I do not suppose," the diary began, "that what I write here will ever be read. It seems to me that the chances are immeasurably against it. Still, there is a possibility that it may fall into the hands of some of my countrymen when, as will surely be the case, the Mahdi's rebellion is crushed and order restored; and I intend, so long as I live, to jot down from time to time what happens to me, in order that the only person living interested in me, my wife, may possibly, someday, get to know what my fate has been. Therefore, should this scrap of paper, and other scraps that may follow it, be ever handed to one of my countrymen, I pray him to send it to Mrs. Hilliard, care of the manager of the Bank at Cairo.

"It may be that this, the first time I write, may be the last; and I therefore, before all things, wish to send her my heart's love, to tell her that my last thoughts and my prayers will be for her, and that I leave it entirely to her whether to return to England, in accordance with the instructions I left her before leaving, or to remain in Cairo.

"It is now five days since the battle. It cannot be called a battle. It was not fighting; it was a massacre. The men, after three days' incessant fighting, were exhausted and worn out, half mad with thirst, half mutinous at being brought into the desert, as they said, to die. Thus, when the Dervishes rushed down in a mass, the defence was feeble. Almost before we knew what had happened, the enemy had burst in on one side of the square. Then all was wild confusion—camels and Dervishes, flying Egyptians, screaming camp followers, were all mixed in confusion.

"The other sides of the square were also attacked. Some of our men were firing at those in their front, others turning round and shooting into the crowded mass in the square. I was with a black regiment, on the side opposite to where they burst in. The white officer who had been in command had fallen ill, and had been sent back, a few days after we left Khartoum; and as I had been, for weeks before that, aiding him to the best of my powers, and there were no other officers to spare, Hicks asked me to take his place. As I had done everything I could for the poor fellows' comfort, on the march; they had come to like me, and to obey my orders as promptly as those of their former commander.

"As long as the other two sides of the square stood firm, I did so; but they soon gave way. I saw Hicks, with his staff, charge into the midst of the Dervishes, and then lost sight of them. Seeing that all was lost, I called to my men to keep together, to march off in regular order, and repel all assaults, as this was the only hope there was of getting free.

"They obeyed my orders splendidly. Two or three times the Dervishes charged upon them, but the blacks were as steady as rocks, and their volleys were so fatal that the enemy finally left us alone, preferring to aid in the slaughter of the panic-stricken Egyptians, and to share the spoil.

"We made for the wells. Each man drank his fill. Those who had water bottles filled them. We then marched on towards El Obeid, but before nightfall the Dervish horse had closed up round us. At daylight their infantry had also arrived, and fighting began.

"All day we held our position, killing great numbers, but losing many men ourselves. By night, our water was exhausted. Then the soldiers offered to attack the enemy, but they were twenty to one against us, and I said to them, 'No, fight one day longer, if we can hold on. The

Dervishes may retire, or they may offer us terms.'

"So we stood. By the next evening, we had lost half our number. After they had drawn off, one of the Dervish emirs came in with a white flag, and offered life to all who would surrender, and would wear the badge of the Mahdi, and be his soldiers. I replied that an answer should be given in the morning. When he had left, I gathered the men together.

"'You have fought nobly,' I said, 'but you have scarce a round of ammunition left. If we fight again tomorrow, we shall all be slaughtered. I thank you, in the name of the Khedive, for all that you have done; but I do not urge you to reject the terms offered. Your deaths would not benefit the Khedive. As far as I am concerned, you are free to accept the terms offered.'

"They talked for some time together, and then the three native officers who were still alive came forward.

"'Bimbashi,' they said, 'what will be done about you? We are Mahometans and their countrymen, but you are a white man and a Christian. You would not fight for the Mahdi?'

"'No,' I said, 'I would not fight for him, nor would I gain my life, at the price of being his slave. I wish you to settle the matter, without any reference to me. I will take my chance. I may not be here, in the morning. One man might escape, where many could not. All I ask is that I may not be watched. If in the morning I am not here, you can all say that I disappeared, and you do not know how. I do not, myself, know what I am going to do yet.'

"They went away, and in a quarter of an hour returned, and said that the men would surrender. If they had water and ammunition, they would go on fighting till the end; but as they had neither, they would surrender.

"I felt that this was best. The Soudanese love battle, and would as readily fight on one side as on the other. They have done their duty well to the Khedive, and will doubtless fight as bravely for the Mahdi.

"The men lay in a square, as they had fought, with sentries placed to warn them, should the Dervishes make a night attack. British troops would have been well-nigh maddened with thirst, after being twenty-four hours without water, and fighting all day in the blazing sun, but they felt it little. They were thirsty, but in their desert marches they are accustomed to thirst, and to hold on for a long time without water.

"I was better off, for I had drunk sparingly, the day before, from my water bottle; and had still a draught left in it. I waited until I thought that the men were all asleep; then I stripped, and stained myself from head to foot. I had carried stain with me, in case I might have to go out as a native, to obtain information. In my valise I had a native dress, and a native cloth, in which I could have passed as a peasant, but not as one of the Baggara. However, I put it on, passed through the sleeping men, and went up to a sentry.

"'You know me,' I said. 'I am your Bimbashi. I am going to try and get through their lines; but if it is known how I have escaped, I shall be pursued and slain. Will you swear to me that, if you are questioned, you will say you know nothing of my flight?'

"'I swear by the beard of the Prophet,' the man said. 'May Allah protect you, my lord!'

"Then I went on. The night was fairly dark and, as the Dervishes were nearly half a mile away, I had no fear of being seen by them. There were many of their dead scattered about, seventy or eighty yards from our square. I had, all along, felt convinced that it would be impossible to pass through their lines; therefore I went to a spot where I had noticed that a number had fallen, close together, and went about examining them carefully. It would not have done to have chosen the dress of an emir, as his body might have been examined, but the ordinary dead would pass unnoticed.

"I first exchanged the robe for one marked with the Mahdi's patches. It was already smeared with blood. I then carried the body of the man whose robe I had taken off, for some distance. I laid him down on his face, thinking that the absence of the patches would not be seen. Then I crawled some thirty or forty yards nearer to the Dervishes, so that it would seem that I had strength to get that far, before dying. Then I lay down, partly on my side, so that the patches would show, but with my face downwards on my arm.

"I had, before dyeing my skin, cut my hair close to my head, on which I placed the Dervish's turban. The only property that I brought out with me was a revolver, and this pocketbook. Both of these I buried in the sand; the pocketbook a short distance away, the pistol lightly covered, and within reach of my hand, so that I could grasp it and sell my life dearly, if discovered.

"Soon after daylight I heard the triumphant yells of the Dervishes, and knew that my men had surrendered. Then there was a rush of horse and foot, and much shouting and talking. I lifted my head slightly, and looked across. Not a Dervish was to be seen in front of me.

"I felt that I had better move, so, taking up my pistol and hiding it, I crawled on my hands and knees to the spot where I had hidden this book; and then got up on to my feet, and staggered across the plain, as if sorely wounded, and scarcely able to drag my feet along. As I had hoped, no one seemed to notice me, and I saw three or four other figures, also making their way painfully towards where the Dervishes had encamped.

"Here were a few camels, standing untended. Everyone had joined in the rush for booty—a rush to be met with bitter disappointment, for, with the exception of the arms of the fallen, and what few valuables they might have about their person, there was nothing to be gained. I diverged from the line I had been following, kept on until there was a dip in the ground, that would hide me from the sight of those behind; then I started to run, and at last threw myself down in the scrub, four or five miles away from the point from which I had started.

"I was perfectly safe, for the present. The Dervishes were not likely to search over miles of the desert, dotted as it was with thick bushes. The question was as to the future. My position was almost as bad as could be. I was without food or water, and there were hundreds of miles of desert between me and Khartoum. At every water hole I should, almost certainly, find parties of Dervishes.

"From time to time I lifted my head, and saw several large parties of the enemy, moving in the distance. They were evidently bound on a journey, and were not thinking of looking for me. I chewed the sour leaves of the camel bush; and this, to some extent, alleviated my thirst.

"I determined at last that I would, in the first place, march to the wells towards which we had been pressing, when the Dervishes came up to us. They were nearly three miles south of the spot where the square had stood. No doubt, Dervishes would be there; but, if discovered by them, it was better to die so than of thirst.

"Half an hour before the sun sank, I started. No horsemen were in sight, and if any were to come along, I could see them long before they could notice me. Knowing the general direction, I was fortunate enough to get sight of the palm grove which surrounded the wells, before darkness set in.

"It lay about two miles away, and there were certainly moving objects round it. I lay down until twilight had passed, and then went forward. When within two or three hundred yards of the grove, I lay down again, and waited. That the Dervishes would all go to sleep, however long I might wait, was too much to hope for. They would be sure to sit and talk, far into the night, of the events of the last three or four days.

"Shielding myself as well as I could, by the bushes, I crawled up until I was in the midst of some camels, which were browsing. Here I stood up, and then walked boldly into the grove. As I had expected, two or three score of Dervishes were sitting in groups, talking gravely. They had destroyed the Turks (as they always called the Egyptians, and their infidel white leaders), but had suffered heavily themselves. The three hundred Soudanese who had surrendered, and who had taken service with the Mahdi, were but poor compensation for the losses they had suffered.

"'A year ago,' one old sheik said, 'I was the father of eight brave sons. Now they have all gone before me. Four of them fell in the assaults at El Obeid, two at Baria, and the last two have now been killed. I shall meet them all again, in the abode of the blessed; and the sooner the better, for I have no one left to care for.'

"Others had tales of the loss of relations and friends, but I did not wait to listen further. Taking up a large water gourd, that stood empty at the foot of one of the trees, I boldly walked to the well, descended the rough steps at the water's edge, and drank till I could drink no longer; and then, filling the gourd, went up again.

"No one noticed me. Had they looked at me they would have seen, even in the darkness, the great patches down the front of the robe; but I don't think anyone did notice me. Other figures were moving about, from group to group, and I kept on through the grove, until beyond the trees. I came out on the side opposite to that which I had entered, and, as I expected, found some of the Dervish horses grazing among the bushes.

"No guard was placed over them, as they were too well trained to wander far. I went out to them and chose the poorest, which happened to be farther among the bushes than the others. I had thought the matter well over. If a good horse were taken, there would be furious pursuit, as soon as it was missed; and this might be soon, for the Arabs are passionately fond of their favourite horses—more so than they are of their families. While I had been waiting at the edge of the wood, more than one had come out to pat and fondle his horse, and give it a handful of dates. But a poor animal would meet with no such attention, and the fact that he was missing was not likely to be discovered till day-light. Probably, no great search would be made for it. The others would ride on, and its owner might spend some hours in looking about, thinking it had strayed away, and was lying somewhere among the bushes.

"I had no thought of trying to return to Khartoum. The wells were far apart, and Dervish bands were certain to be moving along the line. It seemed to me that El Obeid was the safest place to go to. True, it was in the hands of the Mahdists, but doubtless many wounded would be making their way there. Some, doubtless, would have wives and children. Others might have come from distant villages, but these would all make for the town, as the only place where they could find food, water, and shelter.

"Riding till morning, I let the horse graze, and threw myself down among the bushes, intending to remain there until nightfall. In the afternoon, on waking from a long sleep, I sat up and saw, a quarter of a mile away, a Dervish making his way along on foot, slowly and pain-fully. This was the very chance I had hoped might occur. I got up at once, and walked towards him.

"'My friend is sorely wounded,' I said.

"'My journey is well-nigh ended,' he said. 'I had hoped to reach El

Obeid, but I know that I shall not arrive at the well, which lies three miles away. I have already fallen three times. The next will be the last. Would that the bullet of the infidel had slain me, on the spot!'

"The poor fellow spoke with difficulty, so parched were his lips and swollen his tongue. I went to the bush, where I had left the gourd, half full of water. The man was still standing where I had left him, but when he saw the gourd in my hand he gave a little cry, and tottered feebly towards me.

"'Let my friend drink,' I said. I held the gourd to his lips. 'Sip a little, first,' I said. 'You can drink your fill, afterwards.'

"'Allah has sent you to save me,' he said; and after two or three gulps of water, he drew back his head. 'Now I can rest till the sun has set, and then go forward as far as the well, and die there.'

"'Let me see your wound,' I said. 'It may be that I can relieve the pain, a little.'

"He had been shot through the body, and it was a marvel to me how he could have walked so far; but the Arabs, like other wild creatures, have a wonderful tenacity of life. I aided him to the shelter of the thick bush, then I let him have another and longer drink, and bathed his wound with water. Tearing off a strip from the bottom of his robe, I bound it round him, soaking it with water over the wound. He had been suffering more from thirst than from pain, and he seemed stronger, already.

"'Now,' I said, 'you had better sleep.'

"'I have not slept since the last battle,' he said. 'I started as soon as it was dark enough for me to get up, without being seen by the Turks. I have been walking ever since, and dared not lie down. At first, I hoped that I might get to the town where my wife lived, and die in my own house. But that hope left me, as I grew weaker and weaker, and I have only prayed for strength enough to reach the well, to drink, and to die there.'

"'Sleep now,' I said. 'Be sure that I will not leave you. Is it not our duty to help one another? When the heat is over, we may go on. I have a horse, here, which you shall ride. How far is it from the well to El Obeid?'

"'It is four hours' journey, on foot.'

"'Good! Then you shall see your wife before morning. We will stop at the well to give my horse a good drink; and then, if you feel well enough to go on, we will not wait above an hour.'

"'May Allah bless you!' the man said, and he then closed his eyes, and at once went to sleep.

"I lay down beside him, but not to sleep. I was overjoyed with my good fortune. Now I could enter El Obeid boldly and, the wounded man being a native there, no questions would be asked me. I had a house to go to, and shelter, for the present.

"As to what might happen afterwards, I did not care to think. Some way of escape would surely occur, in time. Once my position as a Mahdist was fully established, I should be able to join any party going towards Khartoum, and should avoid all questioning; whereas, if I were to journey alone, I should be asked by every band I met where I came from; and might, at any moment, be detected, if there happened to be any from the village I should name as my abode. It was all important that this poor fellow should live; until, at least, I had been with him two days, in the town.

"From time to time, I dipped a piece of rag in the gourd, squeezed a few drops of water between his lips, and then laid it on his forehead. When the sun began to get low, I went out and caught the horse. As I came up, the Dervish opened his eyes.

"'I am better,' he said. 'You have restored me to life. My head is cool, and my lips no longer parched.'

"'Now,' I said, 'I will lift you into the saddle. You had better ride with both legs on the same side. It will be better for your wound. There is a mound of earth, a few yards away. If you will stand up on that, I can lift you into the saddle, easily. Now put your arms round my neck, and I will lift you in the standing position. If you try to get up, yourself, your wound might easily break out again.'

"I managed better than I had expected and, taking the bridle, led the horse towards the well.

"'You must tell me the way,' I said, 'for I am a stranger in this part, having come from the Blue Nile.'

"'I know it perfectly,' he said, 'having been born in El Obeid. I fought against the Mahdists, till we were starved out; and then, as we all saw that the power of the Mahdi was great, and that Allah was with him, we did not hesitate to accept his terms, and to put on his badges.'

"In less than an hour, we saw the trees that marked the position of the well; and, in another half hour, reached it. At least a score of wounded men were there, many of them so sorely hurt that they would get no farther. They paid little attention to us. One of them was known to Saleh—for the wounded man told me that that was his name—he also was from El Obeid. He was suffering from a terrible cut in the shoulder, which had almost severed the arm. He told my man that it was given by one of the infidel officers, before he fell.

"I thought it was as well to have two friends, instead of one; and did what I could to bind his wound up, and fasten his arm firmly to his side. Then I said to him:

"'My horse, after three hours' rest, will be able to carry you both. You can sit behind Saleh, and hold him on with your unwounded arm.'

"'Truly, stranger, you are a merciful man, and a good one. Wonderful is it that you should give up your horse, to men who are strangers to you; and walk on foot, yourself.'

"'Allah commands us to be compassionate to each other. What is a walk of a few miles? It is nothing, it is not worth speaking of. Say no more about it, I beseech you. I am a stranger in El Obeid, and you may be able to befriend me, there.'

"Three hours later Abdullah, which was the name of the second man, mounted, and assisted me to lift Saleh in front of him, and we set out for El Obeid. We got into the town at daybreak. There were few people about, and these paid no attention to us. Wounded men had been coming in, in hundreds. Turning into the street where both the men lived, we went first to the house of Saleh, which was at the farther end, and was, indeed, quite in the outskirts of the place. It stood in a walled enclosure, and was of better appearance than I had expected.

"I went to the door, and struck my hand against it. A voice within asked what was wanted, and I said, 'I bring home the master of the house. He is sorely wounded.'

"There was a loud cry, and the door opened and a woman ran out.

"'Do not touch him,' Abdullah exclaimed. 'We will get him down from the horse, but first bring out an angareb. We will lower him down onto that.'

"The woman went in, and returned with an angareb. It was the usual Soudan bed, of wooden framework, with a hide lashed across it. I directed them how to lift one end against the horse, so that Saleh could slide down onto it.

"'Wife,' the Arab said, when this was done, 'by the will of Allah, who sent this stranger to my aid, I have returned alive. His name is Mudil. I cannot tell you, now, what he has done for me. This house is his. He is more than guest, he is master. He has promised to remain with me, till I die, or am given back to life again. Do as he bids you, in all things.'

"Abdullah would have assisted to carry the bed in, but I told him that it might hurt his arm, and I and the woman could do it.

"'You had better go off, at once, to your own people, Abdullah. There must be many here who understand the treatment of wounds. You had better get one, at once, to attend to your arm.'

"'I will come again, this evening,' the man replied. 'I consider that I also owe my life to you; and when you have stayed a while here, you must come to me. My wives and children will desire to thank you, when I tell them how you brought me in here.'

"'Is there any place where I can put my horse?' I asked.

"'Yes,' the woman replied; 'take it to that door in the wall. I will go and unfasten it.'

"There was a shed in the garden. Into this I put my horse, and then entered the house.

"Most of the Arab women know something of the dressing of wounds. Saleh's wife sent out the slave, to buy various drugs. Then she got a melon from the garden, cut off the rind, and, mincing the fruit in small pieces, squeezed out the juice and gave it to her husband to drink. When she had done this, she set before me a plate of pounded maize, which was boiling over a little fire of sticks, when we went in.

"'It is your breakfast,' I said.

"She waved her hand.

"'I can cook more,' she said. 'It matters not if we do not eat till sunset.'

"I sat down at once, for indeed, I was famishing. The food had all been exhausted, at the end of the first day's fighting. I had been more than two days without eating a morsel. I have no doubt I ate ravenously, for the woman, without a word, emptied the contents of the pot into my bowl, and then went out and cut another melon for me.

"When the slave woman returned, she boiled some of the herbs, made a sort of poultice of them, and placed it on the wound. Saleh had fallen asleep, the moment he had drunk the melon juice, and did not move while the poultice was being applied.

"The house contained three rooms—the one which served as kitchen and living room; one leading from it on the right, with the curtains hanging before the door (this was Saleh's room); and on the opposite side, the guest chamber. I have not mentioned that there were four or five children, all of whom had been turned out, as soon as we entered; and threatened with terrible punishments, by their mother, if they made any noise.

"When I finished my meal I went into the guest chamber, threw myself down on the angareb there, and slept till sunset. When I awoke, I found that a native doctor had come, and examined Saleh. He had approved of what the woman had done, told told her to continue to poultice the wound, and had given her a small phial, from which she was to pour two drops into the wound, morning and evening. He said, what I could have told her, that her husband was in the hands of Allah, If He willed it, her husband would live.

"Of course, I had seen something of wounds, for in the old times—it seems a lifetime back—when I was, for two years, searching tombs and monuments with the professor, there had been frays between our workmen and bands of robbers; and there were also many cases of injuries, incurred in the work of moving heavy fragments of masonry. Moreover, although I had no actual practice, I had seen a good deal of surgical work; for, when I was at the university, I had some idea of becoming a surgeon, and attended the courses there, and saw a good many operations. I had therefore, of course, a general knowledge of the structure of the human frame, and the position of the arteries.

"So far the wound, which I examined when the woman poured in what I suppose was a styptic, looked healthy and but little inflamed. Of course, a skilled surgeon would have probed it and endeavoured to extract the ball, which had not gone through. The Soudanese were armed only with old muskets, and it was possible that the ball had not penetrated far; for if, as he had told me, he was some distance from the square when he was hit, the bullet was probably spent.

"I told the woman so, and asked her if she had any objection to my endeavouring to find it. She looked surprised.

"'Are you, then, a hakim?'

"'No, but I have been at Khartoum, and have seen how the white hakims find which way a bullet has gone. They are sometimes able to get it out. At any rate, I should not hurt him; and if, as is likely, the ball has not gone in very far—for had it done so, he would probably have died before he got home—I might draw it out.'

"'You can try,' she said. 'You have saved his life, and it is yours.'

"'Bring me the pistol that your husband had, in his belt.'

"She brought it to me. I took out the ramrod.

"'Now,' I said, 'it is most important that this should be clean; therefore, heat it in the fire so that it is red hot, and then drop it into cold water.'

"When this had been done, I took a handful of sand, and polished the rod till it shone, and afterwards wiped it carefully with a cloth. Then I inserted it in the wound, very gently. It had entered but an inch and a half when it struck something hard, which could only be the bullet. It was as I had hoped, the ball had been almost spent, when it struck him.

"Saleh was awake now, and had at once consented to my suggestion, having come to have implicit faith in me.

"'It is, you see, Saleh, just as I had hoped. I felt sure that it could not have gone in far; as, in that case, you could never have walked twenty miles, from the battlefield, to the point where you met me. Now, if I had a proper instrument, I might be able to extract the bullet. I might hurt you in doing so, but if I could get it out, you would recover speedily; while if it remains where it is, the wound may inflame, and you will die.'

"'I am not afraid of pain, Mudil.'

"I could touch the ball with my finger, but beyond feeling that the flesh in which it was embedded was not solid to the touch, I could do nothing towards getting the ball out. I dared not try to enlarge the wound, so as to get two fingers in. After thinking the matter over in every way, I decided that the only chance was to make a tool from the ramrod. I heated this again and again, flattening it with the pistol barrel, till it was not more than a tenth of an inch thick; then I cut, from the centre, a strip about a quarter of an inch wide. I then rubbed down the edges of the strip on a stone, till they were perfectly smooth, and bent the end into a curve. I again heated it to a dull red, and plunged it into water to harden it, and finally rubbed it with a little oil. It was late in the evening before I was satisfied with my work.

"'Now, Saleh,' I said, 'I am going to try if this will do. If I had one of the tools I have seen the white hakims use, I am sure I could get the ball out easily enough; but I think I can succeed with this. If I cannot, I must make another like it, so as to put one down each side of the bullet. You see, this curve makes a sort of hook. The difficulty is to get it under the bullet.'

"'I understand,' he said. 'Do not mind hurting me. I have seen men die of bullets, even after the wound seemed to heal. I know it is better to try and get it out.'

"It was a difficult job. Pressing back the flesh with my finger, I succeeded, at last, in getting the hook under the bullet. This I held firmly against it, and to my delight felt, as I raised finger and hook together, that the bullet was coming. A few seconds later, I held it triumphantly between my fingers.

"'There, Saleh, there is your enemy. I think, now, that if there is no inflammation, it will not be long before you are well and strong again.'

"'Truly, it is wonderful!' the man said, gratefully. 'I have heard of hakims who are able to draw bullets from wounds, but I have never seen it done before.'

"If Saleh had been a white man, I should still have felt doubtful as to his recovery; but I was perfectly confident that a wound of that sort would heal well, in an Arab, especially as it would be kept cool and clean. Hard exercise, life in the open air, entire absence of stimulating liquors, and only very occasionally, if ever, meat diet, render them almost insensible to wounds that would paralyse a white. Our surgeons had been astonished at the rapidity with which the wounded prisoners recovered.

"Saleh's wife had stood by, as if carved in stone, while I performed the operation; but when I produced the bullet, she burst into tears, and poured blessings on my head.

"I am writing this on the following morning. Saleh has slept quietly all night. His hand is cool this morning, and I think I may fairly say that he is convalescent. Abdullah's wife came in yesterday evening, and told the women here that her husband was asleep, but that he would come round in the morning. I warned her not to let him stir out of doors, and said I would come and see him.

"It has taken me five hours to write this, which seems a very long time to spend on details of things not worth recording; but the act of writing has taken my thoughts off myself, and I intend always to note down anything special. It will be interesting to me to read it, if I ever get away; should I be unable to escape, I shall charge Saleh to carry it to Khartoum, if he ever has the chance, and hand it over to the Governor there, to send down to Cairo.

"A week later. I am already losing count of days, but days matter nothing. I have been busy, so busy that I have not even had time to write. After I had finished my story so far, Saleh's slave woman took me to Abdullah's house. I found that he was in a state of high fever, but all I could do was to recommend that a wet rag should be applied, and freshly wetted every quarter of an hour; that his head should be kept similarly enveloped, in wet bandages; and that his hands should be dipped in water very frequently.

"When I got back, I found several women waiting outside Saleh's house. His wife had gossiped with a neighbour, and told them that I had got the bullet out of his wound. The news spread rapidly, and these women were all there to beg that I would see their husbands.

"This was awkward. I certainly could not calculate upon being successful, in cases where a bullet had penetrated more deeply; and even if I could do so, I should at once excite the hostility of the native hakims, and draw very much more attention upon myself than I desired. In vain I protested that I was not a hakim, and had done only what I had seen a white hakim do. Finding that this did not avail, I said that I would not go to see any man, except with one of the native doctors.

"'There are two here,' one of the women said. 'I will go and fetch them.'

"'No,' I said; 'who am I, that they should come to me? I will go and see them, if you will show me where they live.'

"'Ah, here they come!' she said, as two Dervishes approached.

"I went up to them, and they said: 'We hear that you are a hakim, who has done great things.'

"'I am no hakim,' I said. 'I was just coming to you, to tell you so. The man I aided was a friend, and was not deeply wounded. Having seen a white hakim take bullets from wounded men, I tried my best; and as the bullet was but a short way in, I succeeded. If I had had the instruments I saw the infidel use, it would have been easy; but I had to make an instrument, which sufficed for the purpose, although it would have been of no use, had the bullet gone in deeper.'

"They came in and examined Saleh's wound, the bullet, and the tool I had made.

"'It is well,' they said. 'You have profited by what you saw. Whence do you come?'

"I told the same story that I had told Saleh.

"'You have been some time at Khartoum?'

"'Not very long,' I said; 'but I went down once to Cairo, and was there some years. It was there I came to know something of the ways of the infidels. I am a poor man, and very ignorant; but if you will allow me I will act as your assistant, as I know that there are many wounded here. If you will tell me what to do, I will follow your instructions carefully.'

"The two hakims looked more satisfied, at finding that I was not a dangerous rival. One said:

"'Among the things that have been brought in here is a box. Those who brought it did not know what it contained, and it was too strong for them to open, though of course they were able to hammer it, and break it open. It contained nothing but many shining instruments, but the only one that we knew the purport of was a saw. There were two boxes of the same shape, and the other contained a number of little bottles of drugs; and we thought that maybe, as the boxes were alike, these shining instruments were used by the white hakim.'

"'I can tell you that, if I see them,' I said, and went with them.

"In a house where booty of all sorts was stored, I saw the chests which I knew were those carried by Hicks's medical officer. The one contained drugs, the other a variety of surgical instruments—probes, forceps, amputating knives, and many other instruments of whose use I was ignorant. I picked out three or four probes, and forceps of different shapes.

"'These are the instruments,' I said, 'with which they take out bullets. With one of these thin instruments, they search the wound until they find the ball. Sometimes they cannot find it, and even when they have found it, they sometimes cannot get hold of it with any of these tools, which, as you see, open and shut.'

"'What are the knives for?'

"'They use the knives for cutting off limbs. Twice have I seen this done, for I was travelling with a learned hakim, who was searching the tombs for relics. In one case a great stone fell on a man's foot, and smashed it, and the hakim took it off at the ankle. In another case a man had been badly wounded, by a bullet in the arm. He was not one of our party but, hearing of the hakim's skill, he had made a journey of three days to him. The wound was very bad, and they said it was too late to save the arm, so they cut it off above the elbow.'

"'And they lived?'

"'Yes, they both lived.'

"'Could you do that?'

"I shook my head. 'It requires much skill,' I said. 'I saw how it was done, but to do it one's self is very different. If there was a man who must die, if an arm or a leg were not taken off, I would try to save his life; but I would not try, unless it was clear that the man must die if it were not done.

"But you are learned men, hakims, and if you will take me as your assistant, I will show you how the white doctors take out balls, and, if there is no other way, cut off limbs; and when I have once shown you, you will do it far better than I.'

"The two men seemed much pleased. It was evident to them that, if they could do these things, it would widely add to their reputation.

"'It is good,' they said. 'You shall go round with us, and see the wounded, and we will see for ourselves what you can do. Will you want this chest carried?'

"'No,' I said. 'I will take these instruments with me. Should it be necessary to cut off a limb, to try and save life, I shall need the knives, the saw, and this instrument, which I heard the white hakim call a tourniquet, and which they use for stopping the flow of blood, while they are cutting. There are other instruments, too, that will be required.'"

CHAPTER 18:

A Hakim.

"I succeeded in getting out two more bullets, and then handed the instruments to the hakims, saying that I had shown them all I knew, and would now leave the matter in their hands altogether; or would act as their assistant, if they wished it. I had no fear that harm would come of it; for, being so frequently engaged in war, I knew that they had, in a rough way, considerable skill in the treatment of wounds. I had impressed upon them, while probing the wounds, that no force must be used, and that the sole object was to find the exact course the ball had taken.

"As to the amputations, they would probably not be attempted. A fighting Dervish would rather die than lose a limb; and, were he to die under an operation, his relatives would accuse the operator of having killed him.

"I remained at work with them, for two or three days. In nearly half the cases, they failed to find the course of the ball; but when they did so, and the wound was not too deep, they generally succeeded in extracting it. They were highly pleased, and I took great pains to remain well in the background.

"They were very friendly with me. Their fees were mostly horses, or carpets, or other articles, in accordance with the means of the patients; and of these they gave me a portion, together with some money, which had been looted from the chests carrying silver, for the purchase of provisions and the payment of troops. Although they made a pretence of begging me to remain always with them, I refused, saying that I saw I could no longer be of assistance to them. I could see they were inwardly pleased. They gave me some more money, and I left them, saying that I did not, for a moment, suppose that I could tell them anything further; but that if, at any time, they should send for me, I would try and recall what I had seen the white hakims do, in such a case as they were dealing with.

"In the meantime, Saleh was progressing very favourably; and, indeed, would have been up and about, had I not peremptorily ordered him to remain quiet.

"'You are doing well,' I said. 'Why should you risk bringing on inflammation, merely for the sake of getting about a few days earlier?'

"Abdullah was also better, but still extremely weak, and I had to order that meat should be boiled for some hours, and that he should drink small quantities of the broth, three or four times a day. Many times a day women came to me, to ask me to see to their husbands' wounds; and sometimes the wounded men came to me, themselves. All the serious cases I referred to the hakims, and confined myself simply to dressing and bandaging wounds, which had grown angry for want of attention. I always refused to accept fees, insisting that I was not a hakim, and simply afforded my help as a friend.

"I had the satisfaction, however, of doing a great deal of good, for in the medicine chest I found a large supply of plaster and bandages. Frequently mothers brought children to me. These I could have treated with some of the simple drugs in the chest, but I refused to do so; for I could not have explained, in any satisfactory way, how I knew one drug from another, or was acquainted with their qualities. Still, although I refused fees, I had many little presents of fowls, fruit, pumpkins, and other things. These prevented my feeling that I was a burden upon Saleh, for of course I put them into the general stock.

"So far, I cannot but look back with deep gratitude for the strange manner in which I have been enabled to avert all suspicion, and even to make myself quite a popular character among the people of El Obeid.

"One bottle I found in the medicine chest was a great prize to me. It contained iodine and, with a weak solution of this, I was able to maintain my colour. I did not care so much for my face and hands, for I was so darkened by the sun that my complexion was little fairer than that of many of the Arabs. But I feared that an accidental display, of a portion of my body usually covered by my garments, would at once prove that I was a white man. I had used up the stuff that I had brought with me, when I escaped from the square; and having no means of procuring fresh stain, was getting uneasy; but this discovery of the iodine put it within my power to renew my colouring, whenever it was necessary.

"About a month later. I have been living here quietly, since I last wrote in this journal. The day after I had done so, the Emir sent for me, and said he had heard that I had taken bullets out of wounds, and had shown the two doctors of the town how to do so, by means of instruments found in a chest that was among the loot brought in from the battlefield. I repeated my story to him, as to how I had acquired the knowledge from being in the service of a white hakim, from Cairo, who was travelling in the desert; and that I had no other medical knowledge, except that I had seen, in the chest, a bottle which contained stuff like that the white doctors used in order to put a patient to sleep, so that they could take off a limb without his feeling pain.

"'I have heard of such things being done by the Turkish hakims at Khartoum, but I did not believe them. It is against all reason.'

"'I have seen it done, my lord,' I said. 'I do not say that I could take off a limb, as they did, but I am sure that the stuff would put anyone to sleep.'

"'I wish you to put it to the trial,' the Emir said. 'One of my sons came back, from the battle, with a bullet hole through his hand. The hakim said that two of the bones were broken. He put bandages round, and my son said no more about it. He is a man who does not complain of slight troubles, but yesterday evening the pain became so great that he was forced to mention it; and when I examined his arm, I found that it was greatly swelled. Slaves have been bathing it with cold water, ever since, but the pain has increased rather than diminished.'

"'I will look at it, my lord, but I greatly fear that it is beyond my poor skill to deal with it.'

"The young man was brought in and, on removing the bandage, I saw that the wound was in a terrible state, and the arm greatly inflamed, some distance up the wrist. It was a bad case, and it seemed to me that, unless something was done, mortification would speedily set in.

"'The two doctors saw it an hour ago,' the Emir went on, 'and they greatly fear for his life. They told me that they could do nothing, but that, as you had seen the white hakim do wonderful things, you might be able to do something.'

"'My lord,' I said, 'it is one thing to watch an operation, but quite another to perform it yourself. I think, as the doctors have told you, your son's life is in great danger; and I do believe that, if there were white doctors here to take off his arm, he might be saved. But I could not undertake it. The skill to do so is only acquired by long years of study. How can I, a poor man, know how to do such things? Were I to attempt and fail, what would you say?—that I had killed your son; and that, but for me, he might have recovered.'

"'He will not recover,' the Emir said, moodily.

"'What say you, Abu? You have heard what this man says; what do you think?'

"'I think, Father, that it were well to try. This man has used his eyes, so well, that he has taken the white man's instruments, and drawn out bullets from wounds. I feel as if this wound will kill me; therefore, if the man fails, I shall be none the worse. Indeed, it would be better to die at once, than to feel this fire burning, till it burns me up.'

"'You hear what my son says? I am of the same opinion. Do your best. Should you fail, I swear, by the head of the Prophet, that no harm shall come to you.'

"The wounded man was a fine young fellow, of three or four and twenty.

"'If it is my lord's will, I will try,' I said; 'but I pray you to bear in mind that I do so at your command, and without much hope of accomplishing it successfully. It would, I think, be advisable that the limb should be taken off above the elbow, so that it will be above the spot to which the inflammation has extended.'

"The Emir looked at his son, who said:

"'It matters not, Father. 'Tis but my left arm, and I shall still have my right, to hurl a spear or wield a sword.'

"I need not tell how I got through the operation. Everything required for it—the inhaler, sponges, straight and crooked needles, and thread—was in the chest. The young Arab objected to be sent to sleep. He said it might be well for cowards, but not for a fighting man. I had to assure him that it was not for his sake, but for my own, that I wished him to go to sleep; and that if I knew he was not suffering pain, I might be able to do the thing without my hand trembling; but that if I knew he was suffering, I should be flurried.

"I insisted that the hakims should be sent for. When they came I called them to witness that, at the Emir's command, I was going to try to do the operation I had seen the white doctor perform, although I was but an ignorant man, and feared greatly that I might fail. I really was desperately nervous, though at the same time I did feel that, having seen the operation performed two or three times, and as it was a simple one, I ought to be able to do it. Of course, I had everything laid handy. The tourniquet was first put on the arm, and screwed tightly. Then I administered the chloroform, which took its effect speedily. My nerves were braced up now, and I do think I made a fair job of it—finding and tying up the arteries, cutting and sawing the bone off, and making a flap. A few stitches to keep this together, and it was done, and to my relief the Arab, who had lain as rigid as a statue, winced a little when the last stitch was put in.

"This was the point on which I had been most anxious. I was not sure whether the amount of chloroform he had inhaled might not have been too strong for him.

"'Do not try to move,' I said, as he opened his eyes and looked round, as if trying to remember where he was.

"As his eyes fell upon me, he said, 'When are you going to begin?'

"'I have finished,' I said, 'but you must lie quiet, for some time. The slightest movement now might cause the flow of blood to burst out.'

"The Emir had stood staring at his son's quiet face, as if amazed beyond the power of speech. Four Dervishes had held the patient's limbs, so as to prevent any accidental movement. A female slave had held a large basin of warm water, and another handed me the things I pointed to. I had begged the hakims to keep their attention fixed on what I was doing, in order that these also might see how the white doctor did such things.

"When his son spoke, the Emir gave a gasp of relief. 'He lives,' he murmured, as if even now he could scarcely believe that this was possible; and as he put his hand upon my shoulder it trembled with emotion.

"'Truly the ways of the white infidels are marvellous. Abu, my son, Allah has been merciful! He must have meant that you should not die, and thus have sent this man, who has seen the white hakims at work, to save your life!

"What is to be done now?' he went on, turning to me.

"'He should be raised very gently, and clothes put under his shoulder and head. Then he should be carried, on the angareb, to the coolest place in the house. He may drink a little juice of fruit, but he had best eat nothing. The great thing is to prevent fever coming on. With your permission I will stay with him, for if one of the threads you saw me tie, round these little white tubes in the arm, should slip or give way, he would be dead in five minutes; unless this machine round the arm is tightened at once, and the tube that carries the blood is tied up. It would be well that he should have a slave to fan him. I hope he will sleep.'

"The Emir gave orders for the bed to be carried to the room adjoining his harem.

"'His mother and his young wife will want to see him,' he said to me, 'and when the danger that you speak of is past, the women will care for him. You will be master in the room, and will give such orders as you please.'

"Then he turned off, and walked hastily away. I could see that he had spoken with difficulty, and that, in spite of his efforts to appear composed and tranquil, his mouth was twitching, and his eyes moist.

"As soon as the bed had been placed, by my directions, near the open window, the four Dervishes left the room. The hakims were on the point of doing so, when I said:

"'I will stay here for a few minutes, and will then come out and talk this matter over with you. I have been fortunate, indeed, in remembering so well what I saw. I heard a white hakim explain how he did each thing, and why, to the sheik of the wounded man's party; and I will tell you what I remember of it, and you, with your wisdom in these matters, will be able to do it far better than I.'

"When they had retired, the door leading into the harem opened, and a woman, slightly veiled, followed by a younger woman and two slave girls, came in. I stopped her, as she was hurrying towards her son.

"'Lady,' I said, 'I pray you to speak very quietly, and in few words. It is most important that he should not be excited, in any way, but should be kept perfectly quiet, for the next two or three days.'

"'I will do so,' she said. 'May I touch him?'

"'You may take his hand in yours, but do not let him move. I will leave you with him for a few minutes. Please remember that everything depends upon his not being agitated.'

"I went out and joined the hakims.

"'Truly, Mudil, Allah has given you strange gifts,' one of them said. 'Wonderful is it that you should have remembered so well what you saw; and more wonderful still is it, that you should have the firmness to cut and saw flesh and bone, as if they were those of a dead sheep, with the Emir standing by to look at you!'

"'I knew that his life, and perhaps mine, depended upon it. The Emir would have kept his oath, I doubt not; but when it became known in the town that Abu, who is known to all for his bravery and goodness, died in my hands, it would not have been safe for me to leave this house.'

"I then explained the reason for each step that I took. They listened most attentively, and asked several questions, showing that they were intensely interested, and most anxious to be able to perform so wonderful an operation themselves. They were greatly surprised at the fact that so little blood flowed.

"'It seems,' I said, 'from what I heard the white hakim say, that the blood flowed through those little white tubes. By twisting the tourniquet very tight, that flow of blood is stopped. The great thing is to find those little tubes, and tie them up. As you would notice, the large ones in the inside of the arm could be seen quite plainly. When they cannot be seen, the screw is unloosed so as to allow a small quantity of blood to flow, which shows you where the tubes are. You will remember that I took hold of each, with the bent point of a small wire or a pair of these nippers; and, while you held it, tied the thread tightly round it. When that is done, one is ready to cut the bone. You saw me push the flesh back, so as to cut the bone as high up as possible; that is because the white doctor said the flesh would shrink up, and the bone would project. I cut the flesh straight on one side, and on the other with a flap that will, when it is stitched, cover over the bone and the rest of the flesh, and make what the hakim called a pad. He said all cutting off of limbs was done in this way, but of course the tubes would not lie in the same place, and the cutting would have to be made differently; but it was all the same system. He called these simple operations, and said that anyone with a firm hand, and a knowledge of where these tubes lie, ought to be able to do it, after seeing it done once or twice. He said, of course, it would not be so neatly done as by men who had been trained to it; but that, in cases of extreme necessity, anyone who had seen it done once or twice, and had sufficient nerve, could do it; especially if they had, ready at hand, this stuff that makes the wounded man sleep and feel no pain.

"'I listened very attentively, because all seemed to me almost like magic, but I certainly did not think that I should ever have to do such a thing, myself.'

"'But what would be done if they had not that sleep medicine?'

"'The hakim said that, in that case, the wounded man would have to be fastened down by bandages to the bed, and held by six strong men, so that he could not move in the slightest. However, there is enough of that stuff to last a hundred times or more; for, as you see, only a good-sized spoonful was used.'

"The Emir, who had passed through the harem rooms, now opened the door.

"'Come in,' he said. 'My son is quiet, and has not moved. He has spoken to his mother, and seems quite sensible. Is there anything more for you to do to him?'

"'I will put a bandage loosely round his arm, and bind it to his body so that he cannot move it in his sleep, or on first waking. It will not be necessary for me to stay with him, as the ladies of the harem can look after him; but I must remain in the next room, so as to be ready to run in, at once, should they see that the wound is bleeding again. I have asked the hakims to make a soothing potion, to aid him to sleep long and soundly.'

"As I went up to the side of the bed, Abu smiled. I bent down to him, and he said in a low voice:

"'All the pain has gone. May Allah bless you!'

"'I am afraid that you will feel more pain, tomorrow, but I do not think it will be so bad as it was before. Now, I hope you will try to go to sleep. You will be well looked after, and I shall be in the next room, if you want me. The hakims will give you a soothing draught soon, and you can have cool drinks when you want them.'

"Things went on as well as I could have wished. In four or five days the threads came away, and I loosened the tourniquet slightly, and strapped up the edges of the wound, which were already showing signs of healing. For the first twenty-four hours I had remained always on watch; after that the hakims took their turns, I remaining in readiness to tighten up the tourniquet, should there be any rush of blood. I did not leave the Emir's house, but slept in a room close by that of the patient.

"There was now, however, no longer need for my doing so. The splendid constitution of the young Baggara had, indeed, from the first rendered any attendance unnecessary. There was no fever, and very little local inflammation; and I was able to gladden his heart by telling him that, in another fortnight, he would be able to be up.

"The day I was intending to leave, the Emir sent for me. He was alone.

"'The more I think over this matter,' he said, 'the more strange it is that you should be able to do all these wonderful things, after having seen it done once by the white hakim. The more I think of it, the more certain I feel that you are not what you seem. I have sent for Saleh and

Abdullah. They have told me what you did for them, and that you gave up your horse to them, and dressed their wounds, and brought them in here. They are full of praise of your goodness, and but few of my people would have thus acted, for strangers. They would have given them a drink of water, and ridden on.

"Now, tell me frankly and without fear. I have thought it over, and I feel sure that you, yourself, are a white hakim, who escaped from the battle in which Hicks's army was destroyed.'

"'I am not a hakim. All that I said was true—that although I have seen operations performed, I have never performed them myself. As to the rest, I answer you frankly, I am an Englishman. I did escape when the black Soudanese battalion surrendered, three days after the battle. I was not a fighting officer. I was with them as interpreter. I may say that, though I am not a hakim, I did for some time study with the intention of becoming one, and so saw many operations performed.'

"'I am glad that you told me,' the Emir said gravely. 'Your people are brave and very wise, though they cannot stand against the power of the Mahdi. But were you Sheitan himself, it would be nothing to me. You have saved my son's life. You are the honoured guest of my house. Your religion is different from mine, but as you showed that you were willing to aid followers of the Prophet and the Mahdi, although they were your enemies, surely I, for whom you have done so much, may well forget that difference.'

"'I thank you, Emir. From what I had seen of you, I felt sure that my secret would be safe with you. We Christians feel no enmity against followers of Mahomet—the hatred is all on your side. And yet, 'tis strange, the Allah that you worship, and the God of the Christians, is one and the same. Mahomet himself had no enmity against the Christians, and regarded our Christ as a great prophet, like himself.

"Our Queen reigns, in India, over many more Mohamedans than are ruled by the Sultan of Turkey. They are loyal to her, and know that under her sway no difference is made between them and her Christian subjects, and have fought as bravely for her as her own white troops.'

"'I had never thought,' the Emir said, 'that the time would come when I should call an infidel my friend; but now that I can do so, I feel that there is much in what you say. However, your secret must be kept. Were it known that you are a white man, you would be torn to pieces in the streets; and even were you to remain here, where assuredly none would dare touch you, the news would speedily travel to my lord the Mahdi, and he would send a troop of horse to bring you to him. Therefore, though I would fain honour you, I see that it is best that you should, to all save myself, continue to be Mudil. I will not even, as I would otherwise have done, assign you a house, and slaves, and horses in token of my gratitude to you for having saved the life of my son.

"'Something I must do, or I should seem utterly ungrateful. I can, at any rate, give you rooms here, and treat you as an honoured guest. This would excite no remark, as it would be naturally expected that you would stay here until my son is perfectly cured. I shall tell no one, not even my wife; but Abu I will tell, when he is cured, and the secret will be as safe with him as with me. I think it would please him to know. Although a Baggara like myself, and as brave as any, he is strangely gentle in disposition; and though ready and eager to fight, when attacked by other tribes, he does not care to go on expeditions against villages which have not acknowledged the power of the Mahdi, and makes every excuse to avoid doing so. It will please him to know that the man who has saved his life is one who, although of a different race and religion, is willing to do kindness to an enemy; and will love and honour you more, for knowing it.'

"'I thank you deeply, Emir, and anything that I can do for members of your family, I shall be glad to do. I have a knowledge of the usages of many of the drugs in the chest that was brought here. I have not dared to say so before, because I could not have accounted for knowing such things.'

"So at present I am installed in the Emir's palace, and my prospects grow brighter and brighter. After the great victory the Mahdi has won, it is likely that he will be emboldened to advance against Khartoum. In that case he will, no doubt, summon his followers from all parts, and I shall be able to ride with the Emir or his son; and it will be hard if, when we get near the city, I cannot find some opportunity of slipping off and making my way there. Whether it will be prudent to do so is another question, for I doubt whether the Egyptian troops there will offer any resolute resistance to the Dervish hosts; and in that case, I should have to endeavour to make my way down to Dongola, and from there either by boat or by the river bank to Assouan.

"A month later. I have not written for some time, because there has been nothing special to put down. All the little details of the life here can be told to my dear wife, if I should ever see her again; but they are not of sufficient interest to write down. I have been living at the Emir's house, ever since. I do not know what special office I am supposed to occupy in his household—that is, what office the people in general think that I hold. In fact, I am his guest, and an honoured one. When he goes out I ride beside him and Abu, who has now sufficiently recovered to sit his horse. I consider myself as medical attendant, in ordinary, to him and his family. I have given up all practice in the town—in the first place because I do not wish to make enemies of the two doctors, who really seem very good fellows, and I am glad to find that they have performed two or three operations successfully; and in the second place, were I to go about trying to cure the sick, people would get so interested in me that I should be continually questioned as to how I attained my marvellous skill. Happily, though no doubt they must have felt somewhat jealous at my success with Abu, I have been able to do the hakims some service, put fees into their pockets, and at the same time benefited poor people here. I have told them that, just as I recognized the bottle of chloroform, so I have recognized some of the bottles from which the white hakims used to give powder to sick people.

"'For instance,' I said, 'you see this bottle, which is of a different shape from the others. It is full of a white, feathery-looking powder. They used to give this to people suffering from fever—about as much as you could put on your nail for men and women, and half as much for children. They used to put it in a little water, and stir it up, and give it to them night and morning. They call it kena, or something like that. It did a great deal of good, and generally drove away the fever.

"'This other bottle they also used a good deal. They put a little of its contents in water, and it made a lotion for weak and sore eyes. They called it zing. They saw I was a careful man, and I often made the eye wash, and put the other white powder up into little packets when they were busy, as fever and ophthalmia are the two most common complaints among the natives.'

"The hakims were immensely pleased, and both told me, afterwards, that both these medicines had done wonders. I told them that I thought there were some more bottles of these medicines in the chest, and that when they had finished those I had now given them, I would look out for the others. I had, in fact, carried off a bottle both of quinine and zinc powder for my own use, and with the latter I greatly benefited several of the Emir's children and grandchildren, all of whom were suffering from ophthalmia; or from sore eyes, that would speedily have developed that disease, if they had not been attended to.

"I had only performed one operation, which was essentially a minor one. Abu told me that his wife, of whom he was very fond, was suffering very great pain from a tooth—could I cure her?

"I said that, without seeing the tooth, I could not do anything, and he at once said:

"'As it is for her good, Mudil, I will bring her into this room, and she shall unveil so that you can examine the tooth.'

"She was quite a girl, and for an Arab very good looking. She and the Emir's wife were continually sending me out choice bits from their dinner, but I had not before seen her face. She was evidently a good deal confused, at thus unveiling before a man, but Abu said:

"'It is with my permission that you unveil, therefore there can be no harm in it. Besides, has not Mudil saved my life, and so become my brother?'

"He opened her mouth. The tooth was far back and broken, and the gum was greatly swelled.

"'It is very bad,' I said to Abu. 'It would hurt her terribly, if I were to try and take it out; but if she will take the sleeping medicine I gave you, I think that I could do it.'

"'Then she shall take it,' he said at once. 'It is not unpleasant. On the contrary, I dreamt a pleasant dream while you were taking off my arm. Please do it, at once.'

"I at once fetched the chloroform, the inhaler, and a pair of forceps which looked well suited for the purpose, and probably were intended for it. I then told her to lie down on the angareb, which I placed close to the window.

"'Now, Abu,' I said, 'directly she has gone off to sleep, you must force her mouth open, and put the handle of your dagger between her teeth. It will not hurt her at all. But I cannot get at the tooth unless the mouth is open, and we cannot open it until she is asleep, for the whole side of her face is swollen, and the jaw almost stiff.'

"The chloroform took effect very quickly. Her husband had some difficulty in forcing the mouth open. When he had once done so, I took a firm hold of the tooth, and wrenched it out.

"'You can withdraw the dagger,' I said, 'and then lift her up, and let her rinse her mouth well with the warm water I brought in. She will have little pain afterwards, though of course it will take some little time, before the swelling goes down.'

"Then I went out, and left them together. In a few minutes, Abu came out.

"'She has no pain,' he said. 'She could hardly believe, when she came round, that the tooth was out. It is a relief, indeed. She has cried, day and night, for the past three days.'

"'Tell her that, for the rest of the day, she had better keep quiet; and go to sleep if possible, which I have no doubt she will do, as she must be worn out with the pain she has been suffering.'

"'I begin to see, Mudil, that we are very ignorant. We can fight, but that is all we are good for. How much better it would be if, instead of regarding you white men as enemies, we could get some of you to live here, and teach us the wonderful things that you know!'

"'Truly it would be better,' I said. 'It all depends upon yourselves. You have a great country. If you would but treat the poor people here well, and live in peace with other tribes; and send word down to Cairo that you desire, above all things, white hakims and others who would teach you, to come up and settle among you, assuredly they would come. There are thousands of white men and women working in India, and China, and other countries, content to do good, not looking for high pay, but content to live poorly. The difficulty is not in getting men willing to heal and to teach, but to persuade those whom they would benefit to allow them to do the work.'

"Abu shook his head.

"'That is it,' he said. 'I would rather be able to do such things as you do, than be one of the most famous soldiers of the Mahdi; but I could never persuade others. They say that the Mahdi himself, although he is hostile to the Turks, and would conquer Egypt, would willingly befriend white men. But even he, powerful as he is, cannot go against the feelings of his emirs. Must we always be ignorant? Must we always be fighting? I can see no way out of it. Can you, Mudil?'

"'I can see but one way,' I said, 'and that may seem to you impossible, because you know nothing of the strength of England. We have, as you know, easily beaten the Egyptian Army; and we are now protectors of Egypt. If you invade that country, as the Mahdi has already threatened to do, it is we who will defend it; and if there is no other way of obtaining peace, we shall some day send an army to recover the Soudan. You will fight, and you will fight desperately, but you have no idea of the force that will advance against you. You know how Osman Digna's tribes on the Red Sea have been defeated, not by the superior courage of our men, but by our superior arms. And so it will be here. It may be many years before it comes about, but if you insist on war, that is what will come.

"'Then, when we have taken the Soudan, there will come peace, and the peasant will till his soil in safety. Those who desire to be taught will be taught; great canals from the Nile will irrigate the soil, and the desert will become fruitful.'

"'You really think that would come of it?' Abu asked, earnestly.

"'I do indeed, Abu. We have conquered many brave peoples, far more numerous than yours; and those who were our bitterest enemies now see how they have benefited by it. Certainly, England would not undertake the cost of such an expedition lightly; but if she is driven to it by your advance against Egypt, she will assuredly do so. Your people—I mean the Baggaras and their allies—would suffer terribly; but the people whom you have conquered, whose villages you have burned, whose women you have carried off, would rejoice.'

"'We would fight,' Abu said passionately.

"'Certainly you would fight, and fight gallantly, but it would not avail you. Besides, Abu, you would be fighting for that ignorance you have just regretted, and against the teaching and progress you have wished for.'

"'It is hard,' Abu said, quietly.

"'It is hard, but it has been the fate of all people who have resisted the advance of knowledge and civilization. Those who accept civilization, as the people of India—of whom there are many more than in all Africa—have accepted it, are prosperous. In America and other great countries, far beyond the seas, the native Indians opposed it, but in vain; and now a great white race inhabit the land, and there is but a handful left of those who opposed them.'

"'These things are hard to understand. If, as you say, your people come here some day to fight against us, I shall fight. If my people are defeated, and I am still alive, I shall say it is the will of Allah; let us make the best of it, and try to learn to be like those who have conquered us. I own to you that I am sick of bloodshed—not of blood shed in battle, but the blood of peaceful villagers; and though I grieve for my own people, I should feel that it was for the good of the land that the white men had become the masters.'"

CHAPTER 19:

The Last Page.

"Khartoum, September 3rd, 1884.

"It is a long time since I made my last entry. I could put no date to it then, and till yesterday could hardly even have named the month. I am back again among friends, but I can hardly say that I am safer here than I was at El Obeid. I have not written, because there was nothing to write. One day was like another, and as my paper was finished, and there were no incidents in my life, I let the matter slide.

"Again and again I contemplated attempting to make my way to this town, but the difficulties would be enormous. There were the dangers of the desert, the absence of wells, the enormous probability of losing my way, and, most of all, the chance that, before I reached Khartoum, it would have been captured. The Emir had been expecting news of its fall, for months.

"There had been several fights, in some of which they had been victorious. In others, even according to their own accounts, they had been worsted. Traitors in the town kept them well informed of the state of supplies. They declared that these were almost exhausted, and that the garrison must surrender. Indeed, several of the commanders of bodies of troops had offered to surrender posts held by them.

"So I had put aside all hope of escape, and decided not to make any attempt until after Khartoum fell, when the Dervishes boasted they would march down and conquer Egypt, to the sea.

"They had already taken Berber. Dongola was at their mercy. I thought the best chance would be to go down with them, as far as they went, and then to slip away. In this way I should shorten the journey I should have to traverse alone; and, being on the river bank, could at least always obtain water. Besides, I might possibly secure some small native boat, and with the help of the current get down to Assouan before the Dervishes could arrive there. This I should have attempted; but, three weeks ago, an order came from the Mahdi to El Khatim, ordering him to send to Omdurman five hundred well-armed men, who were to be commanded by his son Abu. Khatim was to remain at El Obeid, with the main body of his force, until further orders.

"Abu came to me at once, with the news.

"'You will take me with you, Abu,' I exclaimed. 'This is the chance I have been hoping for. Once within a day's journey of Khartoum, I could slip away at night, and it would be very hard if I could not manage to cross the Nile into Khartoum.'

"'I will take you, if you wish it,' he said. 'The danger will be very great, not in going with me, but in making your way into Khartoum.'

"'It does not seem to me that it would be so,' I said. 'I should strike the river four or five miles above the town, cut a bundle of rushes, swim out to the middle of the river, drift down till I was close to the town, and then swim across.'

"'So be it,' he said. 'It is your will, not mine.'

"Khatim came to me afterwards, and advised me to stay, but I said that it might be years before I had another chance to escape; and that, whatever risk there was, I would prefer running it.

"'Then we shall see you no more,' he said, 'for Khartoum will assuredly fall, and you will be killed.'

"'If you were a prisoner in the hands of the white soldiers, Emir,' I said, 'I am sure that you would run any risk, if there was a chance of getting home again. So it is with me. I have a wife and child, in Cairo. Her heart must be sick with pain, at the thought of my death. I will risk anything to get back as soon as possible. If I reach Khartoum, and it is afterwards captured, I can disguise myself and appear as I now am, hide for a while, and then find out where Abu is and join him again. But perhaps, when he sees that no further resistance can be made, General Gordon will embark on one of his steamers and go down the river, knowing that it would be better for the people of the town that the Mahdi should enter without opposition; in which case you would scarcely do harm to the peaceful portion of the population, or to the troops who had laid down their arms.'

"'Very well,' the Emir said. 'Abu has told me that he has tried to dissuade you, but that you will go. We owe you a great debt of gratitude, for all that you have done for us, and therefore I will not try to dissuade you. I trust Allah will protect you.'

"And so we started the next morning. I rode by the side of Abu, and as all knew that I was the hakim who had taken off his arm, none wondered. The journey was made without any incident worth recording. Abu did not hurry. We made a long march between each of the wells, and then halted for a day. So we journeyed, until we made our last halt before arriving at Omdurman.

"'You are still determined to go?' Abu said to me.

"'I shall leave tonight, my friend.'

"'I shall not forget all that you have told me about your people, hakim. Should any white man fall into my hands, I will spare him for your sake. These are evil times, and I regret all that has passed. I believe that the Mahdi is a prophet; but I fear that, in many things, he has misunderstood the visions and orders he received. I see that evil rather than good has fallen upon the land, and that though we loved not the rule of the Egyptians, we were all better off under it than we are now. We pass through ruined villages, and see the skeletons of many people.

We know that where the waterwheels formerly spread the water from the rivers over the fields, is now a desert; and that, except the fighting men, the people perish from hunger.

"'All this is bad. I see that, if we enter Egypt, we shall be like a flight of locusts. We shall eat up the country and leave a desert behind us. Surely this cannot be according to the wishes of Allah, who is all merciful. You have taught me much in your talks with me, and I do not see things as I used to. So much do I feel it, that in my heart I could almost wish that your countrymen should come here, and establish peace and order.

"'The Mohamedans of India, you tell me, are well content with their rulers. Men may exercise their religion and their customs, without hindrance. They know that the strong cannot prey upon the weak, and each man reaps what he has sown, in peace. You tell me that India was like the Soudan before you went there—that there were great conquerors, constant wars, and the peasants starved while the robbers grew rich; and that, under your rule, peace and contentment were restored. I would that it could be so here. But it seems, to me, impossible that we should be conquered by people so far away.'

"'I hope that it will be so, Abu; and I think that if the great and good white general, Governor Gordon, is murdered at Khartoum, the people of my country will never rest until his death has been avenged.'

"'You had better take your horse,' he said. 'If you were to go on foot, it would be seen that there was a horse without a rider, and there would be a search for you; but if you and your horse are missing, it will be supposed that you have ridden on to Omdurman to give notice of our coming, and none will think more of the matter.'

"As soon as the camp was asleep, I said goodbye to Abu; and took my horse by the reins and led him into the desert, half a mile away. Then I mounted, and rode fast. The stars were guide enough, and in three hours I reached the Nile. I took off the horse's saddle and bridle, and left him to himself. Then I crept out and cut a bundle of rushes, and swam into the stream with them.

"After floating down the river for an hour, I saw the light of a few fires on the right bank, and guessed that this was a Dervish force, beleaguering Khartoum from that side. I drifted on for another hour, drawing closer and closer to the shore, until I could see walls and forts; then I stripped off my Dervish frock, and swam ashore.

"I had, during the time we had been on the journey, abstained from staining my skin under my garments, in order that I might be recognized as a white man, as soon as I bared my arms.

"I lay down till it was broad daylight, and then walked up to the foot of a redoubt. There were shouts of surprise from the black soldiers there, as I approached. I shouted to them, in Arabic, that I was an Englishman; and two or three of them at once ran down the slope, and aided me to climb it. I was taken, at my request, to General Gordon, who was surprised, indeed, when I told him that I was a survivor of Hicks's force, and had been living nine months at El Obeid.

"'You are heartily welcome, sir,' he said; 'but I fear that you have come into an even greater danger than you have left, for our position here is well-nigh desperate. For months I have been praying for aid from England, and my last news was that it was just setting out, so I fear there is no hope that it will reach me in time. The government of England will have to answer, before God, for their desertion of me, and of the poor people here, whom they sent me to protect from the Mahdi.

"'For myself, I am content. I have done my duty as far as lay in my power, but I had a right to rely upon receiving support from those who sent me. I am in the hands of God. But for the many thousands who trusted in me, and remained here, I feel very deeply.

"'Now the first thing is to provide you with clothes. I am expecting Colonel Stewart here, every minute, and he will see that you are made comfortable.'

"'I shall be glad to place myself at your disposal, sir,' I said. 'I speak Arabic fluently, and shall be ready to perform any service of which I may be capable.'

"'I thank you,' he said, 'and will avail myself of your offer, if I see any occasion; but at present, we have rather to suffer than to do. We have occasional fights, but of late the attacks have been feeble, and I think that the Mahdi depends upon hunger rather than force to obtain possession of this town.

"This evening, I will ask you to tell me your story. Colonel Stewart will show you a room. There is only one other white man—Mr. Power—here. We live together as one family, of which you will now be a member.'

"I felt strange when I came to put on my European clothes. Mr. Power, who tells me he has been here for some years, as correspondent of the *Times*, has this afternoon taken me round the defences, and into the workshops. I think the place can resist any attacks, if the troops remain faithful; but of this there is a doubt. A good many of the Soudanese have already been sent away. As Gordon said at dinner this evening, if he had but a score of English officers, he would be perfectly confident that he could resist any enemy save starvation.

"September 12th:

"It has been settled that Colonel Stewart and Mr. Power are to go down the river in the Abbas, and I am to go with them. The General proposed it to me. I said that I could not think of leaving him here by himself, so he said kindly:

"'I thank you, Mr. Hilliard, but you could do no good here, and would only be throwing away your life. We can hold on to the end of the year, though the pinch will be very severe; but I think we can make the stores last, till then. But by the end of December our last crust will have been eaten, and the end will have come. It will be a satisfaction to me to know that I have done my best, and fail only because of the miserable delays and hesitation of government.'

"So it is settled that I am going. The gunboats are to escort us for some distance. Were it not for Gordon, I should feel delighted at the prospect. It is horrible to leave him—one of the noblest Englishmen!—alone to his fate. My only consolation is that if I remained I could not avert it, but should only be a sharer in it.

"September 18th:

"We left Khartoum on the 14th, and came down without any serious trouble until this morning, when the boat struck on a rock in the cataract, opposite a village called Hebbeh. A hole has been knocked in her bottom, and there is not a shadow of hope of getting her off. Numbers of the natives have gathered on the shore. I have advised that we should disregard their invitations to land, but that, as there would be no animosity against the black crew, they would be safe; and that we three whites should take the ship's boat, and four of the crew, put provisions for a week on board, and make our way down the river. Colonel Stewart, however, feels convinced that the people can be trusted, and that we had better land and place ourselves under the protection of the sheik. He does not know the Arabs as well as I do.

"However, as he has determined to go ashore, I can do nothing. I consider it unlikely, in the extreme, that there will be any additions to this journal. If, at any time in the future, this should fall into the hands of any of my countrymen, I pray that they will send it down to my dear wife, Mrs. Hilliard, whom, I pray, God may bless and comfort, care of the Manager of the Bank, Cairo."

CHAPTER 20:

A Momentous Communication.

Gregory had, after finishing the record, sat without moving until the dinner hour. It was a relief to him to know that his father had not spent the last years of his life as he had feared, as a miserable slave—ill treated, reviled, insulted, perhaps chained and beaten by some brutal taskmaster; but had been in a position where, save that he was an exile, kept from his home and wife, his lot had not been unbearable. He knew more of him than he had ever known before. It was as a husband that his mother had always spoken of him; but here he saw that he was daring, full of resource, quick to grasp any opportunity, hopeful and yet patient, longing eagerly to rejoin his wife, and yet content to wait until the chances should be all in his favour. He was unaffectedly glad thus to know him; to be able, in future, to think of him as one of whom he would have been proud; who would assuredly have won his way to distinction.

It was not so that he had before thought of him. His mother had said that he was of good family, and that it was on account of his marriage with her that he had quarrelled with his relations. It had always seemed strange to him that he should have been content to take, as she had told him, an altogether subordinate position in a mercantile house in Alexandria. She had accounted for his knowledge of Arabic by the fact that he had been, for two years, exploring the temples and tombs of Egypt with a learned professor; but surely, as a man of good family, he could have found something to do in England, instead of coming out to take so humble a post in Egypt.

Gregory knew nothing of the difficulty that a young man in England has, in obtaining an appointment of any kind, or of fighting his way single handed. Influence went for much in Egypt, and it seemed to him that, even if his father had quarrelled with his own people, there must have been many ways open to him of maintaining himself honourably. Therefore he had always thought that, although he might have been all that his mother described him—the tenderest and most loving of husbands, a gentleman, and estimable in all respects—his father must have been wanting in energy and ambition, deficient in the qualities that would fit him to fight his own battle, and content to gain a mere competence, instead of struggling hard to make his way up the ladder. He had accounted for his going up as interpreter, with Hicks Pasha, by the fact that his work with the contractor was at an end, and that he saw no other opening for himself.

He now understood how mistaken he had been, in his estimate of his father's character; and wondered, even more than before, why he should have taken that humble post at Alexandria. His mother had certainly told him, again and again, that he had done so simply because the doctors had said that she could not live in England; but surely, in all the wide empire of England, there must be innumerable posts that a gentleman could obtain. Perhaps he should understand it better, some day. At present, it seemed unaccountable to him. He felt sure that, had he lived, his father would have made a name for himself; and that it was in that hope, and not of the pay that he would receive as an interpreter, that he had gone up with Hicks; and that, had he not died at that little village by the Nile, he would assuredly have done so, for the narrative he had left behind him would in itself, if published, have shown what stuff there was in him.

It was hard that fate should have snatched him away, just when it had seemed that his trials were over, that he was on the point of being reunited to his wife. Still, it was a consolation to know he had died suddenly, as one falls in battle; not as a slave, worn out by grief and suffering.

As he left his hut, he said to Zaki:

"I shall not want you again this evening; but mind, we must be on the move at daylight."

"You did not say whether we were to take the horses, Master; but I suppose you will do so?"

"Oh, I forgot to tell you that we are going to have camels. They are to be put on board for us, tonight. They are fast camels and, as the distance from the point where we shall land to the Atbara will not be more than seventy or eighty miles, we shall be able to do it in a day."

"That will be very good, master. Camels are much better than horses, for the desert. I have got everything else ready."

After dinner was over, the party broke up quickly, as many of the officers had preparations to make. Gregory went off to the tent of the officer with whom he was best acquainted in the Soudanese regiment.

"I thought that I would come and have a chat with you, if you happened to be in."

"I shall be very glad, but I bar Fashoda. One is quite sick of the name."

"No, it was not Fashoda that I was going to talk to you about. I want to ask you something about England. I know really nothing about it, for I was born in Alexandria, shortly after my parents came out from England.

"Is it easy for anyone who has been well educated, and who is a gentleman, to get employment there? I mean some sort of appointment, say, in India or the West Indies."

"Easy! My dear Hilliard, the camel in the eye of a needle is a joke to it. If a fellow is eighteen, and has had a first-rate education and a good private coach, that is, a tutor, he may pass through his examination either for the army, or the civil service, or the Indian service. There are about five hundred go up to each examination, and seventy or eighty at the outside get in. The other four hundred or so are chucked. Some examinations are for fellows under nineteen, others are open for a year or two longer. Suppose, finally, you don't get in; that is to say, when you are two-and-twenty, your chance of getting any appointment, whatever, in the public service is at an end."

"Then interest has nothing to do with it?"

"Well, yes. There are a few berths in the Foreign Office, for example, in which a man has to get a nomination before going in for the exam; but of course the age limit tells there, as well as in any other."

"And if a man fails altogether, what is there open to him?"

The other shrugged his shoulders.

"Well, as far as I know, if he hasn't capital he can emigrate. That is what numbers of fellows do. If he has interest, he can get a commission in the militia, and from that possibly into the line; or he can enlist as a private, for the same object. There is a third alternative, he can hang himself. Of course, if he happens to have a relation in the city he can get a clerkship; but that alternative, I should say, is worse than the third."

"But I suppose he might be a doctor, a clergyman, or a lawyer?"

"I don't know much about those matters, but I do know that it takes about five years' grinding, and what is called 'walking the hospitals,' that is, going round the wards with the surgeons, before one is licensed to kill. I think, but I am not sure, that three years at the bar would admit you to practice, and usually another seven or eight years are spent, before you earn a penny. As for the Church, you have to go through the university, or one of the places we call training colleges; and when, at last, you are ordained, you may reckon, unless you have great family interest, on remaining a curate, with perhaps one hundred or one hundred and fifty pounds per annum, for eighteen or twenty years."

"And no amount of energy will enable a man of, say, four-and-twenty, without a profession, to obtain a post on which he could live with some degree of comfort?"

"I don't think energy would have anything to do with it. You cannot drop into a merchant's office and say, 'I want a snug berth, out in China;' or 'I should like an agency, in Mesopotamia.' If you have luck, anything is possible. If you haven't luck, you ought to fall back on my three alternatives—emigrate, enlist, or hang yourself. Of course, you can sponge on your friends for a year or two, if you are mean enough to do so; but there is an end to that sort of thing, in time.

"May I ask why you put the question, Hilliard? You have really a splendid opening, here. You are surely not going to be foolish enough to chuck it, with the idea of returning to England, and taking anything that may turn up?"

"No, I am not so foolish as that. I have had, as you say, luck—extraordinary luck—and I have quite made up my mind to stay in the service. No, I am really asking you because I know so little of England that I wondered how men who had a fair education, but no family interest, did get on."

"They very rarely do get on," the other said. "Of course, if they are inventive geniuses they may discover something—an engine, for example, that will do twice the work with half the consumption of fuel that any other engine will do; or, if chemically inclined, they may discover something that will revolutionize dyeing, for example: but not one man in a thousand is a genius; and, as a rule, the man you are speaking of—the ordinary public school and 'varsity man—if he has no interest, and is not bent upon entering the army, even as a private, emigrates if he hasn't sufficient income to live upon at home."

"Thank you! I had no idea it was so difficult to make a living in England, or to obtain employment, for a well-educated man of two or three and twenty."

"My dear Hilliard, that is the problem that is exercising the minds of the whole of the middle class of England, with sons growing up. Of course, men of business can take their sons into their own offices, and train them to their own profession; but after all, if a man has four or five sons, he cannot take them all into his office with a view to partnership. He may take one, but the others have to make their own way, somehow."

They chatted now upon the war, the dates upon which the various regiments would go down, and the chance of the Khalifa collecting another army, and trying conclusions with the invaders again. At last, Gregory got up and went back to his hut. He could now understand why his father, having quarrelled with his family, might have found himself obliged to take the first post that was offered, however humble, in order to obtain the advantage of a warm climate for his wife.

"He must have felt it awfully," he mused. "If he had been the sort of man I had always thought him, he could have settled down to the life. But now I know him better, I can understand that it must have been terrible for him, and he would be glad to exchange it for the interpretership, where he would have some chance of distinguishing himself; or, at any rate, of taking part in exciting events.

"I will open that packet, but from what my mother said, I do not think it will be of any interest to me, now. I fancy, by what she said, that it contained simply my father's instructions as to what she was to do, in the event of his death during the campaign. I don't see what else it can be."

He drew the curtains he had rigged up, at the doorway and window, to keep out insects; lighted his lantern; and then, sitting down on the ground by his bed, opened the packet his mother had given him. The outer cover was in her handwriting.

"My dearest boy:

"I have, as I told you, kept the enclosed packet, which is not to be opened until I have certain news of your father's death. This news, I trust, you will some day obtain. As you see, the enclosed packet is directed to me. I do not think that you will find in it anything of importance, to yourself. It probably contains only directions and advice for my guidance, in case I should determine to return to England. I have been the less anxious to open it, because I have been convinced that it is so; for of course, I know the circumstances of his family, and there could be nothing new that he could write to me on that score.

"I have told you that he quarrelled with his father, because he chose to marry me. As you have heard from me, I was the daughter of a clergyman, and at his death took a post as governess. Your father fell in love with me. He was the son of the Honorable James Hartley, who was brother to the Earl of Langdale. Your father had an elder brother. Mr. Hartley was a man of the type now, happily, less common than it was twenty years ago. He had but a younger brother's portion, and a small estate that had belonged to his mother; but he was as proud as if he had been a peer of the realm, and owner of a county. I do not know exactly what the law of England is—whether, at the death of his brother, your grandfather would have inherited the title, or not. I never talked on this subject with your father, who very seldom alluded to matters at home. He had, also, two sisters.

"As he was clever, and had already gained some reputation by his explorations in Egypt; and was, moreover, an exceptionally handsome man—at least, I thought so—your grandfather made up his mind that he would make a very good marriage. When he learned of your father's affection for me, he was absolutely furious, told his son that he never wished to see him again, and spoke of me in a manner that Gregory resented; and as a result, they quarrelled.

"Your father left the house, never to enter it again. I would have released him from his promise, but he would not hear of it, and we were married. He had written for magazines and newspapers, on Egyptian subjects, and thought that he could make a living for us both, with his pen; but unhappily, he found that great numbers of men were trying to do the same; and that, although his papers on Egyptian discoveries had always been accepted, it was quite another thing when he came to write on general subjects.

"We had a hard time of it, but we were very happy, nevertheless.

Then came the time when my health began to give way. I had a terrible cough, and the doctor said that I must have a change to a warmer climate. We were very poor then—so poor that we had only a few shillings left, and lived in one room. Your father saw an advertisement for a man to go out to the branch of a London firm, at Alexandria. Without saying a word to me, he went and obtained it, thanks to his knowledge of Arabic.

"He was getting on well in the firm, when the bombardment of Alexandria took place. The offices and stores of his employers were burned; and, as it would take many months before they could be rebuilt, the employees were ordered home; but any who chose to stay were permitted to do so, and received three months' pay. Your father saw that there would be many chances, when the country settled down, and so took a post under a contractor of meat for the army.

"We moved to Cairo. Shortly after our arrival there he was, as he thought, fortunate in obtaining the appointment of an interpreter with Hicks Pasha. I did not try to dissuade him. Everyone supposed that the Egyptian troops would easily defeat the Dervishes. There was some danger, of course; but it seemed to me, as it did to him, that this opening would lead to better things; and that, when the rebellion was put down, he would be able to obtain some good civil appointment, in the Soudan. It was not the thought of his pay, as interpreter, that weighed in the slightest with either of us. I was anxious, above all things, that he should be restored to a position where he could associate with gentlemen, as one of themselves, and could again take his real name."

Gregory started, as he read this. He had never had an idea that the name he bore was not rightly his own, and even the statement of his grandfather's name had not struck him as affecting himself.

"Your father had an honourable pride in his name, which was an old one; and when he took the post at Alexandria, which was little above that of an ordinary office messenger, he did not care that he should be recognized, or that one of his name should be known to be occupying such a station. He did not change his name, he simply dropped the surname. His full name was Gregory Hilliard Hartley. He had always intended, when he had made a position for himself, to recur to it; and, of course, it will be open to you to do so, also. But I know that it would have been his wish that you, like him, should not do so, unless you had made such a position for yourself that you would be a credit to it.

"On starting, your father left me to decide whether I should go home. I imagine that the packet merely contains his views on that subject. He knew what mine were. I would rather have begged my bread, than have gone back to ask for alms of the man who treated his son so cruelly. It is probable that, by this time, the old man is dead; but I should object as much to have to appeal to my husband's brother, a character I disliked. Although he knew that his father's means were small, he was extravagant to the last degree, and the old man was weak enough to keep himself in perpetual difficulties, to satisfy his son. Your father looked for no pecuniary assistance from his brother; but the latter might, at least, have come to see him; or written kindly to him, when he was in London. As your father was writing in his own name for magazines, his address could be easily found out, by anyone who wanted to know it. He never sent one single word to him, and I should object quite as much to appeal to him, as to the old man.

"As to the sisters, who were younger than my husband, they were nice girls; but even if your grandfather is dead, and has, as no doubt would be the case, left what he had between them, it certainly would not amount to much. Your father has told me that the old man had mortgaged the estate, up to the hilt, to pay his brother's debts; and that when it came to be sold, as it probably would be at his death, there would be very little left for the girls. Therefore, certainly I could not go and ask them to support us.

"My hope is, my dear boy, that you may be able to make your way, here, in the same manner as your father was doing, when he fell; and that, someday, you may attain to an honourable position, in which you will be able, if you visit England, to call upon your aunts, not as one who has anything to ask of them, but as a relative of whom they need not feel in any way ashamed.

"I feel that my end is very near, Gregory. I hope to say all that I have to say to you, before it comes, but I may not have an opportunity; and in that case, some time may elapse before you read this, and it will come to you as a voice from the grave. I am not, in any way, wishing to bind you to any course of action, but only to explain fully your position to you, and to tell you my thoughts.

"God bless you, my dear boy, prosper and keep you! I know enough of you to be sure that, whatever your course may be, you will bear yourself as a true gentleman, worthy of your father and of the name you bear.

"Your loving Mother."

Gregory sat for some time before opening the other enclosure. It contained an open envelope, on which was written "To my Wife;" and three others, also unfastened, addressed respectively, "The Hon. James Hartley, King's Lawn, Tavistock, Devon"; the second, "G. Hilliard Hartley, Esquire, The Albany, Piccadilly, London;" the third, "Miss Hartley," the address being the same as that of her father. He first opened the one to his mother.

"My dearest Wife,

"I hope that you will never read these lines, but that I shall return to you safe and sound—I am writing this, in case it should be otherwise—and that you will never have occasion to read these instructions, or rather I should say this advice, for it is no more than that. We did talk the matter over, but you were so wholly averse from any idea of ever appealing to my father, or family, however sore the straits to which you might be reduced, that I could not urge the matter upon you; and yet, although I sympathize most thoroughly with your feelings, I think that in case of dire necessity you should do so, and at least afford my father the opportunity of making up for his treatment of myself. The small sum that I left in your hands must soon be exhausted. If I am killed, you will, perhaps, obtain a small pension; but this, assuredly, would not be sufficient to maintain you and the boy in comfort. I know that you said, at the time, that possibly you could add to it by teaching. Should this be so, you may be able to remain in Egypt; and when the boy grows up, he will obtain employment of some sort, here.

"But should you be unsuccessful in this direction, I do not see what you could do. Were you to go to England, with the child, what chance would you have of obtaining employment there, without friends or references? I am frightened at the prospect. I know that, were you alone, you would do anything rather than apply to my people; but you have the child to think of, and, painful as it would be to you, it yet seems to me the best thing that could be done. At any rate, I enclose you three letters to my brother, father, and sisters. I have no legal claim on any of them, but I certainly have a moral claim on my brother. It is he who has impoverished the estate, so that, even had I not quarrelled with my father, there could never, after provision had been made for my sisters, have been anything to come to me.

"I do not ask you to humiliate yourself, by delivering these letters personally. I would advise you to post them from Cairo, enclosing in each a note saying how I fell, and that you are fulfilling my instructions, by sending the letter I wrote before leaving you. It may be that you will receive no reply. In that case, whatever happens to you and the child, you will have nothing to reproach yourself for. Possibly my father may have succeeded to the title and, if for no other reason, he may then be willing to grant you an allowance, on condition that you do not return to England; as he would know that it would be nothing short of a scandal, that the wife of one of his sons was trying to earn her bread in this country.

"Above all, dear, I ask you not to destroy these letters. You may, at first, scorn the idea of appealing for help; but the time might come, as it came to us in London, when you feel that fate is too strong for you, and that you can struggle no longer. Then you might regret, for the sake of the child, that you had not sent these letters.

"It is a terrible responsibility that I am leaving you. I well know that you will do all, dear, that it is possible for you to do, to avoid the necessity for sending these letters. That I quite approve, if you can struggle on. God strengthen you to do it! It is only if you fail that I say, send them. My father may, by this time, regret that he drove me from home. He may be really anxious to find me, and at least it is right that he should have the opportunity of making what amends he can. From my sisters, I know that you can have little but sympathy; but that, I feel sure, they will give you, and even sympathy is a great deal, to one who has no friends. I feel it sorely that I should have naught to leave you but my name, and this counsel. Earnestly I hope and pray that it may never be needed.

"Yours till death,

"Gregory Hilliard Hartley."

Gregory then opened the letter to his grandfather.

"Dear Father,

"You will not receive this letter till after my death. I leave it behind me, while I go up with General Hicks to the Soudan. It will not be sent to you, unless I die there. I hope that, long ere this, you may have felt, as I have done, that we were both somewhat in the wrong, in the quarrel that separated us. You, I think, were hard. I, no doubt, was hasty. You, I think, assumed more than was your right, in demanding that I should break a promise that I had given, to a lady against whom nothing could be said, save that she was undowered. Had I, like Geoffrey, been drawing large sums of money from you, you would necessarily have felt yourself in a position to have a very strong voice in so important a matter. But the very moderate allowance I received, while at the University, was never increased. I do not think it is too much to say that, for every penny I have got from you, Geoffrey has received a guinea.

"However, that is past and gone. I have been fighting my own battle, and was on my way to obtaining a good position. Until I did so, I dropped our surname. I did not wish that it should be known that one of our family was working, in an almost menial position, in Egypt. I have now obtained the post of interpreter, on the staff of General Hicks; and, if he is successful in crushing the rebellion, I shall be certain of good, permanent employment, when I can resume my name. The fact that you receive this letter will be a proof that I have fallen in battle, or by disease.

"I now, as a dying prayer, beg you to receive my wife and boy; or, if that cannot be, to grant her some small annuity, to assist her in her struggle with the world. Except for her sake, I do not regret my marriage. She has borne the hardships, through which we have passed, nobly and without a murmur. She has been the best of wives to me, and has proved herself a noble woman, in every respect.

"I leave the matter in your hands, Father, feeling assured that, from your sense of justice alone, if not for the affection you once bore me, you will befriend my wife. As I know that the Earl was in feeble health, when I left England; you may, by this time, have come into the title, in which case you will be able, without in any way inconveniencing yourself, to settle an annuity upon my wife, sufficient to keep her in comfort. I can promise, in her name, that in that case you will never be troubled in any way by her; and she will probably take up her residence, permanently, in Egypt, as she is not strong, and the warm climate is essential to her."

The letter to his brother was shorter.

"My dear Geoffrey,

"I am going up, with General Hicks, to the Soudan. If you receive this letter, it will be because I have died there. I leave behind me my wife, and a boy. I know that, at present, you are scarcely likely to be able to do much for them, pecuniarily; but as you will someday—possibly not a very distant one—inherit the title and estate, you will then be able to do so, without hurting yourself.

"We have never seen much of each other. You left school before I began it, and you left Oxford two years before I went up to Cambridge. You have never been at home much, since; and I was two years in Egypt, and have now been about the same time, here. I charge my wife to send you this, and I trust that, for my sake, you will help her. She does not think of returning to England. Life is not expensive, in this country. Even an allowance of a hundred a year would enable her to remain here. If you can afford double that, do so for my sake; but, at any rate, I feel that I can rely upon you to do at least that much, when you come into the title. Had I lived, I should never have troubled anyone at home; but as I shall be no longer able to earn a living for her and the boy, I trust that you will not think it out of the way for me to ask for what would have been a very small younger brother's allowance, had I remained at home."

The letter to his sisters was in a different strain.

"My dear Flossie and Janet,

"I am quite sure that you, like myself, felt deeply grieved over our separation; and I can guess that you will have done what you could, with our father, to bring about a reconciliation. When you receive this, dears, I shall have gone. I am about to start on an expedition that is certain to be dangerous, and which may be fatal; and I have left this with my wife, to send you if she has sure news of my death. I have had hard times. I see my way now, and I hope that I shall, ere long, receive a good official appointment, out here. Still, it is as well to prepare for the worst; and if you receive this letter, the worst has come. As I have only just begun to rise again in the world, I have been able to make no provision for my wife. I know that you liked her, and that you would by no means have disapproved of the step I took. If our father has not come into the title, when you receive this, your pocket money will be only sufficient for your own wants; therefore I am not asking for help in that way, but only that you will write to her an affectionate letter. She is without friends, and will fight her battle as best she can. She is a woman in a thousand, and worthy of the affection and esteem of any man on earth.

"There is a boy, too—another Gregory Hilliard Hartley. She will be alone in the world with him, and a letter from you would be very precious to her. Probably, by the same post as you receive this, our father will also get one requesting more substantial assistance, but with that you have nothing to do. I am only asking that you will let her know there are, at least, two people in the world who take an interest in her, and my boy.

"Your affectionate Brother."

There was yet another envelope, with no address upon it. It contained two documents. One was a copy of the certificate of marriage, between Gregory Hilliard Hartley and Anne Forsyth, at Saint Paul's Church, Plymouth; with the names of two witnesses, and the signature of the officiating minister. The other was a copy of the register of the birth, at Alexandria, of Gregory Hilliard, son of Gregory Hilliard Hartley and Anne, his wife. A third was a copy of the register of baptism of Gregory Hilliard Hartley, the son of Gregory Hilliard and Anne Hartley, at the Protestant Church, Alexandria.

"I will write, someday, to my aunts," Gregory said, as he replaced the letters in the envelopes. "The others will never go. Still, I may as well keep them.

"So I am either grandson or nephew of an earl. I can't say that I am dazzled by the honour. I should like to know my aunts, but as for the other two, I would not go across the street to make their acquaintance."

He carefully stowed the letters away in his portmanteau, and then lay down for a few hours' sleep.

"The day is breaking, master," Zaki said, laying his hand upon Gregory's shoulder.

"All right, Zaki! While you get the water boiling, I shall run down to the river and have a bathe, and shall be ready for my cocoa, in twenty minutes."

"Are we going to put on those Dervish dresses at once, master? They came yesterday evening."

"No; I sha'n't change till we get to the place where we land."

As soon as he had breakfasted, he told Zaki to carry his portmanteau, bed, and other belongings to the house that served as a store for General Hunter's staff. He waited until his return, and then told him to take the two rifles, the packets of ammunition, the spears, and the Dervish dresses down to the steamer. Then he joined the General, who was just starting, with his staff, to superintend the embarkation.

Three steamers were going up, and each towed a barge, in which the greater part of the troops was to be stowed, and in the stern of one of these knelt two camels.

"There are your nags, Mr. Hilliard," the General said. "There is an attendant with each. They will manage them better than strangers, and without them we might have a job in getting the animals ashore. Of course, I shall take the drivers on with us. The sheik told me the camels are two of the fastest he has ever had. He has sent saddles with them, and water skins. The latter you will probably not want, if all goes well. Still, it is better to take them."

"I shall assuredly do so, sir. They may be useful to us, on the ride, and though I suppose the camels would do well enough without them, it is always well to be provided, when one goes on an expedition, for any emergency that may occur."

An hour later, the steamer started. The river was still full, and the current rapid, and they did not move more than five miles an hour against it. At the villages they passed, the people flocked down to the banks, with cries of welcome and the waving of flags. They felt, now, that their deliverance was accomplished, and that they were free from the tyranny that had, for so many years, oppressed them.

The banks were for the most part low; and, save at these villages, the journey was a monotonous one. The steamers kept on their way till nightfall, and then anchored.

They started again, at daybreak. At breakfast, General Hunter said:

"I think that in another two hours we shall be pretty well due west of El Fasher, so you had better, presently, get into your Dervish dress. You have got some iodine from the doctor, have you not?"

"Yes."

"You had better stain yourself all over, and take a good supply, in case you have to do it again."

Gregory went below, and had his head shaved by one of the Soudanese; then re-stained himself, from head to foot, and put on the Dervish attire—loose trousers and a long smock, with six large square patches, arranged in two lines, in front. A white turban and a pair of shoes completed the costume. The officers laughed, as he came on deck again.

"You look an out-and-out Dervish, Hilliard," one of them said. "It is lucky that there are none of the Lancers scouting about. They would hardly give you time to explain, especially with that rifle and spear."

Presently they came to a spot where the water was deep up to the bank, which was some six feet above its level. The barge with the camels was brought up alongside. It had no bulwark, and as the deck was level with the land, the camels were, with a good deal of pressing on the part of their drivers, and pushing by as many Soudanese as could come near enough to them, got ashore.

None of the Soudanese recognized Gregory, and looked greatly surprised at the sudden appearance of two Dervishes among them. As soon as the camels were landed, Gregory and Zaki mounted them.

"You had better keep, if anything, to the south of east," General Hunter's last instructions had been. "Unless Parsons has been greatly delayed, they should be two or three days' march farther up the river, and every mile you strike the stream, behind him, is so much time lost."

He waved his hand to them and wished them farewell, as they started, and his staff shouted their wishes for a safe journey. The black soldiers, seeing that, whoever these Dervishes might be, they were well known to the General and his officers, raised a cheer; to which Zaki, who had hitherto kept in the background, waved his rifle in reply. As his face was familiar to numbers of the Soudanese, they now recognized him, and cheered more heartily than before, laughing like schoolboys at the transformation.

CHAPTER 21:

Gedareh.

"Abdul Azim was right about the camels," Gregory said, as soon as they were fairly off. "I have never ridden on one like this, before. What a difference there is between them and the ordinary camel! It is not only that they go twice as fast, but the motion is so pleasant, and easy."

"Yes, Master, these are riding camels of good breed. They cost twenty times as much as the others. They think nothing of keeping up this rate for twelve hours, without a stop."

"If they do that, we shall be near the Atbara before it is dark. It is ten o'clock now, and if General Hunter's map is right, we have only about eighty miles to go, and I should think they are trotting seven miles an hour."

They carried their rifles slung behind them and across the shoulders, rather than upright, as was the Arab fashion. The spears were held in their right hands.

"We must see if we can't fasten the spears in some other way, Zaki. We should find them a nuisance, if we held them in our hands all the way. I should say it would be easy to fasten them across the saddle in front of us. If we see horsemen in the distance, we can take them into our hands."

"I think, Master, it would be easier to fasten them behind the saddles, where there is more width, and rings on the saddle on both sides."

A short halt was made, and the spears fixed. Gregory then looked at his compass.

"We must make for that rise, two or three miles away. I see exactly the point we must aim for. When we get there, we must look at the compass again."

They kept steadily on for six hours. They had seen no human figure, since they started.

"We will stop here for half an hour," Gregory said. "Give the animals a drink of water, and a handful or two of grain."

"I don't think they will want water, Master. They had as much as they could drink, before starting, and they are accustomed to drink when their work is over."

"Very well. At any rate, we will take something."

They opened one of the water skins, and poured some of the contents into a gourd. Then, sitting down in the shadow of the camels, they ate some dates and bread. They had only brought native food with them so that, if captured and examined, there should be nothing to show that they had been in contact with Europeans. Gregory had even left his revolver behind him as, being armed with so good a weapon as a Remington, it was hardly likely that it would be needed; and if found upon them, it would be accepted as a proof that he was in the employment of the infidels.

It was dusk when they arrived at the bank of the river. No incident had marked the journey, nor had they seen any sign that Dervishes were in the neighbourhood. The Atbara was in full flood, and was rushing down at six or seven miles an hour.

"Colonel Parsons must have had great difficulty in crossing, Zaki. He is hardly likely to have brought any boats across, from Kassala. I don't know whether he has any guns with him, but if he has, I don't think he can have crossed, even if they made rafts enough to carry them."

They kept along the bank, until they reached a spot where the river had overflowed. Here the camels drank their fill. A little grain was given to them, and then they were turned loose, to browse on the bushes.

"There is no fear of their straying, I suppose, Zaki?"

"No, Master. They are always turned loose at night. As there are plenty of bushes here, they will not go far."

After another meal, they both lay down to sleep; and, as soon as it was light, Zaki fetched in the camels and they continued their journey. In an hour, they arrived at a village. The people were already astir, and looked with evident apprehension at the seeming Dervishes.

"Has a party of infidels passed along here?" Gregory asked the village sheik, who came out and salaamed humbly.

"Yes, my lord, a party of soldiers, with some white officers, came through here three days ago."

"How many were there of them?"

"There must have been more than a thousand of them."

"Many more?"

"Not many; perhaps a hundred more. Your servant did not count them."

"Had they any cannon with them?"

"No, my lord. They were all on foot. They all carried guns, but there were no mounted men, or cannon."

"Where is Fadil and his army, that they thus allowed so small a force to march along, unmolested?"

"They say that he is still near the Nile. Two of his scouts were here, the day before the Turks came along. They stayed here for some hours, but as they said nothing about the Turks coming from Kassala, I suppose they did not know they had crossed the river."

"Well, we must go on, and see where they are. They must be mad to come with so small a force, when they must have known that Fadil has a large army. They will never go back again."

Without further talk, Gregory rode farther on. At each village through which they passed, they had some news of the passage of Colonel Parsons' command. The camels had been resting, from the time when Omdurman was taken; and, having been well fed that morning, Gregory did not hesitate to press them. The troops would not march above twenty-five miles a day, and two days would take them to Mugatta, so that if they halted there but for a day, he should be able to overtake them that night.

The character of the country was now greatly changed. The bush was thick and high, and a passage through it would be very difficult for mounted men. There was no fear, therefore, that they would turn off before arriving at Mugatta; from which place there would probably be a track, of some sort, to Gedareh. It was but a thirty-mile ride and, on arriving near the village, Gregory saw that a considerable number of men were assembled there. He checked his camel.

"What do you make them out to be, Zaki? Your eyes are better than mine. They may be Colonel Parsons' force, and on the other hand they may be Dervishes, who have closed in behind him to cut off his retreat."

"They are not Dervishes, master," Zaki said, after a long, steady look. "They have not white turbans. Some of their clothes are light, and some dark; but all have dark caps, like those the Soudanese troops wear."

"That is good enough, Zaki. We will turn our robes inside out, so as to hide the patches, as otherwise we might have a hot reception."

When they were a quarter of a mile from the village, several men started out from the bushes, rifle in hand. They were all in Egyptian uniform.

"We are friends!" Gregory shouted in Arabic. "I am an officer of the Khedive, and have come from Omdurman, with a message to your commander."

A native officer, one of the party, at once saluted.

"You will find the bey in the village, Bimbashi."

"How long have you been here?"

"We came in yesterday, and I hear that we shall start tomorrow, but I know not whether that is so."

"Are there any Dervishes about?"

"Yes; forty of them yesterday afternoon, coming from Gedareh, and ignorant that we were here, rode in among our outposts on that hill to the west. Three of them were killed, and three made prisoners. The rest rode away."

With a word of thanks, Gregory rode on. He dismounted when he reached the village, and was directed to a neighbouring hut. Here Colonel Parsons and the six white officers with him were assembled. A native soldier was on sentry, at the door.

"I want to speak to Parsons Bey."

The Colonel, hearing the words, came to the door.

"Colonel Parsons," Gregory said in English, "I am Major Hilliard of the Egyptian Army, and have the honour to be the bearer of a message to you, from General Rundle, now in command at Omdurman."

"You are well disguised, indeed, sir," the Colonel said with a smile, as he held out his hand. "I should never have taken you for anything but a native. Where did you spring from? You can never have ridden, much less walked, across the desert from Omdurman?"

"No, sir. I was landed from one of the gunboats in which General Hunter, with fifteen hundred Soudanese troops, is ascending the Blue Nile, to prevent Fadil from crossing and joining the Khalifa."

"Have you a written despatch?"

"It was thought better that I should carry nothing, so that even the strictest search would not show that I was a messenger."

"Is your message of a private character?"

"No, sir, I think not."

"Then will you come in?"

Gregory followed Colonel Parsons into the hut, which contained but one room.

"Gentlemen," the former said with a smile, "allow me to introduce Bimbashi Hilliard, who is the bearer of a message to me from General Rundle, now in command at Omdurman.

"Major Hilliard, these are Captain MacKerrel, commanding four hundred and fifty men of the 16th Egyptians; Captain Wilkinson, an equal number of the Arab battalion; Major Lawson, who has under his command three hundred and seventy Arab irregulars; Captain the Honorable H. Ruthven, who has under him eighty camel men; also Captain Fleming of the Royal Army Medical Corps, who is at once our medical officer, and in command of the baggage column; and Captain Dwyer. They are all, like yourself, officers in the Egyptian Army; and rank, like yourself, as Bimbashis.

"Now, sir, will you deliver your message to me?"

"It is of a somewhat grave character, sir, but General Rundle thought it very important that you should be acquainted with the last news. The Sirdar has gone up the White Nile, with some of the gunboats and the 11th Soudanese. He deemed it necessary to go himself, because a body of foreign troops—believed to be French—have established themselves at Fashoda."

An exclamation of surprise broke from all the officers.

"In the next place, sir, Fadil, who had arrived with his force within forty miles of Khartoum, has retired up the banks of the Blue Nile, on hearing of the defeat of the Khalifa. Major General Hunter has therefore gone up that river, with three gunboats and another Soudanese battalion, to prevent him, if possible, from crossing it and joining the Khalifa, who is reported to be collecting the remains of his defeated army.

"It is possible—indeed the General thinks it is probable—that Fadil, if unable to cross, may return with his army to Gedareh. It is to warn you of this possibility that he sent me here. Gedareh is reported to be a defensible position, and therefore he thinks that, if you capture it, it would be advisable to maintain yourself there until reinforcements can be sent to you, either from the Blue Nile or the Atbara. The place, it seems, is well supplied with provisions and stores; and in the event of Fadil opposing you, it would be far safer for you to defend it than to be attacked in the open, or during a retreat."

"It is certainly important news, Mr. Hilliard. Hitherto we have supposed that Fadil had joined the Khalifa before the fight at Omdurman, and there was therefore no fear of his reappearing here. We know very little of the force at Gedareh. We took some prisoners yesterday, but their accounts are very conflicting. Still, there is every reason to believe that the garrison is not strong. Certainly, as General Rundle says, we should be in a much better position there than if we were attacked in the open. No doubt the Arabs who got off in the skirmish, yesterday, carried the news there; and probably some of them would go direct to Fadil, and if he came down upon us here, with his eight thousand men, our position would be a desperate one. It cost us four days to cross the river at El Fasher, and would take us as much to build boats and recross here; and before that time, he might be upon us.

"It is evident, gentlemen, that we have only the choice of these alternatives—either to march, at once, against Gedareh; or to retreat immediately, crossing the river here, or at El Fasher. As to remaining here, of course, it is out of the question."

The consultation was a short one. All the officers were in favour of pushing forward, pointing out that, as only the 16th Egyptians could be considered as fairly disciplined, the troops would lose heart if they retired; and could not be relied upon to keep steady, if attacked by a largely superior force; while, at present, they would probably fight bravely. The Arab battalion had been raised by the Italians, and were at present full of confidence, as they had defeated the Mahdists who had been besieging Kassala. The Arab irregulars had, of course, the fighting instincts of their race, and would assault an enemy bravely; but in a defensive battle, against greatly superior numbers, could scarcely be expected to stand well. As for the eighty camel men, they were all Soudanese soldiers, discharged from the army for old age and physical unfitness. They could be relied upon to fight but, small in number as they were, could but have little effect on the issue of a battle. All therefore agreed that, having come thus far, the safest, as well as the most honourable course, would be to endeavour to fight the enemy in a strong position.

Although it may be said that success justified it, no wilder enterprise was ever undertaken than that of sending thirteen hundred only partly disciplined men into the heart of the enemy's country. Omdurman and Atbara, to say nothing of previous campaigns, had shown how desperately the Dervishes fought; and the order, for the garrison of Kassala to undertake it, can only have been given under an entire misconception of the circumstances, and of the strength of the army under Fadil, that they would almost certainly be called upon to encounter. This was the more probable, as all the women and the property of his soldiers had been left at Gedareh, when he marched away; and his men would, therefore, naturally wish to go there, before they made any endeavour to join the Khalifa.

Such, indeed, was the fact. Fadil concealed from them the news of the disaster at Omdurman, for some days; and, when it became known, he had difficulty in restraining his troops from marching straight for Gedareh.

"Do you go on with us, Mr. Hilliard?" Colonel Parsons asked, when they had decided to start for Gedareh.

"Yes, sir. My instructions are to go on with you and, if the town is besieged, to endeavour to get through their lines, and carry the news to General Hunter, if I can ascertain his whereabouts. If not, to make straight for Omdurman. I have two fast camels, which I shall leave here, and return for them with my black boy, when we start."

"We shall be glad to have you with us," the Colonel said. "Every white officer is worth a couple of hundred men."

As they sat and chatted, Gregory asked how the force had crossed the Atbara.

"It was a big job," Colonel Parsons said. "The river was wider than the Thames, below London Bridge; and running something like seven miles an hour. We brought with us some barrels to construct a raft. When this was built, it supported the ten men who started on it; but they were, in spite of their efforts, carried ten miles down the stream, and it was not until five hours after they embarked that they managed to land. The raft did not get back from its journey till the next afternoon, being towed along the opposite bank by the men.

"It was evident that this would not do. The Egyptian soldiers then took the matter in hand. They made frameworks with the wood of the mimosa scrub, and covered these with tarpaulins, which we had fortunately brought with us. They turned out one boat a day, capable of carrying two tons; and, six days after we reached the river, we all got across.

"The delay was a terrible nuisance at the time, but it has enabled you to come up here and warn us about Fadil. Fortunately no Dervishes came along while we were crossing, and indeed we learned, from the prisoners we took yesterday, that the fact that a force from Kassala had crossed the river was entirely unknown, so no harm was done."

The sheik of the little village took charge of Gregory's camels. Some stores were also left there, under a small guard, as it was advisable to reduce the transport to the smallest possible amount.

The next morning the start was made. The bush was so thick that it was necessary to march in single file. In the evening, the force halted in a comparatively open country. The camel men reconnoitred the ground, for some little distance round, and saw no signs of the enemy. They camped, however, in the form of a square; and lay with their arms beside them, in readiness to resist an attack.

The night passed quietly, and at early dawn they moved forward again. At six o'clock the camel men exchanged a few shots with the Dervish scouts, who fell back at once. At eight a village was sighted, and the force advanced upon it, in fighting order.

It was found, however, to have been deserted, except by a few old people. These, on being questioned, said that the Emir Saadalla, who commanded, had but two hundred rifles and six hundred spearmen, and had received orders from Fadil to surrender. Subsequent events showed that they had been carefully tutored as to the reply to be given.

The force halted here, as Gedareh was still twelve miles away; and it was thought better that, if there was fighting, they should be fresh. At midnight, a deserter from the Dervishes came in, with the grave news that the Emir had three thousand five hundred men, and was awaiting them two miles outside the town. There was another informal council of war, but all agreed that a retreat, through this difficult country, would bring about the total annihilation of the force; and that there was nothing to do but to fight.

Early in the morning, they started again. For the first two hours, the road led through grass so high that even the men on camels could not see above it. They pushed on till eight o'clock, when they reached a small knoll. At the foot of this they halted, and Colonel Parsons and the officers ascended it, to reconnoitre.

They saw, at once, that the deserter's news was true. A mile away four lines of Dervishes, marching in excellent order, were making their way towards them. Colonel Parsons considered that their numbers could not be less than four thousand, and at once decided to occupy a saddle-back hill, half a mile away; and the troops were hurried across. The Dervishes also quickened their movements, but were too late to prevent the hill from being seized.

The Arab battalion had been leading, followed by the Egyptians; while the irregulars, divided into two bodies under Arab chiefs, guarded the hospital and baggage. The Dervishes at once advanced to the attack of the hill, and the column wheeled into line, to meet it. Even on the crest of the hill, the grass was breast high, but it did not impede the view of the advancing lines of the Dervishes. Into these a heavy and destructive fire was at once poured. The enemy, however, pushed on, firing in return; but being somewhat out of breath, from the rapidity with which they had marched; and seeing nothing of the defenders of the hill, save their heads, they inflicted far less loss than they were themselves suffering.

The fight was continuing, when Colonel Parsons saw that a force of about three hundred Dervishes had worked round the back of the hill, with the intention of falling upon the baggage. He at once sent one of the Arab sheiks to warn Captain Fleming; who, from his position, was unable to see the approaching foe. Colonel Parsons had asked Gregory to take up his position with the baggage, as he foresaw that, with their vastly greater numbers, it was likely that the Dervishes might sweep round and attack it.

Scarcely had the messenger arrived with the news, when the Dervishes came rushing on through the high grass. In spite of the shouts of Doctor Fleming and Gregory, the escort of one hundred and twenty irregular Arabs, stationed at this point, at once broke and fled. Happily, a portion of the camel corps, with its commander, Captain Ruthven, a militia officer, was close at hand. Though he had but thirty-four of these old soldiers with him, he rushed forward to meet the enemy. Doctor Fleming and Gregory joined him and, all cheering to encourage the Soudanese, made a determined stand.

Gregory and Zaki kept up a steady fire with their Remingtons, and picked off several of the most determined of their assailants. The fight, however, was too unequal; the Dervishes got in behind them, and cut off the rear portion of the transport; and the little band, fighting obstinately, fell back, with their faces to the foe, towards the main body.

One of the native officers of the Soudanese fell. Captain Ruthven, a very powerful man, ran back and lifted the wounded soldier, and made his way towards his friends. So closely pressed was he, by the Dervishes, that three times he had to lay his burden down and defend himself with his revolver; while Gregory and Zaki aided his retreat, by turning their fire upon his assailants. For this splendid act of bravery, Captain Ruthven afterwards received the Victoria Cross.

Flushed by their success, the Dervishes pushed on. Fortunately, at this time the main force of the Dervishes was beginning to waver, unable to withstand the steady fire of the defenders of the hill; and as they drew back a little, the Egyptian and Arab battalions rushed forward.

Shaken as they were, the Dervishes were unable to resist the attack; and broke and fled, pursued by the Arab battalion. The Egyptians, however, obeyed the orders of Captain MacKerrel and, halting, faced about to encounter the attack from the rear. Their volleys caused the Dervishes to hesitate, and Captain Ruthven and his party reached the summit of the hill in safety.

The enemy, however, maintained a heavy fire for a few minutes; but the volleys of the Egyptians, at a distance of only a hundred yards, were so deadly that they soon took to flight.

The first shot had been fired at half-past eight. At ten, the whole Dervish force was scattered in headlong rout. Had Colonel Parsons possessed a cavalry force, the enemy would have been completely cut up. As it was, pursuit was out of the question.

The force therefore advanced, in good order, to Gedareh. Here a Dervish Emir, who had been left in charge when the rest of the garrison moved out, surrendered at once, with the two hundred black riflemen under him. He had long been suspected of disloyalty by the Khalifa, and at once declared his hatred of Mahdism; declaring that, though he had not dared to declare himself openly, he had always been friendly to Egyptian rule.

The men with him at once fraternized with the Arabs of Colonel Parsons' force, and were formally received into their ranks. The Emir showed his sincerity by giving them all the information in his power, as to Fadil's position and movements, and by pointing out the most defensible positions.

None of the British officers had been wounded, but fifty-one of the men had been killed, and eighty wounded. Five hundred of the Dervishes were left dead upon the field, including four Emirs.

Not a moment was lost in preparing for defence, for it was certain that Fadil, on hearing the news, would at once march to retake the town. The position was naturally a strong one. Standing on rising ground was Fadil's house, surrounded by a brick wall, twelve feet high. Here the Egyptian battalion and camel corps were placed, with the hospital, and two brass guns which had been found there.

A hundred yards away was another enclosure, with a five-foot wall, and two hundred yards away a smaller one. The Arab battalion was stationed to the rear of this, in a square enclosure with a brick wall, twelve feet high, in which was situated a well. These four buildings were so placed, that the fire from each covered the approaches to the other. Two hundred yards from the well enclosure was a fortified house, surrounded by a high wall. As the latter would need too many men for its defence, the wall was pulled down, and a detachment placed in the house.

No time was lost. The whole force was at once employed in pulling down huts, clearing the ground of the high grass, and forming a zareba round the town. The greatest cause for anxiety was ammunition. A large proportion of that carried in the pouches had been expended during the battle, and the next morning Colonel Parsons, with a small force, hurried back to Mugatta to fetch up the reserve ammunition, which had been left there under a guard. He returned with it, three days later.

An abundant supply of provisions had been found in Gedareh, for here were the magazines, not only of the four thousand men of the garrison and the women who had been left there, but sufficient for Fadil's army, on their return. There were three or four wells, and a good supply of water.

The ammunition arrived just in time; for, on the following morning, Captain Ruthven's camel men brought in news that Fadil was close at hand. At half-past eight the Dervishes began the attack, on three sides of the defences. Sheltered by the long grass, they were able to make their way to within three hundred yards of the dwellings occupied by the troops. But the intervening ground had all been cleared, and though time after time they made rushes forward, they were unable to withstand the withering fire to which they were exposed.

After an hour's vain efforts their musketry fire ceased; but, half an hour later, strong reinforcements came up, and the attack recommenced. This was accompanied with no greater success than the first attack, and Fadil retired to a palm grove, two miles away. Of the defenders five men were killed, and Captain Dwyer and thirteen men wounded.

For two days, Fadil endeavoured to persuade his troops to make another attack; but although they surrounded the town, and maintained a scattered fire, they could not be brought to attempt another assault, having lost over five hundred men in the two attacks the first day. He then fell back, eight miles.

Three days later, Colonel Parsons said to Gregory:

"I think the time has come, Mr. Hilliard, when I must apply for reinforcements. I am convinced that we can repel all attacks, but we are virtually prisoners here. Were we to endeavour to retreat, Fadil would probably annihilate us. Our men have behaved admirably; but it is one thing to fight well, when you are advancing; and another to be firm in retreat.

"But our most serious enemy, at present, is fever. Already, the stink of the unburied bodies of the Dervishes is overpowering, and every day it will become worse. Doctor Fleming reports to me that he has a great many sick on his hands, and that he fears the conditions that surround us will bring about an epidemic. Therefore I have decided to send to General Rundle, for a reinforcement that will enable us to move out to attack Fadil."

"Very well, sir, I will start at once."

"I will write my despatch. It will be ready for you to carry in an hour's time. You had better pick out a couple of good donkeys, from those we captured here. As it is only nine o'clock, you will be able to get to Mugatta this evening. I don't think there is any fear of your being interfered with, by the Dervishes. We may be sure that Fadil is not allowing his men to roam over the country, for there can be little doubt that a good many of them would desert, as soon as they got fairly beyond his camp."

"I don't think there is any fear of that, sir; and as my camels will have had ten days' rest, I should have very little fear of being overtaken, even if they did sight us."

"We are off again, Zaki," Gregory said. "We will go down to the yard where the animals we captured are kept, and choose a couple of good donkeys. I am to carry a despatch to Omdurman, and as time is precious, we will make a straight line across the desert; it will save us fifty or sixty miles."

"I am glad to be gone, Master. The smells here are as bad as they were at Omdurman, when we went in there."

"Yes, I am very glad to be off, too."

An hour later they started, and arrived at Mugatta at eight o'clock in the evening. The native with whom the camels had been left had taken good care of them; and, after rewarding him and taking a meal, Gregory determined to start at once. The stars were bright, and there was quite light enough for the camels to travel.

The water was emptied from the skins, and filled again. They had brought with them sufficient food for four days' travel, and a sack of grain for the camels. An hour after arriving at the village they again started.

"We will follow the river bank, till we get past the country where the bushes are so thick, and then strike west by north. I saw, by Colonel Parsons' map, that that is about the line we should take."

They left the river before they reached El Fasher, and continued their journey all night, and onward till the sun was well up. Then they watered the camels (they had, this time, brought with them a large half gourd for the purpose), ate a good meal themselves; and, after placing two piles of grain before the camels, lay down and slept until five o'clock in the afternoon.

"We ought to be opposite Omdurman, tomorrow morning. I expect we shall strike the river, tonight. I have kept our course rather to the west of the direct line, on purpose. It would be very awkward if we were to miss it. I believe the compass is right, and I have struck a match every hour to look at it; but a very slight deviation would make a big difference, at the end of a hundred and fifty miles."

It was just midnight when they saw the river before them.

"We can't go wrong now, Zaki."

"That is a comfort. How many miles are we above its junction with the White Nile?"

"I don't know."

They rode steadily on, and day was just breaking when he exclaimed:

"There are some buildings opposite. That must be Khartoum. We shall be opposite Omdurman in another hour."

Soon after six o'clock, they rode down to the river bank opposite the town; and, in answer to their signals, a large native boat was rowed across to them. After some trouble the camels were got on board, and in a quarter of an hour they landed.

"Take the camels up to my house, Zaki. I must go and report myself, at headquarters."

General Rundle had not yet gone out, and on Gregory sending in his name, he was at once admitted.

"So you are back, Mr. Hilliard!" the General said. "I am heartily glad to see you, for it was a very hazardous mission that you undertook. What news have you?"

"This is Colonel Parsons' report."

Before reading the long report, the General said, "Tell me, in a few words, what happened."

"I overtook Colonel Parsons at Mugatta, on the third morning after leaving. We were attacked by nearly four thousand Dervishes, five miles from Gedareh. After a sharp fight they were defeated, and we occupied the town without resistance. Four days later, Fadil came up with his army and attacked the town; but was driven off, with a loss of five hundred men. He is now eight miles from the town. The place is unhealthy and, although it can be defended, Colonel Parsons has asked for reinforcements, to enable him to attack Fadil."

"That is good news, indeed. We have all been extremely anxious, for there was no doubt that Colonel Parsons' force was wholly inadequate for the purpose. How long is it since you left?"

"About forty-six hours, sir."

"Indeed! That seems almost impossible, Mr. Hilliard."

"We started at eleven o'clock in the morning, sir, and rode on donkeys to Mugatta, where I had left my camels; arrived there at eight, and started an hour later on the camels. We rode till nine o'clock the next day, halted till five, and have just arrived here. The camels were excellent beasts, and travelled a good six miles an hour. I did not press them, as I knew that, if we arrived opposite the town at night, we should have difficulty in getting across the river."

"It was a great ride, a great achievement! You must be hungry, as well as tired. I will tell my man to get you some breakfast, at once. You can eat it, while I read this despatch. Then I may have a few questions to ask you. After that, you had better turn in till evening."

Gregory enjoyed his breakfast, with the luxuries of tinned fruit, after his rough fare for the past fortnight. When he went to the General's room again, the latter said:

"Colonel Parsons' despatches are very full, and I think I quite understand the situation. No praise is too high for the conduct of his officers and troops. All seemed to have behaved equally well, and he mentions the gallant part you took in the defence of the baggage, with Captain Ruthven and the doctor, and only some thirty-four soldiers of the camel corps.

"Now, I will not detain you longer. I hope you will dine with me this evening. I should like to hear more of the affair."

Returning to his hut, Gregory found that Zaki had already got his bed, and other things, from the store; and he was just about to boil the kettle.

"I have breakfasted, Zaki. Here is a dollar. Go to one of those big shops, and buy anything you like, and have a good meal. Then you had better take the camels across to Azim's camp. I shall not want you then, till evening."

No time was lost. Three battalions and a half of Soudanese were sent up the Blue Nile, in steamers, and the garrisons stationed at several points on the river were also taken on board. Three companies of camel corps marched along the bank, and arrived at Abu Haraz, a hundred and thirty miles up the river, in fifty-six hours after starting. Five hundred baggage camels were also sent up. As the distance from Gedareh to this point was a hundred miles, and as water was only to be found at one point, it was necessary to carry up a supply for the troops.

Colonel Collinson, who was in command, pushed forward at once with the 12th Soudanese and the camel corps. When Fadil heard of their approach, he made a night attack on Gedareh. This, however, was easily repulsed by the garrison. He then broke up his camp and marched away, intending to cross the Blue Nile, and join the Khalifa.

His troops were greatly demoralized by their failures, and in spite of the precautions he took, the Darfur Sheik, with five hundred of his men, succeeded in effecting his escape; and at once joined us, actively, in the further operations against Fadil. As there was no further danger, the Soudanese marched back again and joined the other battalions, the garrisons on the river were re-established, and part of the force returned to Omdurman.

The Sirdar had returned from Fashoda before Gregory came back, and had left almost immediately for Cairo. On the day after Gregory's return, he had a sharp attack of fever; the result partly of the evil smells at Gedareh, heightened by the fact that the present was the fever season, in the Blue Nile country.

CHAPTER 22:

The Crowning Victory.

It was eight weeks before he recovered, and even then the doctor said that he was not fit for any exertion. He learned that on the 22nd of October, Colonel Lewis, with two companies of the camel corps and three squadrons of Lancers, had started from Omdurman to visit the various villages between the White and Blue Niles; to restore order, and proclaim that the authority of the Khedive was established there. On the 7th of November, following the Blue Nile up, he reached Karkoj, but a short distance below the point at which the navigation of the river ceased. He had come in contact with a portion of Fadil's force, but nothing could be done, in the thick undergrowth in which the latter was lurking; and he therefore remained, waiting for the next move on the part of the Dervish commander, while the gunboats patrolled the Blue river up to Rosaires.

Six weeks passed. His force, and all the garrisons on the river, suffered severely from heat, thirty percent of the troops being down together. The cavalry had suffered particularly heavily. Of the four hundred and sixty men, ten had died and four hundred and twenty were reported unfit for duty, a month after their arrival at Karkoj; while of the thirty white officers on the Blue Nile, only two escaped an attack of fever.

At the end of the month, Colonel Lewis was joined by the Darfur Sheik and three hundred and fifty of his men. He had had many skirmishes with Dervish parties, scouring the country for food, and his arrival was very welcome.

Gregory was recommended to take a river trip, to recover his health; and left on a steamer going up with stores, and some small reinforcements, to Colonel Lewis. They arrived at Karkoj on the 14th of December, and learned that the little garrison at Rosaires had been attacked by the Dervishes.

The fifty fever-stricken men who formed the garrison would have had no chance of resisting the attack, but fortunately they had, that very morning, been reinforced by two hundred men of the 10th Soudanese, and two Maxims; and the Dervishes were repulsed, with considerable loss. Two companies of the same battalion had reinforced Colonel Lewis, who marched, on the day after receiving the news, to Rosaires. The gunboat went up to that point, and remained there for some days.

Gregory went ashore, as soon as the boat arrived, and saw Colonel Lewis, to whom he was well known.

"I am supposed to be on sick leave, sir; but I feel quite strong now, and shall be glad to join you, if you will have me."

"I can have no possible objection, Mr. Hilliard. I know that you did good service with Colonel Parsons, and it is quite possible that we shall find ourselves in as tight a place as he was. So many of our white officers have been sent down, with fever, that I am very short-handed, and shall be glad if you will temporarily serve as my assistant."

On the 20th, the news came that Fadil was crossing the river at Dakhila, twenty miles farther to the south. He himself had crossed, and the women and children had been taken over on a raft. On the 22nd, the Darfur Sheik was sent off up the west bank, to harass the Dervishes who had already crossed. On the 24th two gunboats arrived, with two hundred more men of the 10th Soudanese, and a small detachment of the 9th.

On the following day the little force started, at five in the afternoon; and, at eleven at night, halted at a little village. At three in the morning they again advanced, and at eight o'clock came in contact with the Dervish outposts. Colonel Lewis had already learned that, instead of half the Dervish force having crossed, only one division had done so, and that he had by far the greater part of Fadil's army opposed to him.

It was a serious matter to attack some four or five thousand men, with so small a force at his disposal; for he had but half the 10th Soudanese, a handful of the 9th, and two Maxim guns. As to the Darfur irregulars, no great reliance could be placed upon them.

As the force issued from the wood through which they had been marching, they saw the river in front of them. In its midst rose a large island, a mile and a quarter long, and more than three-quarters of a mile wide. There were clumps of sand hills upon it. They had learned that the intervening stream was rapid, but not deep; while that on the other side of the island was very deep, with a precipitous bank.

It was upon this island that Fadil's force was established. The position was a strong one—the sand hills rose from an almost flat plain, a thousand yards away; and this would have to be crossed by the assailants, without any shelter whatever. The Dervishes were bound to fight their hardest, as there was no possibility of escape, if defeated.

At nine o'clock the Soudanese and irregulars lined the bank and opened fire, while the two Maxims came into action. The Dervishes replied briskly, and it was soon evident that, at so long a range, they could not be driven from their position. Several fords were found, and the irregulars, supported by a company of the 10th, crossed the river, and took up a position two hundred yards in advance, to cover the passage of the rest. These crossed with some difficulty, for the water was three and a half feet deep, and the current very strong; and they were, moreover, exposed to the fire of Fadil's riflemen, from the high cliff on the opposite bank.

Colonel Lewis, determined to turn the left flank of the Dervishes, kept along the river's edge until he reached the required position; then wheeled the battalion into line, and advanced across the bare shingle against the sand hills. Major Ferguson, with one company, was detached to attack a knoll on the right, held by two hundred Dervishes. The remaining four companies, under Colonel Mason, kept straight on towards the main position.

A very heavy fire was concentrated upon them, not only from the sand hills, but from Fadil's riflemen. The Soudanese fell fast, but held on, increasing their pace to a run; until they reached the foot of the first sandhill, where they lay down in shelter to take breath. A quarter of the force had already fallen, and their doctor, Captain Jennings, remained out in the open, binding up their wounds, although exposed to a continuous fire.

This halt was mistaken by the Dervishes, who thought that the courage of the Soudanese was exhausted; and Fadil, from the opposite bank, sounded the charge on drum and bugle; and the whole Dervish force, with banners waving and exultant shouts, poured down to annihilate their assailants.

But the Soudanese, led by Colonels Lewis and Mason, who were accompanied by Gregory, leapt to their feet, ran up the low bank behind which they were sheltering, and opened a terrible fire. The Dervishes were already close at hand, and every shot told among them. Astonished at so unlooked-for a reception, and doubtless remembering the heavy loss they had suffered at Gedareh, they speedily broke. Like dogs slipped from their leash, the black troops dashed on with triumphant shouts, driving the Dervishes from sandhill to sandhill, until the latter reached the southern end of the island.

Here the Soudanese were joined by the irregulars who had first crossed, and a terrible fire was maintained, from the sand hills, upon the crowded mass on the bare sand, cut off from all retreat by the deep river. Some tried to swim across, to join their friends on the west bank. A few succeeded in doing so, among them the Emir who had given battle to Colonel Parsons' force, near Gedareh.

Many took refuge from the fire by standing in the river, up to their necks. Some four hundred succeeded in escaping, by a ford, to a small island lower down; but they found no cover there, and after suffering heavily from the musketry fire, the survivors, three hundred strong, surrendered.

Major Ferguson's company, however, was still exposed to a heavy fire, turned upon them by the force on the other side of the river. He himself was severely wounded, and a third of his men hit. The Maxims were accordingly carried over the river to the island, and placed so as to command the west bank, which they soon cleared of the riflemen.

Over five hundred Arabs lay dead on the two islands. Two thousand one hundred and seventy-five fighting men surrendered, and several hundred women and children. Fadil, with the force that had escaped, crossed the desert to Rung, on the White Nile, where on the 22nd of January they surrendered to the English gunboats; their leader, with ten or twelve of his followers only, escaping to join the Khalifa.

Our casualties were heavy. Twenty-five non-commissioned officers and men were killed; one British officer, six native officers, and one hundred and seventeen non-commissioned officers and men wounded of the 10th Soudanese, out of a total strength of five hundred and eleven. The remaining casualties were among the irregulars.

Never was there a better proof of the gallantry of the black regiments of Egypt; for, including the commander and medical officer, there were but five British officers, and two British sergeants, to direct and lead them.

After the battle of Rosaires, there was a lull in the fighting on the east of the White Nile. The whole country had been cleared of the Dervishes, and it was now time for the Sirdar, who had just returned from England, to turn his attention to the Khalifa. The latter was known to be near El Obeid, where he had now collected a force, of whose strength very different reports were received.

Gregory, whose exertions in the fight, and the march through the scrub from Karkoj, had brought on a slight return of fever, went down in the gunboat, with the wounded, to Omdurman. Zaki was with him, but as a patient. He had been hit through the leg, while charging forward with the Soudanese. At Omdurman, Gregory fell into regular work again. So many of the officers of the Egyptian battalions had fallen in battle, or were down with fever, that Colonel Wingate took him as his assistant, and his time was now spent in listening to the stories of tribesmen; who, as soon as the Khalifa's force had passed, had brought in very varying accounts of his strength. Then there were villagers who had complaints to make of robbery, of ill usage—for this the Arab irregulars, who had been disbanded after the capture of Omdurman, were largely responsible. Besides these, there were many petitions by fugitives, who had returned to find their houses occupied, and their land seized by others.

Gregory was constantly sent off to investigate and decide in these disputes, and was sometimes away for a week at a time. Zaki had recovered rapidly and, as soon as he was able to rise, accompanied his master; who obtained valuable assistance from him as, while Gregory was hearing the stories of witnesses, Zaki went quietly about the villages, talking to the old men and women, and frequently obtained evidence that showed that many of the witnesses were perjured; and so enabled his master to give decisions which astonished the people by their justness.

Indeed, the reports of the extraordinary manner in which he seemed able to pick out truth from falsehood, and to decide in favour of the rightful claimant, spread so rapidly from village to village, that claimants who came in to Colonel Wingate often requested, urgently, that the young Bimbashi should be sent out to investigate the matter.

"You seem to be attaining the position of a modern Solomon, Hilliard," the Colonel said one day, with a smile. "How do you do it?"

Gregory laughed, and told him the manner in which he got at the truth.

"An excellent plan," he said, "and one which it would be well to adopt, generally, by sending men beforehand to a village. The only objection is, that you could not rely much more upon the reports of your spies than on those of the villagers. The chances are that the claimant who could bid highest would receive their support."

Matters were quiet until the Sirdar returned from England, and determined to make an attempt to capture the Khalifa, whose force was reported not to exceed one thousand men. Two squadrons of Egyptian cavalry and a Soudanese brigade, two Maxims, two mule guns, and a company of camel corps were placed under the command of Colonel Kitchener. The great difficulty was the lack of water along the route to be traversed. Camels were brought from the Atbara and the Blue Nile; and the whole were collected at Kawa, on the White Nile. They started from that point, but the wells were found to be dry; and the force had to retrace its steps, and to start afresh from Koli, some forty miles farther up the river.

They endured great hardships, for everything was left behind save the clothes the men and officers stood in, and one hundred rounds of ammunition each; only one pint of water being allowed per head. The country was a desert, covered with interlacing thorn bushes. An eight days' march brought the force to a village which was considered sacred, as it contained the grave of the Khalifa's father, and the house where the Khalifa himself had been born.

Three days later they reached the abandoned camp of the Khalifa, a wide tract that had been cleared of bush. A great multitude of dwellings, constructed of spear grass, stretched away for miles; and at the very lowest compilation it had contained twenty thousand people, of which it was calculated that from eight thousand to ten thousand must have been fighting men, ten times as many as had before been reported to be with the Khalifa. A reconnaissance showed that a large army was waiting to give battle, on a hill which was of great strength, surrounded by deep ravines and pools of water.

The position was an anxious one. The total force was about fourteen hundred strong, and a defeat would mean annihilation; while even a victory would scarcely secure the capture of the Khalifa; who, with his principal emirs, Osman Digna, El Khatim the Sheik of El Obeid, the Sheik Ed Din, and Fadil, would be able to gallop off if they saw the battle going against them. Colonel Kitchener had the wisdom to decide against risking the destruction of his followers by an assault against so great a force, posted in so strong a position. It was a deep mortification to him to have to retreat, and the soldiers were bitterly disappointed; but their commander felt that, brave as the Egyptians and Soudanese had shown themselves, the odds against victory were too great. After a terrible march, and great sufferings from thirst and scanty food, the force reached Koli on the 5th of February, and were conveyed in steamers down to Omdurman.

After this somewhat unfortunate affair, which naturally added to the prestige of the Khalifa, the months passed uneventfully; but, late in October, preparations were made for an attack upon a large scale against the Khalifa's camp, and eight thousand men were concentrated at Karla, on the White Nile. It was known that the Khalifa was at Gedir, eighty miles away; but after proceeding half the distance, it was found that he had marched away, and the column returned, as pursuit through a densely-wooded country would have been impracticable.

The gunboats had gone up the river with a flying column, under Colonel Lewis, to check any of the Khalifa's forces that attempted to establish themselves on the banks. Mounted troops and transport were at once concentrated, and Colonel Wingate was sent up to take command. The force consisted of a brigade of infantry, under Colonel Lewis, with the 9th and 13th Soudanese, an irregular Soudanese battalion, a company of the 2nd Egyptians, six companies of camel corps, a squadron of cavalry, a field battery, six Maxims, and detachments of medical and supply departments, with a camel transport train to carry rations and three days' water—in all, three thousand seven hundred men.

On the afternoon of the 21st of November, the column moved forward and, favoured by a bright moonlight, made a march of fifteen miles; the cavalry scouting two miles in front, the flanks and rear being covered by the camel corps. Native reports had brought in information that Fadil, who had been raiding the country, was now in the neighbourhood, on his way to rejoin the main Dervish army, which was lying near Gadi.

The cavalry pushed forward at dawn, and found that Fadil had retreated, leaving a quantity of grain behind. A sick Dervish who had remained there said that the Dervishes had moved to a point seven miles away. The cavalry, camel corps, and some of the guns advanced, and seized a position within three hundred yards of the Dervish encampment, on which they immediately opened fire.

The rest of the guns were at once pushed forward, to reinforce them, and arrived in time to assist them in repulsing a fierce attack of the Dervishes. Owing to the nature of the ground, these were able to approach to within sixty yards of the guns, before coming under their fire. They were then mowed down by the guns and Maxims, and the musketry fire of the camel corps; to which was added that of the infantry brigade, when they arrived. This was too much even for Dervish valour to withstand, and they fled back to their camp.

The British force then advanced. They met with but little opposition and, as they entered the camp, they saw the enemy in full flight. The infantry followed them for a mile and a half, while the cavalry and camel corps kept up the pursuit for five miles.

Fadil's camp, containing a large amount of grain and other stores, fell into the hands of the captors; with a number of prisoners, including women and children, and animals. Four hundred Dervishes had fallen, great numbers had been wounded, while the British casualties amounted to a native officer of the camel corps dangerously wounded, one man killed, and three wounded.

Gregory had accompanied Colonel Wingate, and acted as one of his staff officers. He had, of course, brought his horse with him. It was an excellent animal, and had been used by him in all his excursions from Omdurman.

"That is rather a different affair from the fight on the Atbara, Zaki," he said, when the force gathered in Fadil's camp, after the pursuit was relinquished; "the Dervishes fought just as bravely, but in one case they had a strong position to defend, while today they took the offensive. It makes all the difference."

"I am glad to have seen some fighting again, Master, for it has been dull work stopping ten months in Omdurman, with nothing to do but ride about the country, and decide upon the villagers' quarrels."

"It has been useful work, Zaki, and I consider myself very fortunate in being so constantly employed. I was desperately afraid that Colonel Wingate would leave me there, and I was greatly relieved when he told me that I was to come with him. It is a fortunate thing that we have beaten our old enemy, Fadil, here. In the first place because, if the three or four thousand men he had with him had joined the Khalifa, it would have given us harder work in tomorrow's fight; and in the next place his arrival, with his followers who have escaped, at the Khalifa's camp, is not likely to inspirit the Dervishes there."

Gregory was occupied, all the afternoon, in examining the prisoners. They affirmed that they had left the former camp, three days before, with the intention of proceeding to Gedid; where Fadil was to join the Khalifa with captured grain, when the whole Dervish force was to march north.

The troops slept during the afternoon, and in the evening set out for Gedid, which they reached at ten o'clock the next morning. A Dervish deserter reported that the Khalifa was encamped seven miles to the southeast. Fortunately, a pool with sufficient water for the whole force was found at Gedid; which was a matter of great importance, for otherwise the expedition must have fallen back.

It was hoped that the Khalifa would now stand at bay, as our occupation of Gedid barred his advance north. Behind him was a waterless, and densely wooded district. The capture of the grain on which he had relied would render it impossible for him to remain long in his present position, and his only chance of extricating himself was to stand and fight.

After twelve hours' rest the troops were roused, and started a few minutes after midnight. The transport was left, under a strong guard, near the water; with orders to follow, four hours later. The cavalry, with two Maxims, moved in advance; and the camel corps on the flanks. The ground was thickly wooded. In many places, a way had to be cut for the guns.

At three o'clock news was received, from the cavalry, that the enemy's camp was but three miles distant from the point which the infantry had reached; and that they and the Maxims had halted two miles ahead, at the foot of some slightly rising ground; beyond which the scouts had, on the previous day, discovered the main force of the enemy to be stationed. The infantry continued to advance, slowly and cautiously, making as little noise as possible.

It was soon evident, however, that in spite of their caution, the enemy were aware of their approach, as there was an outburst of the beating of drums, and the blowing of war horns. This did not last long, but it was enough to show that the Dervishes were not to be taken by surprise. When the infantry reached the spot where the cavalry were halted, the latter's scouts were withdrawn and the infantry pickets thrown out, and the troops then lay down to await daybreak.

The officers chatted together in low tones. There were but two hours till dawn, and with the prospect of heavy fighting before them, none were inclined to sleep. The question was whether the Dervishes would defend their camp, or attack. The result of the battle of Omdurman should have taught them that it was impossible to come to close quarters, in the face of the terrible fire of our rifles. Fadil could give his experience at Gedareh, which would teach the same lesson. On the other hand, the storming of the Dervish camp on the Atbara, and the fight at Rosaires, would both seem to show them that the assault of the Egyptian force was irresistible.

As Gregory had been present at all four of these battles, he was asked to give his opinion.

"I think that they will attack," he said. "The Dervish leaders rely upon the enthusiasm of their followers; and, in almost all the battles we have fought here, they have rushed forward to the assault. It was so in all the fights down by the Red Sea. It was so in the attacks on Lord Wolseley's desert column. It succeeded against Hicks's and Baker's forces; and even now they do not seem to have recognized that the Egyptians, whom they once despised, have quite got over their dread of them, and are able to face them steadily."

There was only the faintest light in the sky, when firing broke out in front. Everyone leapt to his feet, and stood listening intently. Was it merely some Dervish scouts, who had come in contact with our pickets, or was it an attacking force?

The firing increased in volume, and was evidently approaching. The pickets, then, were being driven in, and the Dervishes were going to attack. The men were ordered to lie down, in the position in which they were to fight. In five minutes after the first shot all were ready for action, the pickets had run in; and, in the dim light, numbers of dark figures could be made out.

The guns and Maxims at once spoke out, while the infantry fired volleys. It was still too dark to make out the movements of the enemy, but their reply to our fire came louder and louder on our left, and it was apparent that the intention of the Dervishes was to turn that flank of our position.

Colonel Wingate sent Gregory, to order the guns to turn their fire more in that direction; and other officers ordered our right to advance somewhat, while the left were slightly thrown back, and pushed farther out. The light was now getting brighter, and heavy bodies of Dervishes, shouting and firing, rushed forward; but they were mown down by grape from our guns, a storm of Maxim bullets, and the steady volleys of the infantry. They wavered for a moment, and then gradually fell back.

The bugles sounded the advance and, with a cheer, our whole line moved forward down the gentle slope; quickening their pace as the enemy retired before them, and still keeping up a heavy fire towards the clump of trees that concealed the Dervish camp from sight. The enemy's fire had now died out. At twenty-five minutes past six the "cease fire" was sounded and, as the troops advanced, it was evident that resistance was at an end.

As they issued through the trees, many Dervishes ran forward and surrendered, and thousands of women and children were found in the camp. Happily, none of these had been injured, as a slight swell in the ground had prevented our bullets from falling among them. Numbers of Dervishes who had passed through now turned and surrendered, and the cavalry and camel corps started in pursuit.

Gregory had learned, from the women, that the Emir El Khatim, with a number of his trained men from El Obeid, had passed through the camp in good order, but that none of the other emirs had been seen; and the 9th Soudanese stated that, as they advanced, they had come upon a number of chiefs lying together, a few hundred yards in advance of our first position. One of the Arab sheiks of the irregulars was sent to examine the spot, and reported that the Khalifa himself, and almost all his great emirs, lay there dead.

With the Khalifa were Ali Wad, Helu, Fadil, two of his brothers, the Mahdi's son, and many other leaders. Behind them lay their dead horses, and one of the men still alive said that the Khalifa, having failed in his attempt to advance over the crest, had endeavoured to turn our position; but, seeing his followers crushed by our fire and retiring, and after making an ineffectual attempt to rally them, he recognized that the day was lost; and, calling on his emirs to dismount, seated himself on his sheepskin, as is the custom of Arab chiefs who disdain to surrender. The emirs seated themselves round him, and all met their death unflinchingly, the greater part being mowed down by the volleys fired by our troops, as they advanced.

Gregory went up to Colonel Wingate.

"I beg your pardon, sir, but I find that Khatim, and probably his son, who were so kind to my father at El Obeid, have retired with a fighting force. Have I your permission to ride forward, and call upon them to surrender?"

"Certainly, Mr. Hilliard, there has been bloodshed enough."

Being well mounted, Gregory overtook the cavalry and camel corps, before they had gone two miles; as they were delayed by disarming the Dervishes, who were coming in in large numbers. Half a mile away, a small body of men were to be seen keeping together, firing occasionally. Their leader's flag was flying, and Gregory learned, from a native, that it was Khatim's. The cavalry were on the point of gathering for a charge, as he rode up to the officer in command.

"I have Colonel Wingate's orders, sir, to ride forward and try to persuade the emir to surrender. He does not wish any further loss of life."

"Very well, sir. I am sure we have killed enough of the poor beggars. I hope he will give in."

As Gregory neared the party, which was some five hundred strong, several shots were fired at him. He waved a white handkerchief, and the firing ceased. Two emirs rode forward to meet him.

"I have come, sir, from the English General, to ask you to surrender. Your cause is lost. The Khalifa is dead, and most of his principal emirs. He is anxious that there should be no further loss of blood."

"We can die, sir, as the others have done," the elder emir, a man of some sixty years old, said sternly.

"But that would not avail your cause, sir. I solicited this mission, as I owe much to you."

"How can that be?" the chief asked.

"I am the son of that white man whom you so kindly treated, at El Obeid, where he saved the life of your son Abu;" and he bowed to the younger emir.

"Then he escaped?" the latter exclaimed.

"No, sir. He was killed at Hebbeh, when the steamer in which he was going down from Khartoum was wrecked there; but I found his journal, in which he told the story of your kindness to him. I can assure you that you shall be well treated, if you surrender; and those of your men who wish to do so will be allowed to return to El Obeid. I feel sure that when I tell our General how kindly you acted, to the sole white officer who escaped from the battle, you and your son will be treated with the greatest consideration."

"I owe more to your father than he did to me," Abu exclaimed. "He saved my life, and did many great services to us.

"What say you, Father? I am ready to die if you will it; but as the Khalifa is dead, and the cause of Mahdism lost, I see no reason, and assuredly no disgrace, in submitting to the will of Allah."

"So be it," Khatim said. "I have never thought of surrendering to the Turks, but as it is the will of Allah, I will do so."

He turned to his men.

"It is useless to fight further," he said. "The Khalifa is dead. It were better to return to your wives and families than to throw away your lives. Lay down your arms. None will be injured."

It was with evident satisfaction that the Arabs laid musket and spear on the ground. They would have fought to the death, had he ordered them, for they greatly loved their old chief; but as it was his order, they gladly complied with it, as they saw that they had no chance of resisting the array of cavalry and camel corps, gathered less than half a mile away.

"If you will ride back with me," Gregory said to the emir, "I will present you to the General. The men had better follow. I will ride forward, and tell the officer commanding the cavalry that you have surrendered, and that the men approaching are unarmed."

He cantered back to the cavalry.

"They have all surrendered, sir," he said. "They have laid down their arms at the place where they stood, and are going back to camp, to surrender to Colonel Wingate."

"I am glad of it. My orders are to push on another three miles. On our return the camel corps shall collect the arms, and bring them in."

Gregory rode back to the emirs, who were slowly crossing the plain, but who halted as the cavalry dashed on.

"Now, Emirs," he said, "we can ride quietly back to camp."

"You have not taken our arms," Khatim said.

"No, Emir, it is not for me to ask for them. It is the General to whom you surrender, not me."

"I mourn to hear of the death of your father," Abu said, as they rode in. "He was a good man, and a skilful hakim."

"He speaks always in the highest terms of you, Emir, in his journal, and tells how he performed that operation on your left arm, which was necessary to save your life; but did so with great doubt, fearing that, never having performed one before, he might fail to save your life."

"I have often wondered what became of him," Abu said. "I believed that he had got safely into Khartoum, and I enquired about him when we entered. When I found that he was not among the killed, I trusted that he might have escaped. I grieve much to hear that he was killed while on his way down."

"Such was the will of Allah," Khatim said. "He preserved him at the battle, He preserved him in the town, He enabled him to reach Khartoum; but it was not His will that he should return to his countrymen. I say, with Abu, that he was a good man; and while he remained with us, was ever ready to use his skill for our benefit. It was Allah's will that his son should, after all these years, come to us; for assuredly, if any other white officer had asked us to surrender, I would have refused."

"Many strange things happen by the will of God," Gregory said. "It was wonderful that, sixteen years after his death, I should find my father's journal at Hebbeh, and learn the story of his escape after the battle, and of his stay with you at El Obeid."

Gregory rode into camp between the two emirs. He paused for a minute, and handed over their followers to the officer in charge of the prisoners; and then went to the hut formerly occupied by the Khalifa, where Colonel Wingate had now established himself. Colonel Wingate came to the entrance.

"These are El Khatim and his son Abu, sir. They surrendered on learning that I was the son of the British officer whom they had protected, and sheltered, for a year after the battle of El Obeid."

The two emirs had withdrawn their swords and pistols from their sashes; and, advancing, offered them to the Colonel. The latter did not offer to receive them.

"Keep them," he said. "We can honour brave foes; and you and your followers were ready to fight and die, when all seemed lost. Still more do I refuse to receive the weapons of the men who defended an English officer, when he was helpless and a fugitive; such an act would,

alone, ensure good treatment at our hands. Your followers have surrendered?"

"They have all laid down their arms," Khatim said.

"Do you give me your promise that you will no more fight against
us?"

"We do," Khatim replied. "We have received our weapons back
from you, and would assuredly not use them against our conquerors."

"In that case, Emir, you and your son are at liberty to depart, and
your men can return with you. There will, I trust, be no more fighting
in the land. The Mahdi is dead. His successor proved a false prophet
and is dead also. Mahdism is at an end, and now our object will be to
restore peace and prosperity to the land.

"In a short time, all the prisoners will be released. Those who
choose will be allowed to enter our service. The rest can return to their
homes. We bear no enmity against them. They fought under the orders
of their chiefs, and fought bravely and well. When they return, I hope
they will settle down and cultivate the land; and undo, as far as may be,
the injuries they have inflicted upon it.

"I will write an order, Mr. Hilliard, to release at once the men you
have brought in. Then I will ask you to ride, with these emirs, to a point
where there will be no fear of their falling in with our cavalry."

"You are a generous enemy," Khatim said, "and we thank you. We
give in our allegiance to the Egyptian government, and henceforth
regard ourselves as its servants."

"See, Mr. Hilliard, that the party takes sufficient food with it for
their journey to El Obeid."

Colonel Wingate stepped forward, and shook hands with the two
emirs.

"You are no longer enemies," he said, "and I know that, henceforth, I shall be able to rely upon your loyalty."

"We are beaten," Khatim said, as they walked away, each leading
his horse. "You can fight like men, and we who thought ourselves brave
have been driven before you, like dust before the wind. And now, when
you are masters, you can forgive as we should never have done. You can
treat us as friends. You do not even take our arms, and we can ride into
El Obeid with our heads high."

"It will be good for the Soudan," Abu said. "Your father told me,
often, how peace and prosperity would return, were you ever to
become our masters; and I felt that his words were true. Two hours ago
I regretted that Allah had not let me die, so that I should not have lived
to see our people conquered. Now, I am glad. I believe all that he said,
and that the Soudan will some day become, again, a happy country."

Khatim's men were separated from the rest of the prisoners. Six
days' supply of grain, from the stores found in the camp, were handed

over to them; together with ten camels with water skins, and they started at once on their long march. Gregory rode out for a couple of miles with them, and then took leave of the two emirs.

"Come to El Obeid," Khatim said, "and you shall be treated as a king. Farewell! And may Allah preserve you!"

So they parted; and Gregory rode back to the camp, with a feeling of much happiness that he had been enabled, in some way, to repay the kindness shown to his dead father.

CHAPTER 23:

An Unexpected Discovery.

The victory had been a decisive one, indeed. Three thousand prisoners, great quantities of rifles, swords, grain, and cattle had been captured; together with six thousand women and children. A thousand Dervishes had been killed or wounded. All the most important emirs had been killed, and the Sheik Ed Din, the Khalifa's eldest son and intended successor, was, with twenty-nine other emirs, among the prisoners. Our total loss was four men killed, and two officers and twenty-seven men wounded in the action.

"I am much obliged to you, Mr. Hilliard," Colonel Wingate said to him, that evening, "for the valuable services you have rendered, and shall have the pleasure of including your name among the officers who have specially distinguished themselves. As it was mentioned by General Rundle and Colonel Parsons—by the former for undertaking the hazardous service of carrying despatches to the latter, and by Colonel Parsons for gallant conduct in the field—you ought to be sure of promotion, when matters are arranged here."

"Thank you very much, sir! May I ask a favour?

"You know the outline of my story. I have learned, by the papers I obtained at Hebbeh, and others which I was charged not to open until I had certain proof of my father's death, that the name under which he was known was an assumed one. He had had a quarrel with his family; and as, when he came out to Egypt, he for a time took a subordinate position, he dropped a portion of his name, intending to resume it when he had done something that even his family could not consider was any discredit to it. I was myself unaware of the fact until, on returning to Omdurman from Hebbeh, I opened those papers. I continued to bear the name by which I am known, but as you are good enough to say that you will mention me in despatches, I feel that I can now say that my real name is Gregory Hilliard Hartley."

"I quite appreciate your motives in adhering to your former name, Mr. Hartley; and in mentioning your services under your new name, I will add a note saying that your name mentioned in former despatches, for distinguished services, had been erroneously given as Gregory Hilliard only."

"Thank you very much, sir!"

That evening, when several of the officers were gathered in Colonel Wingate's hut, the latter said, when one of them addressed Gregory as Hilliard:

"That is not his full name, Colonel Hickman. For various family reasons, with which he has acquainted me, he has borne it hitherto; but he will, in future, be known by his entire name, which is Gregory Hilliard Hartley. I may say that the reasons he has given me for not having hitherto used the family name are, in my opinion, amply sufficient; involving, as they do, no discredit to himself; or his father, a brave gentleman who escaped from the massacre of Hicks's force at El Obeid; and finally died, with Colonel Stewart, at Hebbeh."

"I seem to know the name," Colonel Lewis said. "Gregory Hilliard Hartley! I have certainly either heard or seen it, somewhere. May I ask if your father bore the same Christian names?"

"Yes, sir."

"I have it now!" Colonel Lewis exclaimed, a minute or two later. "I have seen it in an advertisement. Ever since I was a boy, that name has occasionally been advertised for. Every two or three months, it appeared in the *Times*. I can see it plainly, now.

"'Five hundred pounds reward will be given for any information concerning the present abode, or death, of Gregory Hilliard Hartley; or the whereabouts of his issue, if any. He left England about the year 1881. It is supposed that he went to the United States, or to one of the British Colonies. Apply to Messieurs Tufton and Sons, solicitors, Lincoln's Inn Fields.'

"Do you know when your father left England?"

"He certainly left about that time. I am nineteen now, and I know that I was born a few weeks after he came out to Alexandria."

"Then there ought to be something good in store for you," Colonel Wingate said. "People don't offer a reward of five hundred pounds, unless something important hangs to it. Of course, there may be another of the same name, but it is hardly likely that anyone would bear the two same Christian names, as well as surname. Is it indiscreet to ask you if you know anything about your father's family?"

"Not at all, sir. Now that I have taken his name, I need have no hesitation in relating what I know of him. Previous to his leaving England, he married without his father's consent; and, failing to make a living in England, he accepted a situation in Alexandria; which he gained, I may say, because he was an excellent Arabic scholar, as he had spent two years in exploring tombs and monuments in Egypt. He was the second son of the Honourable James Hartley; who was brother, and I believe heir, of the Marquis of Langdale, and I should think by this time has succeeded to the title. At his death, my father's eldest brother would, of course, succeed him."

"Then, my dear fellow," Colonel Mahon said, giving him a hearty slap on the shoulder, "allow me to congratulate you. I can tell you that the title has been in abeyance, for the past fourteen years. Everyone knows the facts. Your grandfather died before the Marquis. Your uncle succeeded him, lived only three years and, being unmarried, your father became the next Earl; and has been advertised for, in vain, ever since. As, unhappily, your father is dead also, you are unquestionably the Marquis of Langdale."

Gregory looked round with a bewildered air. The news was so absolutely unexpected that he could hardly take it in.

"It seems impossible," he said at last.

"It is not only impossible, but a fact," the Colonel said. "There is nothing very surprising in it. There were only two lives between your father and the peerage; and as one was that of an old man, the second of a man certainly in the prime of life, but unmarried, why, the Jews would have lent money on the chance.

"I fancy your uncle was a somewhat extravagant man. I remember he kept a lot of race horses and so on, but he could not have dipped very seriously into the property. At any rate, there will be fourteen years' accumulations, which will put matters straight.

"I hope you have got papers that will prove you are your father's son, and that he was brother of the late Earl."

"I think there can be no difficulty about that," Gregory said. "I have letters from both my parents, a copy of their marriage certificate, and of the registers of my birth and baptism. There are some persons in Cairo who knew my father, and a good many who knew my mother."

"Then I should say that it would be quite safe sailing.

"I don't know, Lewis, whether you are not entitled to that five hundred pounds."

"I am afraid not," the other laughed. "Mr. Hartley; or rather, I should say, the Earl; would have discovered it, himself. I only recognized the name, which plenty of people would have done, as soon as they saw it in despatches."

"It will be a great disappointment to someone," Gregory said; "if they have been, for fourteen years, expecting to come in for this."

"You need not fret about that," another officer said. "The next heir is a distant cousin. He has been trying, over and over again, to get himself acknowledged; but the courts would not hear of it, and told him that it was no use applying, until they had proof of the death of your father. I know all about it, because there was a howling young ass in the regiment from which I exchanged. He was always giving himself airs, on the strength of the title he expected to get; and if he is still in the regiment, there will be general rejoicings at his downfall."

"Then I have met him," Gregory said. "On the way up, he made himself very unpleasant, and I heard from the other officers that he was extremely unpopular. The Major spoke very sharply to him, for the offensive tone in which he addressed me; and an officer sitting next to me said that he was terribly puffed, by his expectations of obtaining a title shortly, owing to the disappearance of those who stood before him in succession. Some of the officers chaffed him about it, then. I remember now that his name was Hartley; but as I had no idea, at that time, that that was also mine, I never thought anything more about it, until now. As he was the only officer who has been in any way offensive to me, since I left Cairo nearly three years ago, certainly I would rather that he should be the sufferer, if I succeed in proving my right to the title, than anyone else."

"I don't think he will suffer, except in pride," the officer said. "His father, who was a very distant cousin of the Earl's, had gone into trade and made a considerable fortune; so that the young fellow was a great deal better off than the vast majority of men in the army. It was the airs he gave himself, on the strength of being able to indulge in an expenditure such as no one else in the regiment could attempt—by keeping three or four race horses in training, and other follies—that had more to do with his unpopularity, than his constant talk about the peerage he was so confident of getting."

"Of course you will go home to England, at once," Colonel Wingate said. "The war is over now, and it would be rank folly for you to stay here. You have got the address of the lawyers who advertised for you; and have only to go straight to them, with your proofs in your hand, and they will take all the necessary steps.

"I should say that it would facilitate matters if, as you go through Cairo, you were to obtain statements or affidavits from some of the people who knew your mother; stating that you are, as you claim to be, her son; and that she was the wife of the gentleman known as Gregory Hilliard, who went up as an interpreter with Hicks. I don't say that this would be necessary at all, for the letters you have would, in themselves, go far to prove your case. Still, the more proofs you accumulate, the less likely there is of any opposition being offered to your claim. Any papers or letters of your mother might contain something that would strengthen the case.

"It is really a pity, you know, when you have done so well out here, and would be certain to rise to a high post under the administration of the province; (which will be taken in hand, in earnest, now), that you should have to give it all up."

"I scarcely know whether to be pleased or sorry, myself, sir. At present, I can hardly take in the change that this will make, or appreciate its advantages."

"You will appreciate them, soon enough," one of the others laughed. "As long as this war has been going on, one could put up with the heat, and the dust, and the horrible thirst one gets, and the absence of anything decent to drink; but now that it is all over, the idea of settling down here, permanently, would be horrible; except to men—and there are such fellows—who are never happy, unless they are at work; to whom work is everything—meat, and drink, and pleasure. It would have to be everything, out here; for no one could ever think of marrying, and bringing a wife, to such a country as this. Women can hardly live in parts of India, but the worst station in India would be a paradise, in comparison with the Soudan; though possibly, in time, Khartoum will be rebuilt and, being situated between two rivers, might become a possible place—which is more than any other station in the Soudan can be—for ladies."

"I am not old enough to take those matters into consideration," Gregory laughed. "I am not twenty, yet. Still, I do think that anyone permanently stationed, in the Soudan, would have to make up his mind to remain a bachelor."

The next morning, the greater portion of the prisoners were allowed to return to their homes. All the grain and other stores, found in the camp, were divided among the women, who were advised to return to their native villages; but those who had lost their husbands were told that they might accompany the force to the river, and would be taken down to Omdurman, and given assistance for a time, until they could find some means of obtaining a subsistence.

On returning to Khartoum, Colonel Wingate, at Gregory's request, told Lord Kitchener of the discovery that had been made; and said that he wished to return to England, at once. The next day, the Sirdar sent for Gregory.

"Colonel Wingate has been speaking to me about you," he said, "and I congratulate you on your good fortune. In one respect, I am sorry; for you have done so surprisingly well, that I had intended to appoint you to a responsible position in the Soudan Civil Service, which is now being formed. Colonel Wingate says that you naturally wish to resign your present post, but I should advise you not to do so. The operation of the law in England is very uncertain. I trust that, in your case, you will meet with but small difficulty in proving your birth; but there may be some hitch in the matter, some missing link.

"I will, therefore, grant you six months' leave of absence. At the end of that time, you will see how you stand. If things have gone on well with you, you can then send in your resignation. If, on the other hand, you find yourself unable to prove your claim, it will still be open to you to return here, and continue the career in which you have begun so well."

"I am greatly obliged to you, sir, for your kindness; and should I fail in proving my claim, I shall gladly avail myself of your offer, at the end of the six months."

"Now, Zaki," he said, on returning to the hut, of which he had again taken possession, "we must have one more talk. I have told you about the possible change in my position, and that I was shortly leaving for England. You begged me to take you with me, and I told you that if you decided to go, I would do so. I shall be put in orders, tomorrow, for six months' leave. If I succeed in proving my claim to a title, which is what you would call here an emirship, I shall not return. If I fail, I shall be back again, in six months. Now, I want you to think it over seriously, before you decide.

"Everything will be different there from what you are accustomed to. You will have to dress differently, live differently, and be among strangers. It is very cold there, in winter; and it is never what you would call hot, in summer.

"It is not that I should not like to have you with me; we have been together, now, for three years. You saved my life at Atbara, and have always been faithfully devoted to me. It is for your sake, not my own, that I now speak."

"I will go with you, Master, if you will take me. I hope never to leave you, till I die."

"Very well, Zaki, I am more than willing to take you. If I remain in England, you shall always be with me, if you choose to remain. But I shall then be able to give you a sum that will enable you to buy much land, and to hire men to work your sakies, to till your land, and to make you what you would call a rich man here, should you wish to return at the end of the six months. If I return, you will, of course, come back with me."

On the following day, after having said goodbye to all his friends, disposed of his horse and belongings, and drawn the arrears of his pay, Gregory took his place in the train; for the railway had now been carried to Khartoum.

Four days later, he arrived at Cairo. His first step was to order European clothes for Zaki, and a warm and heavily-lined greatcoat; for it was now the first week in December, and although delightful at Cairo, it would be, to the native, bitterly cold in England.

Then he went to the bank, and Mr. Murray, on hearing the story, made an affidavit at the British resident's; affirming that he had, for fifteen years, known Mrs. Gregory Hilliard, and was aware that she was the widow of Mr. Gregory Hilliard, who joined Hicks Pasha; and that Mr. Gregory Hilliard, now claiming to be Mr. Gregory Hilliard Hartley, was her son. Mr. Gregory Hilliard, senior, had kept an account at the bank for eighteen months; and had, on leaving, given instructions for Mrs. Hilliard's cheques to be honoured. Mrs. Hilliard had received a pension from the Egyptian government, up to the date of her death, as his widow; he having fallen in the service of the Khedive.

Gregory looked up his old nurse, whom he found comfortable and happy. She also made an affidavit, to the effect that she had entered the service of Mrs. Hilliard more than eighteen years before, as nurse to Gregory Hilliard, then a child of a year old. She had been in her service until her death, and she could testify that Gregory Hilliard Hartley was the child she had nursed.

After a stay of four days at Cairo, Gregory started for England. Even he, who had heard of London from his mother, was astonished at its noise, extent, and bustle; while Zaki was almost stupefied. He took two rooms at Cannon Street Hotel, for himself and servant, and next morning went to the offices of Messieurs Tufton and Sons, the solicitors. He sent in his name as Mr. Gregory Hilliard Hartley.

Even in the outer office, he heard an exclamation of surprise, as the piece of paper on which he had written his name was read. He was at once shown in. Mr. Tufton looked at him, with a little surprise.

"I am the son of the gentleman for whom, I understand, you have advertised for a long time."

"If you can prove that you are so, sir," Mr. Tufton said, wearily, "you are the Marquis of Langdale—that is to say, if your father is deceased.

"May I ask, to begin with, how it is that the advertisement has, for so many years, remained unanswered?"

"That is easily accounted for, sir. My father, being unable to obtain a situation in England, accepted a very minor appointment in the house of Messieurs Partridge and Company, at Alexandria. This he obtained owing to his knowledge of Arabic. He had been engaged, as you doubtless know, for two years in explorations there. He did not wish it to be known that he had been obliged to accept such a position, so he dropped his surname, and went out as Gregory Hilliard. As the firm's establishment at Alexandria was burned, during the insurrection there, he went to Cairo and obtained an appointment as interpreter to General Hicks. He escaped when the army of that officer was destroyed, at El Obeid; was a prisoner, for many months, at that town; and then escaped to Khartoum. He came down in the steamer with Colonel Stewart. That steamer was wrecked at Hebbeh, and all on board, with one exception, were massacred.

"My mother always retained some hope that he might have escaped, from his knowledge of Arabic. She received a small pension from the Egyptian government, for the loss of my father, and added to this by teaching in the families of several Turkish functionaries. Three years ago she died, and I obtained, through the kindness of Lord Kitchener, an appointment as interpreter in the Egyptian army. I was present at the fights of Abu Hamed, the Atbara, Omdurman, and the late victory by Colonel Wingate. My name, as Gregory Hilliard, was mentioned in despatches; and will be mentioned, again, in that sent by

Colonel Wingate, but this time with the addition of Hartley.

"It was only accidentally, on the night after that battle, that I learned that my father was the heir to the Marquis of Langdale, and I thereupon obtained six months' leave, to come here."

"It is a singular story," the lawyer said, "and if supported by proofs, there can be no question that you are the Marquis, for whom we have been advertising, for many years."

"I think that I have ample proof, sir. Here is the certificate of my father's marriage, and the copies of the registers of my birth and baptism. Here is the journal of my father, from the time he was taken prisoner till his death. Here are his letter to my mother, and letters to his father, brother, and sisters, which were to be forwarded by her should she choose to return to England. Here are two affidavits—the one from a gentleman who has known me from childhood, the other from the woman who nursed me, and who remained with our family till I reached the Soudan. Here also is a letter that I found among my mother's papers, written from Khartoum, in which my father speaks of resuming the name of Hartley, if things went well there."

"Then, sir," Mr. Tufton said, "I think I can congratulate you upon obtaining the title; but at the same time, I will ask you to leave these papers with me, for an hour. I will put everything else aside, and go through them. You understand, I am not doubting your word; but of course, it is necessary to ascertain the exact purport of these letters, and documents. If they are as you say, the evidence in favour of your claim would be overwhelming.

"Of course, it is necessary that we should be most cautious. We have, for upwards of a hundred years, been solicitors to the family; and as such have contested all applications, from the junior branch of the family, that the title should be declared vacant by the death of the last Marquis, who would be your uncle. We have been the more anxious to do so, as we understand the next claimant is a young man of extravagant habits, and in no way worthy to succeed to the title."

"I will return in an hour and a half, sir," Gregory said, rising. "I may say that the contents of this pocketbook, although intensely interesting to myself, as a record of my father, do not bear upon the title. They are a simple record of his life, from the time when the army of Hicks Pasha was destroyed, to the date of his own murder at Hebbeh. The last entry was made before he landed. I mention this, as it may save you time in going through the papers."

Gregory went out, and spent the time in watching the wonderful flow of traffic, and gazing into the shops; and when he returned to the office, he was at once shown in. Mr. Tufton rose, and shook him warmly by the hand.

"I consider these documents to be absolutely conclusive, my lord," he said. "The letters to your grandfather, uncle, and aunts are conclusive as to his identity; and that of your mother, strengthened by the two affidavits, is equally conclusive as to your being his son. I will take the necessary measures to lay these papers before the court, which has several times had the matter in hand, and to obtain a declaration that you have indisputably proved yourself to be the son of the late Gregory Hilliard Hartley, and therefore entitled to the title and estates, with all accumulations, of the Marquis of Langdale."

"Thank you very much, sir! I will leave the matter entirely in your hands. Can you tell me the address of my aunts? As you will have seen, by my father's letter, he believed implicitly in their affection for him."

"Their address is, The Manor House, Wimperton, Tavistock, Devon. They retired there at the accession of their brother to the title. It has been used as a dower house in the family for many years; and, pending the search for your father, I obtained permission for them to continue to reside there. I was not obliged to ask for an allowance for them, as they had an income, under their mother's marriage settlement, sufficient for them to live there in comfort.

"I will not give you the letter addressed to them, as I wish to show the original in court; but I will have a copy made for you, at once, and I will attest it.

"Now, may I ask how you are situated, with regard to money? I have sufficient confidence in the justice of your claim to advance any sum, for your immediate wants."

"Thank you, sir! I am in no need of any advance. My mother's savings amounted to five hundred pounds, of which I only drew fifty to buy my outfit, when I went up to the Soudan. My pay sufficed for my wants there, and I drew out the remaining four hundred and fifty pounds when I left Cairo; so I am amply provided."

Gregory remained four days in London, obtaining suitable clothes. Then, attended by Zaki, he took his place in the Great Western for Tavistock. Zaki had already picked up a good deal of English, and Gregory talked to him only in that language, on their way down from the battlefield; so that he could now express himself in simple phrases.

Mr. Tufton had on the previous day written, at Gregory's request, to his aunts; saying that the son of their brother had called upon him, and given him proofs, which he considered incontestable, of his identity and of the death of his father. He was the bearer of a letter from his father to them, and proposed delivering it the next day, in person. He agreed with Gregory that it was advisable to send down this letter, as otherwise the ladies might doubt whether he was really what he claimed to be, as his father's letter might very well have come into the hands of a third person.

He went down by the night mail to Tavistock, put up at an hotel;

and, after breakfast, drove over to the Manor House, and sent in a card which he had had printed in town. He was shown into a room where the two ladies were waiting for him. They had been some four or five years younger than his father, a fact of which he was not aware; and instead of being elderly women, as he expected, he found, by their appearance, they were scarcely entering middle age. They were evidently much agitated.

"I have come down without waiting for an invitation," he said. "I was anxious to deliver my father's letter to you, or at least a copy of it, as soon as possible. It was written before his death, some eighteen years ago, and was intended for my mother to give to you, should she return to England. Its interest to you consists chiefly in the proof of my father's affection for you, and that he felt he could rely on yours for him. I may say that this is a copy, signed as correct by Mr. Tufton. He could not give me the original, as it would be required as an evidence of my father's identity, in the application he is about to make for me to be declared heir to the title."

"Then Gregory has been dead eighteen years!" the elder of the ladies said. "We have always hoped that he would be alive, in one of the colonies, and that sooner or later he would see the advertisement that had been put in the papers."

"No, madam. He went out to Alexandria with my mother, shortly before I was born. He died some three or four years before his brother. It was seldom my mother saw an English paper. Unfortunately, as it turned out, my father had dropped his surname when he accepted a situation, which was a subordinate one, at Alexandria; and his reason for taking it was that my mother was in weak health, and the doctor said it was necessary she should go to a warm climate; therefore, had any of her friends seen the advertisement, they would not have known that it applied to her. I, myself, did not know that my proper name was Hartley until a year back, when I discovered my father's journal at Hebbeh, the place where he was murdered; and then opened the documents that my mother had entrusted to me, before her death, with an injunction not to open them until I had ascertained, for certain, that my father was no longer alive."

One of the ladies took the letter, and opened it. They read it together.

"Poor Gregory!" one said, wiping her eyes, "we were both fond of him, and certainly would have done all in our power to assist his widow. He was nearer our age than Geoffrey. It was a terrible grief to us, when he quarrelled with our father. Of course our sympathies were with Gregory, but we never ventured to say so; and our father never mentioned his name, from the day he left the house. Why did not your mother send his letter to us?"

"Because she did not need assistance. She was maintaining herself and me in comfort by teaching music, French, and English to the wives and children of several of the high Egyptian officials."

"How long is it since you lost her?"

"More than three years ago. At her death, I was fortunate enough to obtain an appointment similar to that my father had, and at the same time a commission in the Egyptian service; and have been fortunate in being, two or three times, mentioned in despatches."

"Yes; curiously enough, after receiving Mr. Tufton's letter, we saw Colonel Wingate's despatch in the paper, in which your name is mentioned. We should have been astonished, indeed, had we not opened the letter before we looked at the paper.

"Well, Gregory, we are very glad to see you, and to find that you have done honour to the name. The despatch said that you have been previously mentioned, under the name of Gregory Hilliard. We always file our papers, and we spent an hour after breakfast in going through them. I suppose you threw up your appointment, as soon as you discovered that Geoffrey died, years ago, and that you had come into the title?"

"I should have thrown it up, but Lord Kitchener was good enough to give me six months' leave; so that, if I should fail to prove my right to the title, I could return there and take up my work again. He was so kind as to say that I should be given a responsible position, in the civil administration of the Soudan."

"Well, we both feel very proud of you; and it does sound wonderful that, being under twenty, you should have got on so well, without friends or influence. I hope you intend to stay with us, until you have to go up to London about these affairs."

"I shall be very happy to stay a few days, Aunt; but it is better that I should be on the spot, as there may be questions that have to be answered, and signatures, and all sorts of things.

"I have brought my Arab servant down with me. He has been with me for three years, and is most faithful and devoted; and moreover, he once saved my life, at tremendous risk to himself."

"Oh, of course we can put him up! Can he speak English?"

"He speaks a little English, and is improving fast."

"Does he dress as a native?"

"No, Aunt. He would soon freeze to death, in his native garb. As soon as I got down to Cairo with him, I put him into good European clothes. He is a fine specimen of a Soudan Arab, but when he came to me he was somewhat weakly; however, he soon got over that."

"Where is he, now?"

"He is with the trap, outside. I told him that he had better not come in until I had seen you, for I thought that your domestics would not know what to do with him, till they had your orders."

"You brought your portmanteau with you, I hope?"

"I have brought it, but not knowing whether it would be wanted; for I did not know whether you would take sufficiently to me, to ask me to stay."

"The idea of such a thing! You must have had a bad opinion of us."

"No, Aunt. I had the best of opinions. I am sure that my father would not have written as he did to you, unless he had been very fond of you. Still, as at present I am not proved to be your nephew, I thought that you might not be disposed to ask me to stay.

"Now, with your permission, I will go and tell Zaki—that is the man's name—to bring in my portmanteau. I can then send the trap back."

"Do you know, Gregory," one of his aunts said that evening; "even putting aside the fact that you are our nephew, we are delighted that the title and estates are not to go to the next heir. He came down here about a year ago. His regiment had just returned from the Soudan. He drove straight to the hall, and requested to be shown over it, saying that in a short time he was going to take possession. The housekeeper came across here, quite in distress, and said that he talked as if he were already master; said he should make alterations in one place, enlarge the drawing room, build a conservatory against it, do away with some of the pictures on the walls; and, in fact, he made himself very objectionable. He came on here, and behaved in a most offensive and ungentlemanly way. He actually enquired of us whether we were tenants by right, or merely on sufferance. I told him that, if he wanted to know, he had better enquire of Mr. Tufton; and Flossie, who is more outspoken than I am, said at once that whether we were tenants for life, or not, we should certainly not continue to reside here, if so objectionable a person were master at the hall. He was very angry, but I cut him short by saying:

"'This is our house at present, sir; and, unless you leave it at once, I shall call the gardener in and order him to eject you.'"

"I am not surprised at what you say, Aunt, for I met the fellow myself, on the way up to Omdurman; and found him an offensive cad. It has been a great satisfaction to me to know that he was so; for if he had been a nice fellow, I could not have helped being sorry to deprive him of the title and estates which he has, for years, considered to be his."

After remaining four days at the Manor House, Gregory went back to town. A notice had already been served, upon the former claimant to the title, that an application would be made to the court to hear the claim of Gregory Hilliard Hartley, nephew of the late Marquis, to be acknowledged as his successor to the title and estates; and that if he wished to appear by counsel, he could do so.

The matter was not heard of, for another three months. Lieutenant Hartley was in court, and was represented by a queen's counsel of eminence; who, however, when Gregory's narrative had been told, and the various documents put in, at once stated that after the evidence he had heard, he felt that it would be vain to contest the case at this point; but that he reserved the right of appealing, should anything come to light which would alter the complexion of the affair.

The judgment was that Gregory Hilliard Hartley had proved himself to be the son of the late Gregory Hilliard Hartley, brother of and heir to the late Marquis of Langdale, and was therefore seized of the title and estates.

As soon as the case was decided, Gregory went down again to Devonshire, and asked his aunts to take charge for him. This they at first said was impossible; but he urged that, if they refused to do so, he should be driven to go back to the Soudan again.

"My dear Aunts," he said, "what in the world am I to do? I know no one. I know nothing of English customs, or society. I should, indeed, be the most forlorn person in existence, with a large country estate and a mansion in London. I want someone to introduce me into society, and set me on my legs; manage me and my house, and preside at my table. I am not yet twenty, and have not as much knowledge of English ways as a boy of ten. I should be taken in and duped in every way, and be at the mercy of every adventurer. I feel that it would be a sacrifice for you to leave your pretty home here, but I am sure, for the sake of my father, you will not refuse to do so."

His aunts admitted that there was great justice in what he said, and finally submitted to his request to preside over his house; until, as they said, the time came when he would introduce a younger mistress.

Zaki, when his six months' trial was over, scorned the idea of returning to the Soudan; declaring that, if Gregory would not keep him, he would rather beg in the streets than go back there.

"It is all wonderful here," he said; "we poor Arabs could not dream of such things. No, Master, as long as you live, I shall stay here."

"Very well, Zaki, so be it; and I can promise you that if I die before you, you will be so provided for that you will be able to live in as much comfort as you now enjoy, and in addition you will be your own master."

Zaki shook his head.

"I should be a fool to wish to be my own master," he said, "after having such a good one, at present."

Gregory is learning the duties of a large land owner, and is already very popular in his part of Devonshire. The mansion in London has not yet been reopened, as Gregory says he must learn his lessons perfectly, before he ventures to take his place in society.

www.ingramcontent.com/pod-product-compliance
Lightning Source LLC
Chambersburg PA
CBHW021340250626
47155CB00002B/721